Collateral Damage
SHASSII

CONTENT WARNING

Attempted suicide
Suicide ideation
Attempted rape (Not by MFMC)
Explicit violence
Confinement / isolation / Captivity
Mental health representation
Disability representation
Chronic illness
Self harm
Murder / Death
Blackmail
Blood and Gore
Obscene Language
Drug abuse
Vomiting
Parental loss
Torture/Abusive flashbacks
Breaking and entering
Panic attacks
Attempted murder
Selfish sacrifice
Use of guns & sedatives
Domestic abuse (Not to the captured FFMC)
Child abuse
Torture methods/burning/wiping
Negative self image
Homophobia "Dyke" "Faggot"
bullying flashbacks
Night terrors

KINKS

Dubious Consent
Kidnapping
Corruption
Light DDLG
Knife play
Light BDSM
Age gap
Bondage
Begging
Touch me not
Blindfolds
Sex whilst injured
Branding
Breath play
Blood play
Restraints
Praise / degradation
Virgin & experienced
Impact play
Hate sex
Sex toys (Straps)
Spitting

DISCLAIMER

PLEASE BE ADVISED.
The main protagonist in this book has **mental health issues, addictions, toxic behaviour, and heavy trauma** *that leads to them doing extremely questionable things. I am in no way condoning this behaviour, but rather addressing where its origins lie, how characters act it out, how abuse can affect you mentally and what consequences it can have.*
I would also like to warn you that over the course of the book, there will be disturbing behaviour from the MFMC (Masculine female main character).

This behaviour does not correspond to my preferences but rather to share a realistic take on how people may possibly deal with trauma. Detailed disturbing scenes serve to address a complex topic and are described as the character perceives them, and not as I, the author, or moral norms prefer the character to react.

This book touches heavily on broken systems, child abuse, domestic abuse, physical and mental abuse, abduction, sexual assault, and certain torture methods.

If any of this relates heavily **PLEASE** *think twice before reading this book.*

COPYRIGHT TERMS

This is a work of fiction. Unless otherwise indicated, all the names, characters, businesses, places, events and incidents in this book are either the product of the author's imagination or used in a fictitious manner. Any resemblance to actual persons, living or dead, or actual events is purely coincidental. The only things true to their name are areas around the world in which the book is taken place.

copyright © (2025) SHASSII

All right reserved. No parts of this book may be reproduced or used in any manner without writers written permission. Only use of quotations in a book review will be accepted.

No songs are owned by SHASSII

Big thank you to Chlo & Selina

Instagrams: @spicyreadswchlo @bookishblackbird

for the beautiful images within these pages! I.E the playlist page spread and the author note page spread!

LANGAUGE NOTE

I just want to make the readers aware; this book is set in America but it is written in English standard besides particular words such as **'Mom'** instead of **'Mum'** and **'Trailer'** instead of **'Caravan'** to indicate the setting between the two American characters.

As a fellow English speaker who lives in the UK, trying to write in American standard was slightly difficult for me as a beginner to grasp and was distracting me from the flow so I decided to keep to English standard but I do plan to change this in the future to cater to the audience if needed!

<u>You will see words like;</u>

'Colour' with **'our'** instead of **'or'**

'Paralyzed' with a **'Z'** instead of an **'S'**.

'Self-defence' with a **'C'** instead of an **'S'**

DICKTIONARY

Chapter 24	*Chapter 41*
Chapter 25	*Chapter 42*
Chapter 28	*Chapter 44*
Chapter 29	*Chapter 45*
Chapter 35	*Chapter 48*
Chapter 36	*Chapter 53*
Chapter 38	*Chapter 54*
Chapter 39	*Chapter 56*
Chapter 40	*Chapter 60*

CHAPTERS

PROLOGUE
1 - Withering Flower
2 - My Final Act
3 - Plead Your Sins
4 - My Nightmare
5 - Collateral Damage
6 - Damaged Goods
7 - My Inconvenience
8 - Criminals Are Monsters
9 - Fucking See ME!
10 - Not Even In Death
11 - My Prodigy
12 - A Broken Band-Aid
13 - Forced Proximity
14 - Corrupt System
15 - Her First
16 - Love Is Weakness
17 - Secrets That Lie Beneath
18 - Give Me A Smile
19 - Unravelling Truths
20 - Ownership
21 - Solving The Case
22 - Fuelling The Flame
23 - Cut The Rope
24 - Little Masochist
25 - Blurryface
26 - Coping Methods
27 - My Work Of Art
28 - Vulnerability
29 - Behind The Mask
30 - Small Talk
31 - Acts Of Kindness
32 - Happy Dooms Day
33 - What Is Beautiful?
34 - Wonderwall
35 - Twisted Dreams
36 - Delicate Angel
37 - A Helping Hand
38 - My Colour
39 - Willing Surrender

40 - Her Delicacy
41 - All Of You
42 - The Taste Of Sin
43 - Curiosity Killed The Cat
44 - The Devils Lair
45 - Bleed For Me
46 - My Constellation
47 - Feed My Violence
48 - Lustful Quarrel
49 - Guilty Conscience
50 - Consuming Her Monsters
51 - Betrayal
52 - Karma In blood
53 - Consuming My Monsters
54 - My Beginning
55 - Hopes And Dreams
56 - Dessert
57 - Then Never I'll Wait
58 - Freedom
59 - Selfless
60 - My Forever
61 - Repeating History
62 - BLUE
63 - Justice
EPILOGUE

Playlist

Scan me

Mansion - NF & Fleurie
Idfc - Blackbear
Sleepyhead - Jutes (Acoustic)
BITTERSUITE - Billie Eilish
BLUE - Billie Eilish
Breathe me - Sia
Outcast - NF
You've got the love - Florence & TM
Constellations (Piano version) - Jade LeMac
Happiness is a butterfly - Lana Del Rey
Arcade - Duncan Lawrence
Daddy Issues - The Neighbourhood
Hypnosis - Sleep Token
Fix You - Coldplay
Hurts like hell - Fleurie
Beautiful Addiction - NF
Beach - The Neighbourhood
Can you hold me? - NF & Britt
Yellow - Coldplay
Soul tied - Ashley Tied
Plane to paris - Nessa Barrett
Reflection - The Neighbourhood
Halo - Beyonce
End of beginning - Djo
Take a moment to breathe - normal the kid

Nervous - The Neighbourhood
Time - NF
Let Me Go - NF
Obsessed - Jutes
Dig it - Bring Me The Horizon
Still Mine - Ashley Singh
Get You The Moon - Kina, Snøw
Would've been you - Sombr
Out of the picture. Pt. 1. - kilu
Half A Man - Dean Lewis
Go - Delilah
Hostage - Billie Eilish
Sugar On Top - Moonlight Scorpio
Eyes don't lie - Isabel LaRosa
Silver spoon - Erin LeCount
No Love For A Sinner - Shaya Zamora
What I've Done - Linkin Park
Black Out Days - Phantogram
Sunflower - Holly Kushner
Vertigo - Jutes (Acoustic)
To build a home - Cinematic orchestra
Star Shopping - Lil Peep
Look After You - The Fray
Like You Do - Ramsey
Fable - Gigi Perez
The Line - Twenty-One Pilots
Remember Me - D4vd
Fuck Me Like You Hate Me - Jutes
Fields of elation - Sleep Token
Can You Feel My Heart - Bring Me The Horizon
Outro - M83

Dedications

You were born bluer than a butterfly,
Beautiful and so deprived of oxygen.
Colder than your father's eyes,
He never learned to sympathise with anyone.

You were born reaching for your mother's hands,
Victim of your father's plans to rule the world.
Too afraid to step outside,
Paranoid and petrified of what you've heard.

~ Billie Eilish

If you like unhinged, masked, morally greys with a soft spot for her, a past worse than death and a split tongue.

I got you.

Oh, and did I mention,

It's a **Woman?**

This book is for the empaths, the damaged, the people who struggle with grief, the ones who struggle to let go, the ones who love so deeply it could kill them, the ones fucked over by the system, the moral seekers, the ones who see pain in others, the ones who try to fix the broken, the ones who had difficult parental relationships, the ones who have lost them, the ones who need to hear that it is ok to feel and to move on, the ones who have lost so much and keep finding the strength to hold on, the ones scared to love again.

And the ones that don't feel strong enough to keep going.

This is for the Survivors.

I see you. And I hope you see us too.

Your story is not over, keep going.

Love SHASSII

To my Baby.
Thank you for letting me show the world how I see you through my eyes. I know you think you are the Villain in everyone's story. But I just so happen to love the Villain.
You're not difficult to Love.
You are worthy of Love.
Your past does not define you.
You are one of a kind.

" Then Never, I'll wait "

SHASSII

Will you be my Beginning?

Or my END ?

12 YEARS EARLIER...

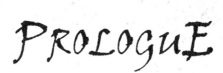

PROLOGUE

Play – 'Mansion – NF'

My blood is stinging as it throttles through my veins. Her cries are haunting me from the hallway and I can't take this anymore. The abuse, the pain. The damage this is doing to the both of us. He needs to be *gone*.

His voice is jarring in my ears, bouncing off the walls of our prison cell.

"I WILL KILL YOU! DO YOU UNDERSTAND ME!?" I can't see, but glass and china chime in symphony as they collide against one another, bringing me closer to the bedroom door.

"I'm sorry! Please! I won't say a word! Just-" I turn the knob slowly, careful not to make much noise over the riot in the kitchen but my blood runs cold as I step out into the hallway just as his fist hits her across her cheek, knocking her into the TV unit.

"No! you won't!" Years of Abuse. Years of submission to the worst kind of torture fuels my rage. My feet take me, storming into the conflict, crashing into his chest as he smashes into the wall.

"Leave her the FUCK alone or so help me GOD." My fingers are tingling, using myself as a human shield as I lift her up off the floor brushing her matted midnight hair out of her damp face.

"Please, baby, go back to your room." Welling pleads are burrowed in her eyes as she squeezes my fingers tightly.

"*Babygirl*. You know better than to pick a fight with Daddy. Sit down and do as Mommy says." He taunts, cracking his neck, hoisting himself up off the wall, rubbing his shoulder where it hit with hard impact and I feel sick to my stomach hearing him call me a name that signifies *protection* and *love* when all he knows is *violence* and *hate*.

"*Over my dead fucking body.*" One of us is not getting out of this alive and he smiles with callous intent, making my spine shudder before he knocks my sight momentarily, seeing the coffee table as I grab for it, trying to gain stability. My jaw throbbing with raw heat.

"*RICK!*"

"Little girl. Do I need to remind you what happens when you disobey me."

"You can try. But you won't be alive long enough to see that through." I wipe the blood oozing from my mouth, clinging to that familiar taste of metal in my gums I've grown to enjoy.

"Was that a threat? *Freak*." My hair is pulled tightly, fighting to mute the dull pain as he pulls me up by my scalp but this infliction is painless compared to the suffering I've endured below me and I smile through it, only winding him up further. His attempts to break me are a waste of time. I'm already *broken*. I'm already accustomed to this abominable hate.

"Yeah. It was." All I have done is train. Train for this exact moment and he has no idea of the strength I have behind me now, but years of child abuse can do that to someone.

My forehead meets his and the sound of bones crunching causes her to yelp in fear from behind me, trying to grab for my hand.

"STOP IT! BOTH OF YOU!" I drown out her voice. I drown out everything as his grip loosens, cradling his nose leaving me wide open to uppercut him under the chin where his teeth crack, throwing him into the coffee table. His weight submerges the wood and centre glass to shatter beneath him and a sickening laugh bellows from his stomach.

"Hays please, please stop!" Her voice is a distant echo as my vision tunnels to hallways of red.

"Is that all you got? *Faggot.*" I pay no mind to the insult, more drawn to the fact that he thinks that was all the rage I have held inside me. I let him stand. Finding his heavy feet, wiping his sweaty arms underneath his nose to stop the bleeding before knocking him down again as I let his demons take a hold of me by the throat. I search for that glimmer of peace and freedom as my fists pummel his face. *Again. And again. And again. And again. And again. And again.*

"Hays! I'm serious! Please!" He gurgles through his broken chords, his face like papier-mâshé smothered in red paint as his blood covers my skin, paying no mind to the murder welded by my hand, so close I can almost smell death in the air.

"You will never be a man. You will never be anything but *weak*. And you're cert-ainly no daught-er of mi-ne." Shortness in my breath leads my hands to wrap around his throat like his noose that's been holding mine since the day I was born, clawing at me with little life as I suffocate him of his pathetic existence.

"*HAYLEY!* Baby! You're going to kill him! Stop it!!" Her voice is a distant hum, fighting the angel on my shoulder to make me let go but I don't. I squeeze tighter, his hands wriggling in the shards of glass scattered across the floor, digging into my knees, both of us bleeding all over the tattered carpet but I'm numb. Witnessing the life drain from his dead eyes, watching my imagination finally come to light, all those years of praying he'd die, now I can finally take his waste of existence myself. I'm doing the world a fucking favour. I squeeze until he's limp but I can't fight this instinct to kill and my fist finds the carpet through his skull, able to hear my heart in my ears, pounding with such force, white noise breaking my sound barrier. I grab a shard of broken glass from the coffee table, stabbing it into his chest until the glass is imbedded in my palm, using his unconscious state to paint a pretty picture across his wrinkly old fucking face, gliding it across his mouth the way he did mine. The way it brings me so much sick joy is only making me push deeper. I was his *Puppet*, but now, I'm his bloody *Puppeteer*.

"Please. Hays, let go. I can't lose you too!" She whispers with aggression as her grip finds my shoulders, eventually sucking me from drowning further as her cries suddenly invade my hearing. I collapse against her chest as we stagger back, her grip tight on me as she sobs into my shoulder blade. I glare at his lifeless entity feeling nothing but accomplishment. This was needed, but suddenly we are both consumed with the realisation as I turn slowly to face her already peering at me in horror. She reaches to caress my blooded cheeks in her palms, shaking her head in fear. Fear that I've just made the worst mistake of my life.

"Oh *babygirl*..." She embraces me into a tight cradle, aiding my pain, coaxing me back to shore as she grips the back of my head.

But in this moment,

His death is my only salvation.

It's my only purpose.

It's my Freedom.

CHAPTER 1

WITHERING FLOWER

Puppet

30th October 2009

Freedom.

I say it like I don't live in the absolute middle of nowhere, the kind of home people could only ever dream of. It takes me an hour just to get to the nearest town by car, if that isn't freedom I don't know what is. But that is not the kind of freedom I mean. I mean no strings attached. It can be so tiresome living with health conditions. I just wish to be normal. Strict parents and absolutely no social life doesn't exactly scream freedom, does it? yet I'm such a free spirit. I live in the clouds, spending the majority of my time daydreaming about the what ifs. I have goals I want to someday achieve, which is not easy when your parents have already plotted out your entire life for you. I love them dearly and I couldn't ask for a better pair of clean freak overly protective, love smothering parents, but having a quick wit and a big house doesn't exactly work in your favour when you can't even hold a conversation.

"You better be coming to my party tomorrow Rara!" My girl Kacey invited me to her annual Halloween party and I am going to feel like an absolute flake if I don't go. She's pretty adamant that I attend and she has been banging on about it for weeks, I just know that the answer will be *no* and it makes me want to rip my hair out so I've avoided the question and tried to make excuses as to why I haven't asked Mommy dearest yet. Besides, she's now made plans and it doesn't matter how many times I tell her, Kacey still won't take no for an answer. She is desperate to hook me up with someone and I'll be quite honest, I am eighteen and I've never even held a boy's hand. It's about time I put myself on the market, *I guess?*

"I'll be there!" I smile awkwardly, praying she can't see the nervousness in my face as we pull up in front of my gate.

"I'm sure your Mom will understand, it's Halloween!"

"I gotta dash, but don't forget to text me! Love ya!" She blows me a kiss before beeping her goodbyes as I hop out of her pearly white Audi and make my way to my front door. It's about a five minute walk so I plug in some tunes until I get inside where Mom is cooking. Only one meal smells this damn good. *Spaghetti Bolognese!*

"Hello baby girl! How was college?" I brave a smile and put my duffle bag down on the counter top. College is so boring and the majority of the time I am on my own but if I say that they will probably kick up a fuss and end up in my head teachers office about how *the girls need to interact with me more.*

"It was good." The only good thing about college these days is the journey home where I can blast music and write my silly little stories.

"Are you still up for the movies tomorrow? I can book your favourite pizza place before we go?" *Oh god,* here we go… I already know where this is going. I could just say I asked Mom and she said no, but Kacey will see straight through me. *I am a terrible liar.*

"About that. Erm. Kacey is holding a small get-together at her place for halloween and I was wondering if I could go?" I'm almost biting my tongue off trying to manifest her saying that it would be totally OK for me to go to a party with alcohol and boys and *probably drugs*. Literally my Mom's worst *nightmare*.

"Sweetheart. You know how I feel about parties. And you know I am not big on her either." This is getting old and I'm starting to lose my patience.

"Mom, it's not a party, just a few friends and food." I tighten my shoulders, giving her puppy eyes to try and cover up my dishonesty. *Friends* meaning hundreds and *food* meaning enough alcohol to knock out a horse.

"You forget I was your age once. Hard to believe I know," she huffs a gentle smile, the golden accents in her hair shimmer against the setting sun through the window. She's right, It is hard to believe when you look at her. She is the perfect Mom, her whole life sorted with the perfect job and she looks so beautiful and pure it's hard to imagine she was ever a rebellious teen once. But she also had the freedom to do so, whereas I do not. Doesn't that count for something? You'd think she'd at least let me experience it once.

"She is a bad influence Lora." I roll my eyes quietly.

Play - 'Wake Up - NF'

"She is the only semi decent friend who's nice to me." Kacey isn't exactly the most amazing person, but she is the only person who's given me the time of day and speaks to me like I am a human being, like our friendship means something. She does some questionable things... Like hooking up with a younger teaching assistant in the disabled toilet... And put alcohol in almost every English teacher's coffee before flirting her way out of a fail... I won't carry on. But besides that, she respects me and likes me for who I am. *I think?*

"Exactly my point. I don't trust her, she's the definition of plastic. You've watched mean girls, and besides, it will ruin your schedule." Kacey is the definition of a blonde baddie. We are complete opposites with her beach wave curls and her sandy skin with a killer body, next to me. A nerdy brunette with the figure of a stick and no appealing features going for me besides my eyes. *I like my eyes.* My parents take her at face value, they have only met her a handful of times and every encounter is more embarrassing than the last, so now we just hang at college or before when we walk together with our coffee.

Dad walks in through the double doors to the kitchen with a crumpled up roll of newspaper, his eyes glued to the pages. He's a former detective but I know he misses it. I will never understand why he dropped out. I have told him multiple times to pick it back up but he tells me he's happy, and that this life is what he wanted *for me*. That he was too absent in the life of catching criminals, yet he spends the majority of his life in the office anyway, so I don't see what the difference is, we barely have a relationship anymore.

"Dad. Please tell her I'm old enough to look after myself." I scowl at him, ready to give him my best face but he doesn't even acknowledge me, still fixated on the passage he's reading, throwing his finger at Mom shaking it gently.

"I'm with your Mother on this munchkin. She has nothing but bad intentions and it's bad enough you being around her at college." I throw my arms in the air before slamming them back down on the marble countertop, *he can't be serious right now.*

"This is not fair!" I'm so tired of being controlled, I'm losing my mind.

"We are only looking out for you, plus; your Mother made plans with you, don't be rude." *Don't be rude!* Are they kidding me! My inner anger spirals in my chest. I am such a quiet person at the best of times, and I also hate confrontation but I'm reaching the end of my tether. I have been eighteen for eight months now and they still treat me as if I'm fresh from the womb.

"I never get to go anywhere or do anything! I'm eighteen now, I'm literally an adult. When are you guys going to see that?" Everything inside me wants to break and scream at the top of my lungs.

"We can see that, but your health comes first and partying and alcohol will not do well with your blood sugar levels, we have talked about this." I've not been able to do anything remotely fun my entire life. The most exciting thing I did was move, which I can barely remember because I was too young. I have never left the country, nor have I done anything that may remotely mess up my schedule. They treat a holiday like a trip to the hospital, it's exhausting and I've had enough. They preach that my health comes first, but mentally I am deteriorating. *What's a life for if you can't live it?*

"You cannot let my diabetes rule my life. And you can't keep using it to control my *freedom!*" Frustration laces my voice, irritation building in the back of my teeth. I've never blown up, about anything, I don't dare disrespect them, but it seems to have gotten me nowhere in life. *I am a doormat.*

"Please do not raise your voice young lady. And you can't be too careful during Halloween. Who knows what is behind those costumes." *He can't be serious right now?* He's going to try and use halloween as a scapegoat for my safety?

"You're actually being ridiculous. You think a serial killer disguised as bad cops and clowns is gonna kill me on the one night in the entire year I've actually left the building besides putting my head in books?" I slouch on the kitchen stool, my index fingers lining between my brows and down the bridge of my nose, rubbing a brewing migraine from this bickering that will get me absolutely nowhere.

"I didn't work in the police force for nothing kiddo. You'll be surprised what kind of sick and twisted people are out there." Why is he bringing this up when he was the one who dropped out? He could be protecting me from the sickos he preaches about but instead he sits at home coddling me like a child. All he ever talks about is a life he no longer lives, a life I have told him to run back to but he refuses to acknowledge that my burden is now his to bear. My fuse blows, pushing myself up from the stool, the legs ringing against the tiled floor as I use all my force to get up off the chair in anguish.

"Yeah well. You can't protect me forever." *I'm hurt and I'm angry* and tomorrow I will probably hate myself for the things I've said but right now I don't care, families have arguments all the time, this is normal. *Right?* Hopefully they will listen to me for once and realise I am not a kid anymore, I am a grown ass woman who's aching to experience things beyond my four walls. From an outsider's perspective I have the perfect life and the perfect parents, and maybe I do, maybe I am the problem. No. *I know I am the problem,* and I cannot change it, I cannot fix it, I can only live with it. I know I shouldn't be angry at them; they didn't give this to me but right now I need someone to blame *for the strings tying me down,* I need to pin my fury on something.

I make my way upstairs, stomping my feet like a child as I do, drowning out the things they should be saying to me right now but they are not. They aren't saying a word, they let me go and my guilt swallows me. They know I don't mean it and they also know that one day they won't be here to tuck me in at night and write out my schedule for the week; set alarms for my pen and have emergency doctors on standby just in case. So what I said was not exactly wrong, but I can be mad at them for a little while, mad at them for being too perfect... Mad at them for caring too much. I'm lucky I have parents who *Love* this hard, but sometimes it's overwhelming and exhausting. If you give a flower *too* much water, you'll drown it. And I feel like I'm *drowning*. My pot is spilling over taking the soil with me.

I throw my bag on the bed before following suit. My back hitting the mattress, arms spread and I glare at the ceiling. My room is made up of all the things that complete me, yet I still feel so empty. Its beige, fluffy blankets and cushions scatter my perfectly pristine bed. My black bass guitar and vinyl records displayed on their shelves hang flush against the wall by my window. I love music. I love all things creative. I love art. It's a symphony I understand, I speak to art like Love. It's how I escape. I make memories through paper, and movies through songs.

After a momentary cool down, I pull my phone from my black knitted cardigan.

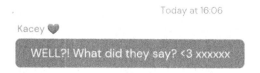

I slip off my little black docs, crawling onto my front, tucking a duck feather pillow underneath my chin exhaling a disappointed sigh.

Today at 17:17

Me
> Bad news. Mom said no. <3 x

Kacey 🖤
> Boooooo, she's such a party pooper. Why don't you just sneek out? I'll get Jack go come get u! Xxxxxx

Me
> Cici. I am not sneaking out! I will literally get grounded. Plus. We just had a tiff. X

Kacey 🖤
> You need to get out, jeeeeeez, I'm sure they won't get mad? They are softies. Xxxxxxxx

Me
> I have loads of homework to do anyways. There is always next time! X

Kacey 🖤
> You're such a little goody two shoes Rara it's adorable, really. But you need a drink and some dick. No offence babe but no ones gonna even look your way or go near you until you have booooo. Xxxx

Me
> Thanks? I guess. Lol x

Kacey 🖤
> You know I just want you to be happy!! Xxxxxx

Me
> Yeah I knowwww. Sorry my parents are being so difficult. X

Kacey 🖤
> Hey! I gotta run, Jack's here. I'm heading out but I'll see you tomorrow bish! Luv ya! <3 xxxxxxxx

Me
> Night x

I glare at the phone, dissociating for a moment, wanting so desperately to tell Jack to pick me up tomorrow. But it will only cause more harm than good and that impulsive thought will feel dumb when I wake with a guilty conscience. So I stare at the chat a little longer, rolling my eyes in frustration as I lock the screen and throw it on my bed.

It's been a few hours and I've ploughed my feelings into a new story I'm writing. It's a story about a girl who escapes her captivity and falls madly in love with a stable boy she runs away with. I'm a sucker for romance, which is funny coming from someone who has never even kissed a boy before. But a girl can *dream*. I was so engrossed in writing that I missed dinner, but I wasn't hungry anyway. I would rather not sit at the table playing with my food in tension as thick as fog. Sleep should wash away the awkwardness by tomorrow.

My alarm goes and I glance down at my phone.

My least favourite time of day. Mom usually does it for me in the evenings, but I'm in no mood to see her right now. Slipping into my jammies, I take my pen from my bedside table, lining the little needle up with my fleshy skin just above my abdomen and click, placing the fresh pen back in the pocket of my shorts.

Timid footsteps creep up the staircase beyond my bedroom door followed by a gentle knock as I run my brush through my cocoa hair.

"Did you take your Lantus sweetie?" Her voice is gentle, a mixture between her natural persona and the way I'm fragile as of right now. She should be angry with me but she's not, caring for me still.

"Yes Mom." I glared at the door expecting her to come in, but she doesn't. I guess this is the first proper argument we've ever had. I know she isn't my biological Mother, but she has been in my life since I can remember and looked after me like I came out of her womb. For a long time I thought she was my biological Mother until I was old enough to understand, but by that time the truth didn't hurt. It never has, she will always be my Mom and I wouldn't ever change that.

"You missed dinner, have you eaten?" *No. I ate enough today to last me all week.*

"Yes." *I lie.* My replies are short and blunt, I don't want her to come in, but at the same time I am craving a hug.

"You know we love you right?" She argues her point, she can hear my hurt and she is never short of reassurance. They are strict but they are good at being gentle.

"I know." I crawl underneath the bed covers, clutching my pillow tightly. I'm not a crier. I can't even remember the last time I cried; I have no reason to cry really. But I won't deny the lump forming in the back of my throat. *I hate crying.*

"We just want to keep you safe." I've heard that a million times before, but for some reason now it just sounds different.

"I know."

"Sweet Dreams Sweetie. I Love You."

"Love you too." I roll onto my back, rubbing underneath my eyes before picking back up my phone and surfing through Facebook at silly memes and what people are up to. I don't really use it, I don't know why I look, seeing everyone out doing things only makes me feel worse, but I look anyway. Smiling away at the life I will never live at this rate. I can keep daydreaming my life away. Living through the ink on my pages, bleeding out my selfish emotions so people don't have to hear me moan about my *perfect life.*

A never-ending cycle of silent melancholy.

SHASSII

CHAPTER 2

MY FINAL ACT

Puppeteer

Play - 'What I've Done - Linkin Park'

J*ustice.*

It's so close now, I can smell it.

I've waited eleven painful years for this very moment. I served my time, but I didn't learn my lesson. Call me relentless but some people don't deserve to breathe, certainly not this sack of shit. I will die withering away in a pool of my own blood if I have to, but not yet. Not until he bleeds her cries.

I swear I've not slept since I was discharged. Four years of searching for a needle in a haystack and boy was he a small ass fucking needle. The little bitch ran, as I suspected. Being part of the Chicago police department still had perks for him, they removed all traces of him to save his ass thinking that would keep him hidden. What a *clown*. Moved his entire life two states away to run from his guilt. Well his guilt caught up. I'm his *guilt*. Walking, breathing fucking guilt. And I'm ten minutes away from releasing eleven years of regret, eleven years of pain, eleven years of anger into his mother fucking skull. I've been thinking about what she'd say if she saw me now and honestly? I think she'd tell me to let it go. But this is all I have left. I will rest with you soon Mom. *Just let me do this for you.*

This son of a bitch is out here living the life kids like me could only ever dream of. This house is bigger than my entire fucking hometown. He sucked up that money once he won his shitty self-defence bullshit in court I bet. It's embarrassing to know what a naive and gullible world we live in, and I wish to be no fucking part of it once this is over.

Indiana is definitely a sight when you have lived in a shacked up broken bungalow and behind bars for the best part of your life. You forget how beautiful nature can be. That is when it hasn't been tampered with by the cunts around us who wanna turn the world into a concrete jungle. The law and power is an ugly place. They will do anything to keep their act up, even if it means locking up a teenager who simply murdered to survive...

OK. Was it self-defence? Yes. But. Did it kind of feel good? Also yes... Was it involuntary? *Who knows.*

Not that prison scared me much anyway. Prison was like LaLa land compared to the Devil I gutted. I'll admit, it wasn't the vacation I was hoping for, but it taught me a lot.

Like *how to kill someone and not get caught this time.*

It wasn't exactly easy, and I earned a few scars I'll never forget but I made it out alive and that was the main goal. Although I bet he's been keeping tabs on me. He knows I'm out, but I've kept a low profile to give him the illusion I've no interest in him. Little does he know I'm finally parked right outside his pretty little farmhouse, not that he made that any easier either. The entire house was smothered in surveillance cameras. *Guilty conscience much?* It's a good job computer tech is my favourite subject otherwise this would've proven to have been a little more difficult.

I know he has a wife, and as much as I am a Mommy's girl at heart; I'm afraid I cannot keep her breathing, as gorgeous as she is, so there's no harm in toying with her a little before I remove her too. I'm doing the bitch a favour anyway, she's too good for him. Not that I've gotten close and personal with her but from a distance she's a looker, and far too intelligent for the likes of him. Dude couldn't even solve a case without murdering the wrong suspect whilst she's out here saving lives.

Speaking of the Devil. He's still awake. I best get this over with. He's made this rather easy for me. Fucker thought moving out into the sticks was going to help him yet it's made this whole process so much cleaner. No witnesses. No busy streets. No street cameras. No nothing. He's exposed and vulnerable, and he's too dumb to realise his cameras are out. *He's gotten too comfortable*, which is exactly what I wanted. But I'm the Clown, right? Damn right I fucking am. I wear it with pride. This face mask is my new purpose. I want him to fucking see me as I shoot him between the eyes though, so I left the face paint off for now.

I turn the key to the ignition, killing the engine. Stolen of course, it's a shame to dispose of it. I've grown a liking to this beast, but evidence is evidence, no matter how beautiful it may seem. Haltering myself from the driver seat, I clip the door to make sure I don't alarm anyone, not that it would. You'd think the dumb cunt would at least have canines or something, but he doesn't which speeds up this process. Dogs are far more reliable than technology these days.

I make my way round to the back of the building where I had already tampered with their locks to give me access. Slipping into the kitchen, I lock it as quietly as I can so there is no means of escape. An island sits in the middle of the room obstructing my way towards the living room where the TV is still blaring. *Perfect.* They won't hear me coming. A horror movie. *How ironic...*

Creeping my way across the tiled floor I pull out my Glock from the back of my jeans, gripping the handle in my thick leather gloves. It's dark, but luckily there are enough windows to leak in natural light. The warm glows illuminate from the room in front of me where I peek to see his wife sitting comfortably slumped in the sofa, completely oblivious to the infiltrator who is approaching her from behind. He's in his office, most likely checking up on my previous hit and run. Detectives have been all over it but found no evidence. I finally gave the judge a little visit, stabbed him a few times. Ok, a few is an understatement, a lot, before leaving a precious little smile across his face, then hung him up for the entirety of the town to see from the courthouse and fuck did it feel good. The look on his face was priceless, not that it relieved me of much pent-up anger, but the fucker had it coming. I'm not the only one who's been objectified by his sexist nature, I'm sure people were relieved to see him gone.

I step slowly out from behind the kitchen door, treading carefully trying not to be too heavy on my boots as I grip my gun by my stomach aiming at the floor, closing in on the sweet smell of lavender and freshly washed hair. She doesn't deserve this, but neither did I. Neither did *she*. I'm going to make him feel my pain as I strip him of the only thing he has. I reach out my arm, extending the barrel of my pistol until it sits gently on the back of her skull before pulling it back to reset the trigger making it click, peaking her fight or flight. She's being such a *good girl* staying quiet for me, this makes it all the more enjoyable to toy with the both of them. I was half expecting her to scream but she hasn't, her breathing has just quickened underneath the muffled cries coming from the TV in front of her. I lean in slowly, pressing the tip of the gun harder into her head as I creep in towards her soft cartilage.

"Would you like to star in a Horror movie Mrs. Blackthorne?... Because you are about to be all over the news..." I watch her body jolt as she trembles beneath me, fighting to keep tears in, wanting so desperately to call out but she is no idiot, she knows that would be a *very*, stupid idea.

"Get up. Slowly." She does as I say, cautiously pushing herself off the sofa with her hands in the air. *She's definitely a sub in the bedroom.* Maybe I was wrong about her. Where's the spunk?

I shuffle around the settee, my gun still firmly aimed at her as I walk in behind her frame, grabbing her forearm to secure her against my torso. She's shaking like a little puppy.

"Don't take this personally," a tiny squeal escapes her mouth, thinning her lips as she sucks them in, squinting her eyes firmly shut as the barrel rubs against her temple.

"Call him in. Calmly." She nods sporadically before using her words to entice her loved one to walk into his grave with her. *And people say romance is dead?*

"Honey. Can you come here? Please." There is a subtle quiver in her pleading as she abruptly throws it on the end. It pains me that she is a part of this. We will see how this goes. Maybe I can spare her.

"One minute darling!" Hearing his voice sends me all sorts of crazy. It grinds against my broken bones, penetrating the open wounds that have never stopped bleeding. Suddenly, my rational thinking is smothered with a red blanket and all I can hear is the beating in my chest cavity. That undeniable ache thumping against my rib cage, pleading to be let out. She is being far too calm considering the circumstances. I let go of her gently, reaching to pull out some duct tape from my back pocket, hovering it in front of her chest still looping my finger through the centre.

"Pull it." She hesitates, lifting her hands to peel the tape away from its roll as I lean in, pulling the bottom portion of my mask up to bite off the access, taking the departed piece and plastering it over her mouth causing the roll to thud on the wooden floor boards underneath us. I can hear him shuffling papers around as his chair scrapes against the varnished floorboards and I'm practically ringing with euphoria. I've embraced the darkest parts of me by now. *I'm sick, twisted,* and hell bent on spilling blood. They should never have let me out and in many ways, I see my Father in me, which makes my blood run cold and nausea sit on the back of my tongue. Yet I can't seem to escape this hunger for revenge. *I'm broken, rotten, lost.* But he created this. *He* made me who I am. I guess it's genetics. I was doomed the day I was conceived. Now I am just being the person he always said I'd be. A fucking CLOWN... A ludicrous circus act of attempted humour. Putting on a show for people only to laugh AT me. The abuse I endured for simply being different really fed me my new identity. Now I've lived and breathed to put on a mind-blowing show, *and this is my final act.*

The office door creaks open from the corridor beyond the living room and his footsteps make their way towards us. I cannot deny the cheshire cat grin plastering my face underneath this mask to mirror the one painted on it. He is now standing ten feet in front of me and the horror in his eyes is my favourite part of this movie. He freezes like a deer in headlights, gripping the wall for stability as he almost stumbled from halting so abruptly and my smirk is disgusting. *What's his move now?* I've waited eleven years for this exact moment. I've dreamt about it, day in and day out and it's finally sitting at the barrel of my gun. *This is so ironically beautiful...* I hope he can see the art behind this.

The barrel tickles her skin, gliding down her soft cheeks to meet the opening of her pyjama shirt. Popping open the buttons as the metal tugs on it to expose her chest to me. She's lucky I am not a sick perverted man, but fuck has she got a nice rack. I toy with her breasts, the cold metal of my pistol dancing against the curves of them before I dig it into her chest plate of bone, urging her to move against the pain.

"Turn around." I whisper down her ear sending the hairs on her neck to stand up as she swivels to face my mask. She has yet to see what I look like, and the look on her face says all I need to know about the way I look. Diabolically terrifying. Her face is soaking wet as she pleads with her eyes, begging without words as I take a step back, both my leather gloves now wrapped firmly around the mag as I aim right for her heart. He has yet to speak. *Some hero he is.*

"Now, doesn't this look familiar..." We are staggered across the living room, she is now standing in between us and his head is shaking, bobbing between the back of her head and my eyes beneath the mask. I'm looking at myself, and he is looking at himself. *History repeating itself.* He really did try to run, but karma always has a way of catching up to you, and now it's standing before him like a beacon of justice. Only this time, for the right fucking reasons.

"I don't know what you want from me, but she has no part of this. Please. Let her go!" A shiver coats the length of my spine as his familiar words spill from his disgusting mouth and I cannot help but let a sinister laugh slip.

"That meant fuck all when I said it." I hiss, spit hitting the back of my mask, his fearful gawk cocks a brow in confusion, and I love watching him try to put the puzzle pieces together.

"Is this some kind of sick Halloween joke?" Is he really suggesting this is a fucking joke right now? I am in two minds to end her life right fucking now. But it will spoil the show. I take a deep breath and recite his words to his beloved wife.

"Move out of the way, or I will not hesitate to shoot you." That decision now rests on her shoulders. Because there is no escaping the bullet I have with his name on it. He will watch as I did. Watch her use herself as a human shield to protect his sorry ass whilst I take the oxygen from her lungs and seek pleasure from the pain in his eyes. Revenge is a sick form of poetry and can be performed in many ways. I guess this is not the prettiest form, but nothing about me or my life ever has been. I have been exposed to so much ugliness that I'm not even sure what pretty is meant to look like. My mind has been permanently damaged. I've been programmed to feed off the abominable, absorb pain and let it drown me, pull me under and fill my lungs. I've accepted that I've sunk, and he has been the rock pinning me between the seabed, but even free of it, I will never be able to reach the surface in time. I have accepted there is a ticking time bomb and all I can do is let it fill up my lungs.

My hands are now shaking, reliving this moment is making me spiral. I can feel myself tightening like a rubber band about to release. Remembering the very moment that bullet punctured her heart the way it punctured mine. I was never shot that day, but it damn well feels like it. This ache is a permanent reminder that I should have done more.

"Look, whatever I did, I am sure there is a better way around this." *Better way*? What better way can I avenge her if not this! I don't want to hear his pitiful lies or his grovelling, I don't give a flying fuck if he bows at my feet and kisses my fucking boots. *NOTHING* will reverse the damage he caused me. I spent six years behind bars while he sat around sipping fucking tea and marrying a woman who had no idea of the man he really is!

"You don't get it do you? There isn't. If it means I have to set this house ablaze with both of us in it to ensure you suffer with me in hell, don't think I won't. You are going down with me like you should have done eleven fucking years ago. *Now Sit!*" He jumps, stumbling for the sofa like a beggar, grovelling like a coward as my gun pushes her onto the sofa next to him.

"Did you really think your demons were not going to catch up with you one way or another? You would just move away and this would all just disappear?" He is still completely clueless. How he ever got a degree I will never know. He can't even put the pieces together when I'm spelling them the fuck out. By the look on her tearful expression, she has no idea what I'm talking about. He really has tried to eradicate every part of his life before her, and she is none the wiser of the killer sat beside her, as well as in front of her. It's ironic really. The most dangerous ones are the people you least expect. The way my father would shake my teachers' hands but burn mine is a perfect example of that. I've had my fair share of betrayal to know that people like that don't *change.*

"It's been a long time, but I remember it like it was yesterday. Every word, every smell. The way you shared her bed only to harm her, the way she pleaded before you and you hurt her anyway, you sick FUCK!" There is a shift in his eyes, that moment of realisation swallowing him, blocking his inability to speak as he looks at me, suddenly fearful of the masked woman in front of him. It makes me throb so hard I clench my jaw to ease my sickening desire to bleed him out. He knows this is no longer a game. The mind is a powerful thing. I had kept myself stable for so long, even when I wanted to let go and fall into my own head I refused to ruin my goal. But now it's finally time to let go. Sanity was never my goal.

"Yeahhhhh...there it is. The realisation is suffocating you, isn't it?" I hum deeply to push his suspicions, my barrel still buried in her breasts as I tap his face gently to congratulate him for using his big boy brain, before sliding my hood down and slipping the mask off my face. By the bulging eyes nearly popping out of both of their heads, my face is clearly even more frightening than my false identity and I can't lie, that brings me so much twisted joy.

He's staring into the face of a woman he stole from, and I wish I could frame the terror in his eyes and put it on my wall. It's like his bad dreams have finally come to life, a movie of his forgotten past replaying on a broken tape, as I glare through him with years of haunting pain. He already knows there is no way out of this by the way his Adam's apple bobs, disappearing into the rapid heartbeat beneath his chest.

"Surprise..."

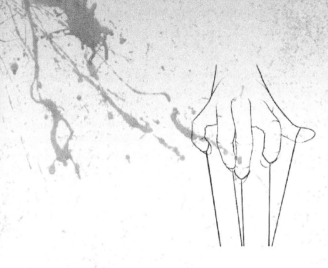

CHAPTER 3

PLEAD YOUR SINS

Puppeteer

Play - 'Destiny - NF'

It looks like he has so much to say but I've sucked the life from him and it's fucking beautiful. Fear is its own font of beauty that I have fallen in love with. I slide the flick knife from my front pocket.

"It doesn't have to be like this. I will do anything you want; I regret what I did every day, she-" he has the audacity to try and victimise himself still when he's staring death in the face? This man's more delusional than I thought. *And they called me crazy?* I cut him off before he can utter another pointless word.

"DONT!... utter her fucking name. I don't want your fucking pity. I don't want to hear your apology. I don't give a flying fuck how you feel. I want your confession!..." Poking the sharp point underneath his chin, digging into his Adam's apple as I direct his focus to lock eyes with mine, I tilt my head in doll-like fashion waiting for his expression to paint a picture of confusion.

"My confession?" *Yes, you sick fuck.*

"I want you to tell me that you had no intention of ever loving her. That you believed my Fathers twisted lies whilst he sat back and watched you tear a family apart. And that you purposely pulled that trigger." Here comes the water works. I can see him conjuring up a sob story to keep him clean, but I know the facts. I was there that night. I saw everything. I saw the way he looked at her and the evidence in his hand from previously searching our home without a warrant. Being in bed with her did not equate to warranting her property. I wish I caught him snooping but I will give him credit. His A+ level acting had me and my Mother both fooled. Maybe that is why I can't let this go. He wasn't a Father by blood, but he gave me a safe sense of security whilst sabotaging our lives behind closed doors. I am the lesser evil amongst men like him who walk this earth.

"Hayl- Hayden... Your Father loved you and your Mother. I couldn't understand why you would take his life." Hearing that sentence almost causes tunnel vision as a surge of untameable rage pumps through my veins, sparking my incessant urge to push his eyes into his skull until they pop under my thumbs and bleed him dry.

"Do you know what he used to do to her behind closed doors?! Huh?! To both of us?! No, you didn't, because you were too tied up in his manipulative little bubble to see the bigger picture! She trusted you. She put her trust in you, even when she had none left to cling to and you shot her in the fucking chest for something I did!" I have him by the scruff of his shirt, my switchblade now surely doing some damage at such close proximity as I shake him around like a rag doll.

"She never told me Hayden. She hid the truth! What else was I meant to do!" I toss him back into the sofa, aiming my barrel square centre to his head watching my sight tremor with pure anger as I rest my finger on the trigger, the corners of my eyes fuzzy with heaving adrenaline. There is just something about someone staring death in the face that makes my eyes fight to not roll into the back of my skull. It's exhilarating. Knowing their life is in the palm of your hands and they either breathe oxygen or choke on their own innards by your choice and your choice alone. It's power. Power that I crave, power that I drown in. Power that I was deprived of for so long while underneath the very people who claim they do good in the world and keep women and children safe. Where were they when I needed them to help? They threw me behind bars and *exiled* me for trying to do exactly what they proclaimed. Where were they when my Mother needed help? They turned a blind eye because they are all sexist pigs. It's amazing what you can get away with in the face of the law and political structure. This man walked free with not so much as a slap on the wrist and the fucker wasn't even remotely in danger. Yet I suffered and endured the worst kind of treatment all because I wasn't wearing a damn badge?

"You were meant to leave us the fuck alone. But you just couldn't do it, could you? You just couldn't leave it the fuck alone." All of this could have been avoided if he had just listened. Read between the lines, *the dumb fuck.*

"She wouldn't want this for you." I clench my jaw so tightly I'm pretty sure I just chipped a tooth, grinding them to ease the dire need to make him choke on his words and vomit them back up, make him gag on my barrel and fire into his sorry excuse of an existence. This vindictive prick is playing the therapist on death's door trying to make me feel something like there is some redemption left inside me. It's amusing. Really. He has no idea of the *monster* he's awoken, the animal he's caged, starved and poked. I want blood and I'm going to get it, but it's fun to watch him think he's getting through to me. It will make it so much more enjoyable for me when he realises the length I will go to just to prove him wrong and watch him suffer.

"Shut your fucking mouth, you aint got a damn clue what she would want. YOU put me behind bars. Remember?" He raises his hands, shielding himself from my aggression

"Let's just talk, ok. You can tell me everything, I will listen and understand." Listen? *Listen*?! He wants to listen now? He's eleven years too fucking late!

"You're kidding right? The damage is DONE. You got what you wanted. You got your freedom, your perfect little life. Nothing you say to me will make me believe you feel remorse. You lied to save your own ass."

"I did what I felt was necessary. I was blind." He can believe in his own lies as much as he wants. Cover it up and pretend he's a saint. But we both know he had a choice.

"No. You were just taking on the role you always have been deep down. A *Murderer*. Admit it. Admit you fired that gun on purpose." He stutters, muttering another lie.

"I told you, the same as I told them, it was self-defence." If I hear those words one more time, I WILL burn this house down with him still breathing.

"Bull shit! You knew damn well she was not going to hurt you! She was just protecting me!" On what planet would someone like my Mother ever lay a hand on him. There was never a bad bone in her body.

"If you kill me now, you are no better than me Hayden. No better than *him*." The difference is, I own what I am and I wear it with pride. I don't hide from it. I don't run away and start a new life built on lies.

"I don't plan on being *better*. So it makes no odds to me." If I planned on being better, I wouldn't have spent the last four years tracking him down? Does he really think that thought hasn't crossed my mind?

"Just listen to yourself. You are turning into the man you feared most." My eye twitches, finding everything within me not to pull the trigger into the back of his throat.

"He was no man. He was the *Devil*. And I pray that when I leave this god forsaken piece of shit we call earth, that he is in hell, waiting for me so I can kill him again." He is the entire reason we are both in this mess. He killed an innocent woman to protect a man who couldn't of given two fucks about it. It's laughable really. *How fucking dumb can you be?*

"Please. Don't do this." I glance to his right, into the eyes of his wife who looks as frightened and as confused as I was that night.

"Those were her words before you pulled that trigger. They meant nothing to you. And they mean nothing to me." As I finish my sentence, she tries to make a run for it, tripping back down onto the sofa as my palm grips her loose hair, yanking her back down with harsh force.

"Sit. The fuck. Down." My teeth grind, throwing her back into the seat. Did she really fucking think that was going to work? Now I take no responsibility for my actions.

"Did you. Or did you not. Pull that trigger knowing full well what you were doing?" The barrel of my gun rests between his eyes.

"I told you!... It was self-defence!" I refrain from pulling the trigger, having too much fun watching him tremor.

"I'm giving you five seconds to answer correctly or I'm firing your lie through her skull," she sobs, glaring at him in desperation and it's a beautiful sight. So fucking ironic.

"Did you. Or did you NOT. Voluntarily fire that gun, *John*." He stays mute, leaning back in the chair trying to escape the metal.

"*Five*."

"I don't know how many times I have to tell you! I didn't fire on purpose!" Even with her life on the line he still lies through his teeth. He really is a good for nothing son of a bitch.

"*Four*."

"You're fucking crazy!" He takes her hand, squeezing it tightly and this act of '*love*' makes my skin crawl.

"Are you really going to fight this when her life is at stake? *Three*." He finally realises I'm not joking, lifting his hands to surrender as those words I've been waiting for finally choke out of his mouth.

"Ok! I fired with intention! I killed her! I was angry and confused! I'm sorry!" Relief eases off my shoulders, rolling it out as I lick my lips with anticipation.

"Good boy..." I grip the back of his neck with callousness, swinging him to face the fear in her eyes.

A bullet finds its home in her skull as I pull the trigger.

"NO-"

...

"It doesn't matter how much you plead your sins to save someone else. They end up taking the bullet meant for you anyway, isn't that right? *Detective*." I hold him there, fighting his reluctance to watch his beloved bleed out all over the couch but he needs to fucking watch, I want him to watch the life drain from her pretty little eyes. My grip tightens as his loose tears turn into heavy flows of guilt, cradling her head in his hands, mumbling sweet little nothings under his breath.

"I just wanted to hear you beg like I did before you killed my Mother. Before I do what I should have done that night." He's angry. *Good.* Everything he's feeling, everything he wants to say is sitting at the tip of his tongue but he's still holding himself back.

"Here's how this is going to go... I'm going to talk. And you're going to listen," the knife dances between my leather tendrils.

"Let me show you, just what kind of *'friend'* you were dealing with," I slip a lighter from my back pocket. Placing it beside me on the coffee table as I take a seat, almost breaking it with my weight, pulling a cigarette from the box.

"What kind of man you called a friend, shall I?" He doesn't look at all pleased, peering at his deceased wife, leaking from the temple of her forehead, staining his white polo shirt.

"That won't be necessary!" Necessary? This is a *necessity.*

"What's the matter? You scared? You know what wasn't necessary? My Mother's fucking *DEATH.*" My fist cracks against his cheek bone, forcing him to glare at her and take it in once more.

"What can I do. Please. Tell me! Anything!"

...

"You can *Feel.*" I draw a flame, burning the tip of my cigarette and sucking in a long puff before pulling it away from my lips, analysing it between my fingers.

...

"Did you know, that a cigarette burns to $752°F$?" Tears pile up until they break down his face, trying to make sense of my words as I hover it in front of him.

"He wouldn't -" he worked with criminals and he sounds surprised?

"No? Wouldn't he?" I blow a gale of smoke causing him to choke on it as my hand lowers, closing the gap between my cigarette and the back of his hand.

"Please, I have a-" before he has a chance to speak, I shove a rag down his throat, watching him squirm like salt on a worm.

"It's rude to talk with your mouth full." My knife slices between his veins, pinning his hand to the arm of the sofa, pushing a hole into his flesh, burning a bullet wound into the hand that wielded his gun.

"The truth hurts. Doesn't it?..." He's being so fucking loud it's just escalating my rage. He has no place to cry like a bitch. The back of my hand finds his cheek as I stand to my feet, towering over him.

"That burning sensation. Imagine that. *Over. And over. And over. Again...*" I rip my leather glove off, revealing my battered hand from within, primarily smothered in ink to cover my wounds but remnants of craters in my flesh still remain.

"For your sake. I'll make this quick. Believe it or not, I'm not as sadistic as my Father. And I'm sick of fucking looking at you. This is *over.*" I shove the barrel of my gun inside his mouth, pushing the fabric to the back of his throat further, choking him until he leans back into the sofa, my boot finding his torso to keep him pinned beneath me before pulling the trigger, effectively using it as an added silencer.

It's finally over.

SHASSII

CHAPTER 4

MY NIGHTMARE

Puppet

I wake abruptly to the voices in my head. Screams down my ear that felt so real I questioned if it was a nightmare but I feel uneasy. I am usually such a heavy sleeper and this insulin knocks me out. *How strange.* My heart is still racing as I check my phone and it's literally midnight? *12:32 AM.* I lay there for a moment, trying to come up with a reason as to why I am awake at this damn time of night when I hear shuffling downstairs. But not them. Unless Dad's digging his way to China to find something.

What is going on?

I sit up in my silky white pyjamas, my legs flooding cold as I slide them out from underneath the duvet and make my way to the hallway. They must still be awake, all the lights are on? I go to knock on their bedroom door. No answer. They are usually in bed by now. Maybe they are having a horror movie night. If they are I'll be mad, they know I love horror movies, regardless of if I went to bed early. *Blasphemy.*

I make my way downstairs quietly and can still hear the TV, white noise now sawing at my ears. Maybe they have fallen asleep and forgot to turn the TV off? Walking into the living room they are both sitting on the sofa. Well... more, slumped? They look asleep. I creep my way to the coffee table reaching for the remote and press the power button glancing up to catch their reflection in the black screen.

Am I still dreaming?

I go to scream but nothing comes out. My feet are nailed to the floor, frozen in fear. *Paralysed*. Squinting my lids so hard I see stars as I reopen them trying to take away this nightmare I'm currently living in.

Come on Alora. Wake up. Wake. UP.

I turn my head slowly, terrified to admit this reality, hoping it was still in my head but this time it's not in my head, it's very much real, *this can't be real.* This has to be a dream. Why aren't I waking up? Both of them are sitting with two clean bullet holes through the centre of their brows, singular tears of blood leaking down the circumference of their faces, dripping onto their white attire, they are staring back at me with their eyes wide open, if nightmares walked among us this would be it. The white in their eyes bloodshot and dull of any glimmer, freeze frame faces, dripping with fear, like they had been frozen and on a tape, the expressions still etched into their lifeless body. Solid like stone. *Pale. Cold. Stiff.*

Dead.

Play - 'That Home - The Cinematic Orchestra'

They are *dead*. I think I'm going to barf... I can't breathe, yelping in oxygen as my chest heaves. I lose all feeling in my legs as I collapse onto the wooden oak floor. The back of the sofa is bleeding red, seeping into the fabric and the stench of metal is tainting the air. I claw for their legs, struggling to steady my breathing as uncontrollable tears begin to flood my face. These bullet wounds are fresh, whoever did this is still in this house, that is what must have woken me up. My bitter face turns to the noises coming from the basement and my heart sinks, lower and lower until it sits in the pit of my stomach, wiping my wet lashes to clear my blurry vision, fumbling for my fathers phone. *Shit.* I don't know the damn password. *FUCK.* And I just touched crucial evidence, *my fingerprints are all over it.* I stand quietly, trembling to hold my weight as my eyes fix to the door down the corridor ahead leading to my least favourite part of the house. I suck in to hold my breath as cries try to escape my mouth. I can feel sweat forming like a rash all over my flesh, burning me from the inside out, adrenaline kick starting causing my head to thump. I've watched enough murder documentaries to see where this is going. But watching it and actually partaking in one is very different and suddenly I can't think.

Think, Alora think!

I need a weapon. Looking over at the kitchen door, I swallow blades down the inside of my throat, building up the courage to move quietly and carefully towards the room. I'm quivering as the mix of fear and the temperature of the night sweep the back of my neck. Reaching the block of knives, I slide one out gently and I can't hear anything over the hollow drumming in my head and the static white noise grating at my hearing, it's nauseating. I'm on the verge of vomiting. Fear I've never experienced is now flooding every nerve aligning my body.

The door.

They got in somehow. The door must be open. Tip toeing lightly around the island I grab the door handle, squeezing my face up like a raisin as I twist it clockwise praying it doesn't make too much sound. I tug it towards me slightly and it jams. *The bastard locked it back up.* I tug it a little harder as my eyes run, cutting down my cheeks, closing my throat to sob silently into the window of the doorframe. I'm going to die tonight. And I'm not ready to die.

I don't understand. Who would do this? Why? What unorthodox deed did my father commit that led to his demise?

Footsteps begin to make their way up the basement staircase and I could have sworn my hearts stopped beating.

Alora. You need to move. NOW.

Shaking off my paralysis, I think of the next best thing. I need a gun. He always has...*had*... Guns in his office. But I haven't a clue what the safe code is. Please have a handgun in arms reach. It's lucky I am so small, you can barely hear me moving across the floorboards as I hover on my toes, sliding inside the room where I'm met with this now cold and empty space. A space he used to sit, a warm and inviting atmosphere now desolate with memories I have yet to comprehend the extent of. I have no time to grieve right now and that is weighing heavily on my need to stay alive. I want nothing more than to let the floor swallow me whole and give up this enviable fight, but something is telling me to fight. To keep pushing. That instinct in the back of your head that keeps you breathing and doesn't let you give up.

I scurry for the desk nearly fumbling over, my balance is totally off right now. I physically cannot feel anything but pins and needles lacing every pore in my skin. I reach for the little drawers sitting either side of his office chair, the varnished wood making it hard to grip with my wet and sweaty hands as I attempt to pull them out. *Nothing.* There is nothing but paperwork and stationery.

As solid taps turn into shallow thumps exchanging levels between the basement and the first floor, heavy boots echo down the corridor making their way straight to the office where their feet cut off the light source leaking in underneath the door from the hallway. I duck behind the desk, covered by only a small barrier of plywood where the legs rest. Placing my hand over my mouth, I begin to push so tightly I nearly cut off my oxygen supply as the door creaks open.

They are in here and I have no way of getting out if they stick around. They are homing in on me and all I can do is close my eyes and pray. I'm not a believer but please, hear me now. My pyjamas are literally stuck to me, soaking with sweat and my hair is smothering my damp cheeks. I'm completely still, like someone has injected aconite into my blood, static electricity coursing through me as I grip tightly to the knife glued to my chest. So focused on being silent that I suddenly notice the silence. They have stopped moving but I can feel them glaring at me through the wood, like they can smell my presence in the room with them. Horror movies aren't so fun in real life. I don't ever wish to star in one.

They shift again, and by the sounds of it they are moving away from me. The hall light that was illuminating the room has now dimmed, leaving only a sliver of light slicing up the wall and ceiling behind me. Maybe they are leaving? I feel like a shell. The body that once inhabited me is no longer present, a cavity replacing the fleshy parts of me, the parts of me that cannot be replaced. I've lost everything I once knew and gained trepidation of the future that I may possibly never even live to see. Even if I do, what now? What's left for me besides mourning for that missing part of me that made me whole. My life will never be the same. How are you supposed to move on when your heart is stuck, beating for a life that doesn't exist as you sit braindead in a void of infinite emptiness. I knew I'd lose them one day, but I wasn't ready for it to be so soon.

The silence is becoming deafening as the space between me and them grows. I have a gap. I need to get upstairs and use my phone. Crawling out from underneath the confinements of the desk, I make my way to the exit, heart in my mouth trying not to vomit it up. My stomach is physically aching as I grip the door to peep out into the hallway. It seems empty and I hear no movement. *Now is my chance.*

I push for the stairs, creeping up them like a kid at Christmas trying to see Santa until I get to my bedroom, the is still open and I run for my phone which I now realise I forgot to charge. The damn thing is dead. *You've got to be kidding me.* The last option I have is my window which leads out onto the roof. It's one you have to push up and it's always jamming so I don't know how the hell I'm going to do this quietly. I cup the wood and push it as gently as I can, the wood grinds against the window frame, the belt squeaking without lubrication as it inches open, barely enough to get my hands through as I grab the bottom and pull it up, cringing at how damn noisy it is in the desolate silence that surrounds me. Everything is two times louder at night.

A sudden surge of heat burns into my legs directing my focus to the tears of crimson running down my outer thigh, I must have caught myself with the knife. Rubbing the warm liquid against my salty skin I follow the trail all the way down to my foot and my heart sinks to the bottom of my abdomen when I peer down at the carpet beneath me, a perfect blood trail haunts me through the bedroom door to where I'm now stood, cutting the room in two like an earthquake. I can't hide, I've just led them straight to me. My muscles seize, growing tighter against my bones as I tense.

Boots begin to climb the stairs, breaking the floorboards beneath them and all I can do is lock this door. I run for the handle, turning the lock anticlockwise until I hear it click before backing away slowly, light on my feet, holding my breathing so tightly I'm beginning to feel lightheaded, and it feels like I've just jumped fully dressed into a pool, heaving in painful silence, fixated on the handle as their thuds becomes deeper.

They stop. Silence filling the grave around me, boxed in with nowhere to go, already making my bed in a coffin. I glare at the window and scan the room for something heavy. A stack of books are perched on the corner of my bedside table. *I need to distract them.* I pick them up and throw them with all the power left in me, shattering the glass until my carpets smothered in shards.

They are still silent. A few minutes go by and I find my feet again, creeping towards the door, the eerie stillness peaking my curiosity as I press my ear gently against the door, listening for any signs of life beyond the dirt. My eyes rattle at the nothingness, only the sound of my beating heart tunnelling my ear drums bouncing back against the wood. *Are they gone? Did they fall for my decoy?*

I press a little harder, cracking the lining of the door slightly before heavy duty nails pierce the barricade just centimetres from my nose pushing a yelp up my throat, throwing my hands flush against my mouth as I leap back from the door.

COLLATERAL DAMAGE

SHASSII

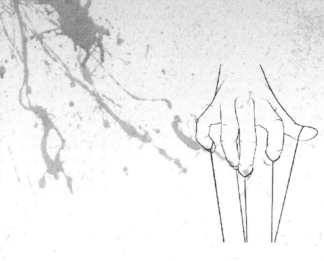

CHAPTER 5

COLLATERAL DAMAGE

Puppeteer

I heard the glass. But I wasn't born yesterday. No idiot is going to clamber through a broken window in pyjamas, most likely barely covering their skin. My bat is now wedged firmly inside the door protecting them from me and a sinister snarl falls slyly against my mouth as a yelp breaches through the walls. I don't hurt children, but they seem too smart to be that young. I was in the middle of setting the house ablaze before whoever this was ruined it. I guess I still could. I'd just have to hang around a while to make sure whoever this is, doesn't get out alive.

Their blood is smeared against the rubber souls of my boots and I can feel their heartbeat through the still air. I've been where they are more times than I would like to admit, fearful of my life. Fearful of evil, fearful of the *Devil*. And although I may not be him, part of his black heart poisoned mine in the process when exchanging my freedom. I inhabit a darkness that finds pleasure in this game of hide and seek, but it won't last long. My patience is slim and they are running it out rapidly.

I wait, even tempered behind the door for around five minutes before they finally buck up the courage to beeline for the front door. *More fun for me.* The door flings open abruptly, thudding echoes through the empty hallway before reaching my leathered hand to grip their forearm. It's pitch black up here but her dark, pin straight hair and blanc skin against the shadows that encapsulate us are nothing short of an eyesore.

Lilies and butterscotch sting my nose as her hair fights with the dead breeze, obstructing her sight as her body swings clockwise to face me and a hearty gush of blood slices my arm. *The bitch caught me with a knife.* I let my guard drop, shaking off the pain as she legs it down the maze of corridors that make up this house, but there is only one way down.

And that is past me.

I yank my weapon from the door frame, tugging it down a notch, wiggling it to release, snapping the bonds and leaving splinters to ride up the centre as I stride after her. Dragging the nails across the wood I stalk the top floor, slowly, with malice waiting for her to run her little legs down the stairs where I will be waiting.

It doesn't take long for her to leg it for the opening and my bat meets the back of her calf muscle, the nails tearing her skin spilling a river down the backs of her sweaty flesh, listening to her sweet cries of pain. I wouldn't have to hurt her if she didn't run. She crawls across the floor slowly, dragging her immobile leg behind her as she floods the floor with her tears.

"Please!" She pleads, but I take no notice. I haven't got time for this. I need to get out of here. My impatience is getting the best of me. Turning her to face me, I'm ready to drive my switch blade across her delicate little throat and watch her bleed out slowly across the floor for me but as our eyes meet, I gently pierce the sharp edge into her jugular and she gapes at the horror that I am with my mask glaring back at her, taking in her final moments, pools spilling over her cheeks. She's blubbering words I cannot understand beneath her breath and I twist my split tongue, rubbing each fork against the piercings in my mouth, sucking in her pain as her eyes catch me completely off guard, so full of sadness and fear. I feel like I am looking at my own reflection, frightening me to let her go. This is unusual, this feeling is foreign to me, *I've never hesitated?*

She thumps to her elbows, ready to crawl away and in my moment of weakness I almost lose her. I grab the bottom of her silky white shirt pulling her back below me as I lace rope around her petite wrists, so tiny I could snap them and prop her up against the nearest wall.

"Please don't do this! Please let me go!" She murmurs as I mute her with tape, blocking out her voice driving my guilt as I begin to pace back and forth collecting my thoughts, her incessant whining breaking beneath me through her muzzle, eating at my frustration. *All of this is wrong, everything is wrong, she wasn't supposed to be here, why is she here, who even is she? How the hell did I miss this? There are no records of a fucking kid. If there was, I would have gone about this entirely differently!* Cries bleed through my subconscious, blocking my concentration until I snap.

"Will you shut the fuck up!... I don't want to hurt you. Don't make me hurt you. Please. Be a good girl and Shhhh..." I slowly kneel to her level, rubbing my leather finger against the soaked tape, smouldered in salty tears as she wriggles away from my touch, snatching her head to the side to unlink us but my grasp finds her chin, yanking her back to look into the eyes of the monster before her, tapping her cheek with sweet abuse three times.

The whining stops.

"There we go..." I can finally hear myself fucking think.

Gasoline. That's what I was doing until I was rudely interrupted. I holster her body over my shoulder carrying her downstairs and place her by the front door before heading to the basement for the gasoline I was searching for buried underneath tools and building materials. *Gotcha.*

I can just burn the evidence, and it will be investigated as a house fire, that way there is no trace of me or this thing I'm now going to have to fucking figure out what to do with, but I will get to that later, right now I just need to get out of here.

I begin to pour gasoline coating the downstairs floor from the basement all the way to the front door, as I close in on her, finding her shuffling her front across the floor towards the exit, dripping her gash all over the floor as she pulls her feeble body towards freedom like I won't catch her. *Stupid girl.* I drop the canister and creep towards her vulnerable body, bleeding under my boot as I grab her by the ankles, dragging her through her own mess, pressing her against the wall as my hand meets her throat.

"Where do you think you're going?" She's trembling, vibrating my fingers with pure fear and I want to let her run, but I can't. *Not now.* So I tie her to the stair banister, securing her in place while I finish ransacking this place. Her glossy sadness sheets her gaze, and I exhale a heavy sigh. *I suppose I am going to have to take her with me now aren't I. Fabulous, just what I fucking needed.* I run for her room, grabbing a bag from the back of her door, filling it with things she may possibly need, clothes, a book sat on her bed side table and an elephant teddy sat on her pillow. *That'll do. She's lucky I'm not a complete dick.*

I get back down to greet her, she's rocking her head back and forth, clamping her eyes closed to shake her nightmare that is very much real, no matter how many times she sits there and tries to wake up, I am her living *nightmare.* I look at the canister and decide against the idea. If she manages to escape me some day, she may need a home to come back to. *Just as I did.*

She refuses to look at me but I stroke away the wet strands of hair from her face anyway. *I'm sorry Love.*

"Sleep tight." The blunt end of my blade finds the side of her temple, quick and sharp, knocking her unconscious.

"Easy does it…" I catch her head in the palm of my hand as she limps her deadweight into me, cradling her fall. I don't have sedatives on me right now, they are in the car so that was the next best thing, I couldn't risk her screaming outside. I know she lives in the middle of butt fuck nowhere but I haven't a clue where the next house is or about the area. The sharp end finds the tie, cutting the rope to free her from the stairs.

"Come on *Princess.* Let's go." I murmur, my arms looping underneath her arms and legs, exiting the front door of the building as I carry her to my car, realising how absolutely ridiculous this is. I've never kidnapped anyone. Holding someone against their will is as far as I've gone. What the fuck am I meant to do now? Do I kill her? Do I let her go? Do I get the fuck out of here before she has a chance to turn me in? Do I just finish what I fucking started and kill us both?

I sedate her to make sure she doesn't wake for at least six hours while I figure out what the hell I'm meant to do from here. I lug her into the back seat along with her bag, propping her up against the window so it looks like she is just sleeping. Luckily no one will be on the road at this time and they won't be found until at least the middle of next week so I'm safe.

For now.

SHASSII

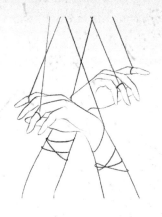

CHAPTER 6

DAMAGED GOODS

Puppet

I break open my eyes, hazy and unaware of my surroundings, worrying I've gone blind when I realise, I've been restricted from sight and my mouth is still taped shut which only heightens my anxiety. I was drugged and I'm still in full effect. My head is spinning, pounding at my frontal skull and all minor strength has been sucked from my feeble muscles. This feeling is something of a living nightmare which only grows worse when I find the energy to move and realise both my wrists are bound to what I can only assume is a bed I'm lying on. The chains clank against the metal sending me into a fit of panic I can't even describe as my clothes stick to my hot skin. I'm still in my pyjamas so at least they were modest enough to keep me clothed.

Trying to keep my composure, I focus on my breathing, sitting in a pool of discomfort as my sore eyes graze my lids. I feel like I've got stones in my sockets where I've shed so many tears that are still spilling over, too focused on my breathing to realise the dirty great gash that has split the back of my calf. I muffle a yelp behind the tape as I try to shuffle it against the bed sheets. It feels wrapped but it doesn't make it any less painful. Even drugged to the high heavens the throbbing is churning the back of my throat, shooting up the back of my leg interrupting my nervous system. I don't think they hit anything vital, but the blood still wants to pour out of the wound like a tap. It's throbbing so hard I squint at the pain, wanting to scream as the tape pulls at my skin surrounding my mouth. I stretch it with pained cheek movements to accommodate the uncontrollable whining, wallowing in this torment as I sway rhythmically to try and ease the urge to lose my mind. I'm lying here like Jesus on a cross and I haven't a clue what's going on beyond my current position. What monstrosity I am currently sitting in. Where I even am?

I tune in to the sounds and smells, using all my senses to my advantage. The air smells stale, thick with must. A place that hasn't been looked after and a potent stench of paint that makes me queasy. I never did like that smell...when we moved that smell lingered around the house for almost a year.

Focusing on distant shuffling, heavy rubber boots graze the wooden floorboards and the sound of water running in the distance sends a shiver along my spine, the gushing tap making the centre of my legs swell with a sudden desperation to use the lavatory but that isn't possible right now. *Hey Mr Killer. May I use your bathroom?*

My heart accelerates tenfold when their footprints approach me, homing in on my personal space. I'm trembling with anticipation. I know what I saw and I know the profile they hold. I'm going to die here and I feel like I've been shot in the chest. This ache is unbearable, like heartburn, like someone lit a match and ignited a fire inside my chest that I can't put out no matter how many tears I cry.

I go to force another sob before a finger meets the outer lining of the tape plastered across my mouth making me freeze like marble, sobbing into the void as I hold my breath, praying they remove my prison mask but it remains on. They smell of leather and men's tacky cologne as I feel them perch on the bed beside me indenting the mattress. I hear a glass hit a wooden surface, as I manoeuvre myself inches away from them in protest. I want to scream but I'm frozen solid and my mouth is restricted, feeling sweat lather my skin like heat rash.

"The longer you fight. The harder this is for both of us." Their voice is like that one song you can't stand, scrunching your face in displease when you hear it play. It's so rough and low it makes my brittle bones rattle.

I can only listen. Shaking like a leaf as their words slice through my open wounds, still bleeding. I don't know how long I've been out but by the way my muscles have seized like a century old pipe. It's been a while and it's making it hard to keep calm. I'm weak, I'm vulnerable, I'm restrained with no way out, stuck in the confinement of my own darkness, accompanied by a monster with incalculable intentions and a suffering worse than torture.

"I never intended for this." They say deeply, a guilty conscience is lingering against their prompt, but I can't read their objective and it's only making this more frightening.

The worst-case scenarios and profound feelings start to engross my conscious mind and I hope I die before they happen.

Rape. Torture. Violence. Psychical abuse. Dismembering.

Disquietude is pumping through my cold veins, warming my fight or flight instinct but I have neither. I'm just helpless prey caught in a trap waiting to be slaughtered and fed to rabid dogs.

"You weren't supposed to be a part of this," their leather gloves stagger my wet cheeks, wiping away my sorrow as I almost swallow my tongue from tensing it to the back of my throat realising their touch is entirely different. *Tender?*

"You need to believe me if you want this to work in your favour. Do you understand? Nod if you understand." I do as I'm told like a good girl, too fearful of the outcome if I do not comply. I will do anything right now to keep the monster at bay. The last thing I want to do is rattle its cage when it's starving.

Killers don't kill for no reason. It's always feeding something, and they play with their food if they aren't yet ready to feast again.

"I'm going to remove your binds when I feel I can trust you with the knowledge you will come to learn." I replay what they say in my head and I'm sensing a twisted kindness. They don't seem to want to harm me, they plan on having me stick around? And the *why* is the part that frightens me the most. They like to lure you into a false sense of security only to tear it from your chest. They said 'come to learn' like I will be sticking around, so I suppose I can be grateful they don't want to end me but I'll be honest that really doesn't ease my mind at all. That could mean so many different things with so many different outcomes. None I see are good right now unless I ended up being kidnapped by a friendly killer. Chances? slim to none. When the hell do you see that on the news? *Never.*

My head rests on a pillow, sinking into it to hold my head which is far more than I expected when held against my will. They push themself back off the bed and I hear the flick of fabric and a gust of cold wind smother my skin in goosebumps. Flinching so hard I tense my torn calf muscle and hiss through the pain as a blanket encapsulates me. I'm afraid they want to suffocate me but instead it rests on my exposed frame, closing me in from the cold.

"You've been out for six hours. Now you're in the land of the living I can finally comfort that pain." What does that mean? What are they going to do? That doesn't sound good at all.

A glass drags against wood and the sound of tinfoil tinkers at my senses, the air is sucked from my lungs as they rip the tape from my mouth, the sound scraping against my ears as I feel a layer of my skin peel off with it, stinging my lips and the sensitive skin around it like lip balm plumper.

"Open." They demand. They don't hesitate but I certainly am. I am already drugged up enough as it is, what could they possibly want to put in my mouth? But their voice is racking my bones and I daren't disobey. I open my mouth slowly to reap my death as a pill rests on my dry tongue, promptly followed with a glass of water to wash it down as they hold it in place for me to drink. I guzzle, like a lost man in a desert, relieving my tense shoulders as the cool liquid soothes my hoarse throat and I'm found unsatisfied as they pull the glass away and repeat the process. I'm so thirsty for relief that the pill goes down like chocolate.

I don't even gag which is strange considering I fear pills like people fear spiders. It's amazing what you'll do in the face of danger. *Why are they comforting my pain though?* This doesn't make any sense, not that I am at all in any position to see sense or conjure up rational thinking right now. I take my pills, and they haven't affected me but I don't think I'd even be able to tell on top of the drugs already in my system. My eyes feel heavy. I pull my chin into my chest as I fight to hold it up but all I want to do right now is sleep and possibly never wake up. I'm full of drugs and I haven't eaten anything since before I got home. I literally missed my favourite meal because I was sulking -

Shit.

My insulin! I've been so caught up in being literally kidnapped that I didn't even take into consideration that I have not taken insulin for most likely over my time frame. But maybe this is a good thing? I mean. I know the side effects are heavy but at least I will no longer be a problem and I will be with my parents. What do I have to gain if I even get out of here now anyway?

Lost in thought I drift off into another timeless sleep from pure exhaustion. Adrenaline is its own drug. When you use too much, the come down is even heavier.

I creep open my eyes expecting to see darkness, and I do see darkness, but this time I see it's 3D with light and shadows casting the room that I can now see in front of me. Particles of dust fill the air like space as the light seeps into the room between the cracks of the plywood plastering the windows shut to my left-hand side, barricading me from the outside world. They're isolating me from my life through rose tinted glasses and I'm only seeing the bleak, desolate numbness in the shade of black that is their house, *or hide out?* Or whatever this is.

It has a poignant stench of trauma and pain that makes my skin writhe. You can feel it in the air. The way the dust is thick on every surface, the stained floorboards with god knows what. *Blood? Mud? Dirt?* and the crooked picture frames. The way the doors creak, echoing through the building like an old Victorian manor and the way the paints peeling from its foundations. *Why would anyone settle here?* It's beyond creepy and makes me pray this process quickens its pace.

I turn my head to catch a digital alarm clock, lit up in red. 13:46.

I've been out for over twelve hours! Suffocating on the smoke invading the air and the smell of fear, my eyes are dry and stiff. Surely this much sleep is not good for the body and I'm beginning to smell. I can't see what I look like right now but I just know that my hair is thick with grease and I have the biggest bags under my eyes, The irregular temperatures of my body during the night have stuck me to this blanket that I can't even remove and my insulin withdrawal is already having a great effect on me.

Not long after my loss in thought, a door chimes in the distance sending the hairs on the back of my neck to stand. *They are here.* Clattering and banging in the rooms surrounding me. This time I can pinpoint where the noises are coming from and they are closing in on the door facing directly to my right. I squeeze my eyes shut in fear but they soon burst back open when I see my parents slumped on the sofa, bleeding out. The clown mask in the darkness, how it followed me through the house. How my screams replay in my own head and remind me how helpless I really am. How I am about to face my greatest fear any second now.

The knob turns on its axis, sending a wave of sweat over my entire body. Behind my blind fold I didn't have to face them but now that I do it makes it much worse. The door creaks open slightly before being pushed harshly sending a heavy force of wind in my direction. They are stood in the doorway cowering in the darkness of the corridor, smothered in black attire and those heavy boots I have come to loathe, a constant reminder of the worst night of my life. But this time the face is different. Still a creepy clown but not so solid, more like paint.

Paint.

It makes sense now.

They gawk at me through the black holes carved into their face, but their eyes look straight through mine, one broken soul to another, a heavy contrast against the moons within and the contorted sculpture of their face that I can now see cutting through the shadows. They are so tall they are almost ducking underneath the door frame mimicking my own paralysis demon as I'm stuck in stone, unable to move or speak and their build is so wide they take up the entire door frame. I have a voice now, but the words don't come out. Fear suffocates my throat, strangling me tightly as I lie helpless. I suddenly don't want to see; I want the blind fold back on.

They tilt their head like a creepy doll, analysing me as if they didn't take my blindfold off, breaching the room, one foot after another, edging closer towards the bed until they are hanging over me gripping the metal bars tightly above my head.

"I thought I almost lost you there..." Their voice is so husky and light on their tongue I feel my spine shuffle at their words. A line with so many meanings. I feel like an abused pet in a cage. Given scraps and chained to a post wanting to retaliate with inner rage but I know I will come off worse. My face remains on them but my eyes wonder, looking for any means of escape.

"There's no way out of those Cuffs. *Puppet.*" My skin crawls at their hideous nickname. *Puppet.* That is exactly what I am right now. I'm even hung like one. It's like they could read my mind. How many times have they done this before? How many girls have been on this bed? How many frightened innocent lives have been exposed to this nightmare.

"Are you going to kill me?" *Why did I ask that?* They are a murderer. Fluttering your lashes and playing innocent is not going to change anything.

"I mean you no harm, but I will if you piss me off. So don't piss me off." That was a warning and a warning I should probably listen to but my fight or flight mode is telling me to do stupid things to survive. They have pledged to keep their hands off me but how am I meant to take their word for it.

"What do you want from me?" My voice is shaky, and my fear is causing tears to travel up my throat. There must be some sort of motive to this sick game they are playing.

"Nothing." They whisper with upmost confidence. I don't know what is worse. Being held captive because they want something from you or being held captive to be their new plaything.

"Then why am I here? Let me go. I promise I won't say a word. I don't even know what you look like!" They took my blindfold off meaning they trust me; they said it themselves. They know with their face paint and creepy face masks that even if I got out and was able to get to a police station. It would be impossible to identify what they look like. It's why they do it. Why you wear a balaclava when you rob a bank. You're hidden in plain sight so you can commit a felony without repercussions and walk amongst the busy street in broad daylight with no suspicions. The mind of a killer is always something I have been so fascinated with and now I have the chance to learn and understand one. All I want to do is crawl into a six-foot grave and bury myself. Being chained to a bed and starved is not quite the same as an interrogation room. They are meant to be the ones cuffed, not me.

"You're *Collateral Damage*. Nothing more." Is that meant to bring me comfort? I have so many questions I'm afraid to ask. Their eyes rip through me like a sharp blade as I endure the sting, conjuring up my courage to ask the most embarrassing question.

"May I use your bathroom?" I know I shouldn't ask but if I don't I'm literally going to piss all over their bed and I would rather keep away from any sort of punishment until I know what I'm really dealing with here.

"As you asked so nicely," my eyes widen at their compliance, suddenly thinking of all the ways I can escape this building once they untie my hands. It can't be sudden as I know I will barely be able to pick myself off the bed, but earning their trust is the closest thing I have right now to meddling with my freedom.

"While we're at it, you can have a shower." Before I even have a moment to reply they are keying my cuffs and my wrists fall limp against the damp bed sheets, mixed with sweat and humid air. My body is so frail right now I don't have the energy to fight or conjure up an escape plan. I tug my right leg to meet the edge of the bed, followed by my left one letting out a bellow scream from my throat as the wound grazes against the bedsheets and the now crusted band-aid. I will barely be able to stand on this. I holster my body up right, my feet touching the grainy wooden floor beneath me, cringing at the texture.

"Walk." They grab my forearm, yanking my dead body weight up off the bed. I hiss and clamber for stability only to realise they have perfect hold of me. I must be featherweight to them and their height has me quivering. They lead me out of the bedroom door, towering over my tiny body, I'm hobbling like a granny and I feel like one. How do these people get pleasure out of doing this? They essentially turn themselves into a caretaker for dummies. My leg is pulsating like my heartbeat through my skin, reviving its rest as the blood pumps through my dormant leg dragging me towards the door ahead that leads to the bathroom. As if the bedroom was not bad enough, the bathroom looks like the set of the first Saw movie. I stand by the entrance to the room for a moment and peer inside, taking in my surroundings. They don't seem to like that very much, tugging me inside where the tiles sting the bottom of my feet.

"You have two minutes." I situate myself as I watch the door close and lock behind me. *Who has a lock on the outside of the bathroom?* I run my fingers over my sore wrists, gliding them across the delicate skin. The restraints weren't tight but being strung for near on twelve hours puts a strain on anyone's skin. A bath is to the right of the door, grimy with limescale, a sink is bolted on the left wall with a cracked-up mirror you can just about see your reflection in and there is a shower and toilet in front of me. It's a walk-in shower which is definitely an upgrade for these kinds of slumps but all my mind envisions is pain and blood on the walls, seeing things that are not there. My eyes search for any means to escape but only a tiny, vented window sits up above the toilet, not even big enough to fit my body through.

I catch my reflection and yesterday's mascara I forgot to wipe off is all smeared down my face, I look just like them. A clown on a budget with bags heavier than bruises. My eyes swell at the girl I do not recognise as my sweaty hair, now dark and inky sticks to my salty skin. In twelve hours, my life has turned from a fairytale into a dark past of a villain's story that they don't tell you about.

I perch myself on the loo, tugging down my dirty pyjamas still smothered in speckled blood when something falls from my pocket.

My insulin.

Of course, I completely forgot I put one in my pocket for safekeeping in case of emergencies. Mom always drilled it into me to keep one on me at all times and I always used to tell her it was silly to sleep with one when I use it before bed and when I wake up. I take it three times a day but I haven't taken it in over twelve hours so I don't have a clue if it will do anything for me apart from make me worse. I've never really missed a shot my entire life, but having strict parents who knew when you pissed and shit I suppose had its perks. A bang rattles the tiled cell.

"You have one minute." They really weren't kidding. I take the pen, and place it just above my abdomen area, injecting myself with my own drugs to keep me breathing. Holding it for five seconds. I realise it's the last 40 units in the pen. It's a sad little life I live really... it's things like this that make me question why I should keep fighting at all. Once I get out, if I get out, it's only one cell to another. My own body imprisons me on a daily basis. A daily reminder that I am damaged goods and will never amount to anything as long as I have this medical condition that is not curable. *I am not curable.* To be truthful. This is probably the most exciting thing that has ever happened to me, and my body is already shutting down. I am like an alcoholic without alcohol. A mad hatter without their meds. It will slowly eat away at me until I'm nothing. I will never be normal. But then I suppose no one is normal. *What is normal?*

"Times up." They bang on the door once more, jumping out of my skin as I sit zoned out staring at my pen.

"One second!" I need to hide this somewhere or they might confiscate it. I climb on top of the toilet and can just about reach for the window ledge where I place it flush against the wall. Hopefully they won't be able to see it, or it will be too small to notice. I jump back down right before they unlock the door, bursting it open with force like they are trying to catch me in the act. I stand stationary like a deer in headlights, startled by their entrance as they put their hand out, holding out a white piece of clothing for me to take.

"Put this on." My brows furrow, opening it up to realise it's a t-shirt. And it's certainly not mine. Staring at them blankly as they keep their eyes on me. *Are they really going to watch me change? Pervert.*

"Do you really have to watch me?" I find my voice, clutching the t-shirt in my hand in protest. There is no way I am stripping naked in front of them.

"What's the matter, *Puppet*. Never been looked at by a woman before?" The air constricts from my lungs, my eyes almost bulging out of my skull. Did they just say *Woman*? There is a deviant grin underneath *her* face paint and I don't know how to react to that damn nickname again.

If this was a mans doing I would understand the harsh nature and sick and twisted stunts they have pulled, but a woman? What woman would treat another woman this way? Although it makes sense as to why she has been kinder than most you see on the news. The pillow. The painkillers. Wrapping up my wound. The shirt to cover up my dignity. I have more understanding, yet it doesn't get rid of the nausea in my stomach. They chuckle, or should I say, *she*. At my clear confusion before slowly turning around to face the bathtub. At least she has some decency.

"Don't worry *Princess*. You're not my type." I think I just barfed in my mouth. Shrivelling up my face in disgust as I quietly undo my pj's letting them fall to the floor and put on my new swimsuit that essentially looks like a hospital gown on me. I'd say she can't be any smaller than 6ft and I'm only 5'4. I look ridiculous, but at least I can rinse off this sweat.

I turn to face the shower, slowly pulling the lever to free the water from its confinement and watch as it falls against my skin, letting out a big sigh. Imagining home, imagining anything but this bathroom I am standing in, where the tiles are cracked and a heavy must lingers. My band-aid begins to soak, water seeping into the fabric and poisoning my wound, it hurts so much. I unravel the cloth until it's free to breathe, clenching my jaw and grinding my teeth to withhold the impending scream that wants to rip from my throat. It's partially healed, gammy and gloopy with dried blood smothering the entrance making me heave. I've never been one for gore in person, it's making me lightheaded and angry, alongside the hunger and the deprivation of everything my body needs right now, my body is fighting me to vomit.

I stand and look at her only to realise she is watching me with no shame. This top is drenched and most likely see through. I feel my cheeks burn, unsure whether it's from the hot water or embarrassment, but even clothed I feel violated and I'm running on so many emotions right now, I don't know which one to feel.

"Why are you being kind to me?" I cower underneath the flow of heat, warming my lifeless body into the face of a clown waiting for an answer, holding my forearms in my hands trying to cover up my chest.

But she says nothing.

I guess the only clown here is me.

For thinking she would give me an answer.

SHASSII

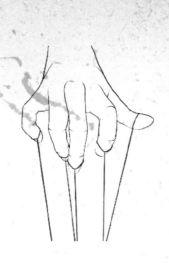

CHAPTER 7

MY INCONVENIENCE

Puppeteer

K*ind?*

She must be joking. I am the furthest thing from kind. Moral maybe. And even that's pushing it. But kind doesn't sit in my vocabulary. The only kindness I give to the world is eradicating the sickness that's poisoned it, which still results in me taking lives and paying the consequences. Kindness never got me fucking anywhere but *hurt*. Kindness only granted me pain.

Kindness only made me realise I was *weak*. Being kind doesn't give you special treatment or help you avoid anything. The last time I was kind I got 10 lashings for using the last of the sugar in a birthday cake. That word makes my skin shrivel up like a decaying corpse. It's acidic in my mouth. I'm not being kind. I'm being considerate. There's a difference.

But I will only be so considerate taking into account the circumstances. I have to be careful what I do and say because if she does get out, she'll show them the first place to look and I can't be around. I'll finish what I started and do what I was meant to do before this inconvenience rolled into my life like an unwanted cockroach. She is nothing but dead weight and I'll be glad to get rid of her, I just need to sort some shit out first.

Who knew babysitting was so tiring. She's a toddler in an adults body. I'm so glad I was an only child so I didn't have to deal with this shit. *Shep* is enough when he's having a tantrum. She's young enough to be a sibling but fuck it's been a while since I've seen some skin and my eyes have a mind of there own watching her rub her skin of my touch, it makes me want to touch her again, grip tighter so she remembers who and what I fucking am. The last thing I want is for her to get comfortable, but I don't exactly wanna kill her either, that would just go against everything that I am. *Or I'm trying to be.*

I just need to wait it out until my next port of call is secure. I have contacts but they aren't exactly clean and the last thing I want is to drag them into my mess and get them thrown behind bars again.

She turns the lever, quivering as the cool air catches up to her now that she's used up all my bloody hot water. Scowling at me with dead eyes, eyes that are telling me a million different things. She hates me. *Good*. She should. I did just murder her parents in cold blood so she's being fairly compliant considering. But I can tell she's not a fighter, she doesn't even have a backbone. She screams *kindness* and I hate it, it means I have to match it and I won't, which means I will just push her to fight me and she will only hate me more.

The absence of heat directs my eyes to the one place they shouldn't and I'm no better than a man but *fuck*, the outlining of her tits against my soaking T-shirt is making me realise I haven't got laid in a long ass time. Far too fucking long. I've been so caught up in finding her *Daddy* that indulging in pussy hasn't exactly been on my to do list. I've no interest in sex beyond numbing my mind. Prison wasn't exactly a strip club but I still got it. I was nearly caught a few times but that was the thrill of it, I had nothing better to do and it helped my brain stop thinking for a while.

She's looking at me in complete and utter distress right now. I will not take my eyes off her, admiring her skinny little figure, plump in all the right places, so breakable. *Focus Hays.* I'm fixated on her in case she tries anything stupid and she needs to change out of her wet t-shirt but she has nothing to change into. Lucky for her I was already two steps ahead. I nod my head towards the door gesturing for her to exit, as much as I love listening to people plead for their life, the bathroom holds enough of that.

"Move." I order, becoming impatient as she creeps towards me, her light feet patting the solid tiles. I grip her moist flesh, still caked in water that has not evaporated yet making it a little trickier but her arms are so small my thumb and middle finger are still touching. So dainty and frail I could snap it, that would solve another problem. If she only has one arm in operation on top of her severed leg there ain't a hope in hell she would try to run, but I always love a good chase and I'm not against being threatened by the idea, just to see how much fight she has in her.

We convert to the bedroom and I watch as her eyes dilate, glaring at her clothes on the bed, clothes I took for her.

Considerate.

I know she wants to say so much but she isn't, she's frightened. I don't even know why I did it. Guilty conscience I guess, and I can't be asked to explain when even I don't know.

I know there is nothing in this room that will benefit her impending escape plan and I could just lock her in and leave her to it but I don't really want to leave her to her own devices in my room right now, without restraints, so I face the door allowing her to change.

"Now what?..." She whispers, uncertainty riddling her voice. I don't respond, only peering down at the bed before pulling out the metal cuffs. Her eyes gloss over but I shove my guilt down. It won't have to be like this forever if she works with me, but I cannot be sure right now how her brain works and how smart she really is. Behind her puppy eyes, those god damn doe eyes I keep finding myself staring into, she could be a mastermind, so a locked door is not enough to ease my mind while I'm out on errands.

She does as she's told, lying back on the bed like a good girl wearing a turtleneck sweater, it's black and frayed at the cuffs. *She's a chewer.* I tug the fabric over her wrist before cuffing it to the bar above her, her natural odour wafting under my nose as I tower over her vulnerable body. I decide against both wrists and I hope for her sake I don't regret how *considerate* I'm being.

I pull away from her and her stomach growls in response. I fight back a smile, or even worse a laugh. My *Puppet* is hungry, and feeding my victims isn't exactly where I thought this would go, but she's looking sorry for herself and giving her something to munch on is the least I can do after what I have put her through. Not that I give a shit personally, but I'd rather she didn't starve to death under my roof. She won't look at me but she knows I heard that too and there is heat illuminating her pale complexion.

I step back, making my way to the kitchen where I shuffle through the cupboards. I barely eat myself; I usually eat on the go when I'm out and about so there is fuck all in the house but I stumble upon a packet of twinkies I got last week. I don't care if she doesn't like them. She'll eat them if she's hungry enough. She side eyes me as I block the door frame, leaning into it before lobbying them in her lap.

"Eat." There is a little humour behind this, but I remain straight faced, laughing on the inside, cocking a brow as she poorly attempts to open the packet with her free hand.

"You're cuffed. Not disabled. Use your mouth," she glares at me in disgust before using those brain cells and biting the seam open. *Maybe she is not as smart as I thought. What an idiot.*

"I'm heading out. I will be back in a few hours. Don't do anything stupid." That look of sarcasm rolls her eyes, like she could do anything stupid cuffed to a bed in a locked room, but it amuses me all the same. She's a plaything. *My plaything.* And if she rolls her fucking eyes at me I'll give her a real reason to roll them.

"Where?" She is asking like a psycho jealous girlfriend. Does she really think I'm going to disclose that sort of information when I've known her for not even 24 hours? I step slowly inside the room until I'm invading her space, the dampness of her hair thick within the air surrounding her. Bending to her level until I'm inches from her face, I whisper through gritted teeth as she peers up at me.

"*The pits of hell…*" The sun slips through the cracks, highlighting the honey glow beneath her timid eyes. The colour is one I've never seen before, the deepest field of sunflowers you could get lost in, a golden compass, a compass I'm slightly worried will deter me away from what I need to do, leading me in a different direction, one I do not want to follow as I find myself staring a little too long.

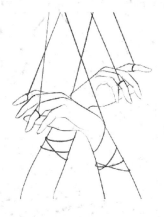

CHAPTER 8

CRIMINALS ARE MONSTERS

Puppet

She's been gone for what feels like days. I know it's only been a few hours but when you're cooped up with nothing to do other than count the markings in the walls, sob until you have no tears left to cry and read a book you've read a million times you start to lose track of time, *lose yourself.*

She took one of my books from my bed side table that night and has given it to me. I already find that strange enough. Why would a killer even give me the time of day, but then again, she hasn't exactly been the worst, not that that makes this any better. I noticed how she put the cuff over the fabric of my shirt and I might be totally delusional but I think that was to protect my wrist.

Uncontrollable sadness breaks my dam, running my eyes sore once more. They already hurt so much from crying but it doesn't seem to stop. I've tried to sleep off their faces but it visits me in my dreams and my lack of insulin has already begun to take effect, the taste of acid is taking up residence in the back of my throat and I wish the process would just hurry up already.

My mind has been overexerting itself so much that I am in a state of numbness, thinking about all the terrible things she could be doing. All the people she could be hurting right now. Maybe she won't even come back and her plan was to flee the country, leave me here to rot. It's either Saturday or Sunday which means no one will find their bodies until perhaps mid-week. No one even knows I'm gone.

Maybe Kacey will realise when I don't respond to her texts, I was meant to be going to that party and there is no way in hell she will take no for an answer, she will turn up and find them, she will call the police. My monster must have left some sort of evidence behind for them to track her down, *fingerprints, footprints?* Even if I am dead before they get here, I hope my monster gets what she deserves. Jail time is too kind, maybe I'll just kill her myself. *Why did I even think that?* I'm a piece of rope, torn between empathy and rage. Seeing the good in people never got me anywhere yet I still do it, and I'm doing it now.

Even on death's door I am still seeking redemption in evil when evil does not deserve forgiveness. People choose to be evil yet I find myself sympathising with the devil, trying to find a reason as to why. What hurt them? What pain did they suffer? Were they just born this way?

Sadness. I had never known the full extent of its wrath until this very moment, as I lay here letting it consume my every breath, every good memory, filling it only with a dull ache. This dull ache that's tearing me apart. I've never experienced grief and it's not at all what I expected. Mourning for an apparition you only see in your nightmares. Pain pinches at my chest so sharply that a dull blade may even hurt less than this unbearable hole inside me, trying to pull itself shut.

After a few hours of mind-numbing cries and puffy eyes, the exhaustion takes me by force, allowing me to chase the sweet notion of escape as the room falls out of focus, concentrating solely on the shallow beating of my own heart.

Play - 'Heal - Tom Odell'

Death.

I'd always wondered what it was like to die. To see that light. People say you see your life flash before your very eyes and I don't know whether that scares me or not. The afterlife always frightened me. What will I see? Darkness? A world beyond this one? A spotlight to the next life? A void of nothingness, an eternity of emptiness. Family? Will we finally be at peace?

I used to worry when I had something to live for. But now? Suddenly not fearing death makes much more sense to me. It's *freedom*. Freedom I have always craved. Who knew death would be my salvation. It now sounds so inviting. The absence of pain, the thought of feeling nothing. 24 hours of grief and I'm already giving up. Some survivor I am right?... I'm so tired of pain, I just want to turn it all off and let death swallow me whole.

She drags herself inside the door, dripping in her leather, I could already hear her coming with the amount of chains she has smothering her attire. She leans against the frame cracking the wood with the metal, staring at me like I'm a museum antique.

"What's the matter with you?" I'll be honest. I can barely see straight as she gawks at me, I'm seeing three of her and my muscles are far from functional, I can feel my lips crusting dry and this nausea is beginning to churn in my stomach. Slurred words slide from my mouth, dragging them out with light effort. My energy is non-existent... I have no fight left to feel anything other than acceptance. It's funny how being deprived of drugs results in poisoning your body as punishment.

"Like you care..." If she does that's a first... a psychopath with feelings beyond murder is unheard of.

"You sound drunk." *Isn't she a charmer*... although fuck I could murder a drink right now. I've never had a sip of alcohol in my life but I can imagine it would be far greater than this discomfort.

"I wish I was... it would make this process much easier." She looks, dare I say, *concerned?* I'm doing her a favour; she should be grateful this doesn't have to get messy.

"What process?" A hiccup-like laugh jumps out of me at her curiosity, slumped into my seat with a now very dead arm, strung up like a skinned pig...It's sweet that she wants the ins and outs of my demise. *Very serial killer of her.*

"I'm alllll out..." I'm not oblivious to the consequences of my own actions, and I knew this insulin wouldn't last long, but quite frankly, I have come to terms with my white light, I find it weirdly beautiful... a means to a tragic ending. Not long now and I will be rested with them. Maybe that's why people aren't afraid to die? When you have nothing else to live for, death becomes your new residence. The dead become friends and the living become foe.

"Out of what?" Her eyes are sinking. Is that guilt catching up to her yet? *Good*. This is her fault, now she can stand there and watch me die. Even if I tell her, there is nothing she can do now.

"Insulin." My eyelids hang heavy over my hazy vision, my body is giving up and I'm waiting for the stage of numbness to take over my body so I can stop feeling this unbearable pain.

"And what does that mean?" Each time she talks, my stomach knots a little tighter. I may be silly to think she actually cares, but there is anguish behind her words, like she is mad that something other than her is going to take my life.

"It meanssss, I have an expiry date..." I roll my head back against the metal frame now digging into my shoulder blades, everything feels twice as painful right now and my head feels twice as big, ready to explode at any given moment.

"What happens if you don't take it?" *Honestly*? I don't know. I've never been this far gone, I don't know exactly what is waiting for me, or how long my body will fight to not give up, but I know it's not pretty, and I'm ok with that. There is no living without fear and no peace without pain, being afraid to live and afraid to die concludes weakness, and that is all I have ever been.

"It's called Hyperglycemia..." I can see her black face paint distort as she quirks her brow in confusion, waiting for me to continue.

"My liver turns into a pool of acid..." I scrunch my face in disgust as the words leave my mouth, and for a moment I don't want to die. I hate vomiting. At this rate I want to ask her to end it quickly so I don't have to suffer, like she did with them. Like she could do for me. But I am her walking karma, and I want her to suffer for the pain she caused me. I want her to feel mine as I deteriorate in front of her very eyes, maybe ignite that sliver of redemption she has inside her, if there is any, and be too late to stop it. As if she ever would. She is a killer.

"And how long does that take?" Maybe she just wants this process over with, but I refuse to give that to her.

"Oh, wouldn't you like to know..." I scoff, almost dribbling as all my muscles relax, contorting against my fragile bones, my blood running cold like fresh tap water.

"How. Long." She's frightened, I can feel it in her abrupt questions, in the quiver against her bottom lip. She's caving, she's cracking. *Maybe there is redemption in her after all.*

"Could be anywhere from. Six hours to four days...depending. But not to worry aye... I'm just saving you the trouble. Now you won't have to dispose of me..." I lie once more, most likely the last lie I will ever tell, two lies in the span of 24 hours, *how rebellious*. At the rate I'm going, I'd say a day would be a miracle.

"I would have saved myself the trouble..." She smiles, but this time it's not sinister. It's genuine. It's a smile to cover up the fact she is lying too, I know it.

"*Such a charmer...*"

"I see you have a sense of humour." She unfolds her arms, the crumpled-up leather rubbing against itself sounds like burning tires. All my senses are amplified right now. She creeps over towards the bed, indenting it as her heavy weight sinks into the mattress by my feet, hunching over with her elbows on the plates of her knees as she glances over at me. Her face will make for a haunting picture when I reach the other side.

"Is it uncomfortable?" I blink subtly acknowledging her concern. *Why would she even ask that?*

"It's bearable…" *For now.* Besides the hot and cold flushes sticking me to the bed, loss of feelings in my legs, the constant nausea lacing the back of my throat and the pounding migraine. *What could get worse.*

"Are you just going to sit there and watch me die a slow and painful death? I'm sure you would enjoy that." I lightly chuckle to myself. Trying to make a joke out of my impending doom hoping it might make me feel slightly better.

"I have better things to do with my time." Her eyes roll slightly, losing the smile she just had, and I strangely miss it, it was comforting in a weird way…a sign I'm not in complete danger. Maybe I'm delusional, these side effects are heavy and I can't exactly think clearly.

"Like… Babysit me?" I mumble sarcastically, trying to revive that hidden cheshire cat smile underneath the fake one painted on her face. It's hideous, but her real one is not so repulsive, either that or I really am losing the plot. "You have beautiful eyes…" I whisper as I stare at her like someone on molly, and all I can concentrate on is how her eyes are piercing through mine, reading all my thoughts like a book. A familiar understanding that I don't quite know the extent of. *Shared pain?* She is a book with empty pages, but I'm a book with a plain cover and thousands of unspoken words inside which she is clearly reading. I focus on the silver jewellery scattered across her face now that she is close enough to look at properly.

"You're hallucinating." She loosely breaks contact, staring down at the grubby floor beneath her boots, like my words disgust her.

"As I'm taking myself out. Do I get to know your name? Not exactly like I can snitch on you now…" My vision is beyond repair at this point, tripping as my lids quiver and my words become shallow and desolate, whispers of the dead walking.

"Nice try *Princess*." She uses these nicknames like we are friends.

"Worth a shot…" I ponder. Trying to numb this incessant pounding. Appreciating the quiet so I can sink in my self-loathing.

…

"Why didn't you tell me?" *Tell her?* Why would I tell her? So she could stop me?

"Because I'd rather die than spend the next three years and last waking moment of my life with my kidnapper..." I was not expecting my last moments to be with a maniac but I guess life is full of surprises...

"Ouch...harsh, you will be." Fabulous. Can't she just walk out and leave me to it.

"Luckyyy me..." My body rolls, facing the wall, squinting in pain with every muscle I move.

"Have you gone through this before?" Her words are quiet but bitter. If she means, starving myself of life until I'm a mummified corpse?

"*Nopeee...*"

"Is there a way to fix it?" Why does she ask so many questions now?

"It's called a Hypopen... and it's back home. You're out of luck if you're looking for redemption..." Part of me can hold onto that sliver of hope, that instinct at the back of my head telling me to keep going, to fight but it's pointless now.

"There is no redemption for me." Her voice is filled with demise but her actions scream repentance.

"Why didn't you kill me?..." I've been playing that night over and over again in my head. She was ready to take my life. Burn my house to the ground but she didn't. I know I'm not stable enough to think rationally right now, but there must be more to it. A killer doesn't hesitate, *right*? She had me in the palm of her hands. All of this could have been avoided so why am I still here?

"I'm a criminal. Not a monster..." I want to laugh in pure disagreement but I don't have the strength to let it out.

"Criminals are monsters." I spit gently. There is no difference between the two. Both are evil. She can try to cover it up but murder is murder. Nothing will ever change what she is to me.

...

"*You got me there, Love...*"

SHASSII

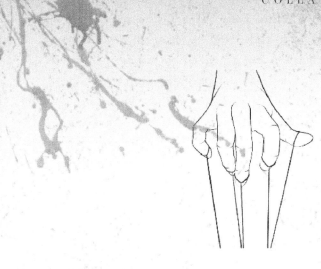

CHAPTER 9

FUCKING SEE ME!

Puppeteer

"Have you ever thought about dying?..." She's asking me so I can comfort her in her decisions, and I don't care what happens to her. Like she said, she is doing the job for me. This way I don't have to dispose of her myself. Maybe just dump her in the sea, or burn her body so it leaves no trace, but a selfish part of me is hating the idea.

"No." I lie. She doesn't need to know she is the reason I am still breathing right now, and for that I want the satisfaction of taking her life myself.

"Why do you do it?..." Because it's all I've ever known. Pain, death, grief, hurt. It's what makes me the monster that I am. Happiness? Happy ever afters? It's all one big joke. We all fucking die, and you can only delay the process. No amount of *Love* can keep you breathing forever. And some people don't even deserve that. I don't deserve that. Death is my gift. I know that, and I have accepted that, just as she has. It's a ticket to freedom. It's a sedative to the suffering.

"Because it calms me." Death keeps my monsters at bay. and it's something I don't expect her to understand, and hopefully she won't have to try much longer. She doesn't even have the energy to react to my words, only stare into the void, a vacant expression paints her gaunt face.

I really don't have time to sit around and watch this. I have shit to do. I stand to my feet, gazing down at her lifeless body, merely conscious. She will hopefully be out by the time I'm back and this shit will all be over. I can go back to my original plan and take myself out once I've finished some business, living a life amongst the dead only makes you want it more. Maybe this resentment I'm feeling is jealousy.

I go to exit the bedroom when weak hands take a gentle hold on my open pockets, tugging with little strength against the mesh fabric.

"Thank you…" My chest constricts. She doesn't know what she just did, but I do, and this changes everything but I can't admit that to myself yet. *Thank you?* Thank you for what? She is dying because of me? And I wish she'd hurry up and get it over with so my mind can fucking relax. Her eyes are closed, her hold on my pockets seemed to be the last strain of strength she had as her arm falls limp to the bed. She said six hours minimum? Maybe she calculated wrong. *Stupid girl.*

I close the bedroom door behind me and gather my things from the garage.

"I'll be back in a bit boy." Shep tilts his head at me, seating himself in his bed. He knows the drill but he is also curious as to why there is someone else in the house right now. We don't do company. He has been my company for the past four years and it's nice to be seen without an insistent voice down my ear. Dogs don't talk. They just whine and tear your shit up instead, but he's tolerable. He's been the only thing keeping me remotely fucking sane.

I lock the front door behind me before making my way to my truck, perching myself in the driver's seat and all I can think about right now is *her* when I should be taking care of other shit. She has been nothing but a hassle. I drive myself down the uneven dirt track which is overgrown with grass up to the bonnet until I meet the main road. The road map in the passenger seat beside me circles my next target. It's in the complete opposite direction from her house. *Why am I even thinking about that right now?*

I drive. And drive. My foot getting heavier on the gas.

It's called a Hypopen... and it's back home. You're out of luck if you're looking for redemption...

The engine roars, mimicking the sound of my rage as I grip the wheel tightly, grinding my back teeth trying to take my mind off the forgiveness in her eyes, her limp body on *my* bed, her acceptance as she lies there and waits for her end like a good little *victim* feeling all sorry for herself, but I'm not the one doing it, it's not enough. This ending is wrong. Her death is wrong. Everything about this is wrong...If anyone is going to kill her it's going to be *me*, how it should be.

Thank you...

Her words repeat like one of my mom's old CD's, grating my gears as she would replay it through till the early hours of the morning just to keep the voices in her head quiet. Voices I have now inhabited. *Her voice.* My very own burnt CD.

She will never forgive me. I know that. I don't want her to. I'm selfish. I'm as selfish as they fucking get, and I will save her ass just to kill her again if I have to. Whatever this is eating her alive is taking my kill. *She is mine to kill.* I didn't do all this shit for something to wipe her out for me. I want to watch her bleed for me, I want to take her last breath.

My boot burns the break.

Fuck this shit.

I run my hands over the leather casing of the steering wheel, whipping it to the left into a side road, reversing the burning tires to come back on myself. I am twenty minutes in the opposite direction, and now almost four hours from Indiana.

What the fuck are you doing Hayden.

My hands and feet take control, my subconscious guilt is eating me alive, boiling my blood red hot as I keep my foot on the gas picturing her lifeless face. I accelerate. Completely oblivious to the speedo. 40...50...60...70...80...90...100...110.

This was not the plan, none of this was ever the fucking plan! I had it all mapped out and she's gone and thrown a curveball in the mix. The needle of the compass is spinning out of control and all I can do is drive. Even if I wanted to stop the car I couldn't. It's like I am not in control of the wheel anymore.

Whatever this is, it needs to quit it. I don't give a flying fuck about her, I only care about my body count. She needs to die by my hand, that is it. Then I can chill out. I don't target women, but everything inside me wants to tear her apart from the inside out. That disgusting purity she brands herself with, it needs to be sucked out. She can't just give the fuck up and take the easy road. She needs to see how ugly the road full of potholes are, where you puncture a tire and you swerve off track. Where it almost kills you and you get the fuck up and get back behind the wheel again. Where you face danger head on and you don't cower.

She is better than this. I don't pity her. I loathe her naivety. She needs to see how ugly the world really is. How ugly the people around her are. She needs to understand why people do bad things, and why she's truly been hidden away for so long. I've never known of her existence because her Father hid her from his past, covered it all up with lies and a fake image. She deserves to know that before she dies.

She needs to understand Me.

I pull up in front of her house expecting to see it smothered in tape and police cars but there is nothing. It's a Saturday and it's Halloween so I suppose my plan worked perfectly. No one has noticed. The house is just how I left it. Desolate and free to enter. It looks like they aren't home. I cleaned up my mess and exposed of the bodies, leaving a note on the front door that says they went on holiday for a week so they probably won't notice for a while. Not until the middle of next week anyway. I force entry in somewhat of a hurry. The house that now homes *my Puppets* memories. I make my way upstairs, facing the door I assaulted and traipse my way inside.

I'm wearing clean gloves so I leave no fingerprints and I start searching her room for the pen. Her bedside table is the first port of call and my suspicions were correct. I pull out the drawer to a grey case full of her prescription and Hypopen, tucking it away in my rucksack as I stand in her bedroom, peering at it now that I'm not chasing her through her house.

Even her room is pure. Bright and simple, plants and homework scatter her desk and dressing table. A Bass guitar hangs on the wall and I cock a brow. *I never took her for the bass guitar type.* I search for other bits and pieces I may possibly need as I have no intention of ever coming back here again. I go draw by draw, sifting through clothes, books, and other various girly things she has. I take more clothes and grab her phone and charger from her bedside table. *Why am I taking her phone? It's not exactly like I'm going to give it to her.*

A calendar hangs by the bedroom door, smothered in so much writing you can barely see the paper. I turn the pages. Times and appointments, reminders and schedules are plastered all over it. No wonder she wants to kick the bucket. What a life to live, does she even get time to breathe? It goes all the way into next year and there is not one holiday? Although she has some interesting things in here. *~Happy Dooms Day to me. Another year older and I'm still single. Yay!~* I laugh to myself, not because it's funny, but because I relate. I've never been in a relationship with anyone and after I got thrown behind bars I stopped waiting for it. It's a waste of time. She's not missing much.

I shove the calendar in my rucksack making a quick exit, being here already far longer than I planned and jump back into the truck, flooring it back to *her*, spending the next three and a half hours convincing myself I am losing my mind. She's my hostage. She means nothing to me. She's *Collateral Damage*. Nothing more. I'm doing my moral part and being *considerate*. She never did anything wrong, none of this is her fault, I ripped her life away selfishly and now I'm trying to make it up to her when I should be cutting people's heads off. *This is ridiculous.* But I won't take back what I did, and I will never apologise for grieving my own way.

Even if it did pass this grief on. She can learn to live with it like I have. Even burnt to ash and dust it never gets better, it doesn't get easier. It just becomes more bearable to withstand, but only if you are strong enough to fight it. If she is my karma for chasing my revenge, then so fucking be it. She is beautiful damn karma to say the least. That much is certain. As much as I hate to admit it to myself. Having her around has given the house a weird aroma I cannot shake. Maybe my loneliness is showing, but having a plaything has kept my mind occupied and stopped the voices in my head. No one's stepped foot in that house apart from me since the day I was dragged out of it into the back of a van. People were so afraid of it, afraid of me, afraid of the stories, that they wouldn't even touch the place when I was gone. I came back six years later exactly how I left it... *We* left it.

Broken.

Play - 'Breathe Me - Sia'

I pull up the drive, it's now dark out and I forgot to leave lights on for her. Not that she would notice, she is in La La land. I drag my heavy-duty bag and rucksack from the passenger seat, striding inside the front door. *I never use the front door?* My bags are thrown to the floor, taking out her prescription she needs. There is no movement or voices from the bedroom as I approach, and I am met with her lifeless corpse, sprawled out on *my* bed, she's practically blue, and a sharp rock slides down my throat as my chest clamps shut.

"Puppet..." I stand frozen. Glaring at the white crust on her lips like frostbite. She can't be dead. There is no way it killed her that quickly. But why do I even care? She's gone. It's done. It's over. *This is over.*

Then why do I feel my jaw clenching and my fists tightening at the sight of her. Why is my chest heaving beneath my rib cage?

"Hey." I reach over to sit beside her, she's stone cold against my skin as I touch her. I lean my ear against her chest, and a shallow heartbeat aches beneath hers. Her body's fighting.

"Wake up." I grab her arm, nudging her to respond to me but I get nothing. "Stop playing." Nothing about this is beautiful, she looks hideous, death looks ugly on her. My mind closes in on memories I don't want to remember. *Mom. Mom! Hey. Wake up. Mom, talk to me! Say something!* My grip tightens against her feeble flesh, squeezing it in the palm of my hand, her brittle bones moulding into my own.

I can't do this shit. I reach over for her case, frantically unzipping it, rummaging for the orange and white Hypopen in its pouch, holding it in my hand as I stare at her. I don't have a fucking clue what I'm doing but something takes a hold of me. I pull off the red lid and inject it into the fleshy part of her upper arm that is exposed to me, clicking it. I don't even know if this is going to work, I don't know if she is too far gone. I sit staring at her waiting for any signs of life and she gives me nothing. Her arm slams hard against the mattress as I let it down from its cuff, finding my thumb rubbing against the red rim of her wrist.

"*Puppet.* Come on." I bite my tongue, both hands clasping at her forearms, my inky fingers tainting her nude skin.

"Wake up." I inhale a large sigh, keeping my composure but my heartbeat has other ideas, rattling its cage as I rattle hers, shaking her arms in frustration, suddenly clinging onto that tiny heartbeat still pumping, but she's floppy and vacant. "Wake the fuck up!"

She's still out, unresponsive, nothing is happening, why isn't anything happening, surely something must have happened by now!

"Come back to me!" I'm quivering, riddled with the past, plagued with the images of my dead Mother, how she laid there on the wooden floor and choked up blood into my lap, unable to speak, unable to move. All I could do was accept that those were her final moments as I pressed my fingers against her open wound. I couldn't do anything. Only watch as the life drained from her body. Nausea crawls up the centre of my chest, nuzzling its way into the back of my throat as I roll her on her side.

"Come on. Come on. Fight it!" *Fucking wake up!* Anger consumes my actions, and without thinking my fist hits the wall, puncturing a hole in the plaster. I can feel unwanted sweat building beneath my eyes, squinting to hide the evidence. Evidence that is very much noticeable. Feelings that are too present for my liking. All of this is *bullshit!*

"Stay with me!" I've spent my entire life pushing that night down, locking it in a box so it didn't destroy me, but the way her dark locks are resting against her porcelain cheeks, the freckles splattered against her soft face, cut out from clouds, sculpted by angels. I miss those damn eyes. I need her to wake up and fucking *LOOK AT ME.* I need her to fucking *see me.* See me for what I am. What she is doing to me and punish her deeply for it.

"God dammit, don't you dare fucking die on me!" *Not now. Not ever.* I shake her relentlessly, digging for a breath, a sound, anything. "I hate you for making me give a shit!" I hate it. I hate it. I hate everything she is. I hate how she's crawled under my skin like the flu. Trembling to chase life back into her inanimate body.

An audible gasp inhales beneath me as she sucks in a deep breath, not chasing it fast enough as she chokes on air, grabbing her throat like I'd slit it open. I wish I had. It means I wouldn't of just had to relive the worst day of my life with a girl I shouldn't even give a fuck about. I've known her for 24 hours. *I'm pathetic.* She claws at her skin, eye's bulging out the sockets as she glares at me and I let go of the heavy breath I'd been holding, exhaling relief as she gawks at me with pits of fear I've never been so happy to see. *She sees me* and I don't know which eye to look at first, bouncing between them like if I look away, I will die. I felt like I was dying all over again, over a timid hostage that should be dead and buried in my back garden. *What the fuck is wrong with me?*

"Hello Stranger…" My voice is calm, deep, most likely shaky. She searches around the room for a reason as to why she should be alive right now, looking into the eyes of a killer who just saved her sorry life.

Because I'm about to make a fucking promise to her.

That the only person that will take her miserable life is me, when I see fit, not when she fucking chooses.

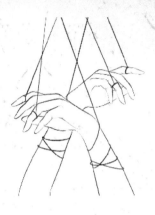

CHAPTER 10

NOT EVEN IN DEATH

Puppet

Am I dead?

I'm choking on life as it suffocates my airways, seeping back inside my throat. *My nightmare* is glaring back at me. Speaking foreign tongue as she comforts my panic, the clown is watching me, studying me as I gasp for breath, *how?* How am I even conscious right now? My blurred vision squints to adjust my fuzzy sight as I pan the room. I'm still here, *why am I not dead?* Darkness cocoons me, but a glint of orange catches my eye.

My *Hypopen?*

"I thought I'd lost you there." I'm still drowsy and my hearing is muffled only just about making out her words. Fuelled with every emotion as my body accustoms to the air around me, my heart shallow but beating, my breathing gentle but heavy.

I need to eat. I need sugar. My arm climbs through the gravitational pull as I lift it in an attempt to make contact but my words are timid and breathless, rolling my head like a stiff doll. I'm seized up and brittle, beyond freezing and trembling at the thought of breathing oxygen. I was ready to let go. I was ready to die. *Why am I still alive?*

"You didn't think I'd let you slip away from me that easy did you?" I barely have the energy to scowl as I roll my stiff neck, facing her with only protruding hate. I don't understand, why couldn't she let me go. *I was making her life easier!* Not that she deserves it. And for that, I will make her regret my kindness.

"Why?..." I ask in search of an answer but I don't know what I want to hear. I don't even know what time of day it is, or if I'm dreaming. Is this my eternal loop of misery for choosing the easy way out? I'm stuck with the monster who is going to grant me pain for trying to run away from my body. Not even in death can I escape her.

"You need to eat and then rest." She speaks so formally and without care, yet the contents of her words speak something entirely different and I cannot work out if I should be angry at her for saving a life that did not want to be saved in some freak attempt to win my company back. She is delusional if she thinks this will change anything, and if anything it's made me resent her more for taking away my death as well as my life. What is she playing at? But right now, I have no energy to fight with her, only succumb to her twisted submission.

She vanishes for fifteen or so minutes and although I am currently uncuffed with a means to finally escape, my shrivelled-up corpse like state with a weak pulse is craving the comfort of this age-old bed with my sweat, blood and tears etched into the mattress that I know has seen far worse than me. I can feel it in the ridged springs beneath me, years of sleepless nights. I nuzzle my head into the stained pillow, crawling underneath the crumpled-up duvet at the end of the bed as she walks back in with a bowl of something steaming from the rim and my body heats just looking at it, although the thoughts of consuming it leaves me heaving. I'm currently stagnant with little life inside me and my body is fighting just to keep me breathing. Let alone eat. I stare down at the bowl of pasta she puts beside me and a subtle soft smile slips, one I didn't intend on, but I'm embarrassed to still be here. I was hoping I would have kicked the bucket by the time she came back. In fact I was, until she plunged a needle inside me.

"Where did you get it?" I glance at the pen on the bed side table, racking my brains trying to understand where the hell she got it from. *Does she have contacts?*

"That's not important right now." There are so many secrets she's hiding. Things she doesn't want me to know and it only makes me more frustrated. There is no way she went all the way back home? *Right?* That would be absurd.

"Now eat." She glances down at the bowl, directing me with just her eyes through her black holes.

"How long was I out for?" I don't remember when she left, I barely remember our previous conversation, did we have one? I hope I didn't say anything stupid.

"Enough questions." I barely have the energy to finish the bowl but I manage to take it down leaving me more exerted than before. She has stood watching me the entire time like a creep. Not uttering a word. She's used to the silence but so am I so it's strangely comforting, when you ignore the fact that my blood is heating my body purely through rage. I want nothing more than to hurt her but that is not possible right now, so I place my half empty bowl down on the bed side table and let my exhaustion straddle me, cupping me by the throat, squeezing until I see my temporary end to seek momentary peace. Darkness pokes at the corner of my eyes until I see black.

I've been in and out of consciousness the last few days. And every time I wake, she's either sitting watching me or there is remnants of her presence scattered across her room, glasses and wrappers on the floor. She's barely left my side and I don't know if I should find comfort in that fact. Being watched by a serial killer for days on end without my knowledge is practically stalking. She is a *freak*. I go to rub my temple to shift the stiffness of my face and my disorientation when I look down, reacting to the heavyweight binding my wrists.

Chains.

She's extended my restraints with chains? *How considerate.* At least I can move a little more freely now I guess.

I hear dull music coming from behind the bedroom door, it's faint but angry, thudding through the building like an earthquake followed by a rhythmic beating, but it's not the music. *That's fists.* She's punching something and a knot sits in the back of my mouth at all the possible reasons I am not her punching bag right now as I lay here wrapped up in a blanket like an ill child being looked after by a parent. She's a serial killer. She's a murderer. She murdered my parents yet I'm sitting here fighting against all the reasons I should feel grateful right now. She put me here. This is all her fault. I nearly died because of her. *No. I did die because of her,* but why do I feel drawn to her Walmart version of kindness. This isn't your typical killer, none of this is as I expected and I certainly didn't think she'd save my life.

I'm left with so many conflicting emotions it makes me want to scream. I want to die. I don't want to be here; she needs to fucking respect that and finish what she started.

I hear a door unlatch, the high pitch grinding against the heavy bass, the volume increasing until the door shuts again, muffling the music. The bedroom door unlocks to reveal her in a black long tee, probably to cover any tattoos I could identify if I got out, and joggers with the pockets hanging out, she's holding a glass of water and a packet in her hand that she slips into her pocket as she heaves like a worn-out dog. Not sweating enough to melt off her hideous face paint though as she puts the glass down next to me.

This has become her routine. I don't know how many days I've been out for. But it's been enough to know this isn't her third, fourth or fifth time. I've been practically unresponsive. I don't see what joy she gets out of this when she could just put me out of my misery and carry on with her psychotic tendencies.

"Don't you have people to murder?..." I sit up slowly, feeling like a sack of bricks as my weak arms hold the weight of me.

"Bold of you to assume I'm not." She dabs her forehead with the towel slumped over her shoulder as she takes a seat on her new bed in the corner of the room. She catches me off guard as she whistles at such high velocity my ears knot, followed by the sight of a four legged friend that strolls in, perching underneath her feet, analysing me like I'm a stranger and I am a stranger, but I am also sort of happy to see another form of life other than hers in my prison cell, despite the size of her canine friend. It's practically twice the size of me and my guard comes back up for a brief moment.

"Are you?" I swallow and I don't know why I even asked, glaring at the both of them.

"Yes." Without hesitation she responds, looking at me through black hooded eyes, darting across the room as she picks up a water bottle off the floor. "Does that scare you, *Puppet*?" I deter my eyes, looking down at my shackles, fiddling with my nails to ease my nerves. It scares me, but the way she is so careless with murder fascinates me.

"Why...why did you save me?" She could get her fix right here but she chooses to do it elsewhere. *Am I not her murdering type?*

"Save isn't exactly the word I'd use." I cock a brow as she leans into the chair, elbows resting on her knees as her fingers interlock. *If that wasn't saving then what the hell was it?* "The only person allowed to take your miserable life. *Is me.*" So she does want to kill me eventually. She's angry I tried to take my life so she couldn't get off to it? "What better kill than completing a triangle aye?"

She knocks her frame back into the seat smiling like a psych ward patient, running the arms of the chair between her hands, like just thinking about it is making her hot and bothered and I feel sick. I know exactly what she means. She means killing off the offspring to end the family name. Like that's a trophy achievement.

"You know. I was starting to think there was just a smidget of *kindness* inside of you. Turns out you're just like the rest of them." My words are feisty, accentuating my letters making it known I'm disgusted by her but that anger quickly turns to fear as she shoots up from her chair making my lifeless body glitch, gripping my delicate throat in her burning hand as she reaches me, it sears into my cold skin and I lose my ability to breathe from lack of oxygen and shock.

"Let's get one thing very fucking clear." She's squeezing tighter. I could retaliate right now. I have the arm room but for some reason I'm sat as still as the dead girl inside of me, peering into the eyes of *my end*. Finding comfort in the thought of blacking out for a few hours.

"Nothing about me is *Kind*. You think me feeding you and keeping you breathing is for your benefit? Keep seeing the good in people and watch where it gets you. You're a body bag. *My plaything*. I take great pleasure in keeping you alive because I know how desperately you want to *die*," my stomach churns with disgust, she is like the rest of them. She is a pig. She's vile and once I gather back my strength. I'm getting the fuck out of here, or I'll die trying. My eyes well but not with sadness as of right now. With anger. *My Plaything?* I'm not a chew toy, I am a human being, I am a grieving girl, captured by the devil disguised inside a human body.

"Do I make myself clear?" My head is thrown forward as she tugs at my limp body, demanding a reply but I refuse to answer with words, so I nod sporadically as a tear slips free.

"Good girl," her thumb runs over my left cheek, catching my tear gently before a sharp sting strikes my right cheekbone, slapping the grief from my face before letting me suck back in air. "But you'll learn to use your words."

She pulls away and takes the packet she was holding out of her pocket containing an insulin pen. She must have been doing it whilst I was unconscious. How does she even know what that is or what to do with it? How did she get it?

She attempts to try and do it for me but over my dead body will she punish me again with my own life as leverage.

"I will do it!..." I snap, narrowing my eyes as I pull my body away from the needle. Her eyes are so dead, like no one is home. Like she's inhabited the body of a corpse as she glares down at me, chucking it on the bed by my side.

"Suit yourself." I take the pen, clawing it underneath my hand as I tuck my knees in on myself glaring up at her like a child who's been told to go to bed. I follow her as she bends to my level, taking the form of my own claustrophobia as her face paint rubs against my cheek.

"If you keep things from me, or *lie* to me again. I will show you just how *'Kind'* I am." she whispers with such aggression my heart flutters, sucking down my urge to test her but I won't.

Not yet.

"Or I might just let him tear you apart..." Her eyes dart to her left where her canine sits, glaring at the both of us and I know I'm not afraid of dogs. But I also know not to mess with one. Who knows what her dog is capable of when its owner is a literal crazy person.

CHAPTER 11

MY PRODIGY

Puppeteer

Y ou've got to be shitting me. I leave her alone for an hour and she's already managed to wangle her way out the cuffs and obliterate my house. I'm taking it she's back to herself again, it's been a week and all I've done is coddle her like a paranoid parent. *I really need to get a grip.*

Call me obsessive, but I've been looking up her treatment and after hours of research and losing fucking brain cells I managed to get my hands on her prescription. *Why is this crap so complicated?* But at least we haven't got to worry about this bullshit again. Can't say the doctor enjoyed my company too much though. It was a risky operation but now I've got enough to supply her until she's grey and old. Not that she will be around for that, but maybe it will come in handy for other shit. Who knows.

I lock the garage door behind me keeping Shep in to stay out of any possible harm as I creep my way deeper inside the house, smashed up plates crunching beneath my steel toe boots. I know she's here because there is no other way out which keeps me calm. I know she's a smart girl but she hasn't spent six years behind bars. There are only a handful of rooms she could be in and most are fairly empty so I don't exactly know where she thought she was going to hide. But fuck it, why not scare her a little.

"One, two, Daddy's coming for you...three, four, *Puppet,* run for that door..." I echo down the hallway. I've spent four years hunting down one singular man across the US and she thinks she can hide from me in my own home? It's rather amusing, although I'll admit, she's good. The living room, my bedroom, bathroom and the kitchen are clear and the door to the garage is still locked which leaves the spare room. She's a petite little thing so hiding in a cupboard would not be far fetched for her.

Making my way down the corridor to the entrance of the room, I push the door forth causing an eerie creek to echo through the empty coffin. You could hear a pin drop it's so quiet but I can't hear her at all. Not even her breathing which peeks my worry a little. There is no way she's got out of this house unless I've completely underestimated her.

Once fully footed inside the room, my heart sinks at the memories held captive here. *She loved this room. It was her escape. Now it is her grave.*

Play – 'Paralyzed – NF'

Lost in thought, as I glare at the dull, burgundy stain underneath my boot, an almighty fit of rage sneaks up from behind me and as I turn around the palm of my hand is met with one of *my* kitchen knives, slicing straight through it with ease as it lodges between my thumb and index finger.

"SHIT!-" Seems I did underestimate her and I can't say I've ever been nailed in the hand before. *FUCK this hurts.* She pushes me off balance straight into the wardrobe behind the door, too distracted by the sheer metal and red river pooling from my hand, but pain is the only way I feel.

It doesn't take me long to pull it out, feeling the sharp edge graze against my open gash making me hold my breath, clamping my teeth shut in fear of biting my own tongue off. I use my remaining force to slam the door shut with my heavy boot, trapping her in where she legs it for the other side of the room, already equipped with another blade, clinging to the chest of draws like it will help her.

I'm leant with my back against the door, the pulse in my hand pushing a flood of blood from my veins decorating the floor with my innards. She's gawking at me and I don't think even she knew she was capable of such violence. I hate to admit how hot this is, but it's been a while since I've tasted psychical pain and my hand isn't the only thing throbbing. Her fear is bringing out her eyes and I could stare at them for hours, pools of the pain she is holding in. I can't even be mad at her for this because I get it. I wanted me dead too, but now she's made this slightly more complicated. She's gripping that knife like a timid doe as if she didn't just stab me with one but I'd prefer she put the bloody thing down. *The game is over now.*

I push off the door slowly, listening to the sound of my bodily fluids hitting the wooden floor, dripping in rhythmic fashion as I approach her.

"DON'T!" she's threatening me as if I should be frightened. I've seen chihuahuas more frightening than her. But it's not her threat that frightens me. It's the way she's crumbling. She's not had a chance to grieve and it's finally catching up to her. I shouldn't have left her to her own devices unattended but that realisation is a little late now. I can't exactly say I am experienced in a parentless teen who's been held against her will...Well... Actually, now that I put it like that. I am very experienced. The difference is, I never got to grieve. I had to suck it the fuck up and take it. I wasn't allowed to feel. I never got chance to process my infliction or heal my fucking harm. She needs to snap out of this if she wants to survive.

"YOU KILLED THEM." she's quivering and I don't even think she knows what she's doing right now but I wanna smack those tears off her fucking face and really give her something to cry about. "YOU RUINED MY LIFE." She's not wrong. I did what I always do. *I'm selfish.* But I wasn't exactly expecting this to be my outcome. She will always be my own personal *Karma*.

"Put. The knife. Down." I wave my bloody hand gesturing for her to give it to me but of course she will not comply. She is breaking. *Good.* She needs to break. She needs to get it out. She needs to feel this pain if she wants to get out of this alive. She needs to pour alcohol on her open wounds and embrace the sting, it's the first stage of healing.

"It hurts! It hurts so much. I- I can't take it!" The cracking in her voice is forming a lump in my throat. I'll be honest, this is a first for me and I feel like an inexperienced mother hearing their baby cry for the first time. Its ear fucking and grating my gears but I have this urge to find a solution to stop her from sobbing like a bloody baby.

"Why are you doing this to me!" She says this like I purposely ruined her life and kidnapped her. I'm a fucking psycho but I'm not a stalker. She's been watching too many murder documentaries. I had no interest in her, she was purely *Collateral damage.*

"I told you. This was not what I wanted!"

"What now huh?! Are you just going to keep me here until I am a rotting pile of bones! Bury me in your back garden with the rest of your victims!" Her back chat is starting to rub me the wrong way. If she carries on and I will fill her mouth to shut her the fuck up, *I am starting to think keeping her sedated was the better option here.*

"The knife *Alora*. I won't tell you again." She's not even listening to me right now, clutching it to her chest, almost dropping it as she trembles like a scared puppy. I know there's adrenaline running through her veins. The impression I get from her is that she never had much control of her own life so I'm sort of proud right now. I'm bringing out that untamed kitten and I don't care if she hates me for it.

"I WILL KILL YOU!" This is adorable, really. But I could snap her in 0.3 seconds. *Her whining is getting annoying.*

"This isn't a horror movie sweetheart. If I kill you, you stay *DEAD*." *Like her mother.* Her expression doesn't change, she knows what I'm capable of and after last week's events I think she wants me to end her quickly.

"Good! You should have let me die! I swear to god I will make your life miserable every second, minute, hour that passes!" You know what. I don't doubt she will. It's been pretty dead round here so I guess she will continue to keep me busy, but if she thinks I'm going to put up with her bratty fucking behaviour she has another thing coming.

"I don't want to hurt you. Don't give me a reason to." A spine-chilling laugh seeps from her mouth as she wipes away the grief damping her cheeks.

"You're funny..." That screamed sarcasm and I want to wrap my hand around her pretty little throat, making my face the last face she sees as I deplete her of oxygen just to show her how *funny* I can really be. "Let me out." Her incessant whining is pushing me to a point I really don't want to reach. Does she really think I'm going to just open that door and let her waltz free? If that was the case I would have done so already.

"Just give me some time. I need time to get my shit together and I will let you go. You'll never have to see me again." I bite creeping forwards, prowling her into the corner of the room where she attempts to threaten me further. I can feel her anger consuming the room like gas, it's becoming harder and harder to breathe. Harder to predict what she is going to do next.

"NO! You don't get to run away from this! I will kill you myself if the cops don't get there first!"

I gently huff in response, making it known that her threat is nothing but useless. There are no houses for miles. We are in the middle of butt fuck nowhere. This place has been abandoned for years after the murders and allegations; people avoid these parts like the plague. If she thinks anyone is coming for her, she is more delusional than I thought. I can't fault her for hoping though. I spent many nights in that cell hoping someone would come for me even though I had no one left to rescue me. Your mind plays with you in the company of loneliness. Your demons begin to take up residence and play the angel in its absence.

"No one is coming for you. You can kick, scream, yell all you like. The windows are boarded up and we are the only sliver of life for miles. So you can either play ball and I can try and make this as comfortable for you as possible, or I can make this ugly. It's your choice." She doesn't quite realise just how lenient I am being with her right now which has proven to do nothing in my favour.

"FUCK YOU!" She screams with malice and I am boiling under my flesh. She knows I don't do kindness. Lucky for her I don't put my hands on women. Not unless self-defence is necessary and I feel there may be quite a lot of that if she carries on being a spoiled little brat, yet by the way she is directing that knife, I don't think she intends on being here much longer.

"Put the fucking knife down. Before I have to get physical." I take another step, holding my arms out to cradle her distress as she reaches forward, attempting to stab my other hand before sitting the tip of the blade against her prominent vein sat flush beneath the skin of her wrist. "Say you did kill me. Then what? Then you'd sit behind bars for murder." I wave my hands in the air to mimic surrender, challenging her at her own morals in this very moment. Fear makes us see them in a different light when you're pushed to meddle between life and death, it makes you commit acts of sin in the name of survival, it makes you kill just to save your own skin.

"I would claim self-defence!" She exclaims. A vindictive cackle bursts from my throat, tilting my head to the ceiling, sighing at the irony. The naivety she still possesses even now. Even though I'm showing her how dark life beyond her perfect little world can be. She still seeks safety in the very system created to break us.

"You know what? They would probably believe you too." I shake my head in despair smiling at her hopeful statement, finding amusement in how history has a way of repeating itself. *Self-defence.* Of course that would work in her favour. She wears no badge but she's still the daughter of an ex-detective who used the same excuse and got away with it.

"What the hell is that supposed to mean?!" She questions, sensing my mockery and my bitterness as I laugh at her for being so fucking foolish.

"You're a Blackthorne after all." My eyes find hers in the anger she's channelling, flickering at her own surname coming from my mouth. I've not told her any specifics, but I can see the dots are slowly connecting. She's not stupid, she knows there is more to this than an unhinged killer with a hunger for blood. She knows there's a reason I was in her house that night and she knows I know more about her family than she does.

"Why am I still here? What are you not telling me!" There are so many things I'm not telling her. Because I find enjoyment in this game of clue. *She will figure it out*. And when she does, I want to watch the sparkle in her eyes fade once she realises the kind of man he really was.

"Daddy's helpless little girl. Defending herself against the big bad monster who killed her parents. *-Finally stops the killer-*. Now that would be a great headline for the papers." I approach once more, swaying my broad shoulders in her direction, egging on her anger so she deters that blade away from her prominent artery.

"Come any fucking closer and I'll add another body count to your list like I should have done last week, you sick FUCK!" My throat tightens as I take in a sharp inhale. She's toying with my weakness and I know she isn't afraid of dying, that much is clear. But for some reason I find myself continuing to give a fuck. This could all be over and I could just let her end this right here, right now, but the pain in her eyes is seeping inside me. She really will do this, and I strangely don't want her to. I refuse to let her be weak, there is a fire inside her that I want to see. I want her to see that she is capable of overcoming this, she needs to realise that life is not all fucking rainbows and fairies. There are people like me, people far worse than the monsters she creates in her head.

"*Alora...*" The closer I get the further she's pushing the knife. I have a few seconds to pursue her before she buries that blade and bleeds out on my floor. I've had enough red mops in my life. I don't particularly want to clean up after her as well if I can help it.

"HOW DO YOU KNOW MY NAME?! DON'T FUCKING SAY MY NAME!" While she is distracted, fighting with her own demons I take it upon myself to lunge for her, gripping her dainty wrist inside my large hands but she won't let up that easily, fighting against my hold to slice her arm clean. She grazes it, not deeply but enough to make its mark as she screams like a banshee down my ear causing it to ring, smoothing both of our arms in our blood as she uses all her might to get out of my grasp. Colliding into the wardrobes and drawers, she yelps in pain, kicking her legs around like a child as I hold her up off the floor, crossing both my arms across her chest to constrict her chest.

"*I didn't ask for any of this! Let me fucking go!*"

"Keep fighting *Princess*. It just makes it more enjoyable for me." It's been awhile since I had a rough and tumble but I can't deny the adrenaline I'm feeling. It's addictive. It feeds my serotonin. Most people get that from puppies or fast cars. I receive it from watching someone fight for their life. If that doesn't tell you everything you need to know about me then I don't know what will.

As I crush her tighter she sinks her teeth into my bicep and I can feel her tearing my flesh away causing me to loosen my grip. "Fucking -" I'm finding out a lot about myself today. Apparently being a punching bag for my *Little Innocence* is proving to relieve me of some pent-up anger and quieting my demons. *Who knew she had that in her.*

"Fight BACK! Fight! COME ON!" She pants, wanting me to retaliate. She wants me to be her outlet. Slamming the flat side of her scrunched up fists into my chest like a drum, she's drawing the monster out of me with her persistent pushing. I'm afraid if I let her carry on I may do something I will regret.

"If you're so eager to die, let me make it quick for you." I waste no time yanking both of her wrists, as I rotate her to face away from my body, locking her forearms in place with one hand as I pull out my firearm from my back pocket with my other, shoving the barrel inside her mouth, I fight against her resistance as she squabbles in my arms, muffling her anger beneath the metal and the plea in her face shows me that deep down she is terrified of dying. "Fucking LISTEN to me!..." *I have no interest in killing her.* The mag is empty, but she needs to be shown the kind of fucking evil she is tampering with.

"I fucking get it! I get this anger you're feeling! I get this hunger for vengeance! I get that swelling ache that feels like it's collapsing your lungs. That overwhelming urge to want to make all the pain go away! But you have to fight it! You have to fucking suck it up and survive! You have to be better than it! *Better than me!...* " She is peering at me with tears welling in her eyes, and I can see by the way they are rounding at the edges that she is taking in my words carefully. I know I am not a saint; I never claim to be and I never will be anything but what she *should* fear.

I am dangerous, but I am dangerous because I've been exposed to nothing but destruction. She is so pure it makes my skin crawl with a selfish need to corrupt her, poison her slowly with every possible means necessary and open her eyes to the world beyond rose tinted glasses. I want to make her question everything she thought she knew. But until I do, I need to know she can handle it. I need her to *fight.*

"You're not a monster. So stop acting like one." I whisper with depth. Every second I am with her I feel like my wall is being lowered and it's driving me insane. Nearly two weeks in and she is already proving to be my biggest problem yet.

I remove the gun slowly watching her bottom lip quiver. She doesn't know whether to be terrified or relieved. I think she gets a kick from being seconds from death knowing deep down I won't let that happen. She is a weakness I'm growing fonder of by the minute. I've spent four years on my own without human company, as violent as it is, it's strangely comforting. All I've known is violence, so it really makes no difference to me. It just coats the deafening silence and the voices in the walls. *She has become my voice in the walls.*

I slide my gun back into my back pocket and peer down at the open gash in her arm where she attempted to off herself *like an idiot*, pulling her wrist to raise her inner arm to me, I gently stroke the flesh surrounding the wound with my thumb wanting so desperately to run my tongue against it. Next time I might not be quick enough, or next time. *I might do it for her.*

"Now. Let's get this wrapped up before you bleed out in your sleep. You foolish girl..."

SHASSII

CHAPTER 12

A BROKEN BAND AID

Puppet

She's resisting me. In a weird, fucked up way. Twice now she has saved my life and twice now I am left confused. I attacked her in search of some sort of closure and answers and I am left even more frustrated than I was before. She could have killed me but she didn't. She could have left me to die last week but she didn't. I wanted her to hurt me. I wanted her to fight back but instead she resisted my harm and took it. I don't understand and I want to rip my hair out. Is she resisting because she cares or is she resisting because she is lonely? I promised her violence and I don't intend on breaking that, but how far can I push before she snaps? Is she sparing me out of pity? If so I don't want her fucking pity. I want the pain to be gone and now I've added to it. She wants me to fight but I am so tired. What exactly am I fighting for? I have nothing left besides the babysitter I have now acquired and the nightmares that have now begun to plague my mind. That night haunts me like a broken tape. Every time I look at her, all I see is *death*.

She makes me want to *die* and she expects me to fight? How am I meant to move on from this?

She's tied me to the metal work of her bed frame as she tends to my wound and there is a knot in my stomach due to how gently she is being with my skin. *Skin I tore.* She is the definition of a mind fuck and I'm finding her kindness nauseating.

"Have you ever hurt yourself before?" Her question catches me off guard, interrupting the way I'm catching myself looking at her hands against my skin. I've thought about it, but I never had the balls. I'd never understood it until now, the pain I inflicted, just for a moment made me forget about everything. It shut off my mind.

"No…" There is a bowl of hot soapy water on the bed side table she's using to clean my wound along with a flannel that she's being so gentle with it's infuriating. *Why is she being so empathetic?*

"Is my company really that unbearable?" I scowl my face at her obscured question. *In what world would she ever think her company would ever be bearable?*

"You are a permanent reminder of everything I've lost. How could I even find comfort in your solitude." The mask she wears makes it even harder to even remotely enjoy looking at her. It's hideous and full of horror I can never erase.

"I don't expect you to." Her manipulation tactics are smooth. I'll give her that. But I have no interest in grovelling at her sorry excuse for a half-arsed apology. She has yet to even apologise to me, not that it would change anything.

"Then why do you care? I certainly don't." I roll my eyes into the back of my head in protest. Refusing to look at her.

"Because what you did was brave, but stupid. And I do not do well with stupidity. Not when I know you're stronger than that." I hiss as she digs the flannel a little deeper into the cut and I don't know if that was for my newfound attitude or because she was digging to clean the wound but it seemed personal. She acts like she's known me my entire life when she's known me for five seconds.

"I will never forgive you so just stop trying so damn hard." I say, glaring at the ceiling pulling focus on the patch work excuse for a paint job and the layers that are peeling off. The house just screams murder house if ever I saw one. It gives me the creeps.

"I don't want you to." My eyes shift to hers and my brows narrow. Why is she not fighting her corner, why is she not fighting back!

"Then what do you want from me!" I thrash around, causing her to grip my arm so tightly it could snap as both our heated glares rest on one another.

"I want you to know the truth. And then I will let you decide whether you want to hand me in or not." If she thinks for one second her little sob story is going to magically change my mind she is highly mistaken…that part of me is long gone. That part of me got hurt. I refuse to be hurt anymore.

"I don't want to be a part of your sick revenge fantasy. The damage is done." I scoff with a sour face. I catch her peering at me through her hideous makeup and she looks me up and down with some sort of approval. I don't know what she is looking at but it makes me shudder.

"Has anyone ever told you how tough you really are?" I gulp on her words, losing sight of my anger as a wave of heat rushes through my system. If only she really knew how much of a baby I really was.

"I'm not…" I cut eye contact, flushed and ashamed that I'm not as brave as I should be. Beneath it all I'm losing it. I'm finding a part of me I didn't even know existed, a part of me I wish I never met. A part of me I'm frightened of because I can't control it. I fear it will eat me from the inside out. I have always been in control. *What do you do when you lose grip of it?*

"It's not every day I get chunks missing out of my arm by an eighteen-year-old girl." As crazy as this sounds, that didn't sound half bad coming out of her mouth. It's also as crazy as the fact she even had to say that, and the way she knows my age. I took a chunk out of her arm just to stay alive. Who even am I?

"It's not every day I have to fight for my life." She's slowly wrapping up my arms in a bandage that has probably been sitting in her bathroom for ten years. I'll probably die of infection before I get out of here.

"Well get used to it, *Puppet*. Welcome to the real world. I am the type of sicko Daddy warned you about, but there are far greater threats than me out there. Trust me…" A look of disgust paints my face. She really thinks murdering my parents and holding me against my will isn't bad? *She really is delusional.*

"And you would know, would you? Do you have a little serial killer fan club?" She's laughing. She's actually laughing at me right now. She actually thinks this is *funny?*

"You have quite the imagination." I can't see it right now but I know she is grinning like the devil underneath her freakish persona and I want to stab knives in her eyes.

"Well, you clearly know a few."

"When you've been to prison you realise just how sugar coated your perfect little lives really are." My heart stops beating as I take in her confession.

She's done time?

"You've been to prison?" My brows relax slightly as she finishes up patching my arm and holds my forearm in her lap, turning to face me like she's about to confess her life story and I'm suddenly nervous to hear it.

"Six years." *Six!!* She did time for six years and she's out killing people again! Did that not teach her anything! She really is fucking crazy!

"Then why did you jeopardise your freedom?" I keep my composure from the outside trying to not burst into a fit of questions. Things I don't even think I want the answers to but find myself asking anyway.

"Revenge has a funny way of clouding your judgement. It's why I refuse to let you make the same mistake I did." The disbelief on my face right now. Did she just try to imply I have serial killer tendencies because I want to imagine stabbing her? Now that I say that, that's what a serial killer would think about… "You're not a killer *Puppet*. You are just shallow." *Ouch.* I don't know whether to take that as a compliment or feel offended.

"If you're trying to build a bridge you keep breaking it." I tug what little movement I can conjure with my restraint wrists to remove it from her lap trying to hold back my visible discomfort. *That hurt.*

"I thought you didn't care." An empty silence fills the room as she speaks dryly. Using my own words against me. And she's right. *I don't care. Why did I even say that?* "Don't feel offended. I'd rather I didn't receive any more holes in my hands, as badass as it might be. I have enough." I glare down at her hand; she's not wrapped, only in ink that travels the length of her fingers.

it's still seeping crimson but she doesn't seem at all phased. On closer inspection I notice indents in her hands, scars that look like tiny bullet holes.

"Are you not going to wrap that up?" it's making me a little dizzy looking at that hole in her hand knowing I caused that. To think I thought I was going to kill her. She's also right again. I'm not a killer. *I'm a pussy.*

"I gave you the last one," she says it so nonchalantly like I'm meant to say thank you or something? Why do I want to? She deserves to bleed. This good guy act isn't going to get under my skin, but there's a small part of me that's smiling. Somewhere in my subconscious. I can feel it.

"What do you like to eat?" This time she's asking me what I want? Now I think about it. I've barely eaten all week which isn't doing any good for my blood sugar levels, not to mention the amount of energy I just exerted attempting to unalive a criminal.

"Nothing you cook if I can help it. You're probably feeding me body parts." You can never be too careful. This nice act always has a motive, but by the expression in her eyes she did not appreciate that assumption.

"Body parts it is." She pushes herself up off the bed, towering over me making me quiver. She's probably more terrifying than my nightmares as she peers at me through her mask like a weirdo. She is so tall not even my own demons could take that down and little me thought I stood a chance.

Revenge has a funny way of clouding your judgement.

"You're vile..." I have absolutely no appetite which is not helping how fatigued I feel right now. Thinking about food makes me want to puke and now I'm thinking about body parts. *Yummy.*

"You're eating." She demands, sounding like my bloody parents. Nothing changes does it. Even dead I cannot get away from this insistent codling.

SHASSII

CHAPTER 13

FORCED PROXIMITY

Puppet

Play - 'Sweat – R Y X'

The air is still, my body so tiny that it cannot keep up with the chill consuming the room. I feel like I'm sleeping outside right now, fighting my body trying to seize up, laying underneath a duvet no thicker than a fluffy blanket. Crisp steam evaporates from my mouth as I exhale into the cool atmosphere, twitching to the rapidly decreasing temperatures. I haven't a clue what the date is but I know we are somewhere into the middle of November and I hate this time of year. I hate the cold, and it doesn't help that I'm skin and bone with barely any layers in a house with no heating, a house that's falling apart and probably missing a few windows.

I don't even hear her approach, too concentrated on the ringing in my ears as I tremble to stay warm.

"You're shaking like a dog." I jolt in response, not expecting her to jump scare me as she states the obvious from behind me, wiping away the remnants of present tears as I sniffle quietly.

"I'm fine." My eyes roll to the back of my head, frustrated that I can't seem to have a moment of peace without her hovering. It's midnight or something stupid, *what is she even doing up?*

"It's only gonna get colder." She can't see my face right now but my brow lines scrunch into my forehead as I cuddle my shackle. It's not exactly the comfiest thing to sleep with.

"How about you just worry about yourself and I will worry about myself." I narrow my eyes, following the woodwork of the wall in front of me. Why can't she just leave me alone?

"I am. And you're in *MY* bed." She emphasises '*my*' like I decided to put myself here and sleep in *HER* bed which only winds me up further.

"You put me here." I turn sharply to face her, codling the duvet in the cold clasp of my dry fingers to find her rubbing her temples, annoyance plastered all over her slender face.

"You need warmth before you freeze to death." Again. Stating the obvious. Don't worry, *I will just get up and grab myself some more blankets.* Oh wait.

"Then give me another blanket." I spit, spiteful with frustration still quivering like an idiot.

"That won't do anything. I have no heating. You need body heat." My eyes shuffle around the room before realisation kicks in. *Is she saying we need to sleep together? In the same bed?*

"Absolutely not. I don't think so, I'd rather sleep with the dog." My protest is pointless as she rolls her dead eyes at me. Somehow, I don't think she is going to take no for an answer.

"You don't exactly have a choice. This is my bedroom and the sofa isn't quite cutting it tonight. Sorry. *Your Highness.*" If I had it my way, I wouldn't even be here right now and she could have had the entire bed to herself. Why is she moaning like she isn't the one keeping me here?

"I'd rather shoot myself in the foot than sleep in the same bed as you." It's not happening. Sharing a bed is intimate. What does she think this is, *a date?*

"That would make my life easier. Means you wouldn't be able to run." The corner of her mouth upturns at the vulgar remark, as if she is trying to be funny and it's getting old. "I can quite happily just take the duvet into the living room with me. It's up to you *Puppet*." Her voice is no longer dull, but sarcastic, trying to make light of the situation, finding much amusement in my detest.

"I will freeze to death." *She's not funny. None of this is funny.*

"That's what you want isn't it?" She questions my wants, edging the temptation of death as she stalks towards the bed slowly, dragging her feet beneath her, eyes on me as she lowers her upper body to grab the opening of the duvet.

"Don't!" ~*Tug*~ "Even think about it!" I leap from the bed, my shackles dragging along with me until the chain pulls tight, keeping me stationary against the edge of the bed and her smile is nothing short of sinister. As both her hands meet the mattress watching my distress, I tug on my restraints knowing full well that my pleas are nothing against her actions if she really wanted to hurt me. "I'm serious!" All I can do is threaten empty words and hold onto the gentle instincts I know she keeps buried somewhere inside her.

"Or what... hmm?" She knows I can't do anything but I think she gets a rise out of watching me try. The sick bitch enjoys pain so inflicting it would be pointless. That wound in her hand is visible evidence of that, she's still not wrapped it and the remaining damage is nothing short of gruesome.

"I will make sure you don't sleep a wince." I bite. My feet are burning against the floor, hosting an entity inside of me at how cold the air is hugging my body but I refuse to let her win. *This is not happening.* I will keep her awake until sunrise if I have to.

"I don't sleep anyway." I would say I am surprised by her insomnia but I'm not. Sleep is for the weak. I sleep to escape but she seems to thrive in her sickness, she likes being this way. Or maybe murdering people likes to tap at her nightmares, I wouldn't sleep either if I took someone else's life. Restless nights equal guilty conscience and she is riddled with it which is a good sign, it means she isn't a complete sociopath.

"Then why do you want to get into bed?" I question her as if this bed is mine.

"Because believe it or not, my bed holds more warmth than my uncomfortable ass sofa I seem to have accommodated, and it's particularly cold out tonight." She slips underneath the duvet wearing her smugness with pride, barely just about fitting into it with the length of her.

"Get out!" I want to burst, gripping at the duvet, tugging towards me before she retaliates, pulling the other side, throwing me over the side of the mattress with sheer strength until I'm inches from her face, the paint choking my nose.

"What are you so afraid of? You think I'm going to hurt you?" There is a knot tightening between my words, torn between my imagination and the reality of the situation. I want to cling to the fact that I'm a victim and I am a victim. But the truth is, her actions have not met her words.

"Do you blame me?" I know she's not actually hurt me yet. *Really hurt me.* When there are many times that she could have. But I've learned my lesson. I don't trust her further than I could throw her. *Which isn't very far.* I can barely see her silhouette against the sliver of moonlight between the cracks but her eyes burrow inside the night like the moon, cutting through the darkness, searching for earth in mine.

"*I won't touch you.*" There is sincerity in her voice for once. And I so desperately want to believe that but for now I will keep my distance.

"Get back into bed. Before you catch hypothermia." Her voice is demanding yet bored as tension lays thick like dust on the furniture. I'm so captivated by her gaze that she rips the duvet from my distracted grip leaving my hand bare.

"And who's fault would that be?" We sound like an old married couple and the only thing keeping my heart beating and my blood pumping right now is the discombobulated rage inside of me. She pulls the duvet back enticing me to slide in, letting the encapsulated heat escape. "You're letting all the heat out!" Irritation rolls through my fingertips, as I rub my upper arms with my icy hands creating friction against my skin.

"Then hurry the fuck up." She bites hard and I hesitate, anticipating the rights and wrongs But she's right. I don't have a place to argue this, and my clothes are barely enough to keep me covered.

"If you lay a hand on me, I will rip your skin off." I snarl, clutching at my body like a fragile ornament. I've never shared a bed with anyone. Not even friends, and I can't exactly say I thought my first bed share would be with a literal murdering psychopath. I shudder at the thought, internally raging at my inner turmoil, at the fact I am even considering this.

"I don't doubt that, *Princess*." These nicknames are really starting to rub me the wrong way and not because I don't like them... Because I do. It shows me there is something there besides evil. It tampers with the relentless mental strength I need to entirely hate her and I don't know why this is proving to be so difficult when I do *hate her*.

"I'm serious." I reach my hands out to grab the sheets, shuddering at the breeze infiltrating the warmth I've settled beneath the palms of my hands.

"I'm quaking in my boots." Her mockery is resenting. It eats away at the wall I've built when all I want to do right now is grin at her smart fucking mouth.

"Are you just going to lie there and watch me like a creep?" On second thought. Being watched whilst unconscious is one thing, but now I'm back to the land of the living, the thought of that makes my skin itch.

"Depends. You're not exactly the most pleasing thing to look at. You dribble in your sleep." I gape my mouth open, trying to find the words but warmth heats my cheeks as I shy in utter embarrassment.

"I'm just going to pretend you didn't say that..." My gaze diverts to the sheets below me, about to plant my ass down with my back facing her, contemplating what the hell in life I did to deserve sharing a bed with the *Devil*.

"Take off your top." My heart tightens in my chest followed by a sharp pain shooting up the pockets of my spine.

"Excuse me?" *She must be joking?*

"You heard." Yeah, I heard her alright, and she is nuts. It's freezing! And my dignity is already stripped from me when she watches me shower in *her* clothes.

"I am not taking off my top!?" What could she possibly want me to take it off for!

"Do you want to stay warm? You have a bra on. Take it off." She's so assertive that my goody two shoes find it hard to fight against her orders, sinking into the bed as I finish sitting, feeling her eyes burning a hole into my back.

"Turn around then..." I can't see her but I can feel her shuffle, tugging the duvet along with her as she follows my order with no hesitation as always which only winds me up more.

I unbutton my upper half, letting it glide against the goosebumps painting my skin as it falls to the mattress and I feel disgusting in my own body, diving under the covers to cover up my humiliation but the chill is biting at my breasts, hardening against the sheets.

Uneasiness plagues the room as I hug my side of the bed trying desperately to create a ravine between us, the sheets brushing like feather weight against my bare body and I am indecisive as to whether I enjoy the feeling. She shuffles some more, subtle tugs pull against the sheets before fabric cushions the floor on her side of the bed. *Did she just take her clothes off?* The space between us immediately radiates with heat and I concentrate solely on the warmth consuming me, closing my eyes to finally chase my escape.

"Closer." *Is sharing a bed not enough for her?* We are already close enough. I don't move but it makes no odds as she plays tug of war with the sheet I'm wrapped in, forcing our proximity until our backs are touching. A silent hitch escapes my mouth as her skin sears mine, burning red hot against me immediately slowing my heart rate. *Comfort* is the only word to explain it and that thought alone makes me grind my teeth with internal annoyance. Nothing about her is comforting. She's like a splinter piercing her way through my decaying heart. Slowly inching her pain inside of me and nothing about that is pleasant. She's already made her grave where whatever this is, is concerned. This is merely a usage of one another to benefit our needs, but I can feel myself yearning for more, crawling inch by inch until our backs are firmly flush against one another, chasing that warmth my glacial landscape so desperately craves right now.

"How are those feet holding up." Her words ooze out as she refers to earliers comment and my tongue runs my teeth as I kiss them, feeling her canine curl up on top of them like a heated blanket.

I would rather shoot myself in the foot than sleep with you.

I hug her back with mine and tell myself I hate it, but she's warm, and my body instantly feels a whole lot better for it. Skin on skin isn't at all what I expected, it's sticky, unsanitary, it's so foreign to me, so not in my jurisdiction and I feel like I'm committing my own felony.

I don't know if this is a one off, or she plans to do this until the temperature picks up again but I'm just going to keep my eyes closed and pretend she's not there. She's merely acting as a hot water bottle. This was her idea not mine. I'm just using the facilities she's willingly supplying.

CHAPTER 14

CORRUPT SYSTEM

Puppeteer

Play - 'Shadow - John Mark Nelson'

After over thirty minutes of protesting getting into the damn bed she's finally passed the fuck out. All that fight *must have been so exhausting.* I know I said I wouldn't watch her, but I lied. She does dribble in her sleep though, that part was true. She isn't unpleasant to look at, I'd rather see her wearing my blood but that's beside the point.

She's been out for around three hours and I've studied her breathing, how her subconscious reacts to me. She won't admit it but she feels safe and part of me hates that. Her damp strands of hair are stuck to her cheek and her mouths slightly open, breathing gently beside me, her wrists curled in under her chin facing my abdomen. I don't plan on doing this forever, but something wanted me close to her tonight and it wasn't invited. I could say I'm being considerate but that doesn't explain the dire urge to touch her tender skin under my fingers. How my eyes are fixated on the plush complexion of her plump lips, how I have to fight a smirk when she makes those sleepy whines against my skin. I'm just fucking horny and I need to get laid. *Jesus*. For some reason the thought of it does nothing for me right now. I say that as I wet my lips just looking at hers. It's freezing but my body is red hot, even sat here half naked. Luckily it's not light enough in here for her to see anything if she was to wake and by how frigid she was to intimacy, it's dawning on me that she hasn't exactly had much experience even without finding a love interest. She's *clean*. Which tempts my urge to corrupt her all the more, in her skimpy little pyjamas and her fragile little frame.

Prison wasn't exactly swarming with Angels. The closest I got; I watched die once again. Right in front of me. Intimacy is something I avoid like the plague. I wouldn't have called it a relationship; *I didn't love her*. We just gave each other what we wanted and that was that. She was rough round the edges but she made for a good fuck and a vent. I'd say she was the closest thing I had to a friend. She was probably the only person on earth I trusted. Maybe there was something there, but it was never love. Loneliness at best. I don't *make love*. I take. I take until I'm satisfied. I've never told anyone I love them and I don't plan on it. The last person I uttered those filthy words to was my mother and look where that got her. *Dead*. When I *'care'* people get hurt, it's a reoccurring curse. After a while you realise you weren't built to consume the touch of purity, only eat away at others in hopes they might warm your cold, hollow heart.

She cares too much for her own good. She finds empathy in the shallowest beating of her own heart, it's how she survives. Or it's my fault for not being harder on her. She is clinging to this premonition that there is good in me when there isn't, that version of me etched herself into the four walls I was confined to for six years. She's fighting me but we both know harming her is the last thing on my mind and maybe that's why she is pushing my fucking buttons. She will come unstuck if she continues to search for this redemption every fucker seems to think I burrow. I chase death, I feed off it. It soothes the monster I've become and she will learn. I don't want her close but keep finding myself moulding myself to benefit *her needs*. Not my own sick and depraved needs.

She should have fought louder. She should hate me deeper, fear me harder, yet she's passed out safe and sound beside me without a care in the world. Even shackled down as her dainty fingers cup the air, she looks peaceful and it's making me gnaw my jaw.

Tomorrow she will deny that my company gave her any comfort but she's not looked this content since the night I brought her here. She's deprived of affection and I've somewhat given her a taste to ease her subconscious when I shouldn't have. I shouldn't give a damn how she feels, yet I'm sat here counting the freckles on her face, withstanding the unbearable metal sinking into my shoulder blades as I suck in nicotine with my bare back against this bed frame, keeping a bed warm for someone who should be buried in my back garden. I exhale from my cigarette slowly, bracing my neck against the bar, staring up at my uneven ceiling remembering the countless nights I'd have to brave my demons until the sun came up and then I realise.

It's silent.

My mind is quiet.

A little too quiet. The only thing taking up residence in my mind right now is *her*, when I should be concentrating on more important shit, like my next target. *I need to sort it out.*

I remove myself from the bed, placing my t-shirt beside her without even thinking, captivated by the crack of light cutting her face in half. She looks ethereal and I question my perception of beauty for a moment as I admire her before making my way out the door to the living room. I tap my leg at Shep, directing him outside for five minutes before a subtle tilt of my head leads him back to the bedroom, slipping on another black tee hanging off the back of the sofa before making my way to *my* part of the house.

I unlock the garage door that's accessible by the kitchen where two doors sit side by side. Neither are the stairway to heaven, but they both serve me the purpose I need. I unlock the right door and slip in, locking it behind me before my ass hits the chair and artificial light almost blinds me.

I've been after a lead for months and the bastards finally slipped up. He recently purchased a new car which gave me access to all the finer details like where he now lives, his place of work, his phone number, and with a little push, access to all of it. He's been out of town all week on a business trip and it was too far for me to travel with my little cockroach in the mix, so I'm patiently waiting for him to come back. I'm sure the sick fuck can't wait to get back and let some anger out on his kids, but hopefully I will catch him before he has chance. I have a day to kill before he's on a flight back to Chicago meaning I have yet another 24 hours to twiddle my thumbs and occupy myself until he lands.

My computer is littered with open tabs, documents, images and personal details. It's my mom's old computer that I've inherited for work usage. I'm disconnected from the Chicago police department but my computer skills are a little more advanced than them, meaning I have access to everything they do without being detected which makes my life a whole lot easier, but also twice as risky.

I do bad things, but only to eradicate worse. I do bad things to tame the trauma inside of me. I do what I do because I realised it was what I needed to do to feel something. It's what kept me alive. I sat in the compounds of my own mind for six years and held on to the part of me that thirst for blood. It is now programmed into me and it's what I will keep doing until I eventually kick the bucket, but until that day this is all I know and I wish I didn't.

The things I had to suffer to get to this point I would only wish on people just as sick and twisted as him. *I am that wish.* But I am not him. Children and women beaters hide amongst a society that covers them up because they raise money for charity and sit on wads of cash. Someone's gotta fucking do it. My consequences are just my count down with a broken clock. I don't know when that will be but when it happens, a bullet will find a home inside my chest where it belongs.

Before I know it the room is glowing with golden accents. I stare at the clock, unphased by the time before exiting my nook and lock the door. There are things in here I'd rather she didn't find, not for my benefit, for hers. She's not strong enough yet. *Yet.* I huff at my own inner words, amused that I think she'll even be around that long.

My feet find the kitchen, dragging my dead weight, reaching for the kettle to make myself a much-needed strong coffee. It's routine, but I must have exerted far too much brain power because I feel like I've been hit by a bus this morning and my face feels drier than the Sahara Desert with yesterday's face paint I couldn't be arsed to wash off. I say couldn't, but I actually couldn't even if I wanted to. Not when playing super nanny anyway.

I take myself to the bathroom and wash the crusty, murky paint off my dry skin before smearing another picture back on. Some might say it's unsanitary to use someone else's blood like makeup but it's my trophy. A reward I wear with pride, it feeds the sadistic freak in me that was drummed into my flesh and carved into my cheek, running the crimson over the ravine travelling the corner of my mouth.

"Give us a smile baby girl. Show Daddy how happy this makes you"

The basin of the sink cracks underneath the palms of my hands, oblivious to my own strength as *IT'S* voice haunts my hollow skull, even dead it speaks to me, the devil on my shoulder, the ghost in the walls, my very own form of insomnia. The only time it seems to shut the fuck up is when I take another waste of oxygen, it's my hit of oxytocin, my own personal remedy. No prescription can quiet the darkness that lives inside me, only *death*, death is my sedative to the war inside my head, others or my own. This is something she will never understand and I don't know why but subconsciously, I hope she does. Something inside me prays that when she realises the truth she will look at me differently, but not with sympathy, with understanding. I don't want her sympathy, nor do I deserve it and something tells me she will cling to it either way. I want her to understand this was not her fault. If anything, she was also a victim to something she was not even aware of, I want her to see that the system failed her too.

SHASSII

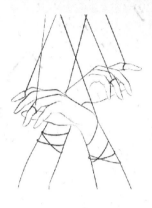

CHAPTER 15

HER FIRST

Puppet

My sleepiness fatigues me as my eyes crack open, holding onto a sudden tightness keeping me from exhaling once I take in my surroundings and last night creeps into the back of my mind, terrified to turn around like I've had a regretful one night stand, so focused on what may possibly be behind me that it takes me a moment to realise there's no longer weight around my wrist. I focus in on my forearm to find it free from its shackle, reacting with a jolt as the mattress wobbles. *She's uncuffed me?* Touching my tender skin where metal was sat last night, I turn slowly to reveal a furry friend glaring back at me. He's a German Shepherd and on closer inspection, he must be three times the size of me as he takes up the majority of the bed. He attempts to lick at my forearms as I rub his velvet ears, feeling a tear in his flesh that feels like it's been there for some time, peering down at the black mound against the stained white sheets where she was lying.

"Hey boy, where is your crazy two-legged friend?" I whisper as an uninvited feeling makes itself known, a feeling of *disappointment* and I scowl, shaking my head in shame once that feeling reaches the surface. As if I wanted her to still be there.

Now who's acting like this is a date.

I slip into her overly large black long sleeve tee that acts as a dress on me, reaching my upper thighs with its length and my fingertips against the sleeves. I tiptoe onto the wood beneath me and her smell encases me. I don't know whether it's that that's making me nauseous or the fact that I'm shackle free in a killer's house. I make my way to the door where the dog jumps up off the bed after me. *Is she here*? Is this a game? Maybe now is my chance. She was an idiot to give me free reign. Did she not learn her lesson last time? She thinks that because we shared a bed together last night that suddenly we are friends? She's highly mistaken, but it holds my plan and keeps it in motion.

Keep your friends close and your enemies closer.

I edge myself towards the door where the knob turns effortlessly and I raise a brow. *Uncuffed and unlocked?...*

Maybe the guilt is catching up to her. I roll my heavy eyes into the back of my head, contemplating whether I should just crawl back into bed a little while longer now that I'm not having to toss and turn against the cuffs but clattering disturbs my urgency for more sleep.

She is still here.

I pitter patter my way out the door until light hits me, where she is standing making something to eat like this is all totally normal. My eyes pan the room slowly, looking for any sign of freedom before stopping in my tracks, distracted by her groggy morning voice, vibrating against the desolate room.

"Morning." My jaw drops at how carefree she's waltzing around her kitchen. A kitchen I've yet to study but it looks like something from the 80s. Those god awful dark plywood cabinets and Granny curtains close off the view from the window to what I'm assuming is the back garden, or what's left of it. A fridge no bigger than me sits by the back door with a heavy-duty padlock most likely meant for me. The absence of personality gives it an entirely new one, one made up of questions and curiosity. Nothing about this place screams family friendly, it's been abandoned and neglected.

Mistreated and abused. The front window is all boarded up. *Why?* Why are they all boarded up like this?

My eyes follow the hideous wallpaper encasing the room where holes puncture the walls, opening out onto a very sad looking living room, practically empty besides a stained patch work sofa, an arm chair with holes burnt into the fabric, a TV flush against the wall on a tiny table and a giant dog bed beside it next to the garage door. The entire place is uncluttered from my stampede, she's cleaned it all up like a house maid.

"Aren't you meant to be out doing whatever you do?" I ask, running my hand through my matted hair, glaring at my feet where her four-legged friend is sitting beside me with his tail brushing against the floor.

"Day off." *Day off*? Is that why she's out most days? She can't work. *Surely not*.

"You work?" My brow tugs, taken back by her words, she's yet to look at me and her face is still painted with another. Clearly still too afraid to show me who she really is.

"If you want to call it that." A knife slices against the chopping board that's firmly in her hand. A weapon I could use, or a weapon she could lodge inside me if I do something stupid, but by the smirk tugging at her cheshire cat smile and her sarcasm, her work is dismembering bodies. Victims like me.

"Of course." I mumble, huffing in annoyance, rolling my head back as I smile in pure disbelief that I even imagined for a mere moment she could possibly obtain a job without the dire need to kill the manager if she was given a task she didn't want to do.

"Don't sound so surprised, *Puppet*." For a moment I imagine using her knife to rip open her stomach and gouge out her bloody eyes. Sickening images flash before me, shaking off my disturbance.

She's already getting into my head.

"So on your day off you've decided to, what? Make pancakes and kick your feet up as a reward?" My upper arm finds the frame of the kitchen door, cupping my elbows as I tilt my head.

"*Precisely.*" She pauses, slowly rotating her neck to look at me, licking the residue of food she's making off her thumb and my tummy knots with a feeling I can't explain as I glare at her tongue, decorated with piercings and split right down the middle making my skin crawl at the thought. *Ouch-* how did I not notice that sooner?

"What is wrong with you? Seriously." She is so careless with the thought of other people's lives so why am I still breathing? None of this makes sense. One minute I feel like I'm starting to *understand* her and then she throws me completely off with the way she walks amongst the simple minded like she herself is one. She is a rubix cube and I've never been good at them, *she is far from simple and she is not like them.*

"Throw another one and I'll lock you back in there." That room is the least of my worries, in fact I feel safer in there, it's become my safe haven. Venturing out is stirring anxiety in me, but being cooped up for weeks does that to a person.

"Am I meant to say thank you?" A ceramic plate scrapes across the concrete countertop, decorated in fluffy pancakes as she nudges it across to me, completely ignoring my hostility.

"Eat. Your insulin is on the table." It sounds crazy, but for just a second, I hear my mom and my heart warms with a thud. I imagine home, sitting at the island in the middle of the room reading the next chapter of my book before college, completely immersed, forgetting to eat the food in front of me. She'd have to remind me multiple times and I'd shove toast in my mouth as I ran out the door. That memory slowly fades as I realise that it is only a memory now, something I will never get back and will only be able to picture like an old tape which sends my blood boiling with anger. I don't know what stage of grief I am in right now, but the feeling never gets easier.

"Why did you uncuff me?" I glare down at my open wrists, stretching out my stiff joints waiting for an answer but she avoids my question.

"Syrup?" *Why is she avoiding the question*?

"Why did you uncuff me?!" I don't want the damn syrup, I don't even want to eat right now, I just want to get out of here and go back to normality which I know will never happen. Even if I did escape, there is nothing left for me. I am a pile of forgotten bones. I wonder if anyone is even looking for me right now.

"Because I can supervise you. I could quite happily put you back if you like?" *Supervise me*? *What am I, five?* Although I do need to stretch my legs, so on further thought I decline.

"No..." I begin to chew the sleeves, standing here drooping in her t-shirt like a one-night stand in a romcom movie and I'm cringing at the sight of me.

"That's what I thought." She knows exactly how to keep me curious and pry for more answers. Answers that I will get when she least expects it. I've already noticed that she doesn't spend any time in here, it's always behind that door by the dining room table. Muffled unexplained noises radiate through that door any moment she is here, like the music the other night. Maybe it's a gym, maybe it's a torture chamber, who knows, but at least I'm not in there, although I can't help but wonder.

"You were supposed to be keeping me warm." I swiftly change the subject so she doesn't catch on that I'm aware of her hide away. The questions will come but not yet.

"I did." She picks up her cup of what I can only assume is coffee by the strong scent of earth lingering. I can't see the bags under her eyes as they are smothered in paint but I just know they are heavy. She swigs from her ugly cup before turning to face me, leaning back on the counter with her plate of food in hand, smothered in black attire. She looks like the dark figure you'd see in a horror movie, yet this isn't a movie, this is real and she frightens me half to death but I'm finding inner strength being cooped up like a caged animal, strength I didn't know I had in me and it feels sort of good.

"You left the bed cold." I reply sternly, crossing my arms to show my disappointment.

"Would you rather I of stayed? I don't sleep with people. Certainly not a hostage young enough to be my sibling." My eyes bulge. I don't believe that for a second. She is the epitome of a *fuck girl* if ever I saw one. I don't know what exactly she's into but it doesn't take a genius to see that men aren't on her shopping list. Maybe I'm just blind. Plus, she looks twice my age, she can't tell me she's never slept with anyone.

"You've never slept with anyone in your *own* bed?" My attention drifts from the food I should be eating, concentrating solely on this conversation and I don't know why it interests me. Maybe it's because this is the most socialising I've had since she locked me away.

"No." She dabs at her pancakes, eating it with her fingers as she smears it in the syrup caking the plate, so much syrup I can feel my mouth foaming. My sugar levels are screaming at me.

"Surely you've had people over?" My body weight rests on my left leg as I hold the countertop next to my plate watching her eye up my hand.

"Oh, wouldn't you like to know *Princess?*" A subtle smirk lifts the corner of her mouth, sucking off the excessive amount of syrup now stuck to her fingers as she locks her eyes on mine. She's making an inappropriate innuendo with an even more inappropriate action like I'm going to find that hot. *I don't,* but the sudden surge of heat in my face is telling me something different.

"That's not what I meant." I shy away, rolling my embarrassment out and a pause settles as she finishes her last mouthful, setting the plate down as she grips the worktop in the palm of her hands holding her body weight. She inhales slowly and exhales sharply, like she's holding back things she wants to say but throws it at me anyway as she gawks out the dirty window.

"You're the first woman to sleep in my bed. *Happy now?*" There's that look again. Look of guilt. Guilt that she's confessing things she shouldn't. Guilt at herself for telling me things that stone cold criminals like her wouldn't tell anyone. *That's embarrassing* but I'm just as embarrassing because neither have I.

"Lucky me." I mock my way through this in hopes she doesn't think I care, because I don't care that I'm the first to sleep in her bed. Nor do I believe her. Me and a million other girls. Hurt no doubt, so what's so special about me? *Nothing is special about you Lora. She's just savouring you for later.*

"Eat. I won't tell you again." She interrupts my thoughts, shifting her carved out diamonds towards the plate in front of me waiting for me to eat and I finally take a bite. *These are actually really good....*

She is staring at me contently as I guiltily enjoy these pancakes.

CHAPTER 16

LOVE IS WEAKNESS

Puppeteer

"**Y**ou can keep that." I taunt, looking her up and down before drinking the last of my now *cold* coffee. I must admit, I never get tired of seeing her drowning in my overly large clothes, I can excuse the lack of water just this once. I forgot how short she is. She looks down at my black tee, scolding in disagreement but I think secretly she likes it too. She's scoffing my food like a beggar and I'm internally grinning at how stupidly adorable she looks trying to pretend she doesn't like it.

I make banging pancakes.

"Wow, thanks. How *kind* of you." Her sarcasm angers me as much as it amuses me and that fucking word is not letting up. She's a tough cookie when she's not crumbling. I'm not sure where exactly we stand right now but I'm hoping for her sake she realises that this is for her benefit. Does she think I enjoy keeping her cooped up like an animal? *No.* But she hasn't exactly been the easiest to work with. I don't hurt women. All I've ever done is protect them. Well... Tried. Maybe that's why my instincts took over when she tried to hurt herself. *Because of me.* I clench my jaw slightly at the thought. This all goes against everything I fucking believe in, but she gives me no choice. The quicker she works with me the quicker this will be over, and she can go back to whatever life is waiting for her outside my walls. Her humour has started to peep back in and she's glaring at my empty cup like she wants some.

"You want one?" I'm trying to treat her more like a guest than a hostage, I guess I'm delusional and probably far too lenient for my own good.

"No. Thank you." She finishes off her last mouthful and puts the plate down gently on the side. *She actually finished it all.* Before walking past me towards the table and her scent is intoxicating. It's far better than the stale must of death.

"Offers there."

She takes her insulin as instructed like a good girl. Facing away, talking towards the wall at me as I dish a bowl for Shep.

"So what now. You think because we shared a bed that we are *friends*?" Friends are the last thing I want out of this. She's a victim, my hostage. My *plaything*. It's sweet that she's thinking about friendship, although I know she's being sarcastic.

"I don't do *friends*." I rock on my feet. Gripping the side of the counter before pushing off to open up the fridge.

"Good. Neither do I." Uncertainty laces her words. A false security. She sounds like me, the little girl inside of me that would beg for friendship and come up short, betrayed and left on my own. I built a wall and told myself I was ok with being alone when really I craved company. She leans against the chair staring at the grooves in the wood between her feet which only confirms my suspicions.

I pull out a beer. Offering her one but she shrugs, turning her nose up.

"I don't drink." She means. *She's never had a drink.* Her purity runs so deep even angels cannot compete. I close the fridge door, shrugging off her decision, remembering when she craved alcohol to numb her pain as I turn to face her, opening the cap with my ring as I cross my arms and legs, leaning my lower back into the ridge of the counter.

"What's his name?" She gestures to my little tornado, chowing down on his beef and I already know where this is going. I'm about to be replaced. She's already clung to him but I was expecting that. It might mellow her out a bit, it's why I let him sleep in there last night.

"*Shep.*" She pulls her lips in, trying not to find amusement in that. Yes it's basic as fuck, but I'm a simpleton. Ain't got time for that shit. "So what do you do?" I ask boldly as she cuddles herself, protecting her body, glaring at me in confusion, most likely wondering why I am asking such a normal question.

"*What do you mean?*"

"You must have things you like to do. *Friendless.*" I emphasise the friendless to remind her that that's exactly what she is searching for and it worries me that I'm asking questions to learn more about her when she means fuck all to me.

"If you must know… I like to write." I wasn't expecting her to actually tell me, but now she has, her bedroom makes a lot more sense, as does her want to escape reality. She lives in the clouds just to get through the day. We all have our ways of coping and sometimes putting your mind somewhere else is the only way to get past the loneliness.

"You're a *Dreamer.*" I wonder what she dreams about. I'd love to pick at her brain. Writing is led by incessant amounts of creativity we cannot contain so we scribble it out on paper. It's like a superpower.

"A what?" She questions me almost in disbelief, like I'm the first person to pay interest in her and understand her.

"You want something far greater than you can comprehend, you live in a realm unknown to the human eye just to escape." Her eyes light up a little, letting her shallow dirty graves bloom into the ocean at sunset as the light hits them through the kitchen window and they are all I seem to be dreaming about lately, *my realm to get lost in.*

"I can't tell if that was a compliment or an insult?" She twirls her fingers through her messy hair unaware she's even doing it and my mind jolts, imagining my hand running through it for a moment. *Snap out of it Hays.*

"It's beautiful. Unique. Different." I take a swig to drown away the betrayal leaving my mouth. In reality I don't even know what beauty entails anymore but something is telling me, *THAT* is and I don't know what I'm referring to anymore, writing or *her*.

"Are you already drunk?" Her expression is bewildered, trying to make sense of my words, but a subtle smile graces her face revealing dimples I've never seen before and my stomach knots, I've not seen her smile before. She's not been conscious around me long enough for me to notice. Her response only tells me she's never been complimented by anyone but her parents which makes me want to compliment her all the more and that just pisses me off. I never compliment anyone. I wasn't even complimenting her; I was referring to her hobby.

"Just honest." I watch her swallow, taking in my words, suddenly embarrassed to look at me.

"What do you do?" She asks shyly, like she shouldn't be asking but she is anyway. This has turned into a fairly normal conversation and it's weirdly unfamiliar to me. I'm so used to gouging out eyes and interrogating my victims for answers, not asking them what they enjoy doing.

"Do you want the serious answer, or the not so serious answer?" I finish my beer and place it down beside me, cracking my neck to release tension as my eyes fall on hers and if looks could kill, I think they might actually out dagger mine, and that's saying something.

"I like to game?" I've never done this shit in my life. Is this what they call the *talking stage?* I don't even know what my favourite colour is, let alone my hobbies. I can't exactly tell her I murder domestic abusers for a living as it will stir questions she's not ready for answers to yet, but what I said seemed to deter her as she let's an adorable snigger slip.

"What, like... Crash Bandicoot?" The devilish little grin on her face tells me she wants to laugh but she's holding it in and part of me wishes she didn't. It's been awhile since I had a good laugh.

"I will have you know that it is a very good game. Have you even played it?" I'll be honest. I can't even remember the last time I played my PlayStation, it probably wouldn't even turn on now but it's all still sitting there under my TV along with my Moms record and video player.

"Absolutely not." She shakes her head, mocking my interests and I want to take her over my knee for laughing *at me,* not with me.

"Diabolical." I see nothing else better to do so I make my way back to the fridge to grab another beer, running out of bottles, moving onto cans as I glare at the empty shelves. I should probably stock up now that I have a *guest* in the house.

"Is that your Mom?..." A wave of sickness raises my temperature, closing the fridge door to see her standing there holding a picture frame of my mom, stroking the glass gently. My heart rate increases like she's holding a knife to her throat. That image is all I have left of her and it's in someone else's hands.

"Yes." My nose flares and the metal can is slowly crumpling underneath the palm of my hand. The laughter subsides and there is a heavy shift in the atmosphere.

"She's really pretty." The way she speaks of her as if she's still alive makes my beer go down in one.

"Was." I've barely shared my past with anyone, but I feel I owe her that and this could go one of two ways. Not that I want her to sympathise. I took her mother from her just as he did mine and I punished her for something that was not her fault but my past is no excuse for that.

"Oh... How did she?..." She's hesitant to ask but she is curious. I've relived that night in my head more times than I spent nights in that prison cell, which was 3,810 days. But I've never said the words out loud.

"Someone killed her." My empty can feels my abuse, crushing it with anger as I picture her lying there with a hole in her heart when it should have been buried inside me. I didn't even get to say goodbye. She has no gravestone and her ashes were spread across Lake Michigan by my Grandmother who unfortunately passed during my time in the cell. His side wanted nothing to do with me after they found out I murdered their son. Not even my own flesh and blood believed I was innocent, even after my statement was aired about his abuse. None of them visited or phoned. He was their golden boy who could do no wrong. It made me sick to listen to the praise they would shower him with on our one family holiday a year. I've not heard anything since my release and I intend for it to stay that way. I never fucking liked them anyway; they are all blind to the fucking Devil they spawned.

"I'm sorry." My mouth parts as I hear those words come from her mouth. *She's sorry?* I killed her mother in cold blood and she's apologising for *my loss?* I urge to smack her for being so fucking naive. I don't want her to apologise for shit. I want her to realise it was her father's fault. "Was it accidental?" I won't tell her the ins and outs of her demise just yet, or even at all so I just go straight to the point.

"No." I wish it was an accident. I wish she had drifted off into a deep sleep so she didn't have to suffer, or even better, still be here with me. But she's not and she did suffer. She suffered for four minutes and thirty-two seconds. It doesn't sound long but when those are your last moments alive and all you can feel is pain, it doesn't feel like it's ever going to end. Luckily for her the suffering eventually stopped but mine didn't and it still hasn't.

"Oh..." Her expression holds a thousand different emotions, ones that feel everything I'm feeling and one's that rebel against me for putting her through the same pain.

"If I knew what I know now, I would have killed the bastard that day but it would have meant missing things I've grown to like."

"What things?" She is peace in the chaos I've slowly built and she doesn't realise the war she's waging against my darkness, but it's peace I've slowly come to enjoy the company of. My silence. An innocence that is corrupting the monster inside of me. She makes me feel something worse than pain. She makes me feel the child inside me left dormant, the child I abandoned when she needed me most. She is getting under my fucking skin and distracting me from the bigger picture.

"Doesn't matter..." I shake off my thoughts, too afraid to admit that she's starting to have a positive effect on me. It's the last thing she needs. I take a seat on my sofa, legs spread wide as I lean into my elbows trying to block out these feelings that keep creeping up on me like an illness.

"Was she a good Mom?" She wasn't perfect. But she was good. She cared for me when no one else would and she stood up for me even when her life was in danger. She would have killed for me and on many occasions she almost did, but I took that responsibility from her in hopes to save her, to *save us*. To keep her safe and in the end, I lost her anyway.

"She was." She finally puts the picture down, being gentle not to break it as she slides it back onto the shelf next to another. A picture that holds her breath for a brief moment. She glides her finger, smearing the dust from the glass to reveal the face of a little girl.

....

"Is that you?" She looks for me in the room as she picks it up, comparing pictures like she will find any resemblance.

"What if it is." I don't know why I kept it. I practically removed all pictures from this house besides Mom and the albums in the loft somewhere, but that picture stayed. It was taken a week before he first laid his hands on me and I suppose it holds meaning. It's to remind me that I will never be that *weak* again. It holds the *innocence* I once inhabited, the pain I endured, the beatings I suffered all in the name of *Love*. All because I was too scared to fight back. It's a lesson.

"You looked cute." I mimic a gag in response, making her contagious smile nearly slip onto my face.

"Your definition of cute and mine is rather different." I rummage around the sofa looking for the remote trying to ignore the compliment. She's stalking me, trying to figure out where it all went wrong and the truth is, there was never a good period in my life, we just covered it up with photos to hide the prison we were both trapped in, this prison. In some ways me and her are a lot alike.

"Do you miss the old you?" An unfaithful laugh escapes me at the thought. She died along with them and I'm much better for it. Why would I miss years of mental and physical abuse? Why would I miss being a punching bag and an experiment to someone sworn to protect me? Why would I miss the fear and the relentless pain, the sleepless nights?

"Not even a little. The old me was *weak*." Weakness is a sickness. If you're weak you're hopeless. Only the strong survive and I'm still here, much to my detest.

"Because you kill people you think that makes you strong?" She bites softly, her approach timid but forceful and my anger spikes, shooting me off the sofa. I stalk towards her slowly until her backs pressed against the shelves of DVDs, she's clutching to the picture of me in her little hands like I'm going to jump out and save her. I inch towards her face, stroking the woody hair from her heated cheek, now raw, red and *vulnerable* as she peers at me through frightened eyes and I whisper gently through my teeth.

"It's power I can control." I clutch to her forearm and she grips the picture harder. Part of me wants to punish her for pushing all the wrong buttons, all the buttons I've kept untouched. I've given her a voice and unleashed a *brat*, I should be happy, this only makes things more fun for me but she's too soft for the sins I would commit on her body, *she wouldn't survive.*

"You said you wouldn't touch me." She rips her arm from me and I'm heaving heavily through my nose in frustration. I don't want to touch her to hurt her. I want to touch her to claim her. She has the same loss in her eyes as I and it's addicting. It's terrifying. It's dangerous. It's fucking consuming.

She is a power I cannot control.

"Do you want to hurt me? Will that give you power?" She has me all wrong and I want so desperately to show her that I'm not one of them but I see the Devil in me every day.

"Don't push me *Little Dreamer*..." I lick my teeth, squeezing my jaw together trying to contain this unbearable urge to rip her fucking clothes off.

"Or what? You'll kill me?" I'll do far more than kill her, I'll bury myself 6ft inside her and listen to her beg for her fucking life as she makes our grave.

"Is this your plan? Push me until I give you what you want?" I ask sternly. She wants to die so badly, even when I'm trying to make this situation more comfortable for her, what fucking more does she want?

"What I want is for you to let me go." My paint cracks as I roll a smile into it, pulling my hands up from my sides, waving them in a mocking fashion.

"Then why are you still standing here..." She huffs harshly, scolding me before pushing against my chest, slipping out from beneath me and heading straight towards the bedroom. I pursue her with little effort as my stride takes up two of hers and my boot wedges between the door as she slams it shut in my face, gripping the edge to stop it from flying back into the already abused wall.

CHAPTER 17

SECRETS THAT LIE BENEATH

Puppet

"Now now *Innocence*. We were finally starting to get somewhere." Ughhhhhh, I hate her! The back of my legs find the bed, stumbling until I sit facing the door waiting for her to barge in behind me.

"Go away." She's gripping the door with her boot wedged between the door and the frame. She holds it and I wait for her to follow me in but she doesn't. Instead, there is a thirty second pause before she slowly lets go, her body slipping away out of sight as she shuts the door for me.

"Fine. Have it your way." My confusion peeks. A minute ago she blew up at me? Now she is leaving me be? I don't understand. Why won't she fight me? Why won't she just snap and end me quickly like she's meant to? There is anticipation between the walls and I wait for her heavy boots to fade away but I hear nothing. She hasn't moved an inch.

"I know you're still standing there." I was an idiot to think today would be any different. Even uncuffed I am still caged. I don't understand why she is being so friendly? What does she think she is going to get out of this, she is nothing but a *monster*.

"I didn't mean to hurt you. *Ok?*" *Ok?* She's attempting to make amends but the fury inside me doesn't allow the empathy I hold to cling to the half-arsed sincerity just yet. I grip the sheets tightly, channelling my anger and the urge to scream through my fingers.

"You know. On second thought, just tie me back to the bed so I don't have to interact with you unless you can be arsed to check up on me." She's messing with my head, I hate her. *I HATE HER.* Just when I think there is something inside her other than *evil* we take ten steps back.

"I don't expect you to understand me. I don't want you to understand. I know an apology isn't going to cut it but I'll say it anyway...it was never meant to be like this. You weren't meant to exist and I wasn't meant to be here much longer, alright? But plans change and there is shit I can't take back, you think I enjoy treating you this way? *I don't.* But I'm fucking trying here. OK?" A rock grazes the back of my throat as I swallow my guilt. Sitting on the conversation we just had. Part of me hates every inch of her for taking away the very thing she rebelled for, but in retrospect, if she hadn't of stopped me that day, I would have easily let the voices in my head take over, I would have murdered her without a second thought, out of pain, out of revenge. If she had allowed me I would have ploughed that knife into her chest until I couldn't breathe.

I would have *killed someone* to try and ease the unbearable ache in my chest. She didn't have to confide in me but she did. She lost someone important and her vengeance got the best of her. I glare at the door trying to find the words but I'm left empty. She doesn't deserve my forgiveness, but she did deserve better too. I'm afraid to learn what went wrong in her life for her to become something she loathed. There is art in that, *dark, potent art.*

A few minutes pass by and we sit in each other's silence before I make my way towards the door. Opening it slowly, I see her leaning against the bathroom door, her foot kicked back into the wood glaring at me like she knew I was going to come out eventually and that in itself frustrates me, I shouldn't even be giving her the time of day but I fear my loneliness is getting the best of me. As much as I hate to admit it to myself, earliers conversation was the most normal I've felt in a long time. She listened; she saw me. No one has ever taken interest in my hobbies, let alone understood them.

"You're really shit at apologising..." I hold the door, rubbing my bare foot against the floor as I refuse to look at her but I know she's rolling her eyes. God forbid she apologise for hurting someone's feelings. "I'm bored." I kick the door gently, leaning my forehead down the seam trying to break the awkward silence that is swallowing us both whole.

"I could put a movie on? Don't think you'd like any of them though." Her brow tugs at me, peeping at me through the hoods of her eyes.

"Try me..." She underestimates me.

"Me and my mom liked horror." I suck in my bottom lip, lost in thought as I think about all the horror movies that I love.

"You got Saw?" I can't see much of her expression underneath the paint but I can tell she is disturbed by my response and it makes me giddy inside.

"I'm sorry. Did you just say, Saw? Isn't that too gory for you?" I glare at her blankly. Considering the crap I have gone through in the last month; a gory movie should be a walk in the park.

"Thanks to you, gore is the least of my worries." A bitter smile makes itself known, grinning at her with ill intent. That was meant to be mean, and I hope it hurts.

"Saw it is." She lifts herself off the door, ready to walk towards the living room and I blurt out like word vomit.

"On one condition..." It comes out without thinking and I don't really know what I'm asking. It could be dangerous, and I know it shouldn't matter but if she's trying as much as she says then I deserve to know.

"Do I have a choice?" She halts and turns to face me, waiting patiently for my response knowing very well she doesn't.

"You tell me your name." I know she doesn't want to tell me, but if she wants us to be *'friends'* then we need to be on a first name basis. She somehow knows mine. It's only fair.

"Big D." I hold back a smile, trying not to laugh as a gaspy huff leaves her mouth.

"*Very funny...*"

SHASSII
"Just call me Hays."

Play - 'Get You The Moon - Kina, Snow'

"Done." She continues her path and I follow quietly behind her. She rummages through her living room for the first movie and sticks it in the video player. Watching her acting so normal is unsettling, unnatural to the monster I know. We sit there all day going through the franchise barely uttering a word, just trying to enjoy normality as Shep sits as a barrier between us. A day without violence, a day without blood, only through a TV screen where it isn't real, the only place it *should* be. She watches unphased while I pretend that certain scenes still don't make me heave as I replay today in my head on loop, barely paying any attention to the screen, analysing everything she told me. She shared so much in the little words that she spoke. I have been unable to think about anything else but one thing stood out to me and I finally cut the silence.

"What did you mean earlier? When you said about not being here much longer?" My knees are tucked under my chest, nuzzled into the sofa she has been sleeping on, God knows what has been on this couch, it looks older than this house.

"Do you think you're the only person who wants the easy way out?" She doesn't move, still fixated on the screen as I burn a hole into the side of her head with my eyes.

"Why haven't you?" I don't understand, if she didn't want to be here, why is she still hanging on and why is she stringing me along with her when we both want the same thing?

"Plans change." She crosses her arms, sinking into the sofa with her legs spread, finding her new comfy spot and by her change of tone, that change of plan is sat in this room.

"You mean me?..." My thumb threads through my fingers, guilty for being the reason she is still breathing but for some reason, part of me feels slightly honoured. There have been multiple times since my arrival things could have gone horrifically different but they haven't, not even with her other plans interrupted by me.

"Something like that." She doesn't agree, but I know I am right. She's drummed it into me that I interrupted her plans, that I was not wanted. But if I am so unwanted then why am I still untouched. Why am I still here?

"Do you still want to?..." Even through her painted smile, I can see hurt all over her face. Not even a fake one can hide your emotions for long, a mask is a temporary fix.

"Yes." She replies sharply without hesitation and my throat closes. I'm trying to understand her but it's encrypted messages, a small part of me aches for her and I hate that she is pinching at my empathy like a vulture. I suppose I am dead. I died that day along with them and I don't think I've been the same since, I don't think I ever will be and that terrifies me, learning this new version of me that has to face life alone. Truly I've spent my entire life living in the clouds. She is right, I chase a world that doesn't exist, I dream of the impossible just to get through life and no one's ever said it like that before. I became a writer to escape my daily life and fall in love with a world beyond this. And she's shown me how ugly it can really be without harming me,

Physically harming me.

"I'm sorry." I whisper under the screams coming from the TV hoping she doesn't hear me but she does.

"Say sorry again and I'll wash your mouth out *Puppet.*" My eyes bulge slightly as I crawl into the corner of the sofa cuddling my legs like a puppy being told off. I can feel my eyes getting heavy, resting my face against the back of my hand as I continue watching the movie.

She said I shouldn't have existed? *What does that mean?* Did she not do her research before she raided my house? Maybe they don't do that but I was under the impression there is a personal vendetta here that I'm missing.

"Was my Dad part of this?" I see her knuckles clench and she ignores my question like the plague as she gets up off the sofa, walking towards the dining room table for my insulin before handing it to me.

"You should get some sleep," my heart drops. Her silence confirms my question without words and I bite my tongue, frustrated that she won't be honest with me. "I will be out tomorrow, not sure when I'll be back." She sits back on the sofa next to me, slightly closer and I gently pull my legs away, afraid to touch her.

SHASSII

"Work?" I ask, knowing the answer beyond that simple and harmless question.

"*Work.*" She replies calmly and glances at me. I shudder knowing what that actually means, but for today, life is normal and it's like she's playing along with me so I can forget.

CHAPTER 18

GIVE ME A SMILE

Puppeteer

Play - 'Face It - NF'

The telly roars and I half expect it to wake her up but she is zonked out next to me. That insulin really does kick her into another dimension. I have a disgusting urge to pick her up and carry her to bed, but that's far too romantic for me. *Eww.* Instead I grab my duvet and place it gently over her, tucking it in underneath her little body. She looks so peaceful when she sleeps it almost makes me jealous. I can't remember the last time I had a decent night's sleep.

I turn the telly off and creep around the living room, biting the bit for a fucking cigarette. I've managed to go all day without smoking one and I'm more than Saw'd out. We watched all bloody six of them, who knew a little thing like her enjoyed watching shit like that. Although now it makes sense as to why she referred to *body parts.*

I make my way outside, careful not to wake her and lock the door silently behind me, heading over to the beaten and bruised car sitting in the middle of the overgrown lawn. This car's nearly as old as me. She loved this pile of junk so it stayed. I was tempted to get it removed but that was too much hassle so now it sits looking ugly, barely visible buried in amongst the overgrown weeds. It's become my comfort place as I climb on top of the roof and perch with my legs over the side, lighting one up as I glare at the night sky. It's not so bad tonight but it's still nippy. *No hot water bottle for her.* After today it feels wrong of me to put her back in that room, I just hope I don't fucking regret it. She's already made a playground of my house once but something shifted in the air today. *I don't know what.*

I look down at my phone.

21 : 52

His flight lands at 3am and luckily I have his registration number, the sick fuck won't even make it back home when I'm finished with him but I've got time to kill so I sit here. Sometimes I can be out here all night. I've nothing else better to do and today is probably the most normal day I've had since I was a kid. Company has never been my thing but it felt strangely nice, even if it was in silence.

There were things today that I said, that I've not said for a long time and things I relived that I'd rather have not thought about and for some reason it was annoyingly easy with her, but it doesn't take away the pent up anger I now need to channel into this man's face to quiet the mind. When I'm not next to her my head is suddenly so fucking loud I want to smash it into the nearest wall. Sometimes I'm nearly successful. I've thought about it recently, but the idea is suddenly not so interesting to me. Yes, I lied to her. Maybe because I have a *plaything* to keep me busy, it stops the intrusive thoughts from clouding my heavy thirst for death.

I've killed three men this month and each time it's been less and less satisfying, it's pissing me off. Hopefully this asshole can relieve me of some emotions. I've been feeling far too much recently when I shouldn't, and what's worse is they are emotions I cannot fucking understand.

COLLATERAL DAMAGE

I'm parked in a stolen vehicle, sat out of sight by the entrance to the airport waiting patiently for his arrival. It's 3:20 and I saw the plane fly in just after three so it won't be much longer now. I roll another cigarette to pass the time, fiddling with my switchblade between my fingers, suddenly imagining it tracing her soft skin and I quickly snap myself out of it. *Focus Hayden. Get your mind out the fucking gutter.*

Why the fuck am I thinking about her right now?

It's a fairly busy airport even at this time, so I have to be strategic and follow him for at least an hour until we are out of the city. *I fucking hate this city.* Everything about it makes me want to vomit. How anyone could enjoy living in this concrete jungle full of narcissistic pricks is beyond me. The air smells of polluted trauma and the quicker I get out of here the better.

Play - 'Death Is No More (Slowed) - BLESSED MANE'

Eventually he pulls out, taking a sharp right driving away from me. The number plate matches so I turn the key and boot up the engine to pursue him with caution, keeping my distance. Luckily the roads are dead so I won't lose him between cars and I tail his ass for around thirty minutes until we reach the outskirts of the city. Clustered forests and open fields are all you see for miles besides the odd house. It's just me and him on the road and adrenaline lines my blood stream, grinning like the Devil as my foot flaws the gas until I'm touching the floor smashing straight into the back of him, *I gotta give it to him he knows how to control a car.*

I flick the nose of my front end, whipping vigorously into the back corner of his car until he spins out of control heading straight for the ditch, both my feet find the brake, slamming to a halt, stopping so hard my back tires are burning and the smell makes me roll my eyes into the back of my skull.

The car is in the ditch headfirst and upside down, smoking like an old steam train as I exit my vehicle, nails scraping across the knobbly concrete as I grip my bat firmly. He's not conscious but I'm sure I can wake him up. Bending to meet the window on the floor, he's spewing blood down his temple but still breathing, he took quite a few tumbles, I'm surprised he's even still alive.

I unplug the seat belt, gripping the scruff off his pristine blazer as I yank him from the seat like a chew toy through the shards of glass tearing him to pieces. I sit him up against the chassis of the car, his limp body leaning into me as I secure him by the shoulder.

"Rise and shine asshole." I take his arm, dislocating it from the elbow forcing him to react to his survival instincts. He wakes abruptly, yelping out like an injured hyena and it's a sweet song I sleep to in my subconscious.

"Please! What do you want from me! I'll give you anything!" He's dreary as he looks for me in my many clones, corrupting his dizzy vision, clutching to his floppy arm like it's going to fall off. Fortunately for him I didn't bring a saw with me. *Bummer. My Little Dreamer had a good idea there.*

"I don't like liars. The only thing valuable to me is your demise." He reeks of money and overly expensive cologne mixed with the metallic stench of blood and that is irony. This is why I do this. To show them that no amount of money can postpone their death. No matter how much dollar you have in the bank, karma is its thief, stealing their security and breaking their walls.

"Who the hell are you!?" I am many things. If I'm honest I don't know who the hell I am. I'm not a who, I'm a what. *'Who'* would imply I'm human, and I'm far from it. *A freak. A Clown. A Monster. An abomination maybe.*

"Your Karma." My blade dances the length of his neck, curving over his apple before pushing the point beneath it.

"I have a wife and kids! Please" I was hoping he'd say that. This makes it so much more ironic.

"Exactly." I lick my lips, savouring the taste of paint, gagging to taste blood. My trophy awaits me as my sinister smile takes a hold of me, imagining all the ways in which I could make him suffer.

"Please don't do this. It's my little girl's birthday tomorrow!" Why do these fucks always bring up their kids on death's door like they give a flying damn? If they did then I wouldn't be removing their stain.

Beating your child until they are begging you to finish it isn't exactly *Love* is it. My blood runs hot at the thought. At the thousands of children suffering in silence without a voice. How these cases get forgotten about to protect the voice of power. It repulses me.

"And I'm sure she will be a whole lot better for it. Maybe one day when she's all grown up, I'll visit her and she can thank me personally for doing her a favour aye?" My gloves meet his cheeks, tapping him to focus on me as his head falls into his chest.

"What the hell are you talking about?! *You freak!*" That word used to keep me hidden in toilet cubicles during lunch hour. Now I kind of like it. It has a ring to it once you fill the expectation. It's almost a compliment.

"Even staring death in the face you are showing your true colours Mr. Jones," running his ugly mouth is only fuelling my drive to pluck his fucking eyes out. I grip his chin roughly, tugging to set his focus on me as my switchblade flicks into view. "Give me a smile."

The cunt spits in my face, fighting what dizzy energy he has trying to release himself from my hold. "Go to hell." I can't lie, the laugh that slips even sends chills down my spine. Hell is where I belong, did he really think that was an insult? I work for the Devil. I deliver evil and in return I save lives.

"Oh we're in it. *Together*. And when you reach the other side, tell big boy, *Hayley Moore sent you.*" I'm not sure who exactly I'm referring to, it could be the Devil. It could be *him*. But either way it's a message.

"You won't get away with this you sick fuck!" Maybe he's right, but I've got far too much blood on my hands now to slip up. I've perfected it, beat the system. He isn't my first and he won't be my last. This is a nerdy hobby for me. There is a reason I've not been found. *Because I don't want to be.*

"You and many others love to tell yourselves you're untouchable. Well, let me tell you something." I lean in close, giving him every opportunity to attack but his arm is slightly getting in the way of that. The tip of my blade greets his eardrum with a cold welcome, holding it, still keeping him hostage beneath me. "Do you think you're the first person, second, third even? To say that?" As I count, I push deeper, piercing the drum until he's screaming like a baby. "This? This isn't for me. This is for your little girl. And as long as she's breathing, I will keep getting away with it." My free hand grips his gel-covered hair, sliding between my fingers as I tug it back vigorously until he's looking up to his non-existent God. I tuck the blade into the corner of his mouth before drawing it out towards his cheek bone in an upwards motion watching it bleed real pretty.

"Give us a smile."

"Please! Plea- FUCK-!" Fleshy muscle, blood and jawbone peer through the gaping hole now opening the side of his face as he thrashes against me. I break the fingers of his mobile hand when he attempts to punch me in the gut. His fight slowly fades, so stunned by overwhelming pain that his body shuts down.

I tie a noose whilst keeping him glued to the chassis of the car, before lacing every inch of it, *and him* with gasoline, taking a few big strides backwards, hopping in my stolen vehicle and parking it up beside his.

My feet are at the foot of my trail as I light a cigarette, stationary in the middle of a road so quiet you could probably hear the wildlife fucking. I intake a few large puffs, seeping in my numbness before I let it go, letting it fall between my feet, watching the road light up like fairy lights at Christmas. *This feels like Christmas.* My eyes slowly follow the flame, inching closer to him like sharks in bloody waters. I kiss the back of my hand and throw it up in the air to send my respects to his family. His pleads echo through the empty fields and a slow, sinister grin grows as both cars go up in flames, sparks of debris and rubber fly through the air creating stars against the clouds. What better way to remove evidence than to make it look like a collision. *Whoopsy.* It does mean I will have to walk miles back to my truck though, but maybe it will clear my head. The fresh air will do me some good.

CHAPTER 19

UNRAVELLING TRUTHS

Puppet

I wake to the beaming sun warming my face through the living room window, lifting my head to realise I'm not in her room. I'm in the living room. I must have conked out after my insulin. A weighted duvet hugs my body. *She literally left me here?* I assess the room and she isn't in the kitchen making pancakes, I peer down to find Shep lying on the floor beneath me as if he's guarding me. *Am I alone?*

Last night's conversation creeps into remembrance and I suddenly realise she said she was out today but I am still shocked she left me access to everything. Maybe she's in her room and isn't up yet? I leap off the sofa, eager to find she trusted me enough to leave me unsupervised and I freeze. The bedrooms empty. This is my chance, *right?* I trundle into the kitchen to find a cup left on the side with coffee granules already inside and I assume that was for her, but it would be a shame to let it go to waste so I make myself at home and put the kettle on. I forget how noisy the damn thing is, even that sounds old.

I sit at the dining room table drinking my coffee from her ugly mug until it's cold thinking about yesterday's gappy conversation and I am left wanting more answers. I'm angry. She refused to talk to me about my father when I know there is more than meets the eye, and she owes me that at least because I'm going crazy here. This was no accident; their deaths were intentional and I want to know *why*.

Glaring at the mysterious door for what feels like ten hours, I think of all the horrendous things that could be lurking behind it and my curiosity gets the best of me. I haven't a clue how to pick locks, *but today I am going to learn.*

I raid the kitchen for things I could potentially use. Draws and draws of clutter and antique looking kitchen utensils fill them to the brim, wondering how many things have been used as torture devices. I spend the next few hours using every method possible to get to whatever's behind that door. Finally, I crack it with a pathetic piece of wire I found and it clicks open, drawing out its squeak through the building like something from a horror movie and my curiosity peaks as I walk in, closing it behind me to keep Shep out.

It's a garage filled to the brim with tools and a bike perched in the middle of the room on its stand. It's old. A Harley Davidson, pristine gloss black with a tire currently missing. I dread to touch it and break something, so I tiptoe around the chaos, careful not to step on any of her equipment as I catch two doors on the back wall. *More rooms?* I turn the knob of one and it's locked so I try the other, the knob turns in my hand slowly until the latch lets the door break free and I'm not so eager to push it open. My hand hovers for a moment, taking in a deep breath before pushing it gently to reveal a dark room. I fumble for a light switch and my gut hits the floor along with my jaw when the warm glow lights it up, as I creep further into the lion's den.

Play - 'Black Out Days - Phantogram'

COLLATERAL DAMAGE

I analyse the sea of paper on the wall; pictures, documents, pins, writing, string, all coat it like paint. My eyes scatter amongst the information before me and I feel violently sick.

It's a case board for my *father*.

His face is plastered all over it along with every possible piece of information he has. CCTV footage of him in stores and streets, time stamps dating back to 2006. *That was three years ago?* Hospital appointments, court cases, w*hat court cases*? My fingers trace the words, reading faster than my brain can process.

Words scream at me.

> *Murder.*
> *Self-defence.*
> *Involuntary Manslaughter.*
> *Chicago police department.*
> *Mother.*
> *Mrs. Lillie Moore.*
> *1999.*
> *Revoked.*

What is all this? What am I missing? What the hell am I in the middle of? I'm churning, fighting the need to pass out. I can't be found in here. *Breathe Alora.* 1999 was the year we moved? That was the year he told me he walked away, that it was all too much, that he wanted to start fresh and leave detective work behind? I don't understand any of this and I want to scream so loud I shatter the windows. I examine what else I can find, turning to find a computer and a phone line. *A phone*! I don't even give my feet time to register before lunging for it, trying to dial 911 into a black void, so shaky I don't register it's doing nothing until I press the green button.

Silence.

"No, no no no, please." I scramble for the lead, following it towards its plug socket only to find it's been cut halfway. "FUCK!..." You've got to be kidding me! There is no way she took that much precaution surely! I plant my ass in the office chair, glaring at my reflection through the monitor. I'm sitting in the seat of a killer and ice runs through my body.

She's smart. Calculated. None of this is coincidence anymore. I'm in amongst a much bigger picture with pieces missing. I am *Collateral Damage* in a game I was not playing. All of this only makes me want to run faster but now I can't, not until I know what I'm dealing with, not until I get into this computer and collect evidence I could use. I press the power button and it does nothing. *Come on!*

Fifteen minutes go by and I've yet to turn the bastard thing on. Scrambling through stacks and stacks of files piled beside the screen, hundreds of cold cases from what I can tell. My heart sinks. These are all domestic abuse cases? My Father was never abusive, if that is what she was targeting then she's got it all wrong but that can't be it, she said I was never in the picture? Or not that she knew of anyway.

I sit my forehead in the palm of my hands trying to collect my thoughts but it's a shamble. This past month I've lost all sense of my time and sustainability. Trying to piece this puzzle together is like a psych patient trying to seek sanity. I feel like I'm losing my mind. I tune into the sound of my own heartbeat, focusing on the movement in my feet like my Mom taught me when I realise the rumble I hear isn't within me.

Shit.

She's home and the sound of her bodged up old truck gurgles from behind the door. I have about two minutes to get myself back in that living room and I choke from lack of oxygen, frantically putting things back in their places, papers nearly flying everywhere. *Shit shit shit.* My adrenaline is piping through me, sending me marching through the door as I close it quickly behind me, clicking it too, nearly tripping over her bloody bike as I run for the living room. I can hear her keys from behind the front door and my hearts humming in my ears, muffling my hearing as I reach for the TV remote and slam the power button finding the sofa just as the door pushes to, followed by her heavy boots breaking the wood beneath her, she's holding a brown paper bag, drenched in black. The smell of petrol overwhelms my senses as she traipses in front of the TV to hand me the bag.

Play - 'EDWARD SCISSOR HANDS – Nessa Barrett'

"Thought you might be hungry." I stare blankly at the bag hovering in front of my face like a homeless man being given a cheque of a million dollars. *Did she actually bring me home food?*

"Thanks." I slowly grip it, taking it out of her hand timidly, opening it up to find a Wendy's inside. I've literally never eaten fast food. Mom always said it was bad for me, but right now I don't really care, *I'm starving.*

"I see you helped yourself to my coffee." I pause rummaging through the bag as I look over like a guilty child with my hand in the cookie jar.

"I'm sorry." That was probably too bold of me, never mess with someone's coffee.

"What did I say, *Puppet.*" She groans deeply, pausing what she's doing, frozen solid making my hairs stand on end remembering her words yesterday. *Say sorry again and I'll wash your mouth out Puppet.* I feel a pulse where I really shouldn't and it repulses me, pushing it to the back of my mind as I look at her grubby wear, quickly changing the subject.

"You look like hell." My hand finds the fries, shoving them in my mouth trying to savour the taste of a proper meal, or as good as I'm gonna get anyway. Shep glares at me from his bed.

"I thought I looked cute?" She questions my statement, and I can feel her grin through the back of her head. *Very funny.*

"Key word. *Looked.* I.e. past tense." My fries find my mouth, unaware that she's turned around to see me stuffing my gob like Oliver Twist.

"And now?" I pause, fries halfway in my mouth glaring at her god awful attire and smeared face paint trying to fight the urge to want to punch her in the face.

"*Hideous.*" My cheeks puff out as I talk with my mouth rammed, chewing to swallow.

"Much better." She praises me for an insult. She wants to look intimidating and unapproachable and it works, it also makes me wonder if she went to Wendy's looking like that? *They must have had a few questions.*

"How was *work?*" I break the ugly tension laying thick in the air with another laughable question, playing on our little roleplay.

"*Tiresome.* And you drank my coffee." Her tone becomes cold, glaring at me from across the living room through crossed arms and for some reason my mouth speaks without permission.

"I'm-" she breaks me halfway, cutting me off with a jump, nearly choking on my fries as it takes her three strides across the floor before she's hovering over me.

"Say it again *Innocence*. Say it and so help me God." My blood runs cold, missing a few beats as I swallow my food hard, peering into the portal of hell as she finds the death sentence in mine.

"You won't hurt me. You said it yourself." I talk back out of nowhere, shocking myself with this sudden bite I seemed to have acquired.

"I said I wouldn't hurt you. No one said anything about making you question your morals, *Princess*." Her hand reaches into my bag, now free from her gloves to take a hand full of *MY* fries, eating them like a heathen and for some perverted reason my eyes are glued to her inky hands as the stench of paint and gasoline suffocate me.

"I'm going for a shower..." She finishes her mouthful, pushing off the sofa towards the bathroom and I'm left sat in utter confusion. *Question my morals? What does that even mean?*

My backs leant against the sofa as I finish off my *junk* food, surfing through the channels for something semi-decent to watch but there is absolutely nothing interesting. I should be trying to run out the door right now but I remain glued to the sofa, listening to the water running. She hasn't even bothered to shut the door? What a weirdo. Does she not care about privacy? Apparently neither do I because I find myself turning to catch the mirror in the bathroom, looking for signs of life. I desperately want to see her face and it's driving me insane. I want to see the coward underneath the mask she hides behind. I continue watching the TV until the rush of water stops, turning on instinct to the noise coming from behind me when I catch her back in the reflection of the mirror, or what I can see of it. It's smothered in tattoos I cannot decipher from this distance. *Omg Alo, stop looking you perv.*

I can't. I'm waiting for her to turn around, resting my head on the top of my pillow like a needy puppy to see her face but instead, she walks out of view leaving the mirror empty and a slight wave of disappointment washes over me. *She's a woman. Why am I even looking at her? Isn't this forbidden or something?* Wait...oh my god. My morals... Does she mean? No. Surely not...eww, absolutely not. Yet I can't seem to look away, fixated on the hazy mirror embodying her through the steam like my own personal entity, always looming, always watching. In some ways it's like she's dead. She's hollow inside. Sometimes I question if there's a beating heart inside her chest, but then she wraps me up in her duvet and brings me food and something tells me I'm wrong, but I don't want to be wrong. She hurts people, she hurts me, she *hurt* me.

I recap the office, the mysteries between paper, the answers right in front of me I can't seem to decipher and I'm furious externally, but internally I'm mourning the simple me, the me that stuck my head in the clouds and tried to drown out the depths of reality in fear they may become mine. The me that only spoke when spoken to, the me that daren't ask questions, the me that would write until the sun came up and head to college on no sleep but it was ok because in my little world, the princess married the prince. The me that saw me getting married one day and slow dancing with my dad. The me that is now just a distant memory and the me that has now become the survivor in my little world, wielding a blade and learning to fight, learning to understand pain and how it affects us. Some wear it, some don't.

She wears it like a trophy yet the achievement has been etched out, *unreadable*, and it fascinates me.

"Have you taken your insulin?" She bellows from the mist and I suddenly feel all warm inside. She doesn't have to care but she does and both are equally as terrifying. She's going about her daily life as if I was now part of the furniture, no longer a prisoner and I should be grateful, but I can't shake the stains she's washing off, the remnants of somebody else beneath her fingernails.

"*Dreamer*," what did she just call me? I feel a yank at my heartstrings, flopping back into the sofa fighting with this endless war in my mind. It's exhausting being able to feel the suffering shared amongst you. My mom used to say it was a gift, but how can it be when I feel empathy for her executioner? Why am I even considering the option? I should despise her. *I do despise her.* For all the wrong bloody reasons, *this is ridiculous.*

"Don't ignore me." She strolls out the bathroom in a fresh coat of paint and a shoulder cut T-shirt this time, my jaw parts slightly. *This is the first time I've seen her arms out.* Although she may as well not have them out. Her tattoo's cover almost every inch of her exposed skin. I knew she had tattoo's but there's more ink than flesh on her and they are the size of tree trunks, what the hell does she do between greeting the Devil? Her pockets are hanging out yet again and I stare at them with annoyance. *Who wears their pockets out like that? It's so dumb.*

"It's annoying isn't it." I taunt. Now she can know how it feels when she avoids all my important questions, although it doesn't last long before I tell her yes. She preaches she won't hurt me and I've pushed a few times, but the reality is she could kill me in one quick headlock and my body shudders at the thought.

"Enjoy the show?" she rubs her towel through her soppy hair as she walks toward the fridge.

Yes. You guessed it, another beer. I don't think I've ever seen her eat a proper meal, all she lives on is *Corona*. Her remark repulses me with a subconscious arousal licking at the surface, eager to get a taste as her grin riddles with ego. *The bitch kept the door open on purpose.*

"Not really, your channels are awful." I play it off, referring to the telly. Which only seems to amuse her further. She knows I saw her and I can feel my cheeks burning. *Burning with anger obviously.*

"I see everything is intact this time." I roll my eyes white, wanting to smash it all up just at that comment, but I refrain. The TV needs to stay intact at least so I can bore myself to death.

"For now." I refrain from a smile, letting my heart smile for me and it kills me.

CHAPTER 20

OWNERSHIP

Puppeteer

My house has stayed intact for around a week now, no smashed up picture frames or holes in the wall which is a relief. We've practically lived in each other's pockets like cat and dog, squabbling over the most ridiculous shit and questioning why I even let her out sometimes. I've semi cleaned the place up a little now I have a *'guest'* to cater for. She's been killing my time while I find another lead and work on my project outside, away from her to keep myself sane. She's like a new puppy under my feet. *Worse than Shep.* I get she's bored but there's not much I can do about that unless I walk around my garden with her on a leash.

    She requested I take the wooden panels off the windows to let some light in and I hesitantly complied. I'm not happy about it but if it keeps her quiet then whatever, being bossed around by an eighteen-year-old girl isn't quite what I had in mind. *For crying out loud.* I kept them covered so she couldn't see beyond her confinement but now that she roams my house it's sort of become redundant. I've caught her intricate gaze a few times coming in and out of the garage and she knows it's out of bounds but I know she is curious. I'm also glad she didn't realise I must have left the door open that day either because I never lock the office door, only the basement door, for reasons I never want to expose her to. I don't think it would break her, I think it would *kill her*. She would never look at me the same and we are finally starting to get somewhere. *Ish*. That part of my life does not need to be reminded of and she certainly doesn't need to be exposed to that level of cruelty. Being cooped up like a bird is more than enough for her snappable little wings. I will clip them. Only I get to corrupt her pretty little head. She sees what I want her to see.

She has gotten a little more comfortable with the sleeping arrangements. We share my bed but she builds a pillow fort between us and it's far too amusing. As if that is going to stop me from touching her delicate skin. *I haven't, b*ut fuck it's tempting. Instead, I imagine how it feels against my fingers as I paint it with my eyes.

I think we have both just accepted that this is how it has to be for now. I've yet to decide what to do with her when I eventually run, but now I've shared too much, I can't exactly let her walk. Her company is tolerable but it's also a major threat. She made it quite clear she would never forgive me, so what makes me think she will let me get away with this when the time finally comes to let her go. I know she's playing along, but I wish she fucking wouldn't. It would make this all much easier.

I enter the living room through the garage door smothered in oil and paint that immediately fills up the room. This motor is taking me for a ride I'll give it that. Trying to get the bastard roadworthy again is a mission in itself and my trailer project is almost finished. It's just missing a few more coats of paint and some lacquer. She gawks at me, wanting to speak but holds her tongue. I'm in and out all day, I don't stick around long enough for her to talk because I know she wants to talk about her father. *It's not happening.*

"What?" I ask dryly as my head rolls to make eye contact with her staring at my dirty attire feeling judgement from the both of them as they glare at me from the couch.

"Are you building your escape plan?" She's been studying me like a hawk and it's unnerving, but if this keeps her out of the garage so be it.

"If you mean a broken pile of machinery. Yes." I continue on my way towards the kitchen sink to clean myself up. I'll have a shower later.

"Yours?" I stop in my tracks, pausing on a small memory sat just below the surface, a memory that keeps my sanity clutching at the strings. It was a birthday present from my mom two years before she died. Just a second-hand piece of junk she found down in the rural areas, they were throwing it and she jumped on it knowing how eager I was to get my own one day and I vowed I'd nurse it back to health. For a long time I let it rot away, refusing to touch it. I resented it in fact.

She got a beating that night.

"Who's pile of junk is that in the front yard, Lillie."

"It was being scrapped so I thought I'd bring it home. You know how much she's wanted to ride, Rick."

She doesn't need a vehicle, she doesn't even have a licence, what were you thinking, giving her that piece of shit? Get it off my fucking property before I blow it up. Ungrateful little bitch barely deserves a cake and you got her a bike?! I hope you didn't pay for that. Tell me you didn't put money towards that heap of metal Lillie."

"Nah, it belongs to the president." I joke it off, pushing it to the back of my head focusing solely on her sickly adorable frown.

"Ha.Ha." There's a smile in there somewhere and it makes me feel violently ill that I'm searching for it.

"It's just a hobby." My oily hands dip beneath the water, lathering them with soap trying to rub out the oily stains.

"It's an awfully dedicated hobby." She's noticed my obsession and I find part of me longing to show her. Scrunching up my face at the thought, my loneliness is showing.

"I'm just trying to avoid you." I'm not half wrong. I am avoiding her, but I feel it's not because she wants an answer. It's because I want answers. Answers to the feelings that seem to completely and utterly consume me whenever I'm within 5ft of her that are withering away at my hard shell.

"Can I ask you something?" *I swear to God if she keeps asking me questions I am going to tape her gob shut.*

"Depends how stupid it is." I turn to face her, leaning against the sink, drying my hands as she's sat cross legged facing me, not even facing the TV. It's just become background noise.

"Why do you wear your pockets out?" *She even noticed that?* My mind chases the day she held mine and stops running when I realise, I bet she doesn't even remember doing it.

"Just habit."

"It looks so silly." She's tilting her head at me like that is going to help her make more sense of it. *She clearly didn't watch enough crime documentaries.*

"Silly didn't really count for much behind bars." She's become less and less spooked by the fact I served six years with convicted murderers, considering her father was trained to track people like me down to the ends of the earth. It seems I have taken his role after he dropped out like a pussy. *I'd have been a great detective Mom.*

"Is it an inmate thing?" She rocks back and forth, eager to hear my response and I have to fight back the dire need to smile, kissing my teeth to disguise the menace inside of me. *Oh if only she knew.*

"It's a symbol of ownership." *This is far too cute for my liking. Why is she suddenly taking interest in things most people wouldn't bat an eyelid at?*

"I'm not following." *Of course she's not.*

"If an inmate held my pocket, they became my *bitch*. An exchange of power to protect them from threats within those four walls." Her puzzled look scans the room, trying to understand prison slang like it's the DaVinci code.

"They submitted to you?" *Oh, they submitted alright. In more ways than one, and I can't lie, her* innocence *is proving to make this far more entertaining for me. She really has no clue how many* bitches *I've had clutching them until they almost tore off.*

"*Clever girl.*" I toy with her a little and watch her highly unnerving glare rapidly disappear as she tries to conceal her shame as blush peppers her cheeks. *It's delicious.*

"And if they didn't?" *Why is she so curious?*

"I'd become their worst nightmare *Puppet*." This conversation is going to run my beers out.

"Because they didn't submit to you, you'd hurt them?" I suddenly realise, she isn't trying to understand prison lingo. She's trying to understand me, and it's getting under my skin.

"Because they chose the wrong side. Prison is a playground for the punishable. A free for all. If you do not protect yourself, you can kiss your ass goodbye." I learnt that the hard way. Being a dyke in a prison full of women who could snap you in two wasn't exactly fun, but it's nothing I'd not dealt with before. My father made sure of that.

"So who was protecting you?" She hits me with a question I wasn't prepared for. Downing my poison to calm the internal rage spreading through the cracks in my skin.

"The demons in my head *Innocence*." No one was protecting me. I had to learn to turn it all off. If you can't feel, nothing can hurt you. I turned it off long before I walked into that cage. It's why I got sent there in the first place. I'd lost my moral compass, or what society deems moral. What I did was more than necessary.

I finish up cleaning, my face lower than the Pacific Ocean trying to numb the memories with another bottle as the TV speaks gibberish in the background to muffle my voices.

"Was this you?" She asks, as I turn to face her, met with Mr Jones plastered all over the screen and I hold the devilish grin trying to crawl onto my face. She was going to see it at some point I guess. Just wrong timing.

"Do you really want me to answer that?" She's searching for answers that will expose the monster I am while she's living under my roof, what is her motive here?

"I just want to understand. Do you have a target?" That's the fucking problem. No one will ever understand me. I don't even fucking understand myself. Why is she trying to find reasoning for my chaos? It's just pissing me off.

"This is not an interrogation. *Quit it*." I storm for the door, ready to slip away from this conversation but she's clearly not finished.

"How many... Have you -" I run my tongue against my teeth, letting out a forced sigh as my hands dig into the door frame.

"Fourteen. Happy now?" I was expecting more of a shocked expression on her face but she doesn't seem shocked at all.

"Have they not even been remotely close to catching you?" Since getting out, I've laid low and I've learnt how to control the world around me. I stay hidden and in plain sight.

"They get as close as I let them." As I say those words her face appears on screen. People are finally onto her disappearance and it's only a matter of time, but for now she's hidden well. Unless CPD put the pieces together which I doubt very much. They are all dumb as fuck and I purposely lead them the wrong way.

...

Play – '16 candles – Isabel LaRosa'

"They will find me, you know." I admire her optimism. But they will only find her if I leave tracks. *Which I don't.*

"It's sweet that you think so." I approach her on the couch, slow and steady, stalking her like prey but she doesn't seem at all phased anymore, standing off with her eyes.

"You can't keep me locked away forever Hays..." I don't do well with people underestimating me. She should know by now that's not a good idea.

"Was that a challenge *Puppet*? Don't tempt me. I will bury you 6ft under still breathing until you decay with the rest of them." My face is so close to hers I could almost kiss her and part of me desperately wants to sink my teeth into her bottom lip until she's bleeding in my fuking mouth.

"I know there are no dead bodies in your back garden, Hays. You're sick but you're also not one to spoil what this place means to you. I don't know what you cling on to so dearly but you wouldn't risk bringing them here. That is why you haven't been caught. And that is why me being in your house has you on edge." *Smart girl...* Does she want a medal? "I see you haven't lost all your intelligence." *She really isn't as dumb and as innocent as she looks.*

"What is it about this place? Why are you still here doing the devil's dirty work? You got out, you were *free!*" That's laughable. Really. Is that what she thinks escaping prison is? Freedom? Being branded with convictions that stop you from living a normal life and exiled to live a lonely, miserable fucking existence?

"Free? There's no such thing as *freedom*, *Puppet*. Your life is a constant tie to shackles far greater than you or I. No one is ever free. We are all chained down to a society and a system that doesn't want us. What about that is freeing? Isn't that why you dream?" My fingers find the bottom of her scalp, not rough but enough to make her look at me and hear my words.

"You've moved from one prison cell to another?" I hate the way she speaks as if she knows me. She doesn't know *shit*.

"I find comfort in my solitude." Being alone is far easier than surrounding yourself with fake pricks who only want something from you.

"That isn't it. What is so special about this place? What are you not letting go of?" She needs to quit it before things get ugly. This house is my own prison as well as my sanctuary. This is where I'm closest to her and it will be that way until I've dropped enough bodies to move on. I endure the terror in these walls for her, because I deserve it. My guilt is embedded in the foundations and that's where it's staying.

"*Alora.*" She likes to push my buttons. So I'll push hers, but she doesn't react at all to me saying her name.

"You've not even given freedom a chance?" She's right. I've not. Because I CAN'T.

"And what? You- you expect me to live a normal life? Find a wife, settle down, have kids? Get a job in a fucking office? I can't *Alora*. I'm a CRIMINAL." I want to rip her hair out and share my grief through her voice as she fucking cries out.

"You could still have lived that life, there was still redemption for you!" Why is she trying to paint me as someone who deserves that!

"And what would you know about me!?..." I deserve this. This life of torment. This life of misery. I wouldn't even know what a normal life looked like. It sickens me and it's an insult to my mother.

"I know nothing, *Hays*. Because you refuse to tell me what I'm sitting in the middle of. So don't act like you're trying to protect me. You're only making it worse!" Her fists find my chest, pushing me with little force.

"This world is ugly. I am ugly! But believe it or not, I am protecting you from answers you don't want to hear!" Does she not see I'm trying to protect her fucking feelings!?

"Why!? What am I missing!?" She barks.

I'm reaching the end of my tether, and her whining is starting to drive me to cut her oxygen. "Because it will kill you!" I shake the sofa with both arms either side of her head, rattling whatever brain cells she has left.

"I'm already dead! And I will only ever be dead whilst still being in your possession!" She definitely knows how to take the air from my lungs.

...

She wants answers? *Fine.* But I'm done going easy. I'm not spoon feeding her shit. I'll drop her in the deep end until she learns to swim without touching the bottom. She wants to understand me? *She has to drown first.*

Without uttering another word I find the garage door, barging through nearly breaking them off their hinges.

"Hey! Where the hell are you going!?" To clear my fucking head before I snap hers. The doors feel my fury as I slam them shut and lock the outside door. I was about to get in my car but I'm intoxicated and that's a risk. Not that it would make any difference to me, I'm still as sober as they come, but as she said. I will do nothing to risk this place being taken from beneath me again and the way she knows that frightens me. It's a threat. I've been to fucking *kind*. This is what I get for being *KIND. Fuck!*

I take off and I dunno where I'm walking but I don't plan on coming back until dark. Maybe I'll feed my anger into someone else's chest just to lessen my load.

She fucking infuriates me! How the hell did she pick me apart? I'm slipping and it's bad.

This is bad.

CHAPTER 21

SOLVING THE CASE

Puppet

She's stormed out the door like a little girl but I'm so repent to find amusement in this right now. I'm just as angry as she is. She's angry because she knows I'm right. I refuse to be left in the dark any longer. I refuse to talk to a wall. I will get to the bottom of this whether she likes it or not because staying in the unknown is eating me alive.

She didn't lock the garage door. Giving me access to the office once more and by the temper that shook the house she isn't going to be back for a while. *Good.* It gives me time to access everything I need to.

Play - 'Panic Room - Au/Ra'

I waste no time legging for the vault of secrets and as I walk in everything is on. The computer is open, sitting on a court case document. Something I don't recognise but it's once again, a domestic abuse case that got dropped. I'm trembling through my fingers as I surf through folders upon folders of files and images. A folder sits pretty with my father's name on it. *Jackpot.* I open it and find it hard to swallow. Hundreds of images plaster the screen including old pictures I've never even seen before. Pictures of him with another woman? *That isn't my mom?* Maybe that's my biological Mother? Is Hays part of my family? What the hell is going on? I scroll a little further and a group photo sits with my father, the same woman, another man and a child. *It's her.* It's the same girl I saw in the living room. Why is she in a photo with my dad?

Endless photos later, I put a few pieces together but still things don't make much sense. They were in the detective scene together? But if so, why have I never heard of this woman before? Maybe he mentioned her but I was too young to remember? I rack my brains trying to remember her name but I'm left blank. These pages are full of writing but they are all blank. Is she Hays Mother? Is that how she knows my father? But that still doesn't explain why she killed him! I'm losing my *MIND*. I stand to face the board on the wall surfing for what feels like centuries and the name *Lillie* seems to pop up quite a few times next to cases my father was working on. I search the computer for a folder potentially holding her name and I eventually find one. All her documents, case files, birth certificate and contract for the Chicago police department are staring me in the face. *Chicago?* Am I back home? If so I'm further away than I thought. That's almost four hours away from Indiana.

Her full name and all her personal information jump out the screen from a document from *1998*.

Lillie Moore. Mother of one. Hayley Moore and wife to Richard Moore who died in 1997. I've never heard any of their names before. I want to rip my hair out, how can this be so complicated! Why is she so fixated on my family!

I search up *Moore* into the search bar of her files and it's just a sea of writing with dotted pictures of her in amongst the chaos. *Is she Hayley?*

```
Hayley Moore
Involuntary manslaughter
6 years
```

The words penetrate the screen in big bold letters, plastered on newspapers and web links.

Six years. She said she served for six years. But this still doesn't tell me why my father is involved? Who the hell did she kill if it wasn't my father? She lost her mother but he wouldn't kill anyone? Certainly not his work colleague. *He's not a killer.* He left the scene because it was too much for him as it is. Where does he come into this? Where does my family come into her shambles of a life?

Father comes up quite a few times. Is that it? Did my father kill her father? I sit on a dark picture, hard to see, heavy on contrast as I sit my forehead in the palm of my hands trying to rub out this impending headache settling on the surface, trying to put these broken pieces together. Hays has never mentioned her father, and he is nowhere to be found around the house. All I have is his name, and that he died in 1997. That was two years before my father walked away and now I'm understanding why, this is exhausting.

I level my head and oxygen is ripped from my lungs as her face peers back at me through the computer screen. But not through an image, her insidious mask. How long has she been standing there?! I jump out my body as I turn to face her, gripping tightly to a blade most likely meant for me but I'm too frustrated and infuriated to care right now.

"Are you ready to talk?!" I challenge her blade, buzzing with fury.

"Are you ready to listen?" The tip of her blade licks under my chin forcing me to look at her and I'm riddled with chills.

"I have been ready since the day I got here! I've demanded you tell me Hays and you've refused!" She closes her eyes and shakes her head gently; I narrow my glare trying to read her rubix cube of a brain.

"Because you're not going to like it." What could possibly be that terrible! I'm not a child, I can handle her past!

"TELL ME, HAYLEY!" I immediately regret speaking that name when her eyes hollow, suddenly seeing innate death in physical form, flaring her nostrils as her split tongue runs her teeth, gripping my throat so tightly my vision goes fuzzy.

"Call me that again. And you'll wish I killed you that night. *Do you understand me?*" She's practically spitting in my face before forcefully throwing me back into the brittle chair, walking backwards, slowly towards the door.

"Where are you going?" We aren't done here. Where the hell does she think she's going? "Hays..." She doesn't respond, slipping out the door shutting it behind her and the lock turns, ringing like a gun shot through my heart. "No! Please! Don't lock me in here! Hays please!" *I can't do this again.* "OPEN THE DOOR!" I tug on the handle, shaking it vigorously trying to escape this nightmare trying to ignore the demons towering over me. This room is drowning me with voices, I can't breathe in here.

"You wanted answers? Look harder." *Is she kidding!* She doesn't even have the decency to tell me even when I'm sitting amongst the answers! What is her problem!? "When you've calmed down. We will talk." I'm far from calm. In fact, I've never been more enraged. I'm a dog locked in a cage, surrounded by my worst nightmare. My fury takes over, paper scatters the air as I throw files off her desk, painting the floor white, scraping at the board tearing down her work. Uncontrollable tears roll down my cheeks, clawing for my sanity between the walls. Why me? Why am I being punished? What did I do to deserve this!? I heave through my chest, trying to focus on the wreckage in front of me. Scattered parts of me bleeding between the pages. I've messed everything up in a fit of rage, how the hell am I going to figure anything out now?

Play - 'Hurricane - Fleurie'

It's been hours and I've lost it. I've exhausted myself beyond comprehension as I sit with my back to the door crawled in on myself creating a puddle against my forearms. I've sifted through everything and still nothing makes sense. I'm at a dead end and I just want to give up. This was punishment in itself for trying to seek answers she was not ready to tell but I was getting impatient. It's been what, two months now? Two months of playing pretend, two months pondering on questions I need answers to. It's killing me. My entire life has become one big joke and I deserve to know what the hell caused this. What caused her to kill mercilessly on my own family.

I've not heard her since she locked the door and I don't know what's more worrying, the fact that I have or the fact that I haven't but for some reason I despise this silence where only the voices in my head are keeping me company. I've gotten so used to having her around I forgot what it was like.

I sit for a few more minutes trying to pull myself together when her voice sinks into me from the other side of the door.

"Are you finished?" She's not even angry. She just sounds fed up with me. I feel her weight shift the door as she sits parallel to me on the other side. We are back-to-back through plywood and that's comforting right now. I know whatever I am about to hear is going to shy me away from embarrassing myself further.

"Yes..." I cross my legs, placing my head against the wood and close my eyes ready to reap what I sow.

"Are you ready to listen?" *No. I don't think I am. But I don't have a choice.*

"Hays please." I squeeze my eyes shut, frustration lingering on my face.

"I need you to know, before I tell you everything, that you were never meant to get caught up in this. And I know I've said it before but I mean it. Whatever you think you know, it's all about to change. Are you prepared for that?" Again. *No.* But how are you meant to prepare to have your life turned on its axis? Luckily, I've already had my fair share of flipped tables but I wish I could say it gets easier.

"Yes..." I hear her shuffle some more, like she's getting comfortable to tell me a bedtime story and I know we may be here some time.

"I served six years in prison for involuntary manslaughter. I killed someone who was meant to protect me. I killed him because he was a threat to me and my mom." I shake out my nerves, listening to her words carefully through the wall.

"Your father?..." I mumble, rolling my throat trying to accept that the woman behind this door killed her own blood.

"Yes. And afterwards things were great. She got her life back together for a while, she was no longer in danger, we were finally at *peace*. She was part of the Chicago police department and she worked alongside *John* for quite a few years, even when my father was alive, due to your father and my mother being case partners, he and John grew quite close. After his passing, my mom told everyone he fled, that he walked away and left a note that he wasn't coming back. *To protect me.* Your father was by her side through it all and that slowly turned into something more for a while, he became a father figure to me."

"When was this? Was I born?" I begin to ponder on my younger years. Trying to pull any possible memories that can link to this part of my life I do not recall, he was a father figure to a child I had no recollection of.

"Your father was a single man at this time from what we knew of. He never mentioned he had a daughter; I assume it was to protect you." At least she can acknowledge he was doing something good.

"He was seeing your mom?" I fiddle with my thumbs, trying to control the lump stuck inside my throat.

"Something like that... That's what we wanted to think. Until one night I woke up to him cursing from her room and instinctively I ran."

My heart throbs for her. She instinctively ran to her mother's aid without a second thought and it only makes me wonder what she went through.

"He was snooping to find evidence against my mom for the disappearance of my father."

This can't be true... He would never use anyone? *Would he?* What kind of man does that make him?

"He was never interested in her that way. He was using her to get her behind bars."

I can hear the anger through her teeth, grinding them together as she speaks.

"I tried to tell him it was me. I pleaded with him to listen to me. She told me to be quiet. That she had it under control, yet he was still aiming at her heart, even after she told him she was just trying to protect me, he wouldn't budge that fucking gun."

I can't picture him wielding a gun to harm another and everything in me is screaming.

"He said, *step aside. Or I will not hesitate to shoot you.* And of course she refused. I told her to move, that it was ok, that punishment for my actions was ok as long as I had her to come back to. But instead she refused to let me go. She just stood there. *She's my baby, John. Don't do this. Please. It was an accident. She was just keeping us safe. She just a kid John!*" She recites her mother's words calmly, painfully. And I knot with guilt not meant for me. "He just glared straight through her. Like she wasn't even there. He was so caught up in the case he wouldn't let it go." I can feel her rage vibrating against me and I know what she's implying. *I feel violently sick.* "He never walked away, *Alora*. He was removed for opening fire on a member of the Chicago police department." Her words bleed down my face, hitching my throat so hard I almost choke trying to hold in my sobs, sobs of uncontrollable culpability.

"He claimed self-defence..." My voice cracks trying to get the words out, remembering the fight we had. The words she spoke that I so desperately wanted to understand. *You know what? They would probably believe you too. You're a Blackthorne after all.* The name of importance.

How doesn't she resent me?

"He walked away without a scratch. Pledged that she was unstable and went for him first. But I saw it all. I watched her die in my arms. I saw the whole fucking thing. The blood was everywhere. I watched him run, leaving me to pick up his mess. Listening to her tell me *she loved me* as she took her final breath. I faced him in court and I got thrown behind bars because my Mother was no longer alive to plead my case. I was almost charged with intentional murder." She was locked up for self-defence but my dad walked free? That only fuels her hatred towards the man who took her mother's life. My *Father*. My Father took her life.

"Was it.... Intentional?" I hesitate, I don't even know why I'm asking and it's probably rude. She also hesitates, sitting on my question for a while and just by the silence, that tells me my question was not completely out of pocket.

"A sick part of me had always wanted to. I'd thought about it, dreamt about it. Envisioned it. And I knew when the time came, if I had to I would. But I didn't seek it out that night. His death was purely to keep me and my mother alive." *But I didn't seek it out that night.* She says it so aimlessly.

That first kill started something. In the last four years she's taken fourteen heads and feels no remorse. It awoke something in her. *Control.* She told me it was power she could control. Her Father's death gave her *control. Freedom.* And she lost it as punishment for trying to save her own life.

SHASSII

I'm taking in so much right now it's hard to process. It's overwhelming and I am trying my hardest to hold it together. The monster behind this door is a monster filled with bullet holes and broken armour. A shattered heart that only knows suffering. Her pain is her architect.

This could all be a lie. It could all be a lullaby to make me see something other than a monster. But she's always made it known that she is nothing but. It's taken around two months for her to be honest with me, if she was just honest with me from the start, maybe things would be different. This changes everything... But now it's too late.

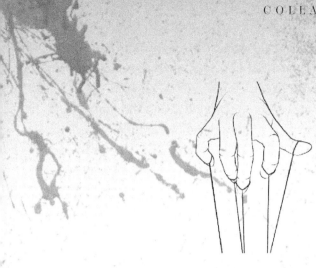

CHAPTER 22

FUELLING THE FLAME

Puppeteer

Play - 'Beautiful Pain - Eminem, Sia'

I'm clinging onto distant memories now so heavily resurfaced I'm almost biting my tongue off trying to contain my pain *for her*. I know she needed to know. But thinking it and saying it are two different things. Maybe it was I who was not ready to relive my past. I've spent so long holding it against its will, caged inside the darkest parts of my vacant heart that I've become accustomed to feeling numb. *She makes me feel*. This is making me feel and it's destroying me.

I can hear her holding in her cries and I want to shake her for being so stupid. I told her this would kill her but she wouldn't listen. So now she can consume just a fraction of my affliction. She needs to see that I was not born this way. *I was created.*

I don't want her forgiveness and I never have, I don't expect her to forgive me for the pain I caused her as I would never have forgiven him. I chased him to the ends of the earth trying to end this ache I endeared only to pass it onto someone else. She has every right to hate me. Hate is too nice a word for the way she should feel about me. I just hope that now she understands my actions were not in vain.

I stand to my feet turning to rest my forehead against the door, holding the key ready to turn it. She needs comfort right now, and as much as I hate human contact, I'll endure it. I turn it slowly to give her time to hold her body up on her own before slowly pulling the door to. She doesn't move. She's completely absent, running for her escape in the clouds but she can't dream right now. My *little Dreamer* needs to keep her feet on the ground for me. There is no escaping this now. The truth is out and she'll either overcome this or let it swallow her whole.

I kneel to her level quietly behind her as not to startle her, the light from the computer screen highlighting her glossy skin that's shedding one too many tears which Shep instinctively wants to try and lick off her soft cheek. He can sense her distress just as much as I can, and all I can see is *myself*.

"Hey…" Even touching her arm she doesn't flinch, she's frozen like stone, in a state of shock and its crippling me seeing her this way. *Why the fuck do I care so much.*

I scrap the talking knowing full well that's the last thing she wants to do and grip her tightly feeling her melt into my hold. Resenting every second I'm comforting her. I never had anyone to comfort me. Maybe I resent it because I mourn for it. Someone to actually give a shit. She collapses her body weight into my chest as she lets go of two months worth of agony, clawing my forearms so tightly her nails are indenting my skin and I know there is direct anger toward me amongst her strength.

She's kept it together for so long and she's finally cracked, she's staining me with her discomfort, trying to find comfort in the very person who put her in this mess, it's like trying to throw water on a roaring fire, you think it's helping when in reality, it's fuelling the *flame further*.

"I'm sorry…" I whisper lightly down her ear, quiet enough that she can't hear my blasphemy. I don't ever apologise. It's something foreign to me and just speaking those words aloud goes against everything I am. I can't apologise when I'm smothered in *Sin*. Sorry will never make up for the damage I've done. I don't know what this means for us, or what we do now. But right now, I hold her, I let her break, I let her crumble. I stop fighting for her to find her strength. *Right now, I am her strength* and we'll figure the rest out later.

Play - *'Save Me – XXXTENTACION'*

She's been out for a few hours, exhausting herself to sleep as I sit here like a relative waiting for her to wake in a hospital bed. The only time she ever looks at peace is when she sleeps, even more so with my boy cuddled up next to her keeping her warm. He's not left her side either and I don't think either of us want to wake her. Just as much as I'm scarily starting to not want to let her out of my sight. I roll my stiff neck out, leaning over my weight, slumped into my hands feeling my leg twitch restlessly my mind going over everything I said. If she hadn't pushed me, I don't ever think I would have told her the truth. Why? Could be fear. Could be guilt. Could be both. I knew telling her may possibly ruin whatever good streak we had going, as messy as it was, it was comfortable.

Now we're back to square one, learning a new me and a new her. Everything she knew was a lie, and when she wakes she's going to have to accept this new version of her life. I just hope I've toughened her up enough for her to be able to handle it.

My impulses win and the back of my finger finds her soft cheek, warm beneath my touch as she rolls into my pillow, cracking open her eyes and I've never felt such relief.

"Hey there *Little Dreamer...*" I stand slowly, approaching her timidly like she's an injured doe.

"I thought I *lost* you there..." She whispers. *Did she just recite my words*? I choke back a smile as she takes a deep breath, pushing her body up off the bed to give all her attention to me.

"How are you feeling?" It's a stupid question. But I ask anyway. Maybe the sleep wore off some of her dejection.

"*Lost.*" I psychically feel my heart sink. Even ripped of everything there was still so much behind those eyes, but right now there is *nothing*.

"If I could take it back. I would." I perch beside her and this time she doesn't move away from me.

"You said you'd of killed him that night." *I did*. And part of me still would. But if I knew she was in the equation I would never have taken her life from her. Not like this. *This was before I met her.* "I won't excuse what he did to you...I'm sorry. You had every right to be angry." There's that damn word again. And if she wasn't so sad right now I'd keep up my end of the deal and make her chew goddamn soap.

"*Innocence*. Just- don't." I'm not going to sit here and listen to her take pity in me. That is not why I did this.

"Do you wanna talk about it... about him...." I know she means the devil himself. And I'd rather take a bullet than bring him up.

"Not right now." Why would I want to talk about that pile of shit...I'd rather eat it.

"I'm not the only one hurting right now. I'm not blind. I'm just trying to help...I'm trying to understand..." This isn't a therapy session. I'm not going to be counselled over my dead father, I'd rather celebrate and shoot shit.

"What more do you want from me *Alora?...*" I can feel my temperature rising at the thought of him as she continues to push me.

"For you to be honest with me." She can't be serious. I've just told her everything and she's still accusing me of hoarding secrets!?

"I've been honest with you!" I shoot up off the bed, pacing to ease my short fuse. The last thing she needs right now is me getting angry.

"Look! I just want to know how you dealt with this! This- pain! This- aching!" She's trying to seek that information from me? Does she forget I find enjoyment in hearing scumbags beg for mercy?

"I didn't! This! This is me dealing with it! I kill people and it makes me feel good! Is that what you wanted to hear?!" I never got time to deal with the shitty card's life dealt me. If I had, maybe I wouldn't repeat my fathers ways as a coping mechanism for my freakish appetite.

"You don't kill just anyone. I read those files Hays. There's a method to your madness." She pays far too much attention; it's starting to get on my nerves. *Wants to know me,* kind of attention.

"I kill people who cheated death." She focuses on my words and reads right between the lines.

"People like your father..." One death is too merciful for a monster like him. His face appears on every life I eradicate, it haunts the very walls I live in until I can't see it anymore, until his face appears inside another and for a mere moment, my serotonin levels spiral as I see his face, until it disappears for a while, and the cycle continues. A never-ending loop of unfulfilled rage, chasing a life that is already dead just to feel something. Just to fill this empty hole that is only getting bigger.

That is how I cope.

"Do you want a gold medal?" There is stillness smothering the room as we sit in one another's musing.

"If things turned out differently. Maybe we would have met in different circumstances."

"Maybe..." She's not wrong... If her father had just let it go, we would most likely have been introduced through them. Although that's a little weird. She would have been my half-sister? *Gross.*

"I can't forgive you. And I certainly can't change the past. You and your mom both deserved better. But so did I. And I understand now that, that was not your fault." She sounds like my mother. But that never works on me. I was indoctrinated to harbour my faults. If I'd been a better daughter, none of this would have happened.

"I will never ask for your forgiveness. I simply wanted you to see the truth." She needed to know of the monster she called her father, just as I did mine.

"Then why did you wait so long?" I won't tell her why. Because it means admitting it to myself.

"Because I was afraid..." *Afraid I'd lose her.*

"My my... Did the monster finally admit she does have a heart after all?" She's smiling and those dimples are making their own personal indent on my damn heart.

"Don't be too optimistic." I don't want her to expect me to care, in fear I may disappoint her if shit goes downhill. She is still my hostage after all. I go to stand, ready to walk out and leave her in peace but I'm interrupted.

"Stay... Please." I guess thinking she needed space was wrong. But I'm certainly not the best company right now. She has a hold on my wrist and I fall into her golden hours lighting up her weary face. I tug at the corner of my mouth, exchanging understanding before crawling in next to her. We've accustomed to sharing a bed with no contact, so I lay on my side and observe her. How she has three perfectly aligned moles on her right shoulder and a tiny white scar grazing her elbow. She shuffles, inching closer to me. Closing the gap between us and I read her signals, gently sliding my right arm beneath her pillow, our frames still not touching but just enough contact to know *I'm here.*

CHAPTER 23

CUT THE ROPE

Puppet

Play - 'Leaving Tonight - The Neighbourhood'

I've slept on the idea and maybe I'm not in the right headspace but all I want to do right now is *run*. How do you run away from a nightmare that you can't wake up from? I turn slowly to face her and she's actually sleeping? *That's a first.* But instead of finding comfort in that, all I'm thinking about is getting out. I just need to get the hell out of here. Back to normality, back to civilization. I can't handle this paradox, it's suffocating me. My father killed someone and he hid that from me, from everyone. My entire life has been one big lie. No amount of sleep will ever change that and now he's no longer alive for me to confront him. All this time I thought he was caring for me when in reality he was scared I'd find out the truth. Find *her*. Or she'd find me.

I don't know what I'm doing but I'll figure that out later. I inch slowly, keeping my muscles as still as possible as I detach from the bed and she doesn't wake. This is so unusual of her, she never sleeps?

Heat warms my body, lathering the back of my neck as I tiptoe lightly against the wooden floor in fear that I'll wake her. *Where would she hide the keys?* She's gotten too comfortable. I pickpocket her jacket hanging off the back of the dining room chair and delicately pull keys out, careful not to jingle them. There are at least ten keys on here. *Fuck sake.*

I dig some more for anything that may possibly help me and my eyes almost burst as I pull a firearm from her pocket. I guess I'm going to need this if she realises I'm gone. Grit rolls down my throat, creeping as slyly as my feet will allow to the front door. I start trying each key. *Come on. It has to be one of them.* I'm running out of time and patience, shaking as I handle them, checking over my shoulder like a paranoid schizophrenic. Finally, a key turns and I gape with optimism. I don't even have shoes on. *This is crazy.* I pull the door towards me scrunching my face as it creaks, echoing through the house and a sudden wave of guilt washes over me that's soon interrupted and swallowed back down when the door slams shut nearly trapping my fingers inside.

"Ouch *Puppet*..." My heart stills, her tone so dangerous it immediately makes my eyes litter with water as she rubs her paint into my neck. "Just when I thought me and you were finally getting somewhere." My hands tighten around the gun, squeezing it as my shoulders stiffen, being pushed against the door like the force of water as her fever etches into my back. "And after I confided in you..." her thumb caresses my cheek, wiping away at my guilt, like she's aiding my betrayal.

"Let me go Hays... Please..." I can feel every muscle lining her torso and I forget how big she actually is. How dangerous she really is, how much blood she has on her hands. I'm meddling with the Devil but something is telling me to keep prodding.

"Now why would I do that?..." Her voice leaves me breathless as I turn to face her, peering up at her blurry face, searching the pits of hell before me and my nerves are spiking my fire.

"I will shoot you." There is no confidence behind my threat. I've never threatened anyone, but I also never thought I'd be chest to chest with a convicted murderer. She finds this laughable, shrieking at my empty threat like a psychopath. Logistically, I know I wouldn't be able to pull this trigger. "Let me OUT!" My grip tightens, indenting the metal into my frail fingers.

...

"Do you know the quickest point on a human's body for collateral impact?" Silence etches itself inside the cracks of unspoken words, but I already know my face is giving away the answer as I struggle to let any words slip out. I choke on the evaporating air seeping from my lungs as she rests her temple against the barrel of the gun. "Judging by the look on your face. I'd take that as a no. So it's a good job I do. Because that's the last thing I want." I stare intensely at her, trying to understand what on earth she is trying to say. *She doesn't want a quick death?*

"If I were you. I'd go for my heart."

She whispers so calmly every nerve ending in my body is trying to burst out my skin.

"And don't miss."

My grip tightens along with every muscle in my body. She says it as if, if I were to mess this up, I'd suffer for it.

"I want it messy. I want you to watch me bleed out slowly. *Innocence*. I want it to hurt."

I can see this death within her dead gaze locked on mine like I'm the key she's been searching for. *She wants to suffer.* "I want to watch the guilt seep out of your pretty little eyes as you realise how foolish you are. Can you handle that, *Puppet?*" She wants us both to suffer. She wants to show me she was right, that killing her will solve nothing but riddle me with guilt she now carries. That removing *My Nightmare* will only create more sufferable sleepless nights. "If you're going to do it. Do it properly." Properly to her is inhumane? Which only peaks me to wonder why she gave my parents such a humane end.

"If you really want out, *Little Dreamer*. It's simple... Pull the trigger." She clasps the barrel pressed firmly against her head, tilting it to align with her chest, holding it hostage against her heart. "All it takes is one *biggggg* squeeze... And you are free. Free to live your life as you wish. In fact, I urge you to do it *Alora*. Because if you don't. I will find you, in every village, town, city and I will not stop until we are this close again because you -" I'm sensing raw pain in her vocals and I don't even think I want her to finish that sentence.

"Are. My. *OXYGEN.*"

My breathing labours as I glare at her with utmost confusion.

"I will stop at nothing to rain hell on anyone who thinks they can take you away from me..."

I'm looking for a meaning behind those words and they are staring me in the face.

"Do it..."

She's testing me. This game of cat and mouse is exhausting.

"Pull the trigger..."

She closes in on the space between us, grazing against my ear lobe, and my tummy flutters again. The hairs are rising and my irrational thoughts take over.

Power. I feel it, I feel that power she speaks of. Her life's at the end of this gun and I am now holding her life in my hands. Pull it and be free of this nightmare. Or get out and suffer her chasing me to the ends of the earth, just as she did my father. Either way, neither are feasible. She's made her stain, wormed her way into my subconscious. Even 6ft under, I will picture her face even when trying to lay at rest and escape my reality.

My impulses win, pulling the trigger until it clicks. Squeezing my eyes to soften my blow.

...

Play - 'Cut The Rope - Charlotte OC'

"Did you really think I'd make it that easy *Puppet?...*" Her paint is rubbing against my cheek and I can no longer feel the heart beating in my chest. She's taken it from me. "Did daddy teach you, *nothing?!...* " The guns ripped from my hand, thrown out of sight and out of mind. Leaving just us as shields against one another but I know she doesn't need a weapon to harm me.

"First rule."

Her fingers trace my chin, tugging my focus to meet her gaze.

"Always, check the mag..."

She's being vigorous yet her words are constructive criticism. Much like training. I've pushed her and still she resists her urges to punish me.

...

"You'd be dead right now." Her middle and index finger rest against my temple, mimicking a blow. Paranoia lacing her tongue. *She's fearful of my death.* That's not the words of someone who wishes to see your end. It's the words of someone who wants to see you fight. She's irritated that I'd of lost that fight for being too timid.

"Are you going to hurt me?..." I think some sick and twisted part of me secretly wants her to break her morals. I'm tampering with her nurture to harm, against her natural instinct to protect what is now her property. Under her roof, that is all I am.

A Puppet.

"Have I hurt you?" It's been two months and truthfully, she's not laid a finger on me that wasn't deserved, and no amount of prodding has driven her to my death. Only drawing *my* curiosity out.

"No..." I look at my feet so she doesn't see the desperation in my face. *Honestly.* I cannot feel right now. I'm in a state of limbo. A numbing sensation worse than death. I feel like I'm trying to chase some sort of high? *Fear.* I should be terrified to face the consequences but instead I'm drawing them out.

"So why would I start now?..." I've done everything I possibly can to make her react and still she resists me, *why is she resisting me!?*

"Because I tried to escape..." Maybe escaping wasn't my goal. Maybe I wanted a fight. Because at least physical pain is tangible. You cannot escape its wrath.

"Do you want me to hurt you?..." I don't make a sound as she forces me to look at her. My silence is her answer. I'm pleading in a language I know she'll understand, too afraid to say the words out loud.

...

"Aahhhhhhh... I get it nowww... This was all a little game. Wasn't it?" I don't want to admit it to myself but I think she is right. My entire life I have been hidden from the world. From danger, from anything that could ruin my perfect little life, I've never experienced adrenaline, *fear*. I'm learning that it's exhilarating. It makes you feel *alive*. And I know I sound crazy, but this house has held much worse. I'm finally beginning to understand the way she was built. Broken pieces from different machinery not meant to go together.

"Are you going to punish me?..." It wasn't a question. It was an invitation, and I don't even know what I'm inviting in but something inside me is yearning for physical touch. To lose myself in someone else. *Is that normal?*

"Do you want me to punish you *sweetheart*? Just say the word *baby* and I will give you the most mind-blowing punishment you've ever fucking had." She made that sound so inviting I drop my jaw as my muscles relax, feeling a beat between my legs as her thumb finds my bottom lip in the dark.

"What does that mean?..." How can pain be pleasurable? Is that what she is implying? *That's absurd.*

"Let's find out *Innocence*." I don't know what the hell that means but it can't be good, and that nickname sends chills up my spine, the irony of the word against the actions we commit on one another. Violence is far from innocent, it's malignant.

The key still sits in its designated hole, the door is still unlocked. She grabs my arm, pulling me away from the door, turning me to face it like a noose as she slowly opens it and for the first time in two months, a breeze cascades beneath my nightgown. My inner voice hums at the sensation. I've not stepped outside since that night and part of me is now intimidated by the idea. She still has a hold of me, so close to my neck I can feel her breathing on it as she groans in a coarse tone.

"You are my *Puppet*. And I, your *Puppeteer*. Your next move will only be determined by my hands *Little Dreamer*. If you think you can outsmart me -" a cold silence surrounds me as her lips run the length of my neck until she reaches behind my ear, sending dead spirits to pass through me.

...

"*Cut the rope...*" A metaphor for the tie we have to one another. She pulls my strings. She has my life in the palm of her hands, orchestrating my every move, every breath I take, every noise I make. Logistically, a puppet is nothing without their puppeteer, but she's letting me try anyway. Try to move without her.

I glare at the overgrown garden lit up only by the reflection of the moon. It's dark out and I have nothing to cover me. It's freezing, but I can't back out now. I wanted this. I wanted to run. She's letting me run but what am I running to? What am I running for? I can feel her eyes scolding the back of my head and my heart is beating so loudly I can hear it in my ears.

"I'll give you a head start." She lets go and I can hear her boots tap the floor as she backs away from me, giving me space. Allowing that dark cloud over my head to fade so I can think clearly.

Play - 'OXYTOCIN - Billie Eilish'

I need to run. Now.

I take off, squinting at the chipped stones and uneven ground beneath my feet, I haven't a clue where I am or where the hell I'm going but there are a cluster of trees surrounding the property. I lunge for the darkness, hiding in amongst them like an animal trying to navigate my way through the pitch black, barely able to see my hands in front of my face. I suddenly fear I may get lost, but why am I worried, that is what I want, to get away from *her*. Away from here. But something is telling me that is near on impossible. I could fly to the other side of the world and she'd still manage to find me in a crowd full of people. She's made sure I am perfectly clear of that. This isn't me escaping. This is me partaking in her little game, and for some reason, *I'm enjoying it.* This is quieting my mind, making me figure out how to survive instead of glossing over my imperfect little life.

I have nothing left. What am I really fighting for if not to fall right back into her hands. I think a part of me has now latched onto her *kindness*. Starving people will do anything. I am starving. Starving for *affection, love, someone to hold me.* She held me yesterday when she didn't need to. She slept beside me when I encompass a picture she should loathe. We are the same words in a different font.

Collateral Damage.

It's been a few minutes and I stop to take a breather, I must be a good quarter of a mile now? I didn't hang about. Searching through the trees for some sort of life but there is nothing. She really does live in the middle of nowhere. I'm so out of breath my vision is going fuzzy trying to concentrate on a focus point. I just need to find a road. I listen to the sound of my own heartbeat, staring up at the moonlit sky between the trees and take in the view just in case this goes south. I know it will, but that's because I secretly want it to.

I knew the mag was empty. That is why I fired it. If there is one thing my father did teach me, it was how to load one up. A father in the force had its perks after all, I just wanted to see how she would react, push her buttons and it worked. She finally snapped.

I get lost in thought, imagining her poor mother and it fuels my motivation to keep running. I need to run that image out of my head but it's buried deep. I stop once more and I've not seen, nor heard any sign of her. I must have lost her now surely. I lean up against a nearby tree, the bark digging into my exposed skin as I try to tune into the noises around me but all I can hear is the rustling of wind in the trees and the odd owl. It's so peaceful it's making me teary. I forgot how beautiful the outside world is, it's almost overwhelming.

A twig cracks behind me and my heart stops in its tracks, eyes glued to the leaves still moving, jumping out my skin as a small animal jumps out from the bushes, rolling my eyes and calming my nerves. *Phew... thank God.* My life flashes before my eyes as her distorted face emerges from between the trees, cracking another twig in her wake, hitching my breath as I turn to run the opposite way. Whiplash almost snaps my neck and I yelp out a cry into the empty void as she grabs the ends of my hair bringing me to my knees, cutting open my porcelain skin against the rough bark, peering down her nose at me like her next victim. Her clown makeup is something of nightmare fuel between the trees, dark and desolate with only us to occupy it.

"Now. About that punishment *Puppet.*"

...

Shit.

CHAPTER 24

LITTLE MASOCHIST

Puppeteer

Play - 'Manipulate - mxze, Clarei'

The *Little Princess* wants to play? No objections here. I'll show her what sin tastes like. She's on her knees before me and my god it's a *beautiful* sight. She has no idea how deeply I want to break her just for betraying me so carelessly. Does she really think I was going to let her walk away after learning the truth? She clearly doesn't know me at all. I was temporarily closing my eyes. It's sweet that she took my vulnerability and tried to use it against me. In fact, I predicted it. She has no idea how much I want to snap her frail little bones until she's a heap on the floor but now, immobilising my *Little Puppet* doesn't seem as fun.

"I said I'd give you your freedom *Little Dreamer,* but I never said you would be free of me. I will haunt your nightmares and plague your pure little mind until the only thing you long for, *IS ME*..." She's trembling under the cold temperatures but I'll soon warm her little body up. "Get up." I tug on her locks of hair to give her a nudge. She knows I won't hurt her. *Really* hurt her. But she's been prodding the lion for far too fucking long and I need to *bite.*

I walk her to the nearest tree stump, throwing her torso over it like a slab of meat. *MY* fucking meat. She whines, uncomfortably laying on damp moss, ruining her tight little nightgown.

"Give me your hands." She does as instructed, cautiously and I place them neatly behind her back, crossing them against the bridge of her spine. I glare at the delightful sight before slowly undoing my buckle, teasing my belt through its hoops until it's looped up in the palm of my hand, almost salivating at my *Little Innocence* bent over before me. She's already beginning to sweat, beads of moisture glisten underneath the moon, but she keeps quiet which surprises me. I thought by now she'd be screaming for help, too bashful to expose her bare thighs to me. The creases of her perky little ass are teasing my imagination from underneath the seam of the dress, I want so desperately to trace her soft flesh, but I refrain. She doesn't deserve that level of intimacy. I'm punishing her for trying to escape with words I confided in her. So I'll just beat them back out of her.

She wants to feel. I get it. She forgets I've been where she is. That denial stage shuts down your emotions like an off switch. She can't feel anything, *and I can fix that.* The tip of my belt runs the length of her inner thigh, taking the dress with it as I drag it to the dimples in her back. I'm aware she probably hasn't endured any sort of pain through intimacy, or intimacy at all for that matter, *so I'll go easy.* Tickling the goosebumps smothering her skin before tapping it lightly to give her a clue, her breathing quickens, probably pumped with adrenaline and embarrassment. She doesn't have to tell me she wants this. I can taste it in the air.

I tap against her skin a little harder, building her tiny tolerance before flicking my wrist lightly with some force behind it. She yelps under her breath, jolting into the tree. I give her thirty seconds or so until I hit her with a *2nd. And a 3rd. A 4th. 5th. 6th.* Each a little harder than the last. Not at all hard enough to do any damage. But it's enough for her to awaken that masochist resting dormant inside of her, and it's working. She lets out a few little whimpers of raw ache and my grin is vile.

"You feel that *Puppet?*..." I'm referring to both her, chasing a high and that foreign ache between her legs. She lays there mute and I know she's trying to wind me up. The little bitch knows I can't stand being ignored so I'll make her *scream* it out. I kneel slowly, inching my mouth towards her backside, tickling her rosy ass with my lips as I lick them, letting her take in the spoonful of pleasure my mouth has to give as I line her skin with my snake like muscle before sinking my teeth into her sore flesh, drawing out a shriek that scares the wildlife nesting in the trees.

"Don't make me repeat myself." She's gripping the tree, holding onto it for dear life as she conceals the aftermath of my bite.

"Yes!..." There is allurement in the way she responds to me that's making me fucking ache. I don't know what's gotten into me but I could draw that helplessness out of her all day every day. She sounds so pretty crying out for me like a *puppy.*

Who knew teasing *my Innocence* would prove to let out some pent-up steam. I've not felt this nourished in months and I've not even had to take her life to gain it. Those cries are feeding me plenty. I push on my feet to stand, towering over her from behind and everything inside me wants to tear that skimpy lace dress off her needy little body and show her just how easily I can make her feel. Feel *me.* But I won't. She's my *plaything,* but I still have my own rules, and she doesn't fucking deserve it.

"Stand up." I hold her shoulder to help pull her body weight into me, my rock form catching her as she stumbles on her feet trying to find balance on her infirm legs, tugging her dress back down to erase her prudishness. Her hands are slumped at her sides and my fingers line her exposed skin, running down each arm until I reach her wrists, pulling them behind her to meet each of my pockets and she grabs them instinctively without demand. She knows exactly what this means *and she just did it willingly.*

"What does this mean, *Puppet?*" Her breathing is irregular, trying to spit out those disgusting words as she wobbles against my torso.

"I'm your bit -...." her voice fades into the whispers between the trees, sending her ugly words down wind.

"Didn't quite catch that." I lean to accommodate her height, towering over the left side of her face, listening closer to her ill confession as my lips graze that spot behind her ear.

"I'm your *bitch*..." She swallows her pride, rolling her eyes trying to keep her head up.

"*Good girl...*" She's exhausted. And understandably so. This can be a lot for someone who reads books and stays well away from the 100m run in college. I don't think she will even remember these words when she wakes tomorrow. She's too high off dopamine to realise what she's actually doing. Your mind craves the most peculiar antidote when trying to cure unexplainable suffering. A pain not controllable. A pain with no cure.

Her legs give way, reaching for my jacket for support and I hold her up with one hand. "Easy there *Love*." The adrenaline is wearing off and she's beginning to shake like a leaf again. I remove my jacket, resting it over her shoulders before picking her up off the floor, looping my forearm under her legs and she's a ball of mush curled up in my chest. After everything I've done, everything she knows, she seems more comfortable now than she ever has done and it's my fault. She wanted me to snap yet I'm cradling her in my arms and her gentle huffs against my white shirt are calming me.

She's become my oxygen tank.

Play - 'Chance with you – Mehro"

I carried her all the way back and she was out for the count. She's lost, and I'm taking it upon myself to help comfort her when I should be telling her to get a fucking back bone. Something is different. *She's different.* I can feel my walls collapsing and it's out of my control, she's tearing them down. She encompasses a power I fear.

Love.

She loves things that don't deserve it. She feels so heavily that her body is shutting down. It doesn't know how to cope with feeling at peace. She internally battles against a raging war she bleeds onto paper and the silence is killing her. She cannot cope without it. Her mind is protecting her heart and in doing so she's forgetting how to function. She's learning why I do what I do. Why I chase for pain, for death like a reward. But with her it's not the same. Her pain only rips out the mercy inside of me. I am merciful with her and her alone. *But why?*

I'm laying in bed next to her, God knows why, staring at her wrapped up like a cocoon for what feels like hours and I think I could draw her blindfolded if given half the chance. She groans softly, rolling about in her semi-conscious state and my throat knots as she mumbles my name underneath her gentle breath.

"*Hays...*" Even half asleep she's calling out for me and I'm indecisive whether that is a good or bad thing, but it makes my heart constrict. I can actually feel it beating inside my broken rib cage. I suddenly love my name in her mouth. *I want her to say it again.*

"Right here *Little Dreamer.*" As I suspected, she rises from the bed completely dazed, gawking at me in utter confusion. Like she blacked out and forgot her previous endeavours. "Is that you in there? Or am I looking at a ghost?" She scrunches her face at me, trying to make sense of my words and that realisation finally smacks her in the face.

"*Oh my god.*" She rips the duvet off her to reveal she's still in her now muddy nightgown and scowls at me.

"Don't worry *Princess.* I have human decency." By the look on her face she doesn't seem to think so, but then punishing her for trying to escape a convicted murderer isn't exactly what the average person would describe as human decency. Nevertheless, I enjoyed myself and I know she did too. Human decency would be letting her go. But I'm afraid I cannot allow that.

"You're a perv..." She throws her pillow in gentle anguish against my chest, trying to muster up just a tablespoon of remorse but she's a terrible liar and I can see straight through those puppy dog eyes and her rosy little cheeks.

"And you're a very good listener." She isn't amused. And I know she's meant to look angry but she looks like a feisty kitten. She's struggling to keep her eyes open and that could be a mix of many things but something tells me she's not just tired. "What's wrong?" She glances at me with a puzzled look on her face. A mixture of disbelief and audacity for different reasons.

"My sugar levels...they are just low, is all." All that adrenaline must have soaked it up like a sponge. And she was a good girl and told me straight.

Without hesitation I get up and head to the kitchen. Grabbing various sweet treats that have accumulated in the cupboard in the last few weeks. If my sperm donor was here to see this he'd turn in his grave. God forbid mom gave me a chocolate bar. She ended up having to hide them from him or he'd throw her money in the bin. Her weary eyes light up without her knowledge as I walk into the room with the goods, handing them to her and I'll never get tired of watching her eat. She's like a kid at Christmas, scoffing cookies and actually smiling.

"These remind me of my favourite chocolate." She's chowing down like a cow and it's bringing out her dimples again. *God dammit.*

"Oh? Do tell." I plant my ass back down next to her. Giving her a side eye as my head rests against the metal bar, taking her stuffed elephant and planting it in my lap as I fiddle with its arms.

"Hersheys." She doesn't seem at all phased by the last hour's antics, either that or she's hiding it well.

"Sorry. We are all out of Hersheys." My arms are now crossed, death gripping her teddy as I stare at the ceiling. Grinning at my stupid humour.

"Get out of it!" Her pathetic strength punches my biceps in a playful manner and a fly could have hit me harder. But I won't have that. I grasp her wrist, flipping myself until my entire body weight is laying heavy on top of her, pinning her firmly to the bed as she grips the cookie tightly in her restrained hand. The curvature or her tiny little waist sits perfectly against the curve of my knees and I scan her with my dead expression. She's frozen like a deer in headlights. She will learn her violence will always be counteracted by my strength. But I'll build that strength. We have all the time in the world. And until I can sort out this transport issue to get my ass out of here, I've nothing better to do.

"Let's get you cleaned up..." I don't have to threaten her further for her to know she shouldn't have laid a hand on me. I take a bite of her cookie, and she pouts at my betrayal.

"Can you stop stealing my food?" I could. But I won't. The uninvited expression on her face makes it worth it. She has no idea what I'm doing to her body, but I do. I'm fraternising with the enemy and I may as well have some fun with it.

After today. It changes everything. And her terrible attempt at escaping was just a ploy to make me give her what she wanted. I've given her so many subtle signs that I yearn for her beneath me and my corruption is slowly seeping into her vulnerable bones.

SHASSII

CHAPTER 25

BLURRYFACE

Puppet

Play - 'WASTE - Slowed Version - KXLLSWXTCH'

I pushed. Maybe a little too far. She terrifies me but I knew she wouldn't hurt me. Not the way she wants to anyway. Call me naive and stupid. Hey, maybe I have learnt my lesson, but even now I don't think I have. She hates that she needs me, she hates the thought of parting with me, and I just needed to push a little harder for her to show me. Prove to me that what I thought about her was right.

She bathes in so much pain and loneliness, guilt and years of abuse that I am still yet to understand but for some reason. I want to understand. I NEED to understand. Maybe that is why I pushed her. I feel sick to my stomach. What I did was inhumane, but it also felt, kind of, *good*? I don't know what that says about me... I'm nothing like her. I don't want to be like her, but everyday I'm stuck with her, I find myself chasing this hunger for excitement. She excites me. Her past. *Our past.* It has opened up a door I was not prepared for, but I don't think I'm mentally stable enough to understand what I'm even doing. All I know is she's been there for me regardless of our shared hatred. Held me, cared for me and dealt with my outbursts without breaking her word. She's shown me without words that she's kind. The affection she so desperately despises has been very much present amongst the chaos of our damaged association and I still broke her trust. But there is no anguish in her eyes when she looks at me. When there should be. There is only concern.

The only reason she inflicted pain is because I begged for it. I'm pathetic. *Who begs for pain?* Or more importantly, why did I beg for it? This is so unlike me. And I enjoyed it, which makes this even worse. Not that I can really remember much of it. My mind is all over the place. All I want to do right now is sleep but I have a feeling she won't let that happen until I've showered and I've not got the energy for that right now either.

"Would you mind if I had a bath?..." I finish off the rest of my cookie as she nods gently, moving off to go and run one. She does so without even thinking about it. No arguments, only compliance, and I rub my lips together, squeezing my hands between my knees trying to shake this relentless feeling niggling at the back of my throat. We are different people now. Learning to understand each other once more. But more so me trying to understand this new information I've been thrown and it's piping hot in my hands. It's going to take me a while to get accustomed to this truth and now I can see why she didn't want to share... She was protecting me but I pushed anyway and I'm still trying to figure out if that was a good move. In some lights it was because now I see her in a completely different light. But I now also see my perfect little life in complete and utter darkness, built on a false prophecy and a false history. *How could he lie to me?*

Ten minutes or so go by and I'm twiddling my thumbs trying not to fall back to sleep, Shep nuzzling me to keep me conscious as his wet nose grazes my arm.

"Hey boy." It's probably around two in the morning and I am ready to knock out for at least forty-eight hours. Sleep doesn't cure pain but it's a temporary fix. If you're asleep you cannot feel. Maybe that's why she doesn't sleep. To tell herself she's still human with a beating heart.

"It's done." She murmurs through the door and I waste no time nearly running for the bath. I've changed into clothes I don't mind getting wet and I lower myself in slowly, embracing that tender sting rising up my body. It hurts but it's soothing. This pain is usually as close as I get so earlier was most definitely new for me. My lip drags through my teeth, frowning a tiny smile at the thought, wanting deep down in the pits of my stomach for her to *hurt* me again.

I never understood the rebellious nature of teenagers but now I'm starting to get it. It's not so much the pain. It's the thrill. The consequences. The hunger for discipline. Which kind of makes sense when you live... Lived... In a house with parents like mine. I was always so lenient. Patient. Not just at home but at school. I was teased for being such a goody two shoes, it's where I got the nickname that Kacey likes to brand me with, and I'll be honest, in my later years it frustrated me. I didn't want to be the sensible idol, but I couldn't even sneak out to a party without panicking over the repercussions. If Kacey could see me now. If I told her what I've been through, I don't know whether she'd be proud or fear for her life.

Play - 'Chasing_(Demo) - NF, Mikayla Sippel'

She stands in the doorway like a creep holding the tip of the frame, watching me as I soak away all my sins, bathing in momentary relaxation. Even after this level of, *trust*? She still won't trust me to wash in peace. I'd like to say I'm surprised but I did just try to run so it's understandable.

It sounds ridiculous but I don't have any instinct to run anymore. There is nothing left on the other side of this, I wanted to die anyway so I may as well go out with a bang. No one's looking for me. No one cares. I have no family left. The relatives I do have live dotted across the world and we barely saw them. I think the last time I saw any family members I was no older than a pup. There's nothing to run to. She's become my safety blanket and it's so wrong, but her venom is flooding my cold veins.

"Do you have family?" The water lines my chin, shrinking to meet the audacity I've stooped to.

"None that care." She really is alone. I bet no one even visited her when she spent six years banging her head against a wall. In fact I'm impressed she still has rational thinking. In most cases, a sentence like that drives someone to do horrific things to achieve their end but she's still very much alive and very much functional.

"What was it like? Prison." I begin to wash, trying to muster up the strength I have left but I'll be honest. I am beyond drained.

"A walk in the park compared to my childhood." What the hell did she go through? What kind of monster was she trapped here with? I take a look around the room and my skin begins to itch.

"The lock on the outside of the bathroom door… That was never for me. Was it." Things are slowly starting to piece together and my stomach is churning with vile imagery. I've never even asked for her age and it makes me feel even more nauseous. I'm eighteen and she has to be at least mid-twenties. She's barely been able to live.

"No." This whole thing. It really was an accident. I don't think she's ever held anyone against their will, not like me anyway, not here. She was quite happy mercilessly killing and I threw a wedge in her plans. This house, the locks, the boarded-up windows, the holes in the wall. This was her prison once too and now it's mine. Deep down I can tell she hates this.

"Enough questions." She moves closer, her chains clanking through the air grating at my ears before she stops by the edge of the bathtub holding out a towel for me and I exchange a quiet smile. A smile I know she understands. A thank you for aiding me through the catastrophe we've endured in the last twelve hours.

I stop pushing, finishing up before attempting to crawl out of the bath, almost falling on my face. *I really do need rest.* Her arms cushion my fall, pulling me back to balance on my feet.

"Next time I'm letting you fall." She voices her irritation. But in reality, she doesn't need to coddle me. She never had to. She chooses to.

"Next time I'll take you with me." She cocks her sinister little brow at me, laughing internally at my unrealistic remark. We both know she wouldn't budge. "Is this the part where you tuck me in and read me a bedtime story?" I giggle quietly to myself and I forgot I had that in me.

"In your Dreams." She's told me enough stories for one day, I'm sure I can give her the night off.

My hair is sopping wet and I don't think it's been tended to at all since I got here. It's probably a matted ball of chaos but I hadn't really thought about it. Luckily my hair doesn't need much attention. I have my mom's genes and usually knot free, but weeks of neglect has finally caught up. I slip into warm clothes trying to shake my chill, looking around at my things littered across her bedroom. Things I've never picked up on until now. My clothes on the chair, blankets multiplying on the bed, my elephant teddy by the pillow and Shep lounging across clean clothes that I'm still unsure how she washes.

"Do you have a brush?" She doesn't respond, only vanishes for a moment and I hear a drawer open from the far bedroom. *Her bedroom*. Before walking back in holding one in her hand. I take it, carefully, like it's made of glass and give her a subtle smile. It feels wrong to use it but she's trusting me with it.

I struggle to untangle my knotted nest, fighting to run the comb through it before my wrist is clamped shut with her fingers, gently pulling the brush from mine and my heart warms. She takes the bristles and begins at the bottom of my hair, slowly working her way up, being delicate not to hurt me. We wallow in the serenity, embracing this moment, taking ourselves somewhere else for a while as I close my eyes until my hairs knot free, she places the brush down on her chest of drawers, running her hand through my sea of hair and down my back so gently I can barely feel her hands on me and my body shudders, rolling an electric shock through my bones. *What the hell was that?*

We crawl into bed and she lays on her side as usual. But tonight, I don't think I want her to. I shuffle discreetly until we're practically touching but she keeps her hands to herself. My body is practically buzzing with this gravitational pull and I don't understand it. I should be repulsed but I can feel my temperature rising. This anticipation is eating away at me like a virus. *I want her to put her hands on me.* She loops her hand around my waist like she can read my thoughts, pulling my featherweight body into her torso and my heart immediately slows down. I feel calm.

I feel,

safe.

I think we both needed this closure. This closeness. Tomorrow we can carry on hating one another, but for right now, this.

This is nice.

SHASSII

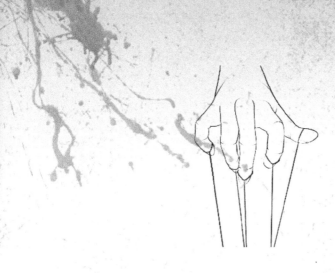

CHAPTER 26

COPING METHODS

Puppeteer

It's been quite a few days since our antics in the woods and I've refrained from speaking about it but I can't get that image out of my head. *Her.* Bent over for me like a good *Little Puppet*. She's submissive at heart and part of me loves it. Her walls are cracking and soon, soon I'll have her exactly where I want her. She's making it extremely difficult to keep my hands off her. It's like she's purposely been dangling herself in front of me. Wearing nothing but her pants and my T-shirts. I suppose I should do a shop run for her at some point but I've never enjoyed shopping and I don't plan on starting now. What does a *sunflower* like her even wear? I'll just have to endure this torture until I can break her. She will crack and I'll show her exactly what she is really craving.

Me.

My boot breaches the front door with a bag and I'm getting army tackled by Shep as she sits reading the book I took for her with her feet up on my coffee table like she owns the joint. But I'm glad to see her looking more comfortable, as bored as she is.

I put the bag by her feet but she's fixated on me, glaring at me like the first time we met.

Play - 'The Beach - The Neighbourhood'

"Your- your arms-" *I suppose I've become too comfortable.*

"You should see the other guy." I grin like a sinner, peering down at the blood smothering my skin, noticeable even over my tattoos. This one got a little messy, but I took what I needed and I'm one step closer to getting the hell out of here. Hell, I may even take my *plaything* with me.

"Will you ever stop?" I wish I could say yes. But I can't. I don't have it in me.

"Do you want me out of your hair?" She's mute, frowning at me with adorable frustration. "That's what I thought..." She knows everything now. It's up to her whether she wants to come to terms with what I do and deal with it. Or we can go back to square one. "Open the bag." I'm trying to make amends here. The quicker she gets over my ways of living the quicker we can move on.

"I'm not hungry..." Her arms cross, peering up at me and I sigh heavily.

"Just- open it." We exchange a heated glance, holding it, until she reaches slowly for the bag, frightful of me which I find highly ironic considering she's been needing for my physical touch every night since our little *game*. Does she think I haven't clocked onto the way her body responds to my presence? We've gone from a pillow fort to a closed space at night.

She pulls from the bag and the little girl inside her comes out, holding onto a bar of chocolate.

"Where did you?-" I suppose she is rubbing off on me. But I couldn't help myself.

"Merry Christmas." I mock. I managed to find one at my nearest gas station. Hershey's was a rare delicacy for me so she better be bloody grateful.

"Thank you..." I've never seen her open something so fast in my life. "Do you celebrate?" Does she mean holidays?

"What?" I walk over to cleanse myself clean. It took far too long to track the bastard down, I suppose I let my anger get the best of me and his face got the brunt of it. It did nothing for me, all I could picture was her god damn face and he wasn't even my average target. He was just an identity I was stealing. I almost thought about letting him walk too. *What the fuck has gotten into me?*

"Christmas?" She asks, I shake off my recent endeavours, wanting to vomit in my mouth at the word.

"God no." Christmas is the last thing I want to be thinking about and I can't escape it when I venture beyond these four walls. It's plaguing the streets and I can't wait for it to be over. Christmas morning is four days away.

"Yeah...I was never much of a fan either. But my mom. She'd cook these really nice shortbread biscuits, and make me help her decorate the tree. She was always awful at it." She breaks a chunk off, laughing to herself as she glares at the ceiling picturing her perfect little life to keep herself sane. I clamp my eyes shut, pushing my guilt down and swallowing it. She probably doesn't even know what day it is.

"I'm sure it looked beautiful." I'll just play along. For right now I'll let her reminisce if it makes her feel better.

"What did I say about this shitty decor Lillie. Take it down. Now."
"Rick. It's for our little girl. It's Christmas. Try to make this memorable. For her."
"NOW LILLIE."
"Please. Rick. Please, don't- don't make me do this."
"We're gonna have a great Christmas. Just the three of us. You'll see Darling. It will be. Perfect..."

"Hays? ...Hays. Hey -" Shit. I have her wrist in my hand, a knee jerk reaction and her eyes are popping out of her skull as Shep nuzzles his nose into my hip. "You ok? It's like you were in some sort of trance?" My fingers are tearing the sofa open as I grip tightly. Trying to erase its voice etched into my motherboard.

"Yeah- yeah I'm fine. Just- enjoy the chocolate." I let her go, and I hate that she's in the middle of this. *I HATE IT.* All I wanna do is show her my anger. *Make her* afraid of me. She is no longer trembling in my space. I gripped her wrist so hard I could have snapped it and she just stood there and took it. I need to punch these demons out of me before they try to inhabit themselves inside of her.

I find the basement, not remembering how I even got down here and I waste no time beating the crap out of my punching bag. *Picturing his face.* Sweat drips down my spine, my tank top is soaked and this fury is not fucking off so I think of the next best thing as my fist meets the wall. I don't flinch. Sucking in a satisfied breath, letting the pain subdue me as I drown in the sharp ache. Her pretty little mark on my hand is a trophy to remind her how strong she really is, and how she weakens me. I've not felt feelings this strong for months. She's like a drip. Slow but steady, keeping my blood pumping when I should be dead. I was meant to die. Now I wanna *run? Fly away?* What's gotten into me? I just killed to steal an identity when I should be drowning at the bottom of Lake Michigan.

Just thinking about her slows my heart rate. My thumb runs the length of her mark on my skin, focusing on her strength, her ability to control. She has this ability to contain this pain, lock it in a box and keep it at bay, but she needs to let it out. I want her to use me as a punching bag. Surely it isn't healthy to hold it all in. She acts like she's totally fine but I know she's losing herself. And I cannot lose the little life left inside her.

Never.

"What are you doing?" I'll be honest. I don't even know, but this attic is the last place I thought I'd be.

"Just don't let go of the ladder." I remind her sternly hearing that giggle, and she dare let go, she'll receive another whooping.

"Maybe I will." I pause. Turning to peer down at her, my white face paint haunting her through the trap door in the ceiling.

"Do you want to bend over again for me, *Puppet?*" Her perky little face glows bright red, staring down at her tiny feet trying to shy away from her guilty desires and avoids the question.

"What are you looking for?" My fingers graze the dusty wooden beams, reaching for corroded boxes and plastic bags. Trying to block out the memories I'm sifting through. It reeks of the past up here so I don't want to be up here any longer than I need to.

"Believe it or not. I have something you might like." I forgot how much junk I had up here. I really need a clear out.

"What could you possibly have that I would like? Besides a baby photo album. Now that, I would love to see." There's that snigger again and it tugs at the corner of my lip.

"You can keep wishing *Little Dreamer.*" *Not happening.* I shuffle through a box of books, old art and stationary and finally come across my little find, pulling it from the wreckage, wiping the dust off the leather cover. "Here." I make my way down the ladder, passing her the ancient scroll of empty pages.

"What is it?" She always looks like she's never received a gift in her life, taking it lightly from my hand.

"I thought you might want to write. Thoughts, feelings, stories. All that soppy stuff." She needs an outlet. Something to vent her emotions into as I know she isn't exactly going to hand them over to me.

"Excuse youuuu. If I remember correctly, you said it was *beautiful.* Or was that just a ruseeee." A ruse? Maybe so. But doesn't mean it wasn't true.

"If you would like to know, I meant what I said." She examines the pages, a blank canvas to stain with words.

"How can I trust you won't read whatever I write?" Awww. How cute. She thinks I'm interested enough to snoop?

"The same way I trust you won't write anything mean about me." I know it will be full of nasty things, but I can make her feel guilty, just this once.

"I can't promise anything." Her dimples light up her face and I just want to pinch them.

"Think of this as a, errr- early Christmas present." If she thinks for one second I'm going to go out and buy her something she has another thing coming.

"Well-"

she inhabits a deep breath.

"Thank you. I shall write all my - '*soppy*'*,* cringy writing." She's acting so, normal? This feels so normal. *A good feeling.* And I'm shrivelling at the thought. Nothing about this should feel good, but she's making this feeling bearable.

"I'll be sure to get you a lock and key *Innocence*." There is that look I've been trying to draw out.

Hope.

"I'm sure you have plenty lying around." She gets snarkier every day and I secretly enjoy her bratty little mouth. It makes it so much more fun to mess with her.

CHAPTER 27

MY WORK OF ART

Puppeteer

Play - 'Unfair - The Neighbourhood'

The fridge opening breaks the silence of the eerily quiet night, a bottle of corona tinkers against the plastic as I pull it out, only to realise it's the last one. I've gone through an entire crate of six in less than an hour hoping for that familiar buzz that sometimes helps me close my eyes for a while. Shep peers at me from the couch waiting for me to plant my ass back down but I close the fridge door and find my bearings for a moment, pulling out a freshly made cigarette before sliding it between my lips waiting for those endorphins to riddle my core. My backsides wedged into the island as I lean back, blowing my ghost into the still air as it lingers like a premonition while I close my eyes and focus on anything but the things that won't stop smothering my every thought. The living room is pitch black at night, not even the nearest streetlamp can reach the windows and it's where

SHASSII

I feel most alive. Most at peace. In darkness where I belong. Where I can imagine death for a while and pretend I'm no longer here.

The bedroom door clicks, causing me to open my eyes, peering up at the pitch-black void that is my kitchen ceiling and momentarily roll my eyes at my disturbance. I hear the chains on Sheps collar clank and a floorboard creek between her tiny feet before I'm met with more silence.

She stands there for a while. Maybe a little too long and I wonder if she knows I can see her through the back of my head with her bourbon eyes burrowing into this glass like she's trying to fill me up with answers to questions I know are sat on the end of her tongue.

"If you stare any longer you may bore a hole into my head." I can almost feel the fright oozing from her chest as she breathes slightly heavier.

"Sorry- I-" Her voice is timid. Quiet. Defeated, as I pull another drag and blow it into the tense atmosphere. By the nervousness in her voice, she wants to tire her tiny mind with chit chat. She's never ventured out of *her* room at this time.

"Couldn't sleep?" My voice feels far louder when the world is quiet and my smokers rasp bounces back off the open space. She's probably wondering why she didn't wake up with me next to her. Routine and all. But like many other nights where she's deep in sleep, I usually don't stick around for long, only until I know she's finally peaceful. I wanted to drown my incessant thoughts of her out with booze but it appears I can't even do that because she's like my little shadow.

"Yeah..." She admits, like it's a bad thing. I don't move, but I can feel her moving closer to me as the air shifts.

"Isn't it bliss." I'm now surrounded by a cloudy haze as we sit in one another's silence for a couple of minutes, paying no mind to her glaring at me like I'll somehow shatter. Her anticipation is practically screaming into the room, I can hear the little slaps of her lips as she continues to open and close them, hanging on faint inhales waiting for her to spit out whatever is clearly weighing heavily on her mind.

...

"How do you do it?" She finally questions, as I rub the back of my neck.

"Do what." Another pause is met, so whatever she's about to ask isn't how I style my hair or deal with the little tornado on my couch.

...

"Hurt people." Now I'm the one hesitating as I ponder on an answer that no matter how I deliver will never sound sane or rational, but I'm sure she knows I'm neither of those things. That's exactly why she's asking.

"I turn it all off." There are many ways she can interpret that. But it's pretty simple. If I don't turn it off, it swallows me like sand beneath the waves. A prisoner to its inevitable crash as it lashes against me, starving me of numbness as I'm forced to fight against the way my lungs are burning.

"Don't you feel anything?" I sit on her question a little while, trying to figure out a way to answer that. I could lie and simply tell her *No*. But we both know that is a lie. She just wants to hear me admit that I'm not as horrible as I think I am, but who's to say I don't enjoy the feeling, I'm a sadist, I feed off people's fear, the way I do hers.

"More than you know." I say barely above a whisper but clearly not quietly enough.

"So why? It clearly keeps you up at night." I rub the corners of my mouth down to my chin as I stretch out my hanging jaw, tilting my head to the right slightly to almost meet her gaze as I attempt to find her over my shoulder.

"Taking a life isn't what keeps me up *Innocence*. Constance is." The finished cigarette meets it's end between my clammy palms.

"*Constance?*"

"I'm a constant reminder of everything I swore I'd never be, but now it's too late to change it." I sigh.

"A murderer?" She whispers through uncertainty, trying to come to terms with the fact that she's stood in the same room as the person who took her loved ones. But I hate the term murderer. It states that my actions are of a mad man, that the crimes I commit are unlawful when I'm anything but. I'm the conscious evil that they should fear. Murder is a word created to label the ill nature of cleansing their kind because they can't admit that they too, are murderers. I will not associate myself with scum. . She's right, I am-

"*A Monster.*" I correct her.

"Insomnia equates to a guilty conscience you know. It shows that you do feel. Somewhere, in that desolate heart of yours." A part of me fights back amusement as I grin into the abyss.

"*Maybe.* Or maybe. I'm just too broken to find peace with rest. It's punishment for all I've done and will continue to do until hell decides it's my time." Another empty silence fills the room besides the gentle huffs from the couch potato as he sleeps. But I know she didn't come out to talk about my inhumane tendencies.

...

"What are you thinking about?" I whisper, wondering through the dark towards the couch where I plant my ass, resting my feet up on the coffee table.

"What do you mean?" *I love picking at her brain.*

"What's keeping you awake?" I can feel my head spinning as I lean my head back into the cushion.

"Oh- I. I'm not sure. I just don't think I could get comfy." Does she think I haven't been reading her like a map? I know that her insulin knocks her out and she was fast asleep thirty minutes ago.

"You and I both know that's a lie. What did I tell you about lying *Puppet?*" I can almost hear her swallow her deception from behind me. "That question didn't come out of nowhere. What are you thinking about?" I demand gently.

"I guess I am just trying to figure out what I'm feeling..." I don't have to look at her to know she is caving in on herself.

"And what might that be?"

"If I'm a bad person." My brows knit. *Bad person?* She doesn't have a bad bone in her body and I'm starting to wonder if that's the reason I'm so perplexed by her.

"And why on earth would you think that?" There are still thousands of questions sitting in the air and she's lucky I'm feeling a sliver of sentiment tonight as I wallow in my temporary peace.

"Doesn't matter..." She sighs, and I remain silent. If I know anything about this peculiar doe, she is almost never afraid to ask questions. *So I wait.*

...

"When you stopped me that day-" She finally blurts out. "From killing you, you said something. You said to be better than *it*. Better than *you*. And at the time, I didn't quite understand the full extent of it. But now I'm wondering why. Why did you fight for me to concur my own downfall when you can't even concur your own?" She needs to stop thinking so much. Her ability to break me down without even trying is something I need to try and stop letting affect me. I don't know if it's because the booze is finally kicking in or I actually have a heartbeat, but her words rip me in ways I didn't think possible and it isn't the first time.

"Because some are stronger than others." I run my inky fingers through Sheps soft coat, reminding me that strength is something only certain people have the ability to obtain and I'm slowly realising that I am not one of them.

"You told me murder is power." She bites and it's a statement more than a question.

"I never said power was good. Power is its own catalyst. Power is someone's greatest foe. It destroys you until you are the very shell of your own." I retort, rubbing my temples, getting more agitated at myself for caving to her ungodly amount of questions.

"Are you saying you want to destroy yourself?" She already knows I didn't plan on being here much longer. Is that really so hard to believe?

"Haven't my actions already answered that." My voice is hoarse and weary.

"Why did you give me the journal?" She snaps back, as if her statement is trying to prove something.

"Because you like to write."

"*The truth.*" She sounds upset. Laced with inner turmoil like she's trying to make me confess something but my wall is transparent right now, feeling what I dred will make me regret my next words.

...

"Because I could see you slipping." I confess. Trying to understand my own jumbled up head. She needed an outlet and I gave it to her.

"Why would you help me?"

"I wouldn't call it that."

"Oh yes, you were being considerate. I got it. Definitely hasn't got anything to do with you actually caring a little?" If I wasn't so drowsy right now I'd have her over my knee for her sarcastic mouth, but instead I grin at the life inside of her.

"Your heart is way too big for your chest *Little Dreamer*. You know that?"

"You can have some if you want?" I can hear her cheeks crinkle as she smiles.

"I'm good. Thanks though." I remark, stretching into a comfier position.

"One day, one day you'll accept that you're not entirely bad." I wish she was right. As much as I wish she wouldn't see that in me considering the pain I've caused her.

"I hope I'm dead by then. Because heaven would laugh at the impossible and hell would shriek with disgust."

"Why must you be so complacent?" I can hear her step closer, her presence invading my already tiny bubble.

"And why must you be so invasive?" I keep my eyes sealed shut, as if her lingering isn't bothering me enough already.

"That's rich coming from you." Her arms are definitely folded, and she is pulling the most adorable face right now, *I just know it*.

"Your sweet tongue will get you nowhere and neither will your sharp teeth." I exhale through a sigh of boredom. "Go to bed *Alora.*"

"You want invasive? Fine." Her feet make light work of my wooden floorboards as she storms round the sofa in the dark, I almost put my foot out to trip her but I refrain, feeling her brush past me to the other side of the sofa, planting her ass down leaving Shep as a divider between us before huffing in annoyance.

"I hope you enjoy silence." I continue to remain unbothered, glaring at the back of my eyelids as I rest my neck in the palm of my hands trying my best to remain composed, but I can feel a smile betraying me as the corner of my lip cracks.

"It's bliss compared to your self-pity. You can't talk about invasiveness when you've invaded every part of my life. Including this stupid thing in my chest." She's not wrong. In fact, that's the smartest thing she's said all night.

"As I said. Your heart's too big for your chest *Innocence*. It'll get you hurt."

"I'd rather feel something than feel nothing." She slumps back into the sofa as we both glare up at my ceiling like it will help us to understand one another better, but all it's ever done is show me the very cell I'm trapped in.

"One day. You will realise just how wrong you are."

Play - 'Wash - Bon Iver'

She's had her head stuck in that thing since I gave it to her and it's kind of nice to see her do something other than stare at my ceiling or pester me. She must have written a whole novel by now with the amount she's writing, I'm gonna have to buy more pens if she keeps this up. I've been tempted a few times to snoop, she's not exactly being discreet with hiding it either, and since our little heart to heart the other night, it's obvious she's been venting through the pages. I don't know how she hasn't torn it apart but at least she eventually fell asleep, even if it did mean I was yet again cast out from my own sleeping arrangement. Her and Shep are growing fonder of that sofa by the day and I'm left on guard duty.

I am absolutely smothered in paint and it's going to be a bitch to wash out. She pulls her head from her pages to raise a brow, trying desperately to hold back a laugh, cuddled in with Shep who has taken more interest in her these days.

"Did you miss your face?" If she's not careful I'll smother her pretty little ass in it.

"*Very funny.*"

"*I'm hilarious*"

"What are you writing in that thing anyway? How has your wrist not fallen off." She's been writing every day and we're nearing the end of January. She wasn't even bothered by Christmas, which was nice for me. It's kept her quiet, maybe a little too quiet. I'm finding myself in the house more and more when I should be keeping my distance rather than making small talk.

"Do you paint?" I have an entire trailer to paint and I could do with a helping hand. I'm sure she will enjoy the distraction.

"Errm- if painting my bedroom at ten years old counts then I guess so?" Yeah, that will do.

"Fabulous." I lug in four large panels from the garage and dump them on the coffee table.

"So you murder people for a living with a side of painting?" *Precisely.*

"It's a project." I haul two large tubs of cream paint in from outside and I know this will end up going everywhere but I'm past the point of caring. The house needs it anyway. I throw her a brush and I'm surprised to see she actually caught it.

"Is this why you're outside all the time?" I like to keep my mind occupied, otherwise I have a tendency to let my anger get the best of me.

"I told you. It's to get away from you." The sarcasm rolls off my tongue, dampening my insult as a grin betrays me.

"That's why you're asking me to help?" I don't actually know why I'm asking her to help. I'm quite capable of painting it by myself. It's purely to speed up the process.

"I can take it back outside and you can wallow in your journal again if you want?" I tug the end of the wooden panel, threatening to remove it.

"No no! I'll do it." She practically jumps on it, keeping it bound to the table and immediately dunks her brush, beginning the painful process and she's clearly not lying. I've never seen a more painful paint job in my life. You'd think I handed a four-year-old a paint brush. I scold her with judgement.

...

"What?" She frowns at my displeasure. Am I really about to give her a lesson on painting? I thought she was meant to be creative?

"Look..." I approach with caution, giving her more than enough warning as I grab the wrist holding the brush, her hip buried into the side of my upper thigh as I lean in calmly, guiding her hand as I move from one side of the panel to the other in rhythmic fashion and her depraved little body is calmly heaving at the bit. This physical touch drives her mad and I love watching her internal struggle.

"What's this for?" She hums softly, her focus glued to the strokes of the brush.

"I'm rebuilding a trailer." My mom was so adamant to get this thing on the road for us but it was a heap of junk for years, even more so when I came back. He wouldn't help. He didn't want us going anywhere so our hope of freedom became a gravestone in the front yard.

Play - 'When You're Around - Jutes'

"Never saw you to be the travelling type." *I'm not.*

"And I thought you could paint, so I guess we're both disappointed." She clearly didn't like my come back, ready to throw hands, wielding her brush as a weapon.

"Hey-!" she dunks the bristles again and I know exactly what she's thinking, her narrow eyes and mischievous grin are going to get her bent over my knee.

"Don't you da-" *~Splat~*

"Right. You asked for it." My hand finds the bucket, drowning it in paint and she jumps away like a frightened cat.

"OMG-! HAYS!" She runs faster than the day I let her out, towards the other side of the bucket moving as quickly as her tiny feet will let her. "I'll tip it, I swear to God!" I know I said the house needed it. But not the bloody carpet.

"And I'll have you over my knee, *Puppet*." If she dares, I will smother her from head to toe and make her *eat* it.

"You'll have to catch me first." She smiles so hard it looks like it hurts and her dimples only make me grin back. She doesn't learn, does she? I never make an empty threat, no matter how adorably cute she is.

"I'd like nothing more..." She doesn't even get out of the living room before I scoop her up with one arm, throwing her feet off the floor, marking her skin with me wishing it was something else and Shep immediately joins in on the commotion, trying to play as his tail wags at an abnormal rate, pawing at my denim jeans.

"No, no, NO, N-o! Eewwwwwwww ew ew ewww!!" I smother her in it as she fights against my grip. Giggling like a child. She's definitely ticklish and that sound never gets old. I suck it out of her, pinching gently under her arms and she sounds disgustingly adorable, collapsing to the floor getting paint on my carpet anyway. She's fighting my grip trying to escape me but secretly she loves this. She's getting a taste of vulnerability. Letting her hair down. Having *fun*. And it looks good on her. In this moment. She actually looks, Happy.

"You're gonna pay for that." She bites playfully, tugging her brows into her forehead as she glares at me, and by pay for that she means give me exactly what I want. She just doesn't know it yet.

My knee rests between her legs, inching its way up her thigh and her flushed cheeks scream at me through her porcelain complexion. She's so frail and delicate. A China doll I want to smash into tiny little pieces.

"I need a showerrrrrrrr-" she wriggles beneath me, showing visible discomfort as she catches me wrong, pushing her groin into the ball of my knee, hiccupping with surprise.

"Soooooo you, didn't? Want to be smothered in paint? Because if I remember rightlyyyyy. I could have sworn you started it?" She smears the excess paint against my inky skin, gripping at my forearm like a vice and she's lucky I *like* her because I'd of shoved her fingers in her own mouth.

"Technicallyyyyy you started it when you insulted me?" She's not wrong. But that's what we do. She bites and she will learn that I bite harder. I will leave a permanent indent on her ass if need be. *Which reminds me.*

"How's that delightful little bite mark by the way?" I speak at a volume only she can hear as my voice vibrates against her ear drum. Her head tilts, rolling her balls of honey at me and she knows exactly what I'm referring to. I wasn't gentle. And she attempts to shove me off her in embarrassment. "What did you say again? It's sat on the tip of my tongue... Oh yes. My Little Bitch..." She loathes how much I'm subconsciously right but I can almost hear her heart beating out of her chest.

"Your ego is so unattractive." I'd half believe that if she wasn't tucking back a smile with her tongue.

"Showerrrrr...I'm going now." She's trying so desperately to avoid how she's feeling right now and all I want to do is fuel it, feed it. I want her to indulge in those cravings niggling beneath her skin.

I let her run, following her towards the bathroom. She knows the drill and each time it tethers my control, because I don't know how long I can keep my hands off her perfect little body before I stain her with my lustful need to rip it all away.

SHASSII

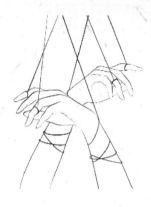

CHAPTER 28

VULNERABILITY

Puppet

Play - 'Butterflies - Isabel LaRosa'

I suck up my nerves, swallowing them sharply down my throat as I drop my loose white tee to the floor. She is looking away as always. Her respect grows on me more and more every day and it scares me... I should not be letting her in this way, but my body is screaming at me in words I don't understand, a different language I cannot decipher. The top I change into is folded up in front of me, waiting for her to turn back around and watch me peal it over my skin without feeling exposed. Something about the way she's been cradling me at night has me almost melting, craving physical affection, her skin on mine, maybe more? I have never been an affectionate person. None of this pairs with my genetic makeup, but I suppose a lot has changed in three months, I am no longer that girl anymore.

I'm a survivor, with a new spark of subtle confidence within myself. Confidence I'm not sure what to do with but right now whatever I'm subconsciously telling myself to do, feels right. She's still facing the wall waiting for the signal but the water hasn't started running yet, I find myself scraping my bottom lip through my teeth just looking at her frame from behind. I've never paid much attention until now, too afraid to give her that satisfaction, keeping eye contact with her makes my eyes burn, fear and devastation is all I feel. I run my hands against my icy flesh, looking down at myself completely bare, my heart palpitating at a rate I've never felt. It knows what I'm about to do, and maybe it's a bad idea but I can't seem to stop myself. I weirdly want this. I want her to see me. I want to defy her in the most disrespectful way. I am curious to know the effect I have on her. That night in the woods. We haven't spoken about it but I haven't stopped thinking about it. It sucked the sadness from me for a temporary moment. It made me *feel*. I want that again. I want to *feel*.

I tiptoe on the cold tiles, almost burning my feet it's so damn cold, I have goose bumps lathering every inch of my skin and my nipples are visibly hard as my hair tickles the dip in my lower back causing me to shudder at the sensation, yet I don't know if that's because of the room temperature or mine. My heart is now on the floor as I stand there for a moment. My hand clenched tightly to the metal lever, breathing in through my nose to calm my now trembling body. This euphoria is scarily addictive...it is fear. But it is inflicted fear, which is an entirely new comfort I can't understand. My toes are now tingling as I face the wall, my curves now completely exposed to her unknowing view. I close my eyes and pull the lever down, letting the initial cold water shake off my state of shock, focusing on anything other than the eyes that are now about to burn into the back of my head.

A few moments feel like hours as I trail the tiles in front of me to distract myself from the fact I am being entirely crude and diabolical right now. I am standing stark naked in front of a woman who committed manslaughter on the only people I had. *This is so unbelievably wrong, what the hell am I doing?* I cover my face with my wet strands of inky hair, rubbing the parts of my arms to create friction where they aren't quite under the now warm water seeping into my skin, hopefully washing away this sin, dripping down my curves, water freeing itself from my hips as it disconnects. I hear a shuffle. The various chains and buckles that smother her rugged attire are clanking against the china bathtub she usually sits on. That can only mean one thing, and the shower seems to get awfully hot, but it's just my blood boiling. I can practically feel her eye fucking me but my inner thighs are throbbing, what is this? *Alora you're crazy... You're literally a virgin. Kacey is so right. No one would ever go anywhere near you.* As I stand there contemplating my impulsive and regretful choices, my throat jams, feeling my spine straighten in fear as she finally speaks. A low growl hums from her mouth.

Play - 'Eyes don't lie - Isabel LaRosa'

"Look at me..." Her damn voice never lets off. How can a woman have a voice I can only describe as honey smothering bark. There is always a harsh undertone, full of fury, but her words roll off her tongue like my own personal lullaby. Sweet and sticky, glueing me in place.

My confidence finally dispatches as I expected, leaving me completely vulnerable to my own stupidity as I hesitate like a jammed clock, lagging as my body and brain battle one another to decide what move to make. I manage to choose and creep round to face her, my eyes fixated on the puddle building underneath me.

"I don't like to repeat myself." I internally jump at her back handed threat, causing me to slowly lift my head until my eyes meet hers and I feel my stomach knot. She's giving me a look I cannot read at all, is she mad? Happy? Surprised? She begins to trail her gaze upon my frame, I can practically see her eyes curving against my curves, like she's following my outline and her eyes are a pen, but she doesn't say anything. Not a damn word. And I don't know whether to feel nervous or relieved. Does she like what she sees? *Am I ugly?*

Her soulless gawk has my chest contracting in ways I didn't think possible as she brings her eyes back up to mine and I suddenly feel the room spinning. This amount of vulnerability is making me lightheaded. Even more so now that she's slowly rising from the basin and her eyes are still heavily locked on mine causing me to hold my breath. This time, I don't feel fear or devastation, I feel nervous and beyond curious to know what she's thinking behind those eyes that could kill, and have. I see a starved animal homing in on its prey. And she is now stalking closer to me.

Omg. Fuck. Fuck. Shit- OK.

Now inches from me, the smell of paint becomes fonder to me by the day. It's her permanent cologne. It's invaded all my senses and buried a home somewhere inside me that now strongly misses it when she is not around. An ugly comfort that makes me feel. *Safe?* I sound crazy. Maybe I am. She's rubbing off on me and it makes me feel sick but not because I don't want her to be. Because I'm allowing her to get close to me. I'm angry at myself for craving such a toxic form of attention.

She has never touched me inappropriately, but recently I find myself wishing she would. Does that make me sick? She has blood on her hands. She's a walking, breathing reminder of everything I've lost, she's a monument of pain I carry, she's everything I was warned to stay away from, but she touches me in a way that shows me, deep down, in that black hollow heart she wears proudly that there is some salvation still left inside her. A kindness stills within her for me. Maybe I am being naive, she will probably end up burying me in her back garden but right now, I've nothing else. She is all I have left and accepting that is becoming easier the sweeter she is. I wish she wasn't, it would make this mental war in my head much easier to bear.

I'm beginning to choke on steam as she crosses her arms to pull her shirt over her head. I've never seen anything like it.

Wait.

She's undressing.

There isn't an inch of her skin that isn't smothered in ink. Thick, bold, linework. The pain is practically seeping into my eyes. How many hours did she endure such agony to cover her flesh? Does it even phase her? Her art signifies death in every sense of the word. It's gothic and raw, hideously beautiful. I have the strangest urge to touch them but my mind stops working as she begins to unbutton her denim jeans letting them fall down her legs, stepping out of each hole one at a time as she pushes closer to me. She's not once broken eye contact with me. Have I just opened Pandora's box?

Her face paint has begun to haunt my dreams, clowns used to terrify me but they are growing on me. Or might I say, *one in particular*. Her piercing eyes contrasted against the black taper smeared around her lids is hypnotising. She looks horrific and disturbing but I'm finding it all the more intriguing to know what lies beneath it.

I walk back to accommodate her size in the shower as she forces me against the wall with only her eyes, bearing witness to my flush complexion, catching me completely off guard as her right arm suddenly raises to rest on the tiles above my head and all I want to do is crumble beneath her. I forget how tall she really is until she's towering above me. I'm only 5'4 and I feel like a troll when stood beside her. It's intimidating, it's humiliating, but it's also strongly assuring of her ability to keep me safe. Not that she needs to save me from anyone but herself.

She is brutal and dangerous, mysterious, capable of terrible things, yet I find myself drawn to her like the ink in her skin. She does things to me I don't want to think about but I find it slipping through the cracks of my now broken perception of good and bad.

It's like she wants to tease me as she leans into my frame between my collar bone and the base of my hair sending electric currents between us, a magnet to the micro hairs lining my skin before pulling away holding a bottle of shower gel.

She was grabbing shower gel Alora you idiot. Calm down.

"Turn around." My heart stops as the base of her voice rumbles against the empty room, bouncing off the tiled walls. I do as she says, slowly rotating to face the wall and my absurd thoughts begin to plague my mind as her rough hands meet my wet skin, rubbing soap in to wash my dirtied flesh. I have thought about this more than I'd like to admit and the bashful smile gracing my face is so embarrassing. I am so glad she cannot see it right now. Travelling both hands around my hips to meet my stomach, pushing her fingers into my frame as soap builds underneath her palms all the way round to my front causing me to ache in a way I've never felt in my life, an ache that physically hurts.

She's inches from my flower and my heart is trying to claw its way out of my chest, I find my breath quicken and my eyes are fighting to focus ahead of me as she pulls my hips into her abdominal area. Her boxers are soaked against my ass and it feels far too good for my liking...this is vile. *I'm a virgin.* Alora you're a virgin, and she's nefarious. This is all types of sin, but I love how she feels against my skin, this twinge between my legs is psychically painful, screaming to be touched as both her hands ride up my front to shape my breasts and I can feel my head limping back.

Get a grip Alora. Focus.

She runs both of her hands around my forearms and cups my neck, digging her thumbs into the sides of my spine, naturally making me face the floor, I struggle to open my eyes at this new found, phenomenal sensation, my mouth parted without my control trying to hold back the moans that want to escape my mouth, but when I do, I'm met with a piece of artwork at my feet where her face paint is seeping into the water creating a river of devilry, like she is letting herself bleed to the floor.

I place my hands firmly against the wall trying to keep my body weight up, almost suffocating on my ability to breathe as the water asphyxiates my access to oxygen. I can hear nothing but the beating of my own heart as the water barricades my hearing and I feel mere moments from passing out only focusing on her touch breaching mine with pure hunger. *Is this lust?* Where your body yearns to feel human contact, because *fuck* this is what I can imagine extasy to feel like. I've never taken any substance, but I feel like I'm drowning in its effects when I'm around her.

"Breathe *Alora*." *Shit*. She can literally sense how anxious I am. Well. That's what I assume until I suddenly realise how stiff I am against her frame, and how my head is submerged under the shower head. I have no choice but to pull my head back and lay it into her chest, sucking in a breath like I'm dying. *I feel like I'm dying*.

She is so tall I can feel her heartbeat against the back of my skull, panting in rhythmic fashion as her hand trails the front of my chest, gently choking my throat to direct my focus to the ceiling where I can see her jawline and partial cheek bone exposed. I'm not at the correct angle to see her face but I think that's what she wants. And I am patient. I don't want to push. This is far more than I was ever expecting, but God that jawline could cut through glass.

I find my hands trying to link with hers before being stunned at her response.

"Hands on the wall." I roll a gulp and follow orders leaving an empty space between us as I reach for it. I can hear the bottle open as she gathers more shower gel and I swear my lungs are evaporating as her hands glide down the curves of my ass and my outer thigh. She is too tall to be standing right now which means she's kneeling and it hurts to swallow as she pushes her fingers to ring my leg like a flannel, lathering soap against the inside of my leg. I can feel her breath brushing against the back of my thigh and an inescapable sigh leaves my throat. I know she's enjoying this far too much. I'm practically a puddle and the urge to turn around just to see her looking up at me with those devilish eyes is driving me beyond insanity.

Three months ago I was nervous to hold a boy's hand and now a killer is kneeling between my legs. *You can't make this shit up.*

SHASSII

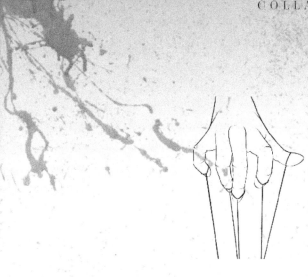

CHAPTER 29

BEHIND THE MASK

Puppeteer

She's aching. Mourning for my touch. She willingly chose to give her body to me and I will take it like my life depends on it. For months I've pictured the dimples in her back, her centre line framing her petite little body. The way her hair brings out her eyes when it's wet. She's a quivering mess as I lean to meet those gorgeous lips. Inches from my mouth, tempting her with the touch of my breath. She has no idea what she's done. I've rubbed my sins into her pure, novice skin. Drowning in the smell of palpable lust.

I will stop at nothing until my tongue is buried deep inside her but not yet. *Not right now*. I want to smash my little dolly first, so she has no structure left. No walls. Only pieces for me to build beneath me. She's succumbing to this loneliness we are both trapped in and I have become her stability but I'm too wrapped up in her hair to protest this new found comfort. This dynamic we have. This black without white. It's tangible.

My *Innocence.*

My *plaything.*

Mine.

She stands with her hands firmly on the wall, and as much as I want to feel her insides, I will stay modest. I run my hands all over her, minding her delicate flowers, claiming this sacred moment she's given me. Savouring it. And I realise it's only fair I return the favour. A mutual understanding. A stuck in stone symbolism of this raw trust. She's trusting me with her work of art so it's only right that I remove mine. I've hidden my identity for so long, she's been so used to the freak that I am, that exposing it to her may ruin this moment.

I continue to wash her clean, washing her auburn hair, running it through my hands like sand, picturing the night she was on her knees for me but only this time I don't have to imagine her bare body. As she stands before me, enticing me to indulge in her helplessness. Inviting me to handle her most sensitive parts.

I peer down at the floor, watching my second identity run down the drain as my face hits the heavy flow of water above us, rubbing my skin clean revealing my ugliness from beneath it. She hasn't moved, staring at the wall in front of us anticipating my next move.

Play - 'Halo - Beyonce'

"Close your eyes." She does as instructed, clamping them shut like her life depends on it. "Turn around..." I guide her with my hands, pulling her to face me, tugging her out from the shower head into my chest. She sucks in a breath being this close to me and this time there are no drugs or heavy traumas involved. It's just *us*. And she can feel *everything.*

I clasp at her hands gently, guiding them up towards my face and place them on either cheek, sucking in my own breath as her light fingers graze my skin. Even under warm water they're still so cold to the touch. I let them go to give her free rein and at first she hesitates, scared to move but eventually she finds the confidence to trace the structure of my face, lining the bridge of my nose, my jaw, feeling around until she finds my lips like she's trying to memorise it by touch alone. She tugs my bottom lip slightly and I'm solely concentrating on the freckles covering her face and the tiny strand of hair invading her mouth. Her other fingers find the ravine in my gaunt cheek, running her index finger along it softly as her breath quickens alongside mine, squeezing my nails into the palms of my hands, her curiosity digging for a story between the uneven surface of my skin until I can no longer take it, pulling her hands away, cradling them into my chest.

She opens her eyes without consent and I melt into them trying desperately to hide my discomfort, finding solitude in her concerned little gawk, being the one clothed but feeling entirely naked, exposed under her new perception of me. She swallows slowly, but not out of fear. There is pain written all over her pretty face.

"Who did-" my finger swiftly finds her lips, shushing her silent. I am not about to go into this shit. She just needs to take this appearance in. My force presses her against the cold tiles causing her to yelp out letting her mouth hang open and the water running against the pink complexion of her lips is niggling at me to put my mouth on them to shut her up. *Don't be ridiculous, Hays.*

Does she want to make it anymore obvious that she's horrified by the gouged-out chunk in my face? She's staring at it, observing its features and she looks like she's about to cry. *She dares and I will give her a reason to cry.*

"We don't talk about it." She nods calmly, respecting my words. I've already revealed too much, she doesn't need to know that crap too, and we stand in an uncomfortable silence as she studies me with new eyes. I'm feeling the most vulnerable I've ever felt and her silence screams a thousand words.

"You're nothing like I pictured." Her voice is so soft against the water I can barely hear her as I raise my brow, intrigued to know what she envisioned when she pictured the monster beneath the mask. I tighten my jaw as she runs slow circular motions against my collarbone.

"What did you picture?" She pauses for a moment, staring into my eyes like a soul snatcher and I still glare inappropriately too long at the colour. It's so unforgettable. Like the first sunset of summer.

"Hideous." A subtle little smile wiggles its way in before she attempts to get out of the shower, leaving me hanging on her sly confession. It's cute. But she doesn't get to walk away from a comment like that.

My hand pulls at her hair, hugging her closely to me, playing with her ear against my lip.

"You're letting your guard down *Princess*. Need I remind you the Devil was once an angel." She finds me in our waltz, staring into my soul like she's found treasure beneath rubble and ash.

"And the Devil was also misunderstood and cast out for rebelling against God. Lucifer was just a *freedom fighter*." My jaw hangs heavy. She's using metaphors to plot out the story of my life. I rebelled against a society and a broken system, which landed me in a cell for trying to do the right thing-

Clever bitch...

"Keep up that smart mouth and I'll give it another use." You could cut the tension with a knife as I pinch her chin and I can't keep my eyes off her mouth, clawing at the side of her face like a depraved man, my mouth quivers with this urge to taste her words in my mouth.

"Only because you know I'm right." My thumb finds her bottom lip in the dim light, staring at Venus in space as it slowly enters her mouth. She doesn't fight, opening it wider for me and I can't ignore the pulse between my legs as I run it along the crevice of her wet tongue imagining her insides around my fingers, revelling in the sensation, fighting everything inside me not to pin her against this wall and claim every inch of her *perfect,* untouched little body.

Mine.

She smart mouths me but deep down I love it, purely so I can put her on her ass when she eventually lets me in.

Her puppy dog eyes are fixated on mine, and if she keeps looking at me like that I don't know if I will be able to keep these intrusive thoughts at bay. I remove my thumb slowly watching her swallow another moment of dignity, now too shy to look at me. I snap her focus with a sharp tap to the cheek.

"Keep it up *Puppet*. Next time my fingers won't be in your mouth. There is more than one way to shut you up." She has this new lease of confidence but underneath it all she is still *Innocent* and she still has no idea how to handle my crude comments. She shies away, pulling herself away from my touch, hopping out of the shower like a sassy minx.

Now that she knows what I look like, I'm in two minds to let her walk free. She now knows everything. Where I live, who's involved, who my parents are, how many people I've killed and my face. But weirdly enough, I trust she won't put me behind bars. Maybe I'm being naive. Maybe this is all just a ploy to let her go but that is not happening. We are too deep in this now to let her walk.

Over my dead body.

I follow her out the shower into my room and she stands there waiting for me to turn around like she didn't just stand there stark naked in front of me. I pull a face and she lifts her frown. *She's got to be joking.* But I do as she says, turning in the door frame to stare at the bathroom rubbing myself dry with my towel. I still have my boxers and sports bra on that are completely drenched but I'll change in a minute.

"You do realise I can't let you go now." I fiddle with my fingers, hanging on her reply.

"Didn't look like you were going to anyway." *Ouch.* I was going to but she's ruined that now. She's gotten too close and I'm not the one who stripped naked.

"Where are we thinking? England? Spain?" I play with her a little, winding her up, but I'm sure she wouldn't pass up a vacation.

"You're crazy." *Nevermind.*

"And you're *Mine.*" That slips from my mouth and I even surprise myself, I've never called anyone *mine,* but I don't mean *Love.* I mean *Possession.* I want to possess and corrupt every part of her. I turn to face her and she's adjusting her top. Pulling it over her perky little breasts in just white knickers, completely unaware of her personal invasion and I can't tell whether I prefer her with or without clothes. I grin to myself as I eye fuck her beautiful frame still damp with loose wet hair falling against her sticky skin.

"Hays! Omg-" A sarcastic chuckle escapes me as she attempts to cover herself up, rolling her annoyance at me and every time she does, it makes my eye twitch. "I barely even know you?" She's not wrong. The small talk we should have had was overridden with trauma and pain. But I've also never felt the need to share my past with anyone. Not until now anyway. She knows things people don't usually learn until they are half a year into a relationship.

"Then get to know me. Besides the- ya know." I point towards my face, if there's one thing I won't talk about it's *him*.

"Is that your attempt at flirting?" *Flirting*? I can flirt if she wants me to but-

"I think we are past that, don't you?" She glares at me profusely, trying her hardest to hold back a grin.

"Fine. Why don't you like being called your birth name?" She respected me enough not to say it. And I won't go into detail. I know I said I wouldn't talk about him but I can't keep avoiding every question.

"Because I changed it for personal reasons." One day I might tell her why but for right now I'll keep that in the basement with everything else.

"Oh? What did you change it to?"

"*Hayden.*"

CHAPTER 30

SMALL TALK

Puppeteer

Play - 'idfc – Blackbear'

"Is that why you're all *macho*?" I mean. She's not wrong, she's clearly never met a dyke before.

"You mean *gay*?" I pull a pair of black joggers and a clean tank top from my drawers before heading to the bathroom to change, hearing her raise her voice through the doors.

"Yeah that name is pretty gay." She continues to insult me but she doesn't realise I get off on that shit.

"You won't be saying that when I make you scream it."

"*In your dreams.*" My foot breaches the bedroom door making her jump.

"Alo. I'm serious. Go ahead, ask me anything. We have all the time in the world." *Literally.* So we may as well kill some time and get to know each other.

"OK...errrm. What is your favourite colour?" A stupid laugh slips out, imagining all the things she *could* have said but she decided to ask the most basic question of all.

"You could have asked me anything and that is the first thing you ask me?" My arm rests against the door frame, watching her as she slumps on the bed like a typical teenager and I'll be honest my eyes are fixated on her bare thighs and those lacey little undies she's wearing. She's definitely doing this shit on purpose.

"I suck at this OK!" *Me and her both.* But we are both getting a giggle out of it and that mischievous little smile is starting to grow on me a little too much.

"It's black, *like my soul.*" She yanks herself up from the bed, clapping her hands in slow rhythmic fashion.

"Did I ever tell you you're an A* comedian?" My wrist rolls, bending slightly to poorly bow at her mockery.

"I'm kidding. It's orange. Yours?" I've never had a favourite colour really, not until now anyway, as I stare into her most rich shade of amber. Her face scrunches in concentration and it's honestly the cutest thing I've ever fucking seen.

"Yellows? Erm... Pastels mostly." *Eew. Really?*

"Yellow is *hideous.*" This conversation is gonna need a beer. I pull myself off the door frame to walk to the kitchen. She bellows like I'm not 3ft away, pitter pattering after me.

"You clearly suck at this too, and what's the difference between yellow and orange!?" I never said I didn't but she was the one who kept pushing and those colours are worlds apart.

"Anyway... *Next.*" I avoid her question, earning me a stern glare of judgement.

"Er- your favourite food?" I barely eat as it is.

"Take out. Quick and easy." *Little miss* 'I eat seven healthy home cooked meals a week' looks mortified.

"Take out? You don't have a favourite meal?" Besides the odd meals Mom managed to make without a fight, most of it was oven shit and slop.

"Does pussy count?" Her face is priceless and I wish I could frame it.

"Ew!- Gross!" She's visibly gagging and it's exactly why I said it.

"Yours?" Her entire aura shifts and I feel I hit a nerve.

"Spaghetti Bolognese. It's been my favourite since I was a kid. Reminds me of home." *Yeah I definitely hit a nerve.*

"I'll have you know I'm an outstanding chef." My poor attempt to draw that smile out doesn't take long, shaking her head as a smirk appears.

"Oh yeah? They give you cooking lessons in prison?" *Oh. Two can play at that game.*

"You're underestimating me again. My turn. *What's your body count?*" Her body stills, side glancing at me with pure and utter disgust.

"You're charming, you know that? Why would I tell you that?" *That's just it. I know she won't.*

"What is it?" I take a beer from the fridge, guzzling it to drown myself in this painfully cringe small talk.

"A few. It was great." *She's lying.*

"Oh yeah?" My ass finds the sofa beside her and she's finally comfortable enough not to flinch, trying to cover her bashful deception. Completely diverting so I don't ask further questions, digging into her *amazing* sex life.

"How old are you?" *I was waiting for that one.* It's been almost four months, and she's never commented on my age. Either that or she was scared too.

"I have scars older than you." Her eyelids drop, kissing her teeth as she attempts to playfully shove me against the arm of the sofa alerting Shep to sit up, trying to get involved in the mischief.

"I'm serious Hayden!" *She's totally worried I'm an old creep and I mean. Eleven years is a pretty big jump.*

"Why? Nervous?" She thins her lips, having a mini tantrum trying to hide the fact that I think she lowkey finds it attractive I'm a decade older than her.

"Just tell me." *I'll make her work for it.*

"Half of 58." She zones out trying to figure out the sum, already terrified at the high number as she glares at me and the penny drops. Leaping off the sofa like this is going to change anything, getting Shep all excited as he paws at her legs. She also got that a lot quicker than I was expecting. *Smartass.*

"You're 29!!!"

"Probably should have asked me that before you stripped in front of me, aye *Puppet*." My legs spread wider in front of her as I melt into the sofa, hugging the back of it as I chug another swig, swimming in confidence as I grace her with a wink and her thighs clench tightly together. She's looking everywhere but at me.

"My turn. When's your birthday?" I know exactly when her birthday is but I have a sneaking suspicion she won't tell me. *Birthday hater and all that.*

"I'm not telling you my birthday. I hate my birthday." *Thought as much.* And just for that she is going to wish she had told me.

What do you even buy a girl you have held captive in your house for her birthday. I stroll through the supermarket grabbing bits and bobs and my shops have been exceedingly pricey since she came into my life. Rinsing my damn wallet. *Typical woman.*

I know I shouldn't give a flying fuck about birthdays but as she's hidden it from me, it makes me want to make a big deal out of it all the more.

I grab ingredients for dinner and a tiny cake because I never said I was good at baking. That was my mother's thing. And I don't even know why I am thinking about this but I think she would have loved my *Little Innocence*. Circumstances aside.

As I make my way towards the checkouts a mannequin catches my eye. It's coming up to spring and this ugly pastel yellow dress is on display. I collar one of the workers, not at all surprised they look terrified of me, glaring at my scar like they've never seen one before. *I get it everywhere.*

"Excuse me. Do you have anymore of these in stock?" She smiles so wide it looks like it hurts but I can feel her nerves through her eyes.

"Yes we do Sir. What size were you looking for?" *Shit.* I didn't think about that. She can be no bigger than a small but I'll get both just in case.

"Small and medium?" Her nerves wash off as she catches the flowers in the basket and it's rather ironic. A few flowers and some chocolates completely changes her tune even though there is a serial killer 1ft away from her.

"Certainly! I'll be right back." I hover for a while, waiting for her to come back and it doesn't take long before she waddles in my direction handing me the dresses.

"Who's the lucky lady?" She eyes up my basket once more and I just cringed so hard. She's the furthest from lucky.

"Er, just a friend." I suppose we are now. She'd deny it and call us acquaintances but acquaintances don't strip naked in front of me. That definitely earned our status an upgrade.

I remove myself from the equation before she asks more questions and speed walk to the checkout. This shit is already way too *'normal'* for my liking. I feel so out of my comfort zone I almost didn't come in at all but the fridge was empty and we needed food.

SHASSII

CHAPTER 31

ACTS OF KINDNESS

Puppet

Play - 'Yellow - Coldplay'

I wake to the smell of bacon wafting under my nose and I'm literally dribbling on my arm. *She wasn't joking.* I really do dribble. Oh my god that is so embarrassing. Bacon is definitely what I need to cheer me up. I trundle out from the bedroom realising I didn't even feel her get up, did she even go to bed? Rubbing my eyes, I try to shift the sleepiness and she slowly falls into focus.

"Morning *Little Dreamer*." A large stack of pancakes and a pot of syrup sit on the kitchen counter. She's gently smiling at me and it's strangely comforting. I've realised she has not been *'working'* for weeks now, she's more interested in her projects. Or maybe to keep me company but I know that's being too optimistic, although I cannot shake these tiny, dare I say it, intimate moments from my head. And I am still mortified that she's eleven years older than me. I don't know whether to feel safe or grossed out. She put her thumb in my mouth, she's seen my bare skin and caressed it so softly it's left permanent memories in my pores. I should feel disgusted but I don't. Not to mention the fact she is a woman, aren't I meant to like boys? Maybe I really am losing it.

A lot has changed between us, I don't really even know what. But since she's opened up to me I no longer see a beast in the night. I see a wounded one in a cage and it's somehow made us, *closer?* I will never admit that to her though. That would mean admitting it to myself and I don't think I am ready for that.

I've not forgotten what she's done to me, and I never will. But I guess the empath inside of me can now see the damaged parts of her that tear at my heart. We have both suffered great loss and she's been through far worse than I have. But she's never disregarded my grief, she's only ever pushed me to fight. To find that strength in myself to move on, just as she did. She didn't have to hold me that night, or cradle me in her arms. She didn't have to do a lot of things but she chose to open up to me, even when she had no idea of my intentions.

"You hungry? I made pancakes." Her focus turns to the plate, edging me to help myself and she definitely isn't acting herself. She's being TOO nice.

"I can see, it smells delicious!" I'm drooling at the sight of it and it feels slightly strange to get my appetite back.

"I also made bacon, I wasn't sure if you wanted any." Who in god's green earth doesn't like bacon?!

"Are you kidding? I love bacon! Is this you showing me your *outstanding chef skills*?" I taunt as I begin to plate up my own pancakes, taking in the sound of the morning song from beyond the window, finding serenity in this weirdly serene little morning and I'm either tripping or she's up to something.

"Just- be quiet and eat the damn pancakes. And don't forget to take your insulin." She tells me now like it's second nature, completely oblivious to her own words as she flips the bacon a few times before laying it on my plate.

I feel so rude but I can't stop pining over her architectural facial structure. How her battered skin hoards so much torment. Every pore, crease and scar hold their own story and three months ago I would have been terrified. She was most likely expecting me to be, but it doesn't scare me at all. I just want to nurse it back to health with a kiss. I don't know what that says about me,

I've never been one for the villain, but I have always understood the broken. She's the villain in her own story. A reflection of her own downfall.

I finish up my plate and take my insulin feeling a whole lot better with a full stomach and look at the clock on the wall reading *8:20*. She finally put batteries in it because I was sick of staring at time that stood still. It's still so early.

"Hey, I'm going to go for a shower." She looks over to me, nodding in response but doesn't move, insinuating I can shower on my own and something inside of me moves. Like the final piece on a chessboard.

"Are you not coming?" She still doesn't move, cleaning up the mess she made.

"Run along. Before I change my mind." This is a huge step and I'm left speechless, my eyes sink slightly, a little disappointed that she isn't joining me and I feel so silly. It should be normal to shower on my own, she's finally giving me some *freedom*.

I hop in the shower, cleaning myself up and the bathroom feels so empty. I've grown accustomed to her company now it feels so bare but it is also the privacy I've craved. Although I can't stop thinking about her hands all over me, feeling my throat close and my thighs clench at the thought.

Showers don't take me long, I'm in and out in about ten minutes, quivering as I wrap myself up in my towel and make my way to her bedroom trying to shake off this strange feeling I seem to keep encountering. She's sitting watching TV which I have never seen her do willingly unless I drag her to endure a movie with me. She looks so, *comfortable*?

The door opens and I shut it behind me before my eyes pulsate and the air's taken from my lungs. Fabric slides through my damp fingers as I analyse the two dresses hanging on the back of the door, leaving me utterly thoughtless, reading the note stuck to one of the dresses with Sellotape.

SHASSII

I didn't know what size you were so I got both

My mouth's barricaded with my hand, admiring the beautiful dresses before me. They are the perfect shade of pastel yellow, pinched at the waist with a frilly bottom and off the shoulder sleeves. *It's stunning.* How did she get that so right? And what the hell is the occasion? I try both on and the small fits snug, grinning at the idiot for buying *two* dresses purely because she didn't know my size. *Who does that?* More importantly, *why is she buying me dresses?*

I tiptoe out of the room, feeling nervous as hell and I haven't a clue why but there are butterflies rattling in my stomach trying to fly away and I bloody wish I could fly away right now, this is so embarrassing. My hair is a mess and I have no shoes on.

"Are you going to tell me what this is for?" She turns her head to meet mine from the couch and it's like I pull her off of it. Standing to face me, eyes full of soft admiration, a thousand emotions are whirling around that peculiar head of hers and she's impossible to read. But something is telling me I look decent. It's nothing like the way she looked at me in the shower. This is gentle. *Kind.* But she still doesn't utter a word. "I thought you hated yellow." If she hates this colour so much, why on earth did she buy me a dress in it?

"I think I can make an exception just this once." I am the brightest thing in the room right now. In fact, I am the brightest thing in this entire house, *I'm a beacon of idiocy.*

"You're ridiculous. I can't believe you bought two of these!" Every time she smiles with her teeth it's like it heals another fraction of my broken heart, knowing I'm healing hers, even if it's only a little.

"Well, what if it didn't fit!?" She shrugs her broad shoulders, and I mean, she has a point, but she shouldn't have gotten them at all!

"I am literally the size of an ant." She claws the back of the sofa and she looks like she's ready to pounce over the top of it.

"I know. *Which means I can do this.*" She does exactly that, heading straight for me and I am NOT about to be thrown around in a dress.

"Hayden-" I warn. "Hay- HAYS! NO!" She tugs these uncontrollable giggles from deep inside me and I don't think I have ever laughed the way I laugh with her as she hoists me up over her shoulder, dragging me to the bedroom without my consent as Shep follows curiously and now I'm worried.

"Hayden! Put me down!" My back meets the bed, nearly breaking it on impact.

"Youuuuuu. Are going to plant your ass on this bed, and you can't come out until I say." You have got to be joking. *I am not sitting in here all day!*

"Are you going to tell me what is going on?" What is with all these secrets and weird gifts. I knew she was acting weird.

"Nope."

Oh come on!

"Write in your journal or something." She takes the journal from the foot of the bed, pressing it into my chest and I panic as the pages fly open scrambling to shut it back up.

"I really need to get you that lock and key, huh?" It's nothing special. But no one has ever read my writing. Call myself a writer and I am too scared to show it off. *The irony.* Plus I don't exactly want her reading what I've written. *About her.*

"Fineeeee..." Now I'm really worried. My feet kick up, forcefully hitting the bed so she can see my annoyance but she doesn't care. She never does. Walking out and shutting the door behind her completely carefree as she leaves me and Shep to snuggle. *Asshole.*

I don't know how long it's been. I've been so engrossed in writing that I've lost track of time, minus the interruption of pots and pans clashing from the kitchen as I try to listen in to what the hell she is up to. Now cuddleless because Shep had to have his dinner and the bed is now cold again.

The door finally opens, like a ghost leading me to a secret garden and I waste no time leaping off the bed ready to beat her ass but I'm distracted by the warm glow coming from the crack in the door.

Exiting the room to an overwhelming sense of pure and utter shock, picking my jaw up off the floor as I tread deeper into the heart of the house. A room that was dead, beaten and abused, now feels warm and safe, scattered with candles and rose petals with a vase sat in the middle of a laid table full of *sunflowers*. A tear breaks my strength, trying to hold in this want to ball my eyes out. I finally realise what this has all been about.

*It's **Valentine's Day.***

CHAPTER 32

HAPPY DOOMS DAY

Puppet

My most resented day of the year. My jaw falls open, unable to close it, wandering over to the table trying to muster up the words to thank her but I'm unable to speak. I feel completely foolish with little to no make up on, no shoes or socks and no time to prepare for this. Meanwhile she's stood there in a black shirt, most likely new, her black denim jeans and boots, cutting up vegetables with the sleeves rolled up and I suck my lips in, trying to ignore the fact that this is unnecessarily attractive.

She always slicks her hair back and I'm growing fonder of it by the minute. Everything about her is everything I would have resented. I was never one for the bad boys but I'm swooning like an idiot right now. She's so dark and still full of mystery I desperately want to uncover.

"What is all this!" My hand takes the back of the chair, admiring the cute little red napkins and petals on the table.

"Well. I thought, as I couldn't exactly take you out for Valentine Day, I'd bring Valentine's Day to you." I frown with confusion. This is all so beautiful but why is she even going through all this for me?

"We aren't even dating?"

"Does it matter?" No. But I hope she doesn't think we are. We are closer now, but we aren't that close. I've never been in any sort of relationship with anyone.

"I never took you for the romantic type." A scary serial killer making me pancakes and doing a Valentines dinner is definitely not how I saw this turning out three months ago. I'll be honest, I thought I would be dead by now, if not from my own idiocy, then her getting sick of me.

"I'm not. I've never done this for anyone, so count yourself lucky." I lace my hair through my fingers, tucking it behind my ear and a fire burns beneath my cheeks. There is something about seeing this sweetness in her that's sending me all sorts of crazy.

"I- I don't even know what to say-" I take another look around, taking in the effort and holding back tears, imagining every birthday like this but being left with no one to share it with.

"You don't need to say anything. *Just sit.*" I sit without hesitation. She's showing kindness but she's still so intimidating it makes my hair stand on end.

"Are you cooking what I think you're cooking?" I see her grin from her side profile, the tea towel tossed over her shoulder like a professional and it's making me smile like a little girl. My head rests in the palm of my hands as my elbow leans on the dining room table.

"I told you. I'm the jack of all trades." She did. I indeed underestimated her. I'm swimming in this overwhelming ecstasy.

"You didn't have to do all this. This is too much."

"Trust me. If it was up to me, I wouldn't have. But you deserve this. You deserve some normality *Alora*," her words bleed into my lifeless bones, giving them strength again. I used to hate it when she said my name. But now it makes me swoon. It sounds so gentle from her mouth. She won't admit it but she cares deeply, and this side of her is building my broken bridge. She pulls the tea towel from her shoulder quickly as she spins on her axis towards the fridge. "Which also means! We are going to break that alcohol virginity today." *How did she know I have never drunk alcohol?*

"Mm, mm. Nope, absolutely not." My Mother would turn in her grave.

"Come on! One drink won't hurt." She pulls one of her beers out, walking over to me and my chest locks with this pressure building between my thighs. That feeling again. That dull ache that subconsciously screams to be touched.

"I was always told it was dangerous." Alcohol was a no go for multiple reasons.

"I never said it wasn't. But you also want to live? Do you not?" *Live?* What has living got to do with consuming alcohol?

"And how exactly do they correlate?" My face scrunches, waiting for her to give me an answer as she gazes over my figure silently for a couple of seconds.

"*Freedom*. Living is all about escaping shackles." She confuses me. She said freedom was not possible.

"I thought you didn't believe in freedom?" She undoes the cap of the bottle with her teeth making mine itch before placing it in front of me.

"I don't. But this is what your clouds up here are for *Little Dreamer*." Her index finger taps my head gently, trailing the tip down against my cheek, trying to read my thoughts as I stare at the bottle, enticing me with her touch to trust her. *Is she trying to tell me that freedom lives inside of me?*

"How do I know you haven't drugged it?" Realistically, I know she hasn't. She just opened it in front of me, but I still love to explore this bratty nature I seem to have acquired.

"*You don't.*" My eyes pulse. Hot waves surging through my insides. Why would she even say that? She still loves to instil this fear in me even though I know she won't hurt me anymore.

"You're not funny." I grab the bottle, fiddling with it against my fingers, gathering the condensation as it wets the tips.

"As you keep saying." Her arms cross, waiting for me to drink it and as if I didn't already feel intimidated enough.

SHASSII

I sip it, squinting as the bitter taste hits the back of my throat, swallowing its coarseness. It's definitely, different. But if it does help me chase some freedom then why not? She is staring at me with achievement and it's making me want to drink more. What even is that? *Validation? Praise?*

"Why sunflowers? They don't exactly scream Valentines Day?" I ask curiously, staring at the beautiful shade of yellow, *almost amber?*

"They match your eyes." Before I even have a chance to respond she stands up and makes her way back to the kitchen where she carries on with her cooking, leaving me with bottle in hand as one swig turns to five, that turns to ten, that turns to an empty bottle and I'm definitely feeling something. The smell of spaghetti Bolognese has never been more orgasmic as I sit here drooling, getting the munchies. I wait patiently for my dinner as I watch her and Shep be nothing but themselves, giving him all the love and tossing food into his mouth.

After what feels like four hours when it's probably been about fifty minutes, she begins to plate up and my tummy growls in the desolate silence of the kitchen. *How embarrassing.* This is probably the first proper meal besides take out and snacks I've had and I'm ready to devour this food if I can help it. She finally walks over, plates in hand as she presents it to me and either I'm already drunk, or that looks fucking fantastic. *Who knew she had that in her.*

She notices my empty bottle, replacing it with a new one before sitting down to eat with me and this feels so weird but this anxiety and doubt, all these negative emotions are suddenly *gone?* I feel strangely content right now. Maybe a little too content. I've seen Kacey drunk and it's slightly terrifying. If she could see me now. *Minus the serial killer who ruined my life.* She would be so proud. This isn't exactly your typical *'date'* but it's strongly comfortable.

She admires me from across the table. Like she's looking straight through me as a tiny grin pulls the corner of her mouth, sitting in momentary silence and my eyes shift, trying to figure out what on earth she's looking at before she raises her beer, slumped in her chair.

"Happy *'Doomsday'* Alora." My throat jams, nearly choking on air as I glare at her with detective eyes.

"How did you- I never told-" the realisation smacks me in the face and I want to crawl up into a ball. I was hoping she would leave my birthday out of this and the only way she could have possibly known that was if she took my calendar.

"You read my calendar... Nothings safe with you, is it?"

I chug another few swigs, now accustomed to the sensation, sinking in my self-loathing. Another year older and I'm on a date with a murderer. *Not quite how I pictured my first date.*

"Are you dead yet?" She has yet to touch her food, still heavily fixated on me. Like she's eating me from the inside out with her eyes. And honestly, she already has. She's buried holes inside of me and chewed away at all my defences that were protecting myself from the caged beast. She's now inside of me, making her mark against my walls.

"No..." My teeth graze my bottom lip as I drag it, pushing against my swollen mouth from biting it sore. I could be dead. But I'm not. Part of me still wants to be but she's making life more tolerable. The person who ruined it is making life look fun. I'm learning slowly to let my hair down, consequences be damned. She's trying to teach me that there is no living without danger, and the more I'm around her, the more that is starting to make sense.

"Then I'd say you're pretty safe, wouldn't you?" My thighs clench together tightly beneath the table trying to remember why I should hate every part of her but it's proving to be very difficult when all I can think about right now is how safe I truly am with her. I'm safer here with her than I ever was at home.

"How long have you known?" I begin to shovel food into my mouth, carefree of her judgement. She can't make a meal this banging and expect me not to inhale it. Plus, I dribble in my sleep. It can't get much worse than that.

"Since we met." My chewing stops. Remembering the hypo pen. She must have gone back home. *But why?* "Close your eyes." She swiftly interrupts me like she knows I'm about to ask her more questions as I finish my mouthful, placing my cutlery down on the table.

"Haydennnnnn, enough surprises." *I literally hate surprises.*

"You'll like this one. I promise." I roll my eyes reluctant to shut them but after trying to protest I close them, listening to her shuffle about in the garage from the door behind me.

"Open." She instructs, but I'm nervous, squinting like someone's about to hit me before my eyes nearly fall out of my head at the sight.

"OH MY GOD! IS THAT MY BASS GUITAR?!" She definitely went home and now I am even more curious as to why she would have gone to that length for me when she'd only known me for not even 48 hours.

"Do you play?" I ask playfully.

"Used to. But I'm more of a traditional player myself." She plays guitar too?! What can't she do?!

"You play acoustic?" I contain my excitement, remaining calm on the outside but inside I want to scream.

"You sound surprised." She takes another mouthful, and her blunt answers on their own are enough to make any woman fold. I'm convinced.

"You're just- full of surprises. It's nice. This. Learning more about you..." I gaze at her softly and I don't know if that was me or the alcohol talking.

"You said you wanted to know more about me."

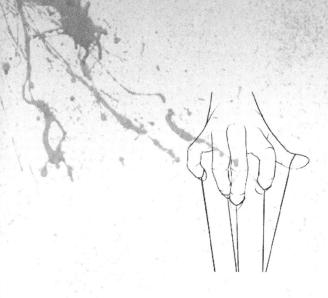

CHAPTER 33

WHAT IS BEAUTIFUL

Puppeteer

Her pupils dilate as she sets her focus on me. I'm finally giving her what she wants and the alcohol is definitely getting to her head. I can almost see heart shaped irises. She's so interested in me that her food is going cold but she has eaten a fair amount. She couldn't get it down her gob quick enough.

"What music do you like?" She asks beaming with excitement.

"Linkin Park. Eminem. Stuff like that." She tilts her head with her thoughts in the clouds.

"Eminem? Who's that?" I nearly drop my beer. What is this blasphemy? How on earth? *God she really was sheltered.*

"I'm sorry. Did you just say, *who's that?*"

"I'm serious! Who's that!" Her. Fucking. Dimples.

"He's only the most iconic rapper in music history!?" She puckers her lips, shrugging her shoulders as she giggles like a ghost in the walls.

"Never heard of him. He can't be that good." Oh, she's playing with fire right now.

"You wanna bet? I'll play a CD right now and you tell me you don't love it." I place my empty bottle down on the table, right about ready to fly out my seat.

"You know what? Music sounds like a great idea actually." She slouches over the table, carelessly drinking from her bottle, nearly spilling it down her chin. *Maybe we lay her off the beer for a bit.*

I make my way over to the TV where a little stereo sits, shuffling through my collection of CD's, VHS tapes and a small collection of DVDs to find my Eminem discs. I plug the stereo in to make sure the tattered thing still works before sliding the CD in and pressing play, completely forgetting that,

'The Real Slim Shady' *is the first song to start playing out the speakers.*

The stereo is crackly and worn but the music is still decent. Her face is a picture, and I can't help but belly laugh at the horrified expression on those rosy little cheeks, clearly sucking in the urge to burst out with laughter but she finally lets it go and my stomach flickers.

"You really are full of surprises-" I'm glad she's finding this amusing as the CD betrays me, trying to suck in air between her hysterical howling that I could listen to for hours. *My own broken little record.*

I assume she's had enough of him as she leaps up off the chair towards me, tipping on her tiny toes playfully, bending down beneath me to have a nosey at my collection of ancient melodies and I never get tired of this view. Her fingers trace the stack of plastic, reading the spines like she's searching for something, pulling a bunch out and shuffling through them. *Shania Twain, Celine Dion, Bon Jovi, Aerosmith, Black Eye Peas, P!nk. Coldplay. Linkin Park-*

"Oh my god! I *LOVE Florence & The Machine!*" My heart buckles. A chilling cold smothers my body with distant memories dancing in the void that is this living room as she takes the CD out, replacing them and I know exactly what song will play. It's the same song she nearly burnt out the CD with. The song she would spend endless hours blasting as she pranced around the room. When life was simpler. When she was happy. Only for a short moment, but that moment holds my humanity and my dormant heart by strings. She slides the CD in and I swallow those memories, now in this one with *her*.

Play - 'Florence & The Machine - You've Got The Love'

She's like an excited little kitten, leaping up off the floor towards the table where she grabs my beer, pulling away from me like she knows I'm going to try and take it away from her and parallels flash before my eyes. Happiness never looked so beautiful on her and I'm frozen, only able to watch as she prances around *my* living room, her messy hair dancing in her chaos amongst the silence. Her dress wraps around her waist like a tight hug as she spins like a music box, angelic but eerie. Paying no mind to my furniture as she uses my sofa as a climbing frame, a beacon of much needed light between these gloomy walls. My beacon of light. Memories serve a purpose. To help you to hold on to happiness and pain, to hold on to the ways they make you feel, both good and bad but happy memories have a way of re-playing in different ways.

"Come on! Dance with me!" *Do I look like a dancer?* I do not dance. But she doesn't seem to care as she leaps off the sofa towards me, grabbing my wrist with little strength, realising I won't budge. "Fine. I'll dance on my own." *Freedom.* She's feeling it. And I suddenly hate that I can't give her more than this. She deserves to see the world. See what life has in store for her, but I'm *selfish*. Possibly *envious*. Maybe something else.

She chugs the bottle, her arms intertwining with the rhythm filling the room and I think I finally understand what *Beauty* is.

It's her.

She's beautiful.

She is that flower in a storm that survived its wrath and kept growing. Blooming. Strong enough to withstand mother nature and all its pain. Standing out against the rest. Standing out to me. That tiny sliver of hope that keeps your heart beating. Some people see beauty in possessions, poetry, art, like it's physical. But it's not. *It's a feeling.* She calms the demons inside of me and makes me view the world differently when I'm around her.

SHASSI

Colours look brighter. Time starts moving. Messy is where she should be. This free-spirited girl in front of me, thriving on the smallest thing fuels my guilt. I'm holding up a mirror with no centre piece. She's always been a prisoner.

She tries again, ushering me to join her and I tilt my head back in annoyance but my feet walk with her, drinking in that euphoria, bumping into me as she sways her body and I take her hand and hold it high above her head. She turns on instinct, floppy and lightweight, giggling to herself on cloud nine nearly stepping on my feet. I'm more worried about hers in my steel toe caps, swigging the remnants of *my* beer, she loses her balance as she tilts her head back into me, crashing into my stomach, sniggering at her clumsiness as she nearly drops the bottle before I catch it.

"Easyyyyy *Love*. I got you." She uses my body as a foundation, trying to correct her balance. I grip her by the waist as her palms find mine with the empty bottle in the other and she's looking up at me like a lovesick puppy, inches from my mouth. My jaw clenches until it hurts, fighting all the reasons I shouldn't crash my lips against hers right now. *She's intoxicated.* This desperation to devour every part of her and strip her of her pure and happy little heart that is beating in sync with mine. This cracked dolly just waiting to be dropped. She is searching for *Love* in the wrong place as she drowns in my eyes, hypnotised by her balls of fire, burning to feel something. I will break her. Burn her. Tear her apart. It will be the death of her and I don't think I'd want to breathe the same air as her if I ruin her life again.

"Hayden…" My name in her mouth is like ecstasy. Pulling me closer without consent, placing my finger against her lips and I don't know who that was for.

"Tell me tomorrow…" I'm terrified to know what she wants to say to me, and I'm sure she would regret saying something silly under the influence. Three beers in and she's ready to pass out, clinging to my shirt to keep her up. She flutters her lashes as she fights to keep her sleepy eyes open that are tugging at my heartstrings. "Let's get you to bed aye?" She protests, moaning and groaning, mumbling under her breath as I pull her tiny body up and slide my forearm underneath the back of her knees. This seems to be a running theme and I hate playing the hero. It doesn't bode well with my image, but I've been doing a lot of it lately.

I carry her to bed, placing her down onto the mattress like she could shatter. And she will. *But just not tonight.*

I wrap her up, tending to her like a wounded doe, brushing her knotty locks out of her face, pushing them behind her ear and my fingers find her soft, warm cheek. She subconsciously nudges into my touch, chasing it with her eyes glued shut, getting cosy underneath the blanket with her arm hanging out to regulate her body temperature but my attempt to escape is cut off as she reaches for my hand and I hold a breath, exhaling slowly.

"You're not a *Monster*..." She mumbles against the pillow. Lightly clutching to my fingers. And I wish she was right. But she's not, and this is the alcohol talking. Tomorrow, she will see me like she's meant to, but for right now I sit back down next to her, inhaling my anticipated regret before sliding in beside her, holding her deadweight as my chest becomes her pillow, completely unphased by the idea as she delicately plays with the fabric of my shirt.

"Do you want to know why you're wrong *Little Dreamer*?" Her distorted gaze meets mine for a short moment before closing them again, squeezing my fingers gently in response. "Because I'm the daughter of a Devil. *Innocence*. A bad man. A man that would take pleasure in harming you. A man that would stop at nothing to see me unhappy. Pain no child should ever have to endure at such a young age. A man who would beat me for polishing his shoes wrong. Burn my skin until I begged for mercy. Cut all my hair off as punishment for liking the wrong gender." A digit rolls down my cheek, my eyes burning from fixating into space for so long that I forgot to blink.

"I'm a *Monster*, because if I'm not. I have nothing left."

I peer down at her peaceful state, now fallen into a heavy sleep, her breathing soft but deep with exhaustion, knowing that she most likely heard none of that. But maybe that was the point. And these tears can fuck off. She makes me feel so many unwanted and unwelcome emotions but a weight is slightly lifted, concentrating on her fragile fingers through mine, running my tips against her scalp consuming her heat. Her life is laying in my hands and this has never felt so right.

SHASSII

CHAPTER 34

WONDERWALL

Puppet

Play – 'Similar minds – Kilu'

I don't know what hurts more, my body or my head as my eyes creep open, wanting to hiss at the sun beaming into the bedroom making my temples pulsate, before I dive underneath the duvet like a hermit.

"How's your head treating you, *Puppet*?" Irritable mumbles leave my mouth against the duvet, slowly creeping back into the land of the living inch by inch until I can see her outside of my hole by the door.

"Never let me drink againnnnn." My hands find the bed, slamming them down in regret before smothering my face with my palms, trying to rub some life into my burning pupils.

"But you were having so much fun?" *She is loving this.*

"I feel like a ninety-year-old woman." My body is stiff and cranky, rolling around the bed trying to loosen my glued-up joints when I realise, I'm in a pyjama top and pants.

"Did you-?"

"Nothing I've not seen before." Just because I stripped in front of her, doesn't give her permission to look at me without my consent. Her cocky grin is so smackable.

"Hayden!"

"You were trying to strip in front of me." My face blows into a heat rash and I squeeze my eyes shut hoping this is a dream. *I really am never drinking again.*

"Calm down *Love*. I kept your underwear on." A sigh of relief protrudes through my mouth, falling limp back into the bed and I want to go and dig my own damn grave in her back garden. "I told you. *I won't touch you.*" I swallow my deceit. Because for some reason, *that doesn't comfort me anymore*. I'm craving her touch like a flower craves the sun to grow. My thoughts take on a mind of their own, sickening sin flashes before me, picturing her using my vulnerable body and I close my legs underneath the duvet to try and ease my disturbed discomfort. She could have had me. *But she didn't.*

She doesn't think I see how she looks at me. How she undresses me with her eyes. Peeling away at my purity like a disease.

Her eyes shift to the glass of water on the bed side table, next to some pain killers and my insulin.

"Hurry up. I want to show you something."

"If you promise not to make me drink again." My body weight slumps into my hands.

"You'll be begging for it when I'm done with you *Puppet*." Her mysterious nature terrifies me. *What the hell is that meant to mean?* But I do as I'm told, swallowing my pills and performing my daily ritual before making my way to the living room, trying to focus on my feet but God I feel rough.

A few cardboard boxes scatter the coffee table and a giant leather gig bag lays on the sofa, a thick layer of grey dust has taken up residence on the lid.

"Is that what I think it is?" Where was she hiding that? She didn't go back up into the loft, surely? She ushers me to open it and I do cautiously, unzipping it, lifting the lid and a beautiful rough auburn acoustic guitar with blistered marking, the same colour as my hair, coated in gloss, pristine, sits in the bag. I line the shapes in the woodwork with the tips of my fingers. This is probably the most prized possession in this prison. It clearly means something to her otherwise it wouldn't be in mint condition. Like an amethyst in amongst basalt rock.

Her presence consumes me, approaching me from behind slowly, reaching for the neck of the guitar and pulling it out carefully up above my head as she sits down to get comfortable with it.

"You're only getting this once." I'm beaming with excitement. *She's actually going to play!* I watch her intensely as she tunes it up, fixated on more stories burrowed inside her flesh I've not seen before as the sun lights up the back of her hands. She squints in pain every time she strums a bum tune until she gets it right and it's like second nature as her fingers begin to fall into a melody I've not heard before.

Wonderwall - Guitar Version

~And backseat, the word is on the street that the fire in your heart is out.
I'm sure you've heard it all before but you never really had a doubt.
I don't believe that anybody. Feels the way I do about you now.

And all the roads we have to walk are winding.
And all the lights that lead us there are blinding.
There are many things that I would like to say to you, but I don't know how.
Because maybe,
You're gonna be the one that saves me.
And after all.
You're my wonderwall. ~

Right now, nothing else in the world matters but this very moment. This normality. This happiness she's trying to give me through acts of reluctant *kindness* just to make me smile. To show me she has a soft side that's buried underneath all the rubble and dirt. The girl who longed for a simple life. A life better than this one.

She has no idea how ethereal she looks right now, tiger light slicing through her olive skin. Her fingers are singing a song I don't know but I don't care because it sounds phenomenal. To still be able to play this well when I know she hasn't touched that guitar for years is astonishing. Her eyes are closed and I'm glad because water is trickling down my cold cheeks breaking down all my feelings. *Happiness, sadness, guilt, contentment*, it's all rolled into one big mess as I sit here, staring at the woman who stole my life from me and gave me a new one. I've accepted that my life as it was, a life I'm clinging to, never will be.

This? This is now. This is real. I've come to grow quite fond of this new little world I'm trapped in, where we play stupid little CD's, dance till the sun goes down and she plays me guitar to brighten up my face.

She is all I have left.

"Did you even know that song?" She laughs with amusement as my focus is completely in my thoughts, staring through her without realising, shaking myself out of it as the room goes quiet again.

"I didn't. What's it about?" She rests the guitar in her lap, the curve mounting her leg as she takes out her papers to roll a cigarette.

"The person you constantly find yourself thinking about." She says she's not the romantic type but if I'm not mistaken. Did she just play me a *Love* song?

"It's beautiful." She won't stop staring at me and I'm so flustered I'm about ready to have a cold shower. Everything she does surprises me when it shouldn't. She murders bad men for a living.

I've just never met anyone like her. She's a damaged engine that needs the right parts to bring her back to life.

We've spent the entire day going through some of her old things. Little heirlooms. I think she needed this as much as I did. I found one of her old high-school sweatshirts amongst some things she kept when she played for their soccer team.

CHICAGO
13
MOORE

She gave me it to wear. It smells of nostalgia. She told me lots of funny stories to try and cover up the pain she also endured during school. I know because we have that in common. She doesn't have to tell me; I can see it in her eyes.

Low music accompanied us as we went through many CDs, giving the house some much needed life. And I've never seen her so,

Normal?

Lounging around the bungalow with just a white tank top on and black joggers, free from her second face that I'm still trying to get accustomed to and a few thick silver chains she never takes off. She looks like your typical teenager, *if you ignore her age*. Like a giant in a hobbit house as she walks around and her size still makes me nervous. I didn't even know it was possible for a woman to have such a bulky build. She could literally pass as a man and I don't know who should be more afraid of her.

Me or them.

There is something so humbling about a woman of her strength removing sickness from this world. Sickness that lies in power, cowards hiding behind screens and paper. The government. People like my father. I've had weeks to get my head around her *work* and the more I think about it, the more I understand. She was let down by a system meant to protect her and as vengeance she's taken it upon herself to become their enemy, *it makes perfect sense.*

She opens the garage door, making her way outside to do something as I'm snuggled up on the couch and I almost leap out of my skin when a four-legged friend runs inside the garage door, meowing with aggressive neediness but Shep doesn't seem at all phased, glaring at it from his bed.

"Oh my god! Hey kitty!" Where on earth did it come from? Hayden follows it back in and she doesn't look at all phased either.

"She must have known I had company." She doesn't take long to crawl towards me, rubbing herself up against my leg.

"Is she yours?" *She never mentioned she had a cat?*

"She's a stray. She comes and goes. Sometimes for months at a time." That explains why I've never seen her before. It also explains the cat food I found under the sink considering she has a *dog*.

"Does she have a name?" I run my fingers through her tough coat. She's a beautiful grey tabby with the eyes of a Disney princess.

"Whiskas." *Again with the originality.*

"Really...Whiskas?" My judgement is oozing out of me.

"What?!... It looked like the box." She's so simple it pains me. Sometimes I wonder if she was a man born into the wrong body.

"Where did she come from? Where does she go when she's not here?"

"I haven't got a clue. I'm not usually home a lot so her food bowl and water are usually outside. She rarely comes inside." She claims she doesn't care about anything. But someone like that wouldn't show acts of kindness towards an animal that's not even hers. She puts up this front but deep down I'm realising her heart is far bigger than I thought.

"She must really like you." There is envy in her gaze as Whiskas sits beside me on the couch, yearning for attention.

CHAPTER 35

TWISTED DREAMS

Puppet

Play - 'Nervous - The Neighbourhood'

"**G**ood girl Puppet. Spread your petals for me." Her warmth invades my skin, wet lips smothering my stomach with hunger worse than a starved man, knocking down my foundations until I am a pile of rubble and concrete. She lowers her hand between my thighs until my hips buckle, choking on my dignity, clutching to my sliver of sanity as the Monster feeds, sucking out the piece of me until there is no ME left -

My eyes burst open, glaring at the ceiling in complete disgust, rubbing my thighs together feeling slick heat between my lips.

"What were you dreaming about?" My upper body shoots up, sitting on my elbows in panic as she's slumped back in the chair, fingers tracing her mouth and I gulp on instinct, imagining how soft they were against my skin.

"Jesus Hayden! You scared me!" I chase my heartbeat, handling my chest like it's injured.

"Don't avoid the question, *Puppet*." My bottom lip disappears as I pull it into my mouth, desperately trying to push those images out of my mind.

"*I wasn't...*"

"*Liar.*"

"I can't remember." It's like she's purposely trying to tease my imagination, sitting in a tight tank top that accentuates her defined muscles beneath that I can't seem to stop glaring at. Her trousers hang low on her waist in the seat exposing the V line that travels up underneath the indented fabric of her top.

"Don't lie to me, *Innocence*." *She knows.* Please don't tell me I was making noises in my sleep.

"Why were you watching me sleep?" I want to move. Cover myself from her dirty glare that's stripping me of all my *Innocence*, feeling entirely too vulnerable in my little white shorts and crop top that feel entirely too tight around my body but it's because they are stuck to my skin and I'm sure my nipples are pinching the fabric right now.

"It's fascinating. Listening to your soft whimpers." I beg for the floor to swallow me whole, tucking my hair behind my ear as I look out the window so she can't see the deceit in my face.

"I don't know what you're talking about." I can't see her, but she stands slowly in my peripheral vision, stalking towards me as my blood runs cold. I'm trying to focus on anything but her looming in my direction, my cheeks betraying me as they sting with blush.

"Yes. You do." The mattress moves, subtly lowering my feet as she mounts the bed. "It's ok. You can tell me," her body encapsulates my legs beneath her, crawling up the bed towards me and all my oxygen fleas from my lungs in fear, terrified to turn my head.

"Why the sudden loss of words, *Little Dreamer*?" My flower is pulsating, aching to be watered. *This pain is crippling me.* "Tell me..."

She whispers to me, leaning into my ear, trapping me against the bed frame as she removes the duvet from underneath us, letting a gust of cold wind to pass through before sliding her knee between my thighs agonisingly slowly. My mouth betrays me, letting a timid sigh of arousal bless her ear, fighting this whirlwind inside of me to break the silence.

...

"You..." Her searing lips engrave my skin, rubbing them gently underneath my earlobe and I realise we haven't been this close since she revealed her devastatingly handsome face to me.

"I what *Princess*? Use your words." Everyday I'm finding it harder to fight her, to resist her. She makes me want to commit the worst kind of sin. *Fornication*.

"Touched me..." I choke out quietly, feeling almost ashamed. I have never touched myself. I've never understood it or felt a need to explore it. *Fornication. Sex*. It's always been a myth to me. Something people indulge in out of boredom, but as she sits between my legs, I realise it's much more than that. It's *intimacy. Lust. Submission*. The way I submitted to her in the woods. That same feeling is throbbing against *her* knee.

"Where. Show me." I shudder against her mouth as she entices me with faint kisses around my throat. Building up the courage to move my hand, I trail the tips of my fingers between my centre line until I'm hovering over my pelvis, too scared to take that next step.

"What did I touch you with?" Her whispers are sending me crazy. I'm holding onto my dignity, afraid to let her hear me but my hand finds hers, craving to feel what my dream opened up to me.

"*You've never touched yourself. Have you.*" I'm nineteen and I'm embarrassed to say I've never been intimate with myself, let alone someone else. But something most likely naive inside of me is telling me I can trust her. I shake my head, rubbing against her cheekbone. She knew I was lying about my body count. She can read me better than I can read myself. Ripping out my pages to keep as souvenirs. "That ache you feel? It means you need to touch it. To relieve it. Can you do that for me?"

My nod is a miss match of yes's and no's. I don't know what I'm doing. This is ridiculous. But this *need*. This pounding between my legs is taking control of me like a second heart leaving my mind dormant.

I finally find the courage to drop my fingers lower, until I find the lining of my knickers, already damp with heat and the sensation scrunches my face.

"Good Girl, *Alora*..." Her words are like venom, paralysing me, crushing my heart and lungs as her hand creeps over mine. "Then what did I do?"

There is barely any space between us as she pins me down with her very existence.

"You- You made it feel, *good*." Her hand guides mine, gently rubbing my fingers in circular motion against the saturation, digging for my songs but I exhale through my nose.

It's there. *That feeling.* That lust that bucks my hips into her, grasping to that sensation ripping down my walls.

"Like this?..." I could drown in *this*, letting it collapse my lungs. *I'm cracking.* I confirm this pleasure between my legs as I nod my head in approval, too nervous to speak.

"Open your mouth *Puppet*. Let me hear you."

Her cologne rubs at my nose. Her smell, her voice, her demons. They have all found refuge inside my heart.

My mouth parts, releasing months of unknowing relief and I feel her cheek move mine as she grins, continuing to teach me this hollow addiction growing inside of me. Soon to take me by force.

I twitch like a rabbit as our fingers mould between the crease of my lips. I'm terrified to venture further but my panties are soaked and I want to rip them off.

"Not so innocent now are we *Love*. So wet for *me*." For *her*. I am. She's becoming my bone marrow. An essential part of my body needed to function. My strings needed to move. My oxygen tank needed to breathe.

I'm her *plaything*.

Her *dolly*.

Hers.

She slides the fabric to the side exposing me and I hitch with sudden embarrassment, feeling my wetness slick against my fingers as I touch it without consent. *Soft. Warm. Swollen velvet.*

"You feel that?" She whispers so gently it makes my muscles spasm as she applies pressure to the back of my fingers, running rings around my clit, nibbling on the tender part of my neck with temptation before pushing the palm of my hand down against my sensitive spot, curving my fingers as she dips me inside myself. "Is that what you felt, *Puppet*?" My head is ringing, pins and needles are attacking every nerve in my body. *Yes. Yes, this is exactly what I felt.*

"Ye-s..." She pushes once more, revelling in these waves crashing into my body and I feel disgusting, but I also feel relieved until she removes my fingers, slowly pulling them towards my mouth. We have not looked at each other once and I think that was purely to keep my confidence but when she pulls away, analysing the redness in my cheeks, the sweat building around my hairline and my fuzzy eyes, my confidence dissipates, sucking in her accomplishment as I lay here, depraved. Deprived. And hungry for release, eating me from the inside now totally fragile and humiliated.

"Why- Why did you stop?" She presses my tainted fingers against my bottom lip, parting instinctively, like they belong there, pushing them inside my mouth to taste myself and I internally scowl at how sinful this is.

"When you're ready." Her eyes are glued to my mouth, inhaling like she's envious, grazing her bottom lip through her teeth before taking my hand and licking between my fingers as she hugs them with the fork of her tongue, never breaking this eye contact that kills me. My stomach swells watching her intensely as she tastes me, how gentle her warmth is against my skin as she cleans up *my mess*. Her eyes quiver, like I'm the most delightful thing she's put in her mouth and it's so warm and mellow that my heart is not the only thing fluttering.

She's right. I don't know if I am ready. I don't know what the hell just happened but I feel violated. Unfulfilled and unsatisfied. *How do I know when I'm ready? Ready for what?* All I can think about is this throbbing between my thighs, calling out to me.

"Coffee?" *Coffee?* She lifts herself up off the bed, acting totally nonchalant and I don't know if I'm relieved, so we can pretend this never happened. Or annoyed. *Did that mean anything to her?*

She kept her word. She still hasn't touched me and it's bringing out this girl inside of me that I don't even know. Immoral acts of desire begin to plague my mind, imagining all the ways I want her to have me until I shake them off, closing my legs back up and sinking into the duvet. She's a mockery and I'm so irritated, lying here staring at the ceiling as she exits the room with a grin so playful I may just entertain it.

SHASSII

CHAPTER 36

DELICATE ANGEL

Puppeteer

I can still hear her singing in my ear and it took everything inside of me to hold myself from destroying her sweet little flower. Unable to touch what is *mine* proved to be highly difficult, but she will not be able to resist me much longer.

I've given her just enough to let her deteriorate, pining for me inside her. She will scream for me, and I will happily suck out all her insecurities. She has nothing to be ashamed of.

She is the definition of *perfect*, and I intend to ruin that. Mould her to chase this high she so desperately craves. Succumb to this darkness she is so undeniably drawn too. She will learn there is no greater feeling than letting yourself go underneath the grasp of malevolence. I want to watch her lose herself as I chase away all her *innocence* until all that purity she holds onto so dearly is infested with unimaginable starvation for transgression. I want her to willingly surrender *to me.*

That is the purest taste of *corruption.*

My *delicate little angel* will fall as I did, and I will show her what it means to relish in pain. Use it to strengthen her will. I know deep down in there somewhere is a little girl curious to know why people like me only function on suffering. I will show her just how bittersweet giving into your own demons can be. Teach her how to control them, to feed and nurture them.

I've left her to her own devices, letting her imagination run wild. I saw an opportunity and I took it. She shouldn't have been moaning my name in her sleep like a needy little *whore.* She has no idea the velocity of my need to fuck her senseless. She's bringing out an animal in me I didn't even know I had. I've never desired anyone the way I do her and it's becoming a weakness untold. She is the noose around my neck and I am terrified that if she said jump. *I would.* Is it normal to yearn for someone so much that you quiver at the mere sight of them in your head? Her skin in my mouth tasted like salted caramel. A delicacy, where you have to hold yourself back from devouring the entire tub.

She's been in there for about thirty minutes, probably trying to muster up the courage to face me but I have no intention of going easy on her now. I will tempt her thoughts until she is on her knees.

Finally, the door opens. And my *Little Puppet* surprises me, wearing only a new pair of lacey knickers and a cropped top I must have thrown in there, exposing her tender skin and the tone in her tummy. She doesn't like being left unsatisfied and now she's dangling herself in front of me so that I give her what she wants. *Clever girl.* But she's going to have to try harder than that.

She wanders over to the kitchen cabinets, overly extending her arms to reach unnecessary heights. Her back is to me so I have a perfect view of her peachy fucking ass and if she's not careful I'll bite a chunk out of it next time.

Testing me further, she claws a glass from the shelf edging it as she glares back at me with mischief beaming from her, once doe eyes that have now inhabited the gaze of a sultry siren, exchanging a threat with words.

"*I dare you, Alora.*"

Play - 'Praying - Isabel LaRosa'

She tugs it a little more letting it smash on the tiled floor, shattering like my patience as I clench my jaw, kissing my teeth before storming over towards her. My boots crush the glass underneath my feet until the palm of my hand finds her throat, lifting her off the floor until her bare ass meets the counter, tilting my head as I stare through her challenging eyes. She's suddenly grown some balls and my plan is working, but she's asking for something her fragile little mind can't handle yet. I'd rip her to shreds, but I'm not opposed to teasing the idea. *Let's test it shall we?*

"You shouldn't have done that..." The way I spoke must have been of a different nature because her eyes explode at my statement. I bend down, picking up the largest piece of glass broken off on the floor, edging it towards her before holding it to her throat, refraining from drawing blood so I can watch it run the length of her centre until it's skimming her pantie line. The thought alone causes me to wet my lips before nipping the thin lace of her undies until it pings free instead. Her challenging little eyes soon become balls of fear as she jumps, clamping them shut so she doesn't have to look at me. They fall down against the counter between her legs as she straddles me, already a breathless mess with her pussy fully exposed against my denim jeans.

"Do you trust me, *Alora*?" She barely responds, hesitant to admit that she feels safe in the arms of a killer but her silence is insufferable. I want to hear her sweet tongue. "I need an answer." She nods sporadically, telling me yes without words and I grind my teeth. "Words."

I hold her firmly in place by the throat with my left hand, grazing the sharp side of the glass against her inner thigh with my right but she doesn't fight. She wants this. That euphoria. *That freedom in losing yourself.*

"Y-es!..." *Good.*

I grip the shard to apply enough pressure to pierce her sensitive flesh, harming us both, only enough to let blood rush to the surface of the cut.

"Ow-!..." My mouth salivates as the little gash fills with red wine, rubbing the fresh wound and she hisses like an injured kitten, tilting her head back to rest on the cabinet. Her red velvet taints my thumb as I grab her chin, forcing her to watch me as I take it in my mouth. She needs to learn to watch me claim what is *Mine*. My eyes roll, seeing only red as my lips find her skin, my teeth chattering to rip her apart as I drop the glass, pulling her groin into mine abruptly. My blood marks her ass from my open wound, listening to her sigh into the void as I crawl down her frame, gripping the bottom of her thigh and lifting it until it's inches from my mouth.

I hover over the wound, warmth preparing it for the sting before I taste her on my tongue. I flatten it against her cut, my piercing indenting her skin, cleaning it up as my teeth carefully nibble around the opening, inches from her sweet spot that's making me salivate at the thought of wearing her sweet liquor on my tongue. I suck her into my mouth, giving her just a glimpse of the plans I have in store for her when she completely and entirely gives her body over to me, *because she will*.

Copper invades my mouth as I tend to *my* harm and I exhale with pent up relief. Feeding off my trauma is my own source of pleasure. I've not killed for weeks. I've not shed blood or tasted its sweetness. I'm deprived and she's letting me feed my cravings. Such a good little *blood bag*.

I suck her skin into my mouth, gripping her tighter as she squirms in my hold, breaking that delicate barrier of tender flesh with a pretty bruise that leaves her inner thigh raw and bloody, marking what will soon belong to me. She doesn't know it yet, but her blood on my tongue is where it belongs, making me hard in my fucking boxers at the thought of making her cry my name.

"Act like a brat. You get treated like one." She's heaving so heavily and I've not even touched her which is making a wicked smile grace my ugly face. This rebellious nature she's exploring is exactly what I wanted. She's spent her entire life walking on eggshells. I want her to hunt for the thrill in danger.

I lift her off the counter and she naturally wraps around me, her essence invading my scent as I walk over the glass so she doesn't injure her feet towards the sofa, placing her face down on the couch with her ass up in the air. Her shins rest against the side of the chair and she stretches out her arms, revealing the perfect arch and the dimples in her lower back as the arm holds her hips up. She likes to go mute when I'm stripping her of her regality. Like it helps her ignore the way I'm conquering her body.

This time, she has no pants to cover up her arousal and she's dripping, as am I at the sight of her. Fighting every impulse to indulge in my dessert laying on a silver platter. But I refrain. Running my fingertips lightly against her inner thigh, lining the outside of her sensitive little rose, so gently that I'm barely touching it. I bite my lip hard at the way she responds to me when a moan slips from her mouth, followed by a heavy gasp when the palm of my hand strikes her ass, already going red raw on impact. This time, *harder*.

"Count for me." She doesn't respond, but I know she heard me, and I strike again, feeling the pulse between my legs harden at my bare skin against hers. It takes her a minute to open her mouth as I massage her skin like putty between my fingers.

"*T-wo!...*"

"*Just like that baby.*" My hand connects again and the sting causes me to fight with my eyes as I lose them in the back of my skull.

"*Three-*"

"*Fo-ur!...*" I grab her left leg, lifting it up to rest on the arm of the chair, spreading her pretty pussy for me and strike between her legs, smacking it to force a yelp to escape her.

"*Five!*" I was gentle with her last time, but she wants this just as much as I do. We will build that tolerance. I take a step to grab her by the scruff of her hair, pulling her back up until she's practically inside of me, wedged between me and the arm of the couch with nowhere to go and I watch her carefully as she pants with all her might.

"Why did you lie to me, *Puppet.*" She knows exactly what I'm referring to and her bottom lip trembles, trying to get the words out.

"I didn't wan-t you to laugh." Being a virgin at nineteen seems to be forbidden. Like a sin in itself purely because you're careful with who you hand your diamonds over to. But she's a good girl. *Sensible.*

"Why would I laugh? At their misfortune maybe." Now she is *Mine* to take. Maybe I'm not worthy of her body, but I'm greedy and selfish. She weeps for me in ways that have me shaking.

"Are- are you going to *fuck* me now?" My brow raises at her bold assumption. She wants me to rid her of her insecurities. She wants me to finally remove a part of her that dreads to face her bullies. Teased for being the odd one out when really she doesn't see just how special she is.

"No." She huffs in disappointment. But I will not fuck her purely to fulfil a ridiculous high school requirement. I will fuck her when she realises her worth and gives that privilege to me. Virginity is to be tended to with care.

It's not something you rip away like you do with someone's miserable life. She will learn to use her words.

She's not a slut. And I won't treat her like one until she's begging for me to fill her up. *When she chooses.* Only then will I rip that clarity from inside of her and fill her with my monsters.

"Is it because I'm untouched? I'm not experienced?" I don't know who the hell made her think that, but my grip tightens around her hair in annoyance.

"No. It's because you're not an object." Her muscles relax against me, like my words relieve her.

"If you want me to, I will. When and *only* when you are ready. Do you understand me?" She nods in agreement, trembling against me now that the adrenaline has worn off. I turn her to face me, all flustered and disorientated. "I need you to tell me you understand *Alora.*" Even in her most vulnerable state, she stands in my hands so comfortably. She trusts me completely and it frightens me the lengths I will go to prove to her I will do anything to keep her safe.

"I- understand." My fingers trace her hot cheeks. She looks lost again and I hate it. She doesn't know what she wants. And that is only for her to decide. She needs to figure that out on her own.

"Go and clean yourself up, *Love.*"

CHAPTER 37

A HELPING HAND

Puppet

Play – 'Running Away – Genevieve Stokes'

It's been about a week and all I've thought about are the words that she spoke.

If you want me to, I will. When and only when you are ready. Do you understand me? I practically threw myself at her and thinking about it, all I've done is throw myself at her but she's rejected me. Maybe she's lying to save her from hurting my feelings. She said I wasn't an object? I never said I was. But I guess I was a little desperate. She's right. I assumed that is all she wanted from me and strangely, she didn't seem at all phased. She didn't want me. Or she did but I expected her to be like any other man I've heard about. But she isn't. *Nor is she a man.*

She's a woman who has only ever put my needs before hers. Now that I think about it. I didn't throw myself at her to please her. I did it to please me.

I've grown this attraction that is now hard to shake. Either that or I'm so lonely that my mind is deceiving me. She has given me all but a spoonful of this darkness she inhabits and I'm drawn to it like a nocturnal animal. I thrive in it. *I feel alive.* She's damaged but she is not broken. There is good in her. Good that's been abused and wronged. But for some reason, when she's with me, I see that redemption inside her that I hoped from day one would keep me safe and it has. *She has.* I know it's wrong of me to even be thinking about her in this light. She's a woman. What does that make me? Am I gay? I don't even know what I am, but I know that when she pulls me close and tempts my thoughts, nothing about it feels disgusting. It feels so unbelievable natural. Looking back, I don't think I've ever found boys *hot*. Not ones I've seen anyway, and the most I've spoken to a boy was in a queue for my morning coffee. I was so taken back by his words I almost dropped it. He told me I have nice eyes and that was a compliment, right? But I hated it. Yet, when she speaks of me like I'm a gift, I can physically feel my cheeks burning. I've spent my entire life around girls, due to being at an all-girls school and college, but only now am I realising that this attraction, this thud in between my legs every time she looks at me? It's not unfamiliar. It's only unfamiliar because I've tried so long to deny the way I really feel. A feeling that's been there way before she walked into my life. Or should I say, forced her way into my life.

I was always so envious of Kacey. Her beautiful blonde hair that reaches her ass and her stunning ocean eyes, far deeper than Hays though. Her defined tummy muscles that slim her waist and look so cute in low rise jeans. Flares that accentuate her ass and lip gloss that make her lips way too unbelievably plump. But now I'm wondering if that was even envy. *Oh god, am I really attracted to women?* Now that I think about it, it makes this so much more terrifying. Does it even count? I mean, Hays is basically a man so now I'm just entirely confused.

My overly stimulated thoughts are pulled from me as the door goes, I take my pen off the paper to look up, finding her smothered from head to toe, yet again in oil and I clamp my legs together at the unwanted rush. *For God sake Alo.* And how has she not fixed that bike yet? I say that like I know anything about bikes.

"You'll be dead by the time that things fixed." She waltzes back into the garage, where her solid voice morphs into an echo.

"*Not if I can help it.* Here. Give me a hand." She talks from the other side of the wall and I frown. Is she asking me to go into the garage? This is new. But I comply. Making my way over to the door, peering in like I'm waiting for the principal to call me in to sit down.

"Hold this for me, *Puppet.*" Her entire off-white tank top is completely ruined with dirty fingerprints and marks, the back end of the bike is jacked up and there are parts scattered all over the floor.

"Are you sure I should be in here? I don't want to mess anything up." She ignores me, like I asked a stupid question and holds a spanner out for me to take, standing there looking like a fish out of water as I hold it for her, drooling at the sight of her on her hands and knees fiddling with God knows what. I haven't a clue what she's doing but she's working those fingers and God I could watch this for hours.

"You see this bolt?" I realise she's talking to me, creeping in closer as she points to the centre of the bike, squinting to focus on what she's showing me. "I need you to hook it." She takes my hand, guiding me to fix the spanner to the bolt. "Like this." I nod. And I probably look terrified. "And I need you to hold it there. Don't move it. Can you do that for me?" I'm staring through her as she speaks to me, gawking at her inky covered hands, guiltily imaging them around my throat.

"*Alora.*"

"Sorry- Yes- yeah. Sure!" I hold it in place. Using all my strength as she does what she does and whatever she is doing she's applying ridiculous force. My hand hurts. "What are you doing?" I don't even know why I'm asking because I haven't a clue what any of this is.

"I'm changing the battery." She still hasn't looked at me, deep in concentration and it's so *cute.*

"A battery? I thought bikes worked on engines." A hysterical laugh leaves her mouth.

"Oh, *baby girl.*" She pinches the bridge of her nose, and it's safe to say, I really am a bike noob, but I'm too concentrated on the fact that she called me *baby girl.* Feeling my cheeks buzz with embarrassment. She's never called me that?

"Every motor needs a battery. Otherwise, it won't turn on. But unfortunately, mine was busted so I've been hunting for a new one. Fingers crossed it boots the old girl up." I nod like I understand but she knows I have absolutely no idea what she's talking about. Completely fixated on listening to her waffle. Another moment to breathe in her inner child she never got to experience as she sits and tells me how it works and all the different parts of the bike. And honestly. I'm only focused on her. Smiling with contentment.

She spends the next ten to fifteen minutes piecing the bike back together, rambling about her favourite hobby like she's never shared it with anyone before.

"Ok. You wanna give it a go?" I look blankly at her. *I don't even have a licence?*

"What? You mean, like- ride it?"

"Noooo. Turn it on. See if she boots up." The palm of my hand hits my forehead, contemplating my IQ right now. Math was my thing. Bikes? Not so much. She ushers me to mount the bike, and I can barely fit my little ass on it, giving me a hand as she holds my waist to help me up, hooking my leg over the seat.

"You see this lever right here? Squeeze it for me." I reach for the handle, just about grabbing it, and she closes my fingers around the lever, holding her hand in place to keep it secure. "That little switch in front of you. Turn it clockwise."

My nerves are ecstatic and I don't know why. I've never been on a bike before. I turn the key, anticipating what it will do but it does nothing.

"You ready?" Excitement is dripping off my face, giggling like a little girl as she squeezes my hand tightly and jacks what looks like a lever by my foot, making the whole bike wobble. Her free hand sits on my lower back to secure me in the seat. She does it a few times and nothing happens, using sheer strength to give it power and suddenly the entire garage rattles.

"Oh my god. OH MY GOD. YOU DID IT!" Vibrations ring through my body, and it's so loud I can't hear myself think but this is so exciting, my hands flail around trying to contain my joy, waving a high five for her little victory and her smile makes my tummy flutter every time. She grabs my hips to lift me back off the seat onto solid ground, pressed up against the side of the bike and she makes me lose all ability to think when we are this close.

"I think that calls for a beer." I lose all sense of reality as she peers down at me through her abnormally long lashes that I've never noticed before, gazing at them for far too long when I realise the disgustingly gorgeous smile on her face. She pulls away from me and I let out a breath I was holding, watching her walk into the kitchen but I take a moment to admire her garage properly now that I am not sneaking around. My fingers trace the wooden bench smothered in tools and dust, catching the doors in the corner of my eye. Her office and...the door I couldn't get into. I stand there for a moment staring at it with curiosity, finding myself moving closer to it like it's speaking to me.

"*You coming?*" I hear her talk but don't register her words, closing the gap between me and this little secret.

"*Alora.*"

Her voice makes me jump as she swings round the garage door and it was almost snappy, pulling me out of my trance. There is a reason it is locked. And by the irritation lacing my name she doesn't want me near it.

"Yeah! Sorry. Coming." I follow her out. I wonder if she even knew it was me who left this door open when I broke in. As far as I know she said she thinks she forgot to lock it. My hand runs the seam of the door, looking at the locked one once more before heading back into the house closing it behind me.

SHASSII

CHAPTER 38

MY COLOUR

Puppeteer

I'll need to keep an eye on her. I don't mind her roaming the house but she needs to stay away from that door. I'm in two minds about warning her but If I warn her she will take that as an invitation to snoop further. We proved that.

"That door. Where does it go?" *Well, there goes that idea.*

"I will say this once. And only once." I lock the garage door behind her, peering over my shoulder at her curious expression, hanging onto my words. "Stay away from it. Do I make myself clear?" She looks down at the floor like I'm telling her off. And I guess I am but she should know by now it's to protect her.

"You said no more secrets, Hays." I stare at the ceiling, rolling my eyes in frustration.

"This is different. This has nothing to do with you." Her throat bobs and I now hate being like this with her as my hands rub her shoulders deeply. "Just- trust me. OK? I promise you. This is to protect you." Her eyes soften as I speak the word *promise* and she drops her hostility.

Play – 'Sink or Swim - Artemas'

"Ok..." She nods with sincerity. She's put so much trust in me that I owe her this. My throat itches at her submission, letting her arms go and she smiles at me softly. She walks over to the sofa where she quickly changes the subject, tracing her fingers over the patchwork and holes in the stitching.

"We need a new sofa." My face scrunches up in surprise.

"Do, *we* now?" *We*? She's moving quickly. Not that I am against the idea.

"Well, If I'm going to be living here, don't I get a say? It's not exactly like I will be going anywhere anytime soon." I'm smiling beneath the surface but I won't show her that.

"And what, pray tell, would you like?" She puts her legs up on the couch, cradling her head with her arms behind her neck looking right at home.

"Now you're spoiling me."

And I'd do it.

"This place needs some much-needed TLC." She states the obvious and I shake my head, staring around the room realising how I vowed this place would stay untouched. It's battered and ugly, but it was what *she* wanted and I'd left it exactly how she did but I also never intended to end up in prison for six years, meaning this home rotted with the apparition of them inside it. This place is all I have left. *But she's right.* Things need attention and I've been so caught up in my lust for revenge that I didn't notice how dead this house is. It's a coffin for the life I lost but she makes me want to tend to it. Like putting flowers on a tombstone to give it colour.

Things that I wouldn't have thought twice about until meeting my *Little Colour.*

"A few coats of paint. Some plants?" My amusement finally slips, leaning against the corner of the sofa until I'm practically sitting on it, peering down my nose at her.

"I think *she'd* like that." At first she looks surprised but then her eyes relax, almost relieved that I spoke about my mother as if she's still with us. I know she wants to learn who I am and dig deep underneath my pain. Make me *feel*. And it's working. But she knows that too, and that's the problem. She's like ivy, crawling her way inside my walls. *These walls. This house. My prison.* Weaving her way inside my heart with her poison.

I catch myself staring at her lips a little too long, pulling my focus away. I glare at the dry and flaky paint which is meant to be cream but is now warped greys with dirt marks dulling its colour.

"I'll see what I can do." Her smile lights up my day. This drive to give her anything and everything she wants, this provider and protector inside of me is breaking through my mask.

She grabs her journal from the other end of the sofa. A little spot she's designated to hibernate with blankets and pillows.

"Are you ever going to tell me what you're writing?" She clutches the book, tucking her legs underneath her.

"If you tell me what's behind that door." Annoyance plagues my face.

"*Alora.*"

"I'm kidding. Sorry-" her fingers graze the paper, contemplating whether or not to tell me the contents of her little world. "I've never shown anyone my writing." My eyes narrow, trying to figure out why she wants to be a writer when she can't even share her work.

"*Why not?*"

"Because it's not worth reading." I want to throw her against a wall and smack her ass for doubting herself.

"And how do you know that if you've never let anyone read it." *She's her own worst critic.*

"I bet you've never read a book in your life." Her messy hair scatters across her nose as she falls back into the couch, blowing it out of her face in irritation.

"Do mechanical books about engines count?" My answer is laced with sarcasm and she knows exactly what I mean, trying to suck back in a smile as she thins her lips, but her dimples betray her.

"You're the last person I'd let read it." I'd believe her if she wasn't grinning like a cheshire cat.

"*Ouch-*" I slide into the seat, slowly creeping my way towards her playfully. Mischief writing my face.

"Haydennnnnn...." Warning laces her tongue before I leap on her, pinning her underneath me watching her stretch her arm out as far as she can to keep it from my reach. "NO!- no! Hayden No!-" I could do this all day just to hear her uncontrollable laughter blessing my ears, purposefully reaching for it without the goal of actually taking it, watching her try to wiggle her way out of my hold. From *underneath me.*

"Just one page." I taunt her, taking my tongue to her throat listening to her gasp with surprise, clutching the book harder so she doesn't drop it.

"It's not happening!" Her fight is fading, breathing heavily down my ear and I want to sink my teeth into her neck to really give her something to fight against. Relight that fading glow with pain.

My hand reaches out grabbing it effortlessly, holding it in the air and she goes limp where her arms gone dead, panting with adrenaline pumping through her gaze. I could easily take it right now. I won't. But that fear licking at her trembling lip is keeping my hand there, watching her fight all the ways to resist her temptations. There is so much *want* in her eyes. Like she's forgotten all about it as our eyes stare into different worlds. Holding it. Her eyes find my mouth, darting back up to my eyes like she's caught herself looking and I pull the book back in, placing it on her chest between us.

"Careful *Puppet*. I might just be the star of your new story." Her cheeks fall strawberry red, gripping it to her body like a vice and that tells me everything I need to know.

She's sleeping peacefully as usual. She hasn't had night terrors for quite a while which eases my mind. That night is finally letting her rest. Can't say the same for me though. It plays on loop thinking of all the ways I could have prevented it, but nothing would have prevented this. I was too hell bent on taking his life. I keep asking myself, would I still have done it if she had made herself known before I pulled the trigger? And in the heat of the moment, I don't think even she would have been able to stop me. I just thank whoever the hell is up there that she didn't watch me pull the trigger that night.

I finish my cigarette, hopping off the trunk of the car and make my way inside. My nightly routine that I've noticed helps me mellow out in the evenings. I slide into bed next to her, pulling the blanket up to cover her bare shoulders where she's moved about and get comfortable. I get about two hours a night now which is more than I ever used to get. Her soft breathing has become my lullaby.

I lay there staring at her for a while, admiring the random tiny curls in her hair and the way she hugs her hand when she sleeps. My fingers find her back, tracing her velvet skin down to her spine and I don't even realise I'm doing it until she moves slightly, whimpering on instinct. Even asleep her body is yearning for me and my groin twitches.

Play - 'Archangel - Burial'

I paint an abstract piece of art on her back with my fingers, crawling up the back of her neck drawing out her timid whines as our bodies slowly close the gap until my torso is flush against her ass. Pushing the blanket to run down her arms exposing the curves in her hips, she digs herself into me like an invitation and I'm way too fucking horny for this shit. Trailing my hand until I find that soft crease in between her lips and her thigh, I rub against the silk of her pyjamas, pulling her in closer until she's practically inside of me, exhaling slowly to calm my mind-numbing temptation, so loud I can't hear myself think.

Her sleepy hand searches for mine cautiously as she quivers slightly, sliding her fingers above mine before slowly guiding my hand as she grabs onto my fingers, moving by millimetres as her soft little breaths quicken their pace. My mouth parts, inching towards the sensitive area at the back of her neck listening to a heavy sigh escape her mouth. *She wants me to touch her.*

I shut out the angel on my shoulder only concentrating on the one in front of me, poking the tips of my tongue against the ridge of her hairline, feeling her shudder against me and her noises make my hairs stand on end. I grip her inner thigh tighter in sync with my jaw as I rock into her frame, grinding against the warmth of her ass, sucking out her fear, pumping her with confidence as her hand finally presses mine between her legs.

"Is this what you want?" My voice is husky and raw, teasing her ear with my teeth, she nods her head in agreement.

"Words, *Innocence*."

A huff of disapproval slips out, pushing her head further back into me giving me access to my delicacy like that will be a better answer but I pull my head away.

"Yes..." Her voice is quiet and smothered in nerves. This time she doesn't want to touch herself. *Needy Little Puppet*. Gripping the back of my hand, edging me to release that agonising throb shooting through her core. This was still not an invitation to conquer her body but it was more than I needed to get my teeth grinding.

My middle and index finger find the crease between her pussy, already feeling how damp she is for me through the fabric. I buck my hips into her from behind pushing a high pitch squeak out of her throat as she moves herself away from me in panic.

"Shhhh... Relax." Almost instantly her muscles mould into mine, embracing my touch as my mouth does the talking against her skin, caressing her jugular with my lips listening to her unfold against me. "There's a *good girl*."

I tug on her pyjama shorts, moving them to give me access and already my fingers are submerged in her juices, parting my mouth to let a silent sigh of pent-up need escape me. I run my fingers against her glossy lips, harshly biting my bottom lip to contain the throb crippling my pelvis. She's so fucking soft I'm salivating, eager to eat her from the inside out. I circle her clit gently, feeling her jolt like a frightened puppy as my other arm slides underneath her head, my palm finding her throat as I rest it to keep her head secure.

"You're already soaked, *Puppet*." My hand eases around her throat a little tighter the more noise she makes, chasing that high she so desperately craves, her broken whimpers fuelling me to lash my fingers over her sweet spot until she's a puddle *for me*. I may know nothing about relationships, but I know how to work my way around a woman's body and the tension in her stomach muscles paint a volatile smirk across my face as I pull my strings, watching how I manipulate her body when she surrenders *to me*. She will come undone for me and I will take great pleasure in feasting on her demons.

She is without a voice, trying to mumble profanities underneath her breath as I indulge in her honey, playing with it between my fingers.

"What was that, *Princess*? I didn't quite hear that?" She seals her mouth shut and she will learn that gets her nowhere. I inch my fingers inside her tight little hole and her mouth bursts open, yelping out a whine.

"I want to hear you."

My teeth find the ravine in her neck, drawing out those sweet moans as she grinds against the palm of my hand, riding in that bliss between her thighs.

"So needy for me..." I will play with what's *mine* until I'm satisfied. I'm enjoying this little game.

The only release she will be gifted is on the end of my fucking tongue.

Where it belongs.

I want to taste that first time like it's my last meal.

SHASSII

CHAPTER 39

WILLING SURRENDER

Puppet

I can barely think, shaking on the end of her fingers trying to keep myself together but I'm cracking. This feeling is so overwhelming and I don't know what to do with it. This burning pressure is trying to claw its way out and my mouth is uncontrollable, moaning like a pathetic little bitch. I know she is loving every second of this. This is exactly what she wanted and I don't know what I hate more. That she most likely planned this, or that I finally fell straight into it but this need has been niggling ever since that night in the woods. The throb I felt, the way my body willingly surrendered without my consent. I *want* that again. I *need* that again.

She rubs my sensitive flower until I am quivering against her, wanting so desperately to say her name. *What is wrong with me?*

Suddenly she slows to a halt. Resting her parted lips against my shoulder blade.

"Hayden..." The palm of her hand finds my mouth in the stillness of the night.

"The only way you will be cumming, *is on my tongue*. Are you prepared for that?" My entire face heats up as her vulgar words hiss down my ear. There is no way I am ready for that. I shake my head and shrug my shoulders against her grip remembering how soft her tongue was against my inner thigh. "Well, you know what I said. And I will happily wait. *You're a delicacy Alora. I want all of you when you willingly surrender yourself to me.*" *A delicacy?* I swallow my insecurities, clinging to her words like my lifeline. She will not give me this until I spell it out, but I am not ready and somehow she knows that, wrapping me back up in my blanket, pulling me into her body for comfort.

"What if I'm never ready?" Her arms wrap around my chest, squeezing me into a bear hug as she fiddles with my hair.

"*Then never, I'll wait.*"

"Anything?" I yell, as she crawls in from outside, completely drenched, her shirt see through and her hair a messy mop on her head, running her hands through it to squeeze out the excess water before she drips all over the floor. We're in the middle of a thunderstorm and I am petrified of them, hiding under the blanket with Shep like a baby while she went to check the power lines. She'd already attempted the power and it's completely dead.

"Nope."

"Great." I fiddle with my hair, trying to ignore the thunder rattling the house but my heart is pounding so vigorously it might just penetrate my chest. "As if I wasn't bored enough already." I burrow underneath the blanket.

Play - 'Shameless – Camila Cabello'

"I'm sure we can kill time." Rumbles echo through the entire building, shaking the foundations making me flinch. "What's the matter *Puppet*? Are you scared?" I've never enjoyed these. They hold a magnitude of darkness that consumes your entire being. You can feel it in your core. It's destructive, dangerous.

"I don't like thunderstorms."

"You've dealt with scarier things than this *Love*." Yeah. I've dealt with her. She's more like a tornado, flattening my life and destroying everything in its path purely out of spite.

"You're not funny." She licks her lips. Locking eyes with me as she walks towards me, leaning over me with her hands on the back of the couch and I can smell the damp on her clothes.

"*Lie again*. And I'll shove it back down your throat." My heart stops. It's practically pitch-black with only a few candles dotted around the room and her face flickers in the horrors of the storm, lighting up the sharp features in her facial structure.

"I'm not lying." I would like to say I'm not, but the hurricane inside of me is heavily contradicting my words.

"*And I'm a saint.*" Her head tilts, studying my eyes through the depth of the room and I want to smack her for being so sarcastic as much as I want to press my mouth against hers. She's far from a saint but her actions contradict the monster she lets control her.

"Is that what you tell yourself?" I hiss, scowling up at her but my eyes won't stop fixating on her lips. She thinks that because she holds my heart in her hands, that makes her powerful?

"No. That's what you tell yourself, so you feel less guilty about that pulse between your legs." My legs instinctively squeeze together, chewing my bottom lip as my pulse reacts to her words like a call.

"I don't know what you're talking about." *Why did I say that?* She smirks like the devil in carnage, letting go of the couch to stroke the flush in my cheeks with her fingers as she finds my face in the dark.

"Are you ready to swallow that?" My body flares like fire beneath my flesh as her thumb slides its way inside my mouth, easing against my tongue before her middle and index finger enter, pushing until they hit the back of my throat making me choke and my eyes leak along with my decorum.

My legs creep apart so naturally, gagging on my purity as I invite the devil in. Unable to see her until light breaks through the shadows.

My Nightmare.

"You take me so well, *Doll*." Her words ring through me like white noise, salivating around her fingers, now dribbling down the centre of my lip, grinding against the apparition of her as she stands between my legs and I'm about to break. I cling onto this compulsion, feeling my tongue glue to her fingers as she draws them out, using my spit as lubricant as she smears it over my bottom lip. Her forehead rests against mine, wetting my face with her damp locks, her hot breath warming my cheek. I'm concentrating on her body weighted against me and the pounding between my inner thighs to shut out the clouds crashing above us, mimicking the sound of the thunder in my chest. How my heart is telling me to lean in and steal a kiss.

My breathing is irregular, trying to keep it steady but the more I move the closer we become until I can practically feel her bottom lip graze mine with *need*. She's fighting this just as much as I am but this gravitational pull is sucking me in like a tidal wave, drawing me in until I crash against the shore and I realise her mouth is my shore, sucking in a sharp breath as our lips meet, drowning in this rapture as my nerves dissipate. Her warmth imprisons mine cautiously, gradually breaking this wall we've both built. I feel her resistance through the trembling of her mouth, merely connecting through severed vibration, trying to figure out if I meant to make a move, teasing my decision as she pulls away, still holding herself back. But I don't want her to.

I want this. I want *her*.

"Please... Don't stop." She's been dipping my feet into the shallow end of the pool, but the truth is. I'm tired of testing waters. I'm tired of being careful. Of being afraid. I want her to pull me under and let me drown in this guilt I carry for wanting to willingly surrender myself to the very woman who made me want to *die*. She vowed to take my life but the problem is. She already has. She had it the moment she saved my life. My perception of life and death, it's all about the part you play. The story you learn. Not all villains are born that way. She was not born a monster. She was brought up to believe that *pain* was *love*, and *love* was *punishable*.

I can see in her eyes that she's just as scared as I am. To let herself feel. *To let go.* But I nuzzle my head against hers, playing with her desires to take what is *hers* until she folds, lapping up the taste of my surrender, quenching her thirst as her tongue slides inside my mouth dancing in rhythm with mine. I've never kissed anyone. I don't know what I'm doing but this feels natural. *Instinctive.* If sinning is as bad as they say then I'm already shunned.

This heavy weight on my chest is lifting the harder she thrashes against me, digging me into the couch as her fingers reach for my throat, cupping it gently with malice, holding my innocence in the palm of her hand with intentions punishable by death but my pussy aches for retribution.

I've learnt more about myself these past few months than I have my entire life. Our kiss is heavier. Sloppier. Sweat is building against my lower back and my hands reach up for her shoulders, hanging onto her as her knee pushes between my thighs, gasping into her mouth with desperation, melting into her grip as she tugs the scruff of my neck. She tastes like the last piece of cake you left for yourself after a long day, just beaming to let it melt in your mouth. To savour its taste and drown in the sweet satisfaction. *A delicacy.* She told me I'm a delicacy. Is that what she meant? My cheeks bloom at the very thought and I speak without thinking.

"Please..." I mutter against her parted mouth, too afraid to tell her exactly what I want. But I know what I want, and so does she.

"Tell me... I want to hear you say it." It's like mother nature knows my confession as the thunder pauses to let me speak, whispering against her sticky cheek with nothing but confidence casing my tongue.

"I'm ready..."

SHASSII

CHAPTER 40

HER DELICACY

Puppet

She takes my invitation without a second thought and her entire demeanour shifts, delicate but heavy, trailing bruises down my neck the more vigorous she handles me. Pulling away to remove her soaked tee shirt, lifting it up over her head exposing my own wounded soldier wearing her scars like a sanctuary and my jaw hangs low as her muscles indent her skin against the warm glow, seeing her in an entirely different light as she towers over my defenceless body. *Death.* Is all she encompasses. Lying here ready to *die* for her. Mimicking a shadow coming to devour my soul.

 Her fingers trace the back of my arm until she reaches my hand, tugging me with so much force my body slams into her torso. I wrap my legs around her waist as she cloaks me with her arms, lifting me off the sofa with little to no effort making her way to the bedroom, unable to keep our mouths off one another. My back meets the door, digging into the wood yelping out a cry before she opens it but we are too frantic to pay mind to the mild ache against my spine as it's now cushioned, falling back onto the bed where thunder rattles in sync with us, hitting it with heavy impact.

This is really happening. Oh my god.

Hunger is driving her thoughts as she devours my skin with her teeth, nearly drawing blood whilst trailing down my chest, licking against the fabric lining my breasts sending waves through my spine, clawing at my skimpy top until it rests under the cups exposing me for her to play with as she sucks on her thumb before rubbing it against my pink little rose buds. I buck my stomach into her chest as her soft kisses run the length of my tummy, lowering herself between my legs and my thighs clamp against her upper arms, riddled with nerves as her hand runs between the ravine of my breasts.

"Ahh ah ah...*Puppet.*" Her teeth threaten to nip my inner thighs, bouncing them back open to accommodate her broad shoulders, her fingers tugging at my pants, unhooking them from underneath my ass dragging them up towards her until they are cuffing my ankles, finishing the job with her teeth until they are on the floor.

"I need you open for me." She lifts her remaining upper bodywear off and over her head. My mouth gapes as her breasts, small but defined, are jewelled with two nipple piercings highlighted in the dull light seeping through the window, smothered in black ink like the rest of her, wrapped around her torso like a demonic entity.

Her arms slide against the bed sheets underneath my thighs, gripping the fleshy cushion of my hips as she lightly pecks near my entrance, sucking my skin into her mouth.

Play - 'Anbu - Iwilldiehere'

"You don't need to hide from me. Do you understand?" I'm too focused on catching my breath to give her a coherent response, my head hitting the pillow in shock.

"Eyes on me, *Alora.*"

The bass in her voice shakes my daze, lifting my head to almost lose it again as I peer down my nose at her just as lightning illuminates the room, sculpting a demon between my thighs as she lowers herself until her mouth disappears only able to momentarily view the unholy corruption within her eyes before my vision goes black. I can't quite tell if it's because I've blacked out or the lightning has paused but my body jolts in satisfaction, chasing her tongue as she ridicules my entire existence with one swift swipe down my slit.

"You will scream for me. So loudly that this thunderstorm will fear you *Love.*" *Love.* She says it with such confidence when she despises every meaning of the word. It's etched into her skin yet she handles mine with such care, gripping me tighter as she buries her tongue deeper inside me, losing control of my voice as her words drum against my thoughts.

"So fucking wet for me *baby...*" She mutters under her breath and I don't think I was meant to hear that, but I did and I feel myself pulse against her tongue as a moan trips from my mouth, melting as her lips marry my skin. "*Good* fucking *girl.*" Her vile praise has me dripping onto her tongue, grinding my hips into her mouth as her words of encouragement push me to use my voice.

"*My Delicacy.*" There it is again, and my throat knots as I listen to her enjoy me like I'm her last meal. *That last piece of cake.* The tips of her tongue flick my clit so vigorously, each slit massaging between my folds. I whine like a needy little puppy feeling her hands ride up my forearms, pinning me in place like human cuffs and the things she can do with her tongue have me completely stunned.

"*Mine.*" She growls against my slit, wiggling the flat side of her tongue to tease me with her jewels that roll against either side of my sensitive bud and pressure builds against my lower stomach, tensing it in ways I never knew possible, crippling me to whimper with overwhelming frustration. "Relax *Puppet.* Focus on my voice," there is motive behind her command and uncertainty spreads goosebumps all over my skin, swallowing my nerves as the tips of her fingers play with our liquids at my entrance. "Breathe for me *Little Dreamer.*" I follow her orders, counting as I inhale and exhale calmly until her digit penetrates me, causing pleasure and pain to dance with one another until her tongue rests against me once more, easing off the uncomfortable insertion.

"Breatheeee..."

Fuck. I'm trying.

It doesn't take long for the feeling to pass, falling completely and entirely into her hold like a drug. My back arches, feeding the motion she's rocking into me and she stretches me out a little further as she adds another finger, curling up inside me making me shriek with shock but she's not wrong. My moans are drowning out the chaos surrounding these walls. All I can hear is my heartbeat in my ears as my surrender echoes through the entire house.

A slick layer of sweat is smothering us both where the air is muggy and her skin is still holding moisture from outside, glueing to my skin as she sinks deeper inside of me, running her free hand up my hips, cupping my breast in her palm, teasing it to edge me further and I have no idea what I'm meant to be feeling but every single muscle is knotting as pools of arousal stir between my groin, desperately clinging to her mouth as she massages my sweet spots. *How the hell am I meant to relax?*

"Ride my face *baby girl*. Don't be shy." Her words are like a key to my confidence, unlocking the lust brewing inside of me waiting to burst its way out. Without permission my hips thrust on impulse, grinding against her vice, stapling me to her soft, fleshy muscles and my body and mind take control.

"Oh- my Go-d..." My words stagger, mumbling under my breath, pushing the back of my head into the pillow as I grip the metal bars for security and my throat jams. She has me chained to this bed with her tongue, glaring at the bars remembering how this started. How I feared for my life and now I'm letting her kill me slowly as she sucks out any remnants left of the old me.

That girl is long gone.

"The correct words are, *fucking hell.*" *I am fucking hell,* burning in the magma, suffocating on its heat as my head buzzes, feeling lightheaded with each stroke of her tongue. She is the match to my kerosene, igniting my fire that wants to tear us both apart.

"I want my name in your mouth as you cum for me *Puppet.*" Her crude words flare up my cheeks, biting on an orgasm I have no idea how to execute but intuition is telling me I don't need to as my whimpers escalate.

"Hold it *Love*. Don't let it go." It's like she can feel it through her fingers, manipulating my every movement as she draws out the last of my virtue.

"*Good girl.* Just like that." Her strokes are rhythmic. A steady pace as she learns my body. Pushing my buttons until I'm shaking like a leaf against her mouth, nearly breaking the headboard as I tug on its railing.

"*Cum.*" My second heartbeat prevails. "*Cum for me Love.*"

My entire anatomy locks, jamming like a scratched record until my entire upper body lifts, forcing out an overwhelming sob to rattle my throat, letting go of my fear. My purity. *My everything.* At this very moment I'm thriving in this sickness she's stained me with.

"Hayden!..." Her name on my tongue only burrows her fingers deeper causing me to scream like a banshee, letting go of the bars, finding her arm as I squeeze her tightly, digging my nails into her wounded skin.

"Feel it. Shatter for me *Innocence.*" My execution is bittersweet, letting my entire being fade as this death consumes me, catching my breath as I fall limp on the bed, twitching with her fingers still inside my walls, gnawing her teeth against my sensitive skin as I descend into liberation.

Her wet mouth, smothered in *me,* works its way up my stomach, smearing me in my own arousal. She wipes the excess off her chin as she pushes my legs apart to accommodate her waist, so wide it makes my muscles stretch. I pinch in an ache as her mouth crashes against mine, tasting myself on her tongue without consent through breathless kisses, clawing at my throat recklessly unable to catch a break, laying in our mess with no thought.

I go to touch her waist when her hands clutch at my wrists, pressing them back down on the bed sheets with warning in her eyes. So intimidating I melt like wax.

I understand. But I want to mould myself to her skin. I want us to be *one* right now.

She glares at me and she's grinning like an idiot.

"Listen..."

She whispers down my ear. I focus on my surroundings and my eyes bulge. *The thunders stopped.*

"You have all the power now *Puppet...*" It's like I've consumed it. Now striking my insides with fierceness.

I am the storm, and I want to do terrible things.

She leans on her knees, pulling me up with her by my neck to remove my top easier, sliding it to my upper arms, leaving it stationary as I'm bound with its fabric, pushing me back with my hands above my head. I sigh out a gentle whimper as her lips take my nipple in her mouth, nibbling carefully as her hand cherishes my body beneath her, memorising its shape in the absence of light. I'm still so sensitive, squirming with little movement, trapped below the Devil.

"Hays!-" a playful giggle fills the room, feeling her smile against my skin.

"You didn't think we were done, did you?" My chest flutters as she rises to align with my mouth, teasing my cupid's bow with the tip of her tongue and I want nothing more right now than to memorise her bone sculpture again. I want so desperately to feel how hot she's burning for me.

"What are you going to do now?" I sink into the mattress, tucking my chin into my chest as I gaze up at her through my lashes and her expression is frightening. It's beaming with misdeed and that look itself is showing me that she's burning, deeply, as her shoulders tower over my tiny frame. I feel so small but right now, I love the feeling of being trapped beneath her. My inability to escape her is only making me more wet.

"I'm going to fill up your desperate, tight little hole with my cock, *Princess.*"

CHAPTER 41

ALL OF YOU

Puppet

Play - 'High For This - The Weeknd'

I am no expert when it comes to Virginity. But am I wrong in thinking that is literally *impossible*? My lips part, gawking at her with internal confusion and by the look on her face she gets off on that reaction.

"What-?" She doesn't speak. Taking my bottom lip in between her teeth and the pinch makes my eyes water, but the thought of something bigger than her fingers inside of me makes my heart race. Exhilaration and fear kiss in rhythm to the beating of my chest, bouncing between her eyes, sucking down my now non-existent purity. There is no point in backing out now. I want that feeling again. I want to consume it and let it build a home to visit.

"My Sweet, Precious, *Little Innocence*." She says, merely above a whisper against the shell of my ear.

"Let me taint your pretty little mind with thoughts only the devil could deem acceptable." Without time to think her groin pushes against my pelvis until her jeans are pressed firmly against me and a sharp hiss forces through my teeth followed by a pleasurable shock as a solid stiffness rubs against my weeping pussy. "I'll be gentle, I promise *Love*."

My throat bobs but I can't ignore how good this feels as her thighs sit underneath the back of mine, radiating heat through both of us. Her hands burning my hips as she holds them, gently rocking into my body as her bulge puts pressure on my clit through her jeans, temporarily relieving me of this unbearable ache that's already wormed its way back inside of me. *Isn't there a cool down period for this stuff?*

"Will it hurt?" I can't deny. I'm nervous. I know how sex works but I thought I'd grow grey and old and be a crazy cat lady. I only really know of sex through Kacey which isn't exactly the best source. She's tried to explain it to me a few times but I was never interested. Until now that is. Now for some reason all I want to feel is her inside me. How can I crave that when I don't even know what it feels like?

Fulfilment. It's like she's a missing piece I need to feel whole.

"It will, to begin with. You just need to relax for me and let me do the work, *ok?*" There is something so calming in her words. I trust her more than I should. I'm afraid to admit I trust her entirely. I nod my head in agreement.

"Can I ask you something?" Her warm breath blankets my face as she leans in, ready to hear whatever I have to say, brushing my loose strands from my face and my cheeks flush with her warmth. "Do you think I'm pretty?" She sits her upper body on her elbow, peering at me and I'm more afraid of this answer than the sin we are about to commit.

"*Alora.*"

...

"You're *beautiful.*" No one has ever called me that. And I'm suddenly all sorts of bashful. She could have just said *yes or no*. I wasn't prepared for that and my breathing escalates as she burrows her face into my neck, planting delicate seeds all over my un-flourished soil, bare and untouched. I go to speak but her finger finds my lips, silencing me to just focus on her before sliding her fingers inside of my mouth, wetting them against my tongue still able to taste myself as she draws them back out, watering my flower as she rubs me softly in circles.

"You want this?" Her words are deep and calm and I can feel her eyes studying my every movement through the darkness. I confirm without words but I should know by now she doesn't like silence. "*Tell me.* What do you want, *Puppet*. Be a good girl and use those words." As she finishes her sentence, metal cracks the silence hosting the air, tightening my throat in knots as she unbuckles her belt sending chills to surf through me pinching at my entrance.

I know what I want. But knowing what I want and being able to handle it are two entirely different things.

"*You...*" Those words are acidic in my mouth. How could I pine for a woman who has hurt me in the most despicable way. Who's broken me down until I'm fragments in her hands. Who ripped me from life as I know it and showed me what it is to be afraid.

"*All of you.*"

My credence deceives me, startled at my own truths. This isn't just about sex anymore. This is about *us*. This is about how, through all my pain and grief, through all my suffering and captivity, her kindness has prevailed. The last fraction of my life resides inside of her. And even if I did one day manage to find a way to be rid of her. A sick part of me would find a way to miss her. Because in the end, I've found refuge in our catastrophe. *Is this Love? Is this utility?* Maybe it's delusion and I've finally lost my mind, but at least this way I don't feel judgement.

Her crescent moons in the midnight sky light up her face at my honesty, biting my lip harshly as the sound of her zipper grates at my ears. Crashing down on my mouth as she gauges my confession from my tongue, grinding against my wet slit, priming me for her to take what is *hers*.

"*Beg me...*"

"Please- *Hays...* I want all of you." It's all I've ever wanted. Since my arrival I've dug deep to find out everything she has to offer me, searching for the human inside of her and everything I've learnt. *It's still not enough*. I need this. I need *more*.

"Breathe with me." Her forehead rests against mine and her eyes are closed. Like she's ready to let me in. Feeling her wet herself against my arousal, heightening my breaths as she tries to guide my pace, calming me as a solid, smooth curve, dips against my hole, stretching it further than her fingers and my mouth gapes as she catches my gasp with a kiss, easing her way in slowly.

It's not real. But whatever it is. It's penetrating my dignity and I whistle through my teeth, trying to wield the pain, almost drawing blood from her bottom lip as I bite down, crying into her mouth.

"That's it." She slides in further, stretching me out to fit her even though it hurts but we hurt. Everything about us hurts. Whatever this is, it's built off pain and I'm finally learning to embrace its sting. "Such a *good girl*. You're doing so fucking good for me *baby*."

She's breathless against me, like she can feel everything I'm feeling and it's encouraging me to let her in easier, yelping against her tongue as we chase a kiss.

"I know. I know it hurts, I'm sorry...shhhhh, *baby girl*... Relax." She holds me, cradling my discomfort as she cups the back of my neck like I'm breaking, pulling me into her collarbone as I breathe through the sting and I don't know how far in she is, but it's tearing me apart.

"Play with yourself..." Her instructions cut through me like blades. *I don't even know how?* But I do as she says, feeling for my throbbing clit, finding myself dripping with need and I run circles around my sensitive bud, already feeling a thousand times comfier. With each gentle thrust she sinks further, filling me to accommodate her inside my walls, breaching that point of no return. *Her weeping angel.*

"That's it. Feel me. Let me worship you. *Let me in.*" Breathless growls vibrate from her throat as she thrusts firmer, stuffing my tight hole with her sins and my teeth tear at the flesh in her neck, biting down harder the deeper she penetrates me as she endures my pain, letting me harm her with my mouth.

"O-h my-" The sting remains but my pussy finally gives in, relaxing around her length as I coat it in my surrender. Sacrificing my body as a gift for *Freedom*. This ability to let go of control when she holds me. *It's compelling.*

It's no longer uncomfortable. Pleasure overriding the pain as I pulse against her, rubbing my clit at a faster pace to keep up with her. She's being gentle for now. But I know she will show me no mercy once she's stretched me out to mould around her and I twitch at the vulgar thoughts. The thought of her inflicting pain on my vulnerable body. Pain I cannot control, only overcome. It tips me over the edge and that pressure builds once more, chasing that relief like a starved animal.

"Yes...Yes. Yes-. Fucking hell-" my words leak out like word vomit, moaning in motion to her rocking me and she grins through a kiss against my bruise lips.

"Yes, you are *baby*." The way she says *baby* has me losing it. There is something comforting about being *Her Baby*. Feeling so safe in her arms. "Let go for me. I'm right here." *She is*. And selfishly, I never want to be away from her again. Maybe this is the hormones talking. But I now couldn't picture a life without her which is ridiculous. This will never be normal. She's a convicted criminal and I am her hostage, but I'm holding the key and I still don't want to run anymore.

"*Mine*." Her tone is coarse and rough down my neck, pushing me to let go and this orgasm is far more intense than my first, crippling every muscle in my body. My mouth gapes as a sob shrieks into the void, my walls tensing around her cock so tightly it paralyses me as I claw my nails into her skin to create my mark as she makes hers, deep inside me. Slowing down her dominating thrusts as she imprints herself against my walls. A mark I will never be able to cleanse myself of. *I'm finally impure*. The feeling is serene as she carefully pulls out as not to hurt me, still hissing at the pressure and the dull sting that will most likely be there for a little while.

She gentle pulls at my wrist until my hands hovering in front of her mouth, kissing each knuckle with a touch so gentle I tremble as she glares right through me, cleaning up my mess with her mouth as she takes my fingers against her soft tongue, wallowing in comforting silence and the sounds of depleting pants, as I struggle to catch my breath.

"How do you feel?..." There are no words to describe how I feel. But I know that the feelings I felt have not run away with my orgasm. And she still looks disgustingly dangerous as she looms over my limp body, laying here completely lifeless trying to comprehend what the hell just happened.

"Dirtied." I've always been under the impression that sex is something only sluts and jockeys did behind shower blocks in college. But that wasn't dirty. It was raw, *passionate*. She didn't fuck me. She made love to me, in the most disgustingly beautiful way possible and I'm still coming down, finding it hard to focus on her as my eyes adjust to the room.

"You better get used to that. Next time I won't be so merciful with your body." I know she won't. But part of me secretly loves it and I don't know why. I want to experiment with this newfound feeling. And it's not like we don't have all the time in the world. But maybe just wait a little first. "You took me so well..." I'm trying to calm down but her words are keeping my heart racing. This praise I'm sick for.

It's going to ruin me.

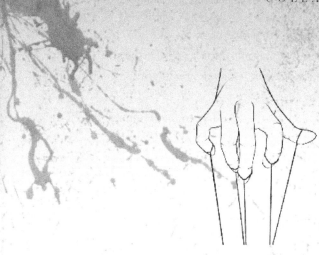

CHAPTER 42

THE TASTE OF SIN

Puppeteer

My sight is aimed for the glass bottle sat on the top of the car bonnet, squinting as I hold my breath before taking my shot, shattering it to pieces. I'm trying to distract myself from the time we spent together last night. I could have stayed in bed with her. I could have woken her up with breakfast and kisses, *but that isn't me.* None of this is me. Instead, I am out here feeling sorry for myself, trying to tell myself I did the right thing. But I shouldn't have done it. *What was I thinking?* I let my own selfish desires get in the way of my actions and now she's lost her virginity to a *monster.*

She should have lost her virginity to a silly little writing nerd with glasses, straight A's and a degree in *how to be a good boyfriend.* But I know that's unrealistic. And how can I count on the fact she would have found the right person. I'm not the right person. But at least this way no one can break her heart. *I will break her heart,* and I've already done that so it won't be difficult for her to get over it. She should hate me anyway so it will only solidify what she should be feeling towards me all along.

I'm fucking selfish. And now I don't think I will ever be able to let her walk away. I'm a fucking idiot. But it felt so right. She felt like home on my fucking tongue. She belongs here. *With me.*

I let my inner frustration out on the bottles lining the bonnet that I should probably clean up later but it's a graveyard of unfulfilled rage that I like to keep. My mag runs out and I go to change it when her sweet little voice calls for me from the front door.

"Damn. Was it really that bad?" She bellows over the ricochet at the end of my gun. I turn to look at her, standing in my doorway with my black tee on and I am assuming nothing else underneath which makes the back of my mouth salivate at the thought. She should know better than to dangle herself in front of me like that.

"Very funny." She's glowing. And I didn't even know it was possible for someone like her to glow more than she already does. She stalks towards me playfully with her hands held behind her back. Her hair is subtle with grease from last night's antics, knotted into a loose bun and her candy apple cheeks are hard to miss. She doesn't seem annoyed that she didn't wake up with me. But honestly, I wasn't sure if she would want to. I don't think either of us expected yesterday to end up how it did.

"Can I have a go?" She rubs up to me like a cat, gazing up at me with her newfound pretty siren eyes as she clings onto my bicep.

"Do you even know how to fire this thing?" I peer down at her, taking my aim off the bottle.

"Ouch!...I will have you know. I have expertise in the matter." I highly doubt that. Don't tell me. *Daddy gave her lessons on how to protect herself.* Look how that's going mate.

"Ok. Give it your best shot." I pass her the gun. It's only a suppressor pistol so it's not heavy but her arm still drops as she takes it from my hand. I forget she's three sizes smaller than me.

She aims at the three bottles left standing on the bonnet and fuck does she look good holding a weapon, fierce and dangerously *beautiful*.

I quietly creep in behind her, pushing her to aim for the far left and I can feel her side eyeing me, gently wrapping my hands around her waist just to listen to her pant with anticipation.

Play – 'Obsessed – Jutes'

"Concentrate *Baby*..." Calling her baby feels weirdly natural. I feel this dire need to protect her. Care for her. Comfort her. When I should be snapping her, bending her and breaking her.

She sucks in a breath, aims and fires, popping the bottle clean off the bonnet and my brow raises in pride, smirking at my *Little Puppet*. She needs to let more of that power in. Her breath hitches, like she's surprised she hit it. She closes her eyes, falling into my touch as my tongues trail up the column of her neck, gripping her hips tighter as she whimpers for me, still desperately trying to hold up the gun with both hands.

"The mag is full this time...I could kill you right now." *Clever girl*. She could. But she won't. She just wants me to put her on her knees.

"Was that a threat?" I mutter, caressing the shell of her ear with my bottom lip.

"*Maybe...*" I'm starting to enjoy this little brat inside of her now that she is willing to bend for me. My left arm reaches round to grab her left wrist, twisting her body to face me cutting her movement with my foot so she stumbles, cradling her fall as her back finds the ground already armed with the pistol in my right hand hooking the barrel underneath her chin as she peers up at me, defenceless and frightened. She squeezes her eyes shut and we both know I could very easily end this right here, *right now*. I've had my fun. *Who's to say I wouldn't?*

"Threaten me again. And I'll make sure I don't hesitate next time, *Innocence*." She wants to believe I wouldn't. But she is also not stupid. At the end of the day, I am still a ruthless killer and I've not exactly had my *fix* lately. She doesn't need to know her existence subdues the monster inside of me but I have no problem letting out my murderous tendencies on her delicious cunt.

"You know, you technically can't call me that anymore." She's not wrong. But now I will just say it out of spite. To remind her who snatched her soul.

"What would you prefer? *My dirty Little Whore?*" I've dirtied her. Smouldered her in my thorns but she doesn't seem to mind and that's exactly what I wanted. She opened her petals for me and now I will pick them, one by one, until the only thing that remains is the skeleton of a flower that once bloomed. She will find beauty in things people deem ugly. *Like me.* A flower with no petals will not get picked, left to decay until the dirty soil consumes her. But her petals were falling long before I came along. They do not grow back, you have to learn to love this new version of you. Like she has to learn to love this new version of herself.

"Yes." She whispers coyly and my mouth cracks, trying to hold in this beast that wants to take great pleasure in showing her how a whore is treated. But I know she's sore, so I will be nice just this once.

"Be careful what you wish for... Let's learn to walk before we run." The tip of the barrel finds its way between her legs, lifting my tee shirt to reveal she is in fact bare underneath, laying helplessly before me. Her pretty pussy glistens in the morning sun and I haven't got a cock, but *fuck* have I got a fucking hard on. I slide the cold metal between her wet slit as she flinches, lathering it in her arousal.

"I thought you liked it when I ran..." She's trying to coax out the brutality in me and I'm fighting everything in me not to ram this barrel into her tight little hole as I pull it to her mouth, slick with her honey, running my tongue along the inside of my cheek.

"Lick it off. *Whore.*" My bitter words paint a picture that lives rent free in my mind. *Fear.* It never ceases to make me throb as her balls of fire erupt, poking out her tongue for me still so willing to please me. I run the metal along her soft muscle, letting her clean off her sins from my weapon before shoving it down her throat instead.

"Does this get you off *Puppet*? Being treated like a *broken dolly?*" She chokes on it, giving me the most adorable evils. The insides of my fingers slap her wet cunt making her jolt against me, taking the barrel further, gagging for air as oxygen leaves her lungs, playing with her sensitive bud as she shudders beneath me, her back grazing against the dirty concrete beneath *us.* "I've not even touched you and you're already dripping for me."

She peers down her nose, trying to avoid eye contact with me but I pull her head back up with the gun still wedged in her gob watching her saliva run down her chin, wanting to smear it over her perky little tits.

"Out in the open with your pussy on show for anyone to see. It's a good job we're alone. *I don't like to share.*" I remove the barrel and she gasps for air, choking as her body rejects it, trying to find her voice again.

"No one would want to fuck me anyway." I grind my back teeth, taking her delicate throat in my hand with intent to bruise it if she keeps up that talk. I want to throttle whoever indoctrinated her with that crap. Some stupid boy no doubt.

"I will wash your mouth out. Careful *Princess*." She pulls away from my hold, trying to stand on her feet, adjusting my tee to cover back up her non-existent dignity.

"I'm going for a shower." She snarls. Storming off towards the house in a huff and just for that, I'm going to show her how fucking wrong she is.

I follow her into the house where she's already stripped off and turned the shower on. She left the door open on purpose, stepping under the water to wash away all her dirty sins. But unfortunately, that won't help her now.

I slip out my cuffs from my jacket pocket on the back of the dining room chair and quietly follow her in, my footsteps drowned out by the running water. She knew this wasn't going to end well for her, but she kept the door open anyway. *Silly Puppet.*

I'm fully clothed but I don't care as I stand there waiting for her to run her hands through her hair, launching for her wrists to clamp them with metal, pushing her closer to the wall so I can thread the chain behind the piping hot shower pole restraining her so she can't move. She screams profanities and I waste no time sliding my fingers through her knotty hair as it moulds around my wrist, tugging her scalp tightly until her face is submerged by water. She thrashes against my grip, holding her breath trying not to drown in it as I spit through my teeth in anguish, enjoying the sound of her gurgle for air, the way her body is chasing for mine as she moulds to my firm torso.

"I want to fuck you!... And if I had it my way, I would fuck your tight, swollen little cunt on every surface of the house until you couldn't walk just to hear your pathetic little whimpers down my ears. *You dumb little girl.* Do you realise just how fucking *perfect* you are? How many men would be lucky to take your body? And so help me god. I'd like to watch them try.

Because as long as I'm still breathing. You belong to me. Do you understand me?"

I hold her there a little longer, watching her hold onto her precious little life before she's just about to break, then throw her head forward, letting her spit out her words, gasping on this life that I've given her. I don't want to kill her anymore. But I can have fun trying.

"Yes..." She doesn't fight. Only obeys, like she needed to hear those words come out of my mouth to finally realise her worth.

"What are you, *Alora*?" I never used to call her by her name because I knew she hated it, but now it makes her a whiny little mess.

"*Beautiful...*"

CHAPTER 43

CURIOSITY KILLED THE CAT

Puppet

Play – 'Yellow Love – Citizen'

"Mash potato?" Just the thought of it churns my stomach.

"Absolutely not." I dismiss the idea as she turns her nose up at me, shrugging her shoulders, trying to figure out what we can eat for dinner with what is left in the house.

"Ok. What about baked potato?" I can deal with that. Not my first choice but I'll take it.

"Ooo yes." She gawks at me in disbelief, trying to rationalise my thought process here, but honestly there isn't one. I will argue this until I'm blue in the face. *They are not the same.*

"THEY ARE THE SAME THING!" She throws her arms up in the air, laughing at my questionable picky eating, and my *god I think she's actually losing it over potatoes.*

"No it's not!" I shut the cabinet, trying to find other nicknacks she is hiding as she rattles on from behind me.

"IT'S MASHED POTATO!" At least there is texture in a jacket potato, mash is just baby food. The texture in my mouth makes me want to hurl.

"It's slop on a plate!" She grabs me by the wrist pulling me into her chest, pinning me up against the island in the middle of the kitchen and my face burns. The past week has been so strange. She hasn't exactly been gentle but she hasn't been rough either. And we have near on fucked against every surface in this house, including this island. I am sore but I don't really care. She kept her word. She's shown me I'm wanted; she's worshipped my body in every sense of the word and I no longer feel disposable. I feel *cherished*. She's made me tell myself I'm beautiful every day since trying to literally kill me in the shower just to make a point. But I have found pleasure in pushing her buttons. I don't know what we are, but whatever we are, it's better than what we were. I've tried to hate her. I've thought tirelessly about what outcome this has. And honestly? None of them are good which makes me so scared. It's like I don't want to be found.

"Spain sounds nice." I say softly. She lifts me up onto the countertop, my ass bare and a loose crop top barely covers my petite breasts. I kind of love wearing practically nothing. She can't keep her hands off me.

She tilts her head, realising what I'm talking about. The day she showed me her face, she asked me where we should travel.

"I was joking." A nervous laugh slips as she kisses my cheek softly.

"I'm not." We should both get away. Chase some normality.

"*Alo*. I would love to travel the world with you. But we both know that is not possible." She fiddles with my fingers before taking the cigarette from behind her ear, placing it in her mouth and holding the lighter out for me to ignite it. I flick the old zipper, running my thumb over the engraving to notice her mothers name carved into the metal.

"Did you two ever travel?" She draws her first puff, exhaling slowly away from my face.

"No." Her eyes meet the floor. Bringing her mother up still hurts. I have tried to talk about her more and she has spoken about her a little lately. Like decorating. She thought of her mother then too. She is like the anchor to her *love* and I intend to try and keep her there if I can help it. She doesn't need to kill anymore. She doesn't have to be the monster she thinks she deserves to be. She hasn't *'worked'* for over a month now and she is definitely using sex to get that pent up frustration out. I know sitting around doing nothing is killing her. But it proves that this is possible. *Her redemption is possible.*

"Where did she want to go?" She draws another puff, leaning her forehead into my chest.

"Alo..."

"Tell me. Please." She needs to do this. For me. I deserve that. Otherwise, my mother really did die for absolutely nothing. I've been able to sympathise with her for her actions. Though they may be unforgivable, I've done my grieving. She can do this for me.

"England. Also travel to other states in the US. It's what the trailer was for." England? That is definitely an interesting one. I glance out the window, searching for the trailer that I have not actually seen yet. It must be behind the garage.

"The one you're rebuilding?"

"The one you did a terrible paint job on, yes." The palm of my hands push against her chest humorously, pinching my cheeks as I smile.

"Hey! There was nothing wrong with my paint job!" I take the cigarette from her mouth gently, holding the centre, careful not to burn myself and she peers menacingly at me like I've stolen from her, flipping it to draw from it myself. I have never smoked in my life, but there is a first time for everything. I've already gotten drunk, so what's the worst that can happen?

I've been keeping on top of my meds, she even wrote me out a new calendar with all my times for my insulin shots so she would remember and to help keep me on top of it, *not very serial killer of her*. She never did tell me where she got such a large supply of my prescription, but in all honesty, I've never felt stronger in my own self-worth and capability than I do right now.

I draw in the cigarette, inhaling with a crippled man's cough, choking on it as it invades my lungs. It's far more attractive when she does it. That's one more thing off the bucket list, but I shan't be doing it again.

"You really suck at being a rebel." She taunts as she chuckles into my mouth, inhaling my smoke and my core heats. *Wow, thanks.* "Right. Well. Honestly, I don't fancy jacket potatoes. So I might just head out and grab us take out."

SHASSII

I smile softly as she puckers her lips before I slide the cigarette back in her mouth.

"Wendys?" I give her puppy dog eyes and I'm sure she's sick of it by now but I've grown an addiction.

"I won't be long." She has barely left the house recently and I desperately want to go with her, but I know I can't. It's not just me involved now, it's her too, and being found equals her going to prison. I don't think I could live with myself if she ended up behind bars *again*. I know morally she deserves it, but maybe now I'm the one being selfish. If she hadn't taken my parents with her, I could completely look past the other people she's taken for good reason. But my parents are different... My father not so much. But it's still taken me five months to come to terms with my mom's death and I still quietly cry at night when she thinks I'm asleep.

She puts her boots and jacket on and it doesn't take long for her to disappear out the driveway, leaving me sitting here looking around for things to do. I find my feet as I jump off the island and run to the garage. This is the first time I've been alone since she took my virginity, but a lot has changed since then. Maybe now she will confess to me what exactly she is hiding. Because for some reason, deep down I am still trying to find reasons to hate her, to feel like my guilt is meaningful. She can't be this *perfect*. Or as perfect as a serial killer could be anyway. When do you ever hear about a hostage becoming their kidnappers' side piece? *Never.*

I tip toe towards the locked door of secrets and lock pick it. I've gotten quite good at that.

The door slowly creeks open, revealing a creepy wooden staircase and a pit of darkness. I would never go down into our basement because I am absolutely terrified of them. I stand there for a moment debating whether I should face my demons, but I've been facing them for five months. Nothing scares me at this point, so I take my first step, the wood creeks underneath my foot as I make my way down the steep stairs. I wonder how anyone walks down there without falling, whilst I scramble to find a switch on the wall.

The room becomes a timid glow of orange light and a single light bulb hangs from a cord in the centre of the ceiling where a punching bag is hanging in the middle of a fairly large open space. Some cardboard boxes scatter the back wall and a worktop cluttered with junk and a boombox are collecting dust. She hasn't been down here for ages from what I can recall, maybe I really am just being paranoid. I don't know what I was expecting but this is pretty normal. Why is she so afraid of me finding out about her man cave? I reach the ground floor, taking a closer look. Even down here, desolate and unused her smell still wafts underneath my nose. A door catches my attention as I continue to snoop in the furthest corner of the room. There is a passageway and a door sits barricaded shut with wooden planks and the fattest nails I've ever seen. Whatever she doesn't want me to find?

I think I've just found it.

SHASSII

CHAPTER 44

THE DEVILS LAIR

Puppet

Play - 'Hate Myself - NF'

I move closer to the door, touching the wood, tracing my fingers over the bolts, studying the way it's been cut off from the rest of the house and I'm so lost. What the hell could she possibly be hiding that is so terrible? She hasn't killed for weeks? *right?*

My breath is taken from my lungs when a hand smothers my mouth. *Her hand.* I can smell her as she wraps her arms around my waist consumed by the waft of ash and leather, dragging me back upstairs as I thrash around trying to escape her hold and I don't know why I bother. It's useless. I can feel it through her grip that she's angry as she yanks me with no remorse. A lump forms in my throat as she hoists me up the steps, kicking my feet against the wood yelping as I hit my Achilles heel. *Fuck!* I'm pulled out the door with my feet dragging across the floor as she slams the door shut so loud my heart jumps into my mouth, throwing me against it by my throat and I freeze. She has never laid her hands on me this way. I can feel her aggression through her fingers as she squeezes with malice, visibly shaking as she glares at me with fury.

"Ouch! You're hurting me!" I stutter through depleting oxygen, clawing at her arm to let go and she doesn't have to say anything, her face tells me what she's thinking. *Good.*

"What did you expect to find, huh?! Dead bodies? A jar of organs! A memorial of all the people I've killed!?" She lets go reluctantly, smashing the palms of her hands against the door either side of my head so volatile that the wall shakes. I rub my sore throat, glaring at her with betrayal, but I can't be angry. We betrayed one another *again*. I should never have gone down there. I didn't realise how angry this would make her.

"I was finding reasons to hate you..." She flares her nostrils, exhaling deeply with frustration and her hand crashes against my cheek leaving a familiar sting that makes my eyes water, holding my harm as I glare at the floor in disbelief.

"Do you hate me now!?" She spits venom as she pinches my chin, making me take in her anger.

"Fuck you!..." I'm hurt. And I know I shouldn't be. I caused this, but she left me no choice. She said no more secrets and she is still hiding things from me.

"I could give you plenty of reasons to fucking HATE ME *Alora*!" She's right. She could. But I don't want to believe she is a saint. I want to find something, *anything* that tells me I am wrong, that she is a *monster*. That all of this is delusional. That she is far worse than I can see so I can stop trying to fix her. Stop seeing the good I see in her.

"What are you so afraid of! What is so bad that you have to hide from me!" I challenge her, pushing my face into her personal space.

"Stop. Fucking. PUSHING!" I've never seen her this angry. *It's frightening*. She's like a fuse about to blow.

"What could you possibly be scared of?! What are you not telling me?!" My back slams against the wood as she tunnels me, pinning me to the door with her eyes.

"If I told you, you would never fucking look at me the same again. Leave it the hell alone!" I bite my tongue out of frustration. That is the problem! I need to know what kind of person I'm sleeping with!

"How can I see you any differently if you don't tell me?!" She frowns with hurt. She always wants to paint herself as a monster, but my words visibly hurt her. Deep down, she doesn't want me to see that in her. She wants me to see the little girl who desperately wants *saving*. I see her.

"You see me for what I fucking am *Alora*, a *Monster*. There is nothing more to it! It's how it should be!" I snap, striking her across the cheek and my stomach drops. Her face shoots to the side and she rolls it out with her jaw, licking the inside of her cheek as she side glances at me with annoyance, her tongue running along her teeth as her eyes meet mine once more full of pent up rage she's desperately trying to resist. I can see it brewing in the storm behind her eyes.

"I don't believe you!" Tears finally fall. We haven't argued like this for so long. We were finally getting somewhere. We were finally learning one another. *This is infuriating.* My fingers find her abuse in the dark, stretching my tendrils over the trauma in her face, the wreckage that is her hollow cheek as I fight back guilt and suppress tears I don't have the privilege of streaming, for damage that was out of my control. I'm pining for answers beneath her skin like braille as I sink into the darkness behind her tired eyes. Wondering what kind of monster would sabotage his own flesh and blood with more flesh and blood.

"You should be afraid of me." She echoes against defeated sighs, like her hauntingly beautiful appearance should scare me away as she digs for signs of fear that I will not give her, visible distress falling from her eyes as I tend to her harm like my touch could cure the years of pain etched into her added smile. "Why? Why aren't you afraid of me?" How can I be afraid of someone who's barely understood what it is to be loved? The most terrifying thing about her is her vulnerability towards a glimmer of peace. She seeks to destroy it like a spider to a fly caught in its web. *Deliberate. Calculated. Doomed.*

"I- I...*Don't know-*" I whisper so quietly through a shaky breath, unsure in myself why being in her arms has never felt safer. Even now, when her aggression is her only prominent emotion and her sweaty palms find my face in the chaos, gripping the hair behind my ear as she pins my body with hers, breathing deeply, cradling my cries. An apology without words.

"I'm bad for you *Alora*...I'm *broken*. Do you hear me? Don't do this to me. Don't make me show you how *broken* I am. Don't make me open that door. *It will kill us both.*" I sob harder, gripping her shirt with so much internal rage. "Why are you doing this to me?"

She questions me, shaking my head vigorously, searching for answers in me, trembling as her lips graze mine and I choke trying to get the words out. Words I didn't ever imagine could drip from my tongue.

"Because I need to know what kind of person I am *falling in love with.!...*" I mutter softly, closing my eyes like it will hide me from my confession as I weep for *us*. She squeezes my hair tighter, leaning her forehead against mine like she's been defeated.

"Don't... Don't say that. *Alora.* You can't. Do you understand me? You can't." *It's too late.* I don't know what love feels like, but I know what I feel for her is far deeper than I can comprehend. Where you would do anything for that person. Where you will find the ounce of good that keeps you holding on. Where no matter how they treat you, you cling to the kindness that is engraved in your heart because you're terrified to lose them. *I'm terrified to lose her.*

"Why...?" it slips from my mouth as I try to find the answer behind the guilt so clearly protruding on her face.

"Because I will never *Love* you back." My heart sinks, releasing my grip on her shirt, dropping my shoulders with vanquish.

I don't know what I was expecting. She doesn't even know the meaning of the word. But if there is nothing between us then what the hell are we doing? I recite her words. Because she is just not ready to let me in. She is too scared to let someone in. To let them help her.

"Then never, I'll wait." She shakes her head but I will not fight her on this. Her tongue glides against my salty cheek, lapping up my cries against the sensitive flesh she struck. The sting makes me squint but her warmth makes me melt into her hold. Her touch makes all the pain go away. *She is fire.* You're drawn to its heat. The way it dances across everything it touches, destroys everything in its path, but you have the urge to touch it. To play with it. To dance with it on a cold night. It's destructively beautiful and its consequences are ugly, but we still light fires, because they keep our blood pumping and our body warm. *There is no beauty without consequence. No happiness without pain. No Love without hate.*

Play - 'Fuck me like you hate me – Jutes'

"You should be terrified of me." She sinks her teeth into my cheek, pinching it until I hiccup a sharp breath, sliding her fingers between my thighs.

"Is that what you want... For me to be afraid? For me to hate you?..." She takes my bottom lip in her teeth, dragging it with just enough force that I follow her as she pulls and I can feel a puddle between my legs every time she touches me like this. *With need.*

"It would be easier that way..." That is what she wants to think but life has been easier since she finally let me in. She needs to realise I'm not going anywhere, that I'm ready to see all the broken parts of her and love her anyway. *It can't get much worse than this.*

"Then *fuck* me like you hate me, *Hayden.*" Her grip indents my skin sinking into my thigh as she glares at me for a moment, like she's shocked that those words even came out of my mouth but she can't resist me and I love it. I love that she can't function unless she's inside of me, *where she belongs.*

"You wanna sit real pretty on my cock *Princess*?" Her famine unravels against my soft tongue as she devours my mouth like she's trying to find something deeper, unzipping her jeans with haste and I will never get used to this. Pulling out her strap before gripping my outer thighs. She lifts me to wrap my legs around her hips and I still flinch as she stretches out my inner thighs with the width of her waist, securing me against the door only holding up my frame with one arm as she plays with my slit, already dripping, ready for her to slide inside me, forcing it in until I whimper into her mouth as I bite down on her lip so hard she growls. Her hold on me is inescapable as she wastes no time fucking me senseless, pounding into me with her jewelled knuckle dusters hot to my neck as I take every inch, choking on the pain she so desperately wants to make me feel. It burns, it burns so hot, but so does this.

"You're nobody to me. *My plaything.*"

Her words are spiteful, talking with her teeth clamped shut down my ear. Disrespecting the secrets I'm leant against, fucking me into oblivion. As the door rattles I grip the handle for support accidentally causing it to swing open leaving nothing but us and a dead drop into the basement. I grab the frame of the door to keep me up, panicking as horror paints my face and she seems totally unphased, grinning at my unfortunate predicament.

"Are you frightened now?..." She tugs at my top, tearing it right down the centre effortlessly as I cling to her with just my legs, letting my breasts free, followed by my pants, ripping them clean off of me with thirst. She squeezes my fleshy thighs as she pounds into me mercilessly, her diamonds glued to my tits as they bounce before her, leaning in to me to take them in her mouth as she pinches them with her teeth, sucking until it bruises me.

"Fu-ck..." My head hangs back, peering into the black void awaiting my arrival, using all my strength to keep me from letting go but it's getting harder, my mind's blank with only the thought of her between my legs. She's already fucked me in the darkness. I feel like I'm consuming her demons every time she makes me scream.

"You get off on this fear, don't you *baby*?" Yes. *It makes me feel alive.* This momentary anchor between life and death. It excites me. "Let go." I pull my head back up, glaring at her. She's crazy. *Let go of the door?!* "Don't make me ask you again."

She fucks me agonisingly slowly, feeling her slide against my walls, curving up into my sweet spot were my legs start to quiver. I do as she says, flinching as I gradually let go of the frame where my upper body falls, squinting as I prepare to hit the floor when she cups the back of my neck, squeezing it tightly in the palm of her hand to support me. *I knew she wouldn't let me fall.*

"Do you hate me, Puppet?..."

"Yes." I hate her for all the ways she makes me feel whole. She is three times the size of me so holding me up must be like holding a feather. Her nails dig into my scalp as she claws her fingers into the scruff of my neck, pushing my head forward to make me look down at her sliding into my wet hole as she spits on my chest making me gasp at the sensation, dirtying me with her foul mouth as it drips down the ravine of my breasts sending a chill up my spine.

"Say it." She loves to be hated. She loves to feel feared. And I do feel all those things, but because once she has her way with me, none of it matters.

"I hate you..." She thrusts harder at her love language. She's punishing me with her cock, spitting between my legs and I pulsate, taking my fingers to play with my clit like I know she wants me to. I don't realise how close I am, jolting through the pain as this pleasure overtakes me, grinding against her desperately chasing this release between my thighs, crying out until I hit it.

"*Say it again.*" Her lips part like she's trying to moan out silently, glaring at her penetrating my hole but god I want to hear it. I want to hear her lie through her moans.

"*I hate you!...*"

"Desperate fucking *Whore.*" She holds me tightly, letting me let go on her cock, twitching as I cling onto that feeling, screaming out her name with wrath and I'm so sore. She's not fucked me that roughly yet but I knew it was coming.

She tugs me sharply, tasting my tongue as she kisses me and it doesn't matter how many times we kiss, butterflies batter against my chest.

I will be her plaything if she wants me to.

I will be anything she wants me to be. All she has to do is ask.

SHASSII

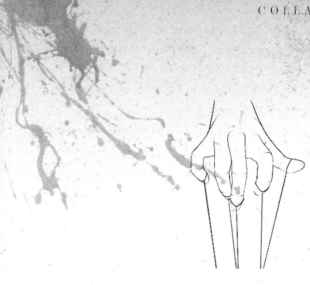

CHAPTER 45

BLEED FOR ME

Puppeteer

I lay my head back into the sofa, chain smoking away my thoughts. I've not stopped thinking about her idiotic confession and I'm so angry. Angry at myself for letting her get this close to me. She should not have told me that. I will never be able to say it back. I don't have that in me. I am incapable of loving anyone. She is merely an *obsession* and things have gotten so out of hand.

She pokes her head round the door with a towel wrapped around her tiny body.

"So like... Do you have any more plugs? We've sort of ran out." I crack my neck, thinking of all the vulgar ways I can continuously corrupt her body. She is far from innocent now but she certainly hasn't seen it all yet.

"If you want me to fuck your ass all you have to do is ask." I am not looking at her but I can see her crumpled face of disapproval through the back of my head.

"OH MY GOD NOT THOSE KIND OF PLUGS!" Not now, but I will happily punish her tight little ass if she steps out of line.

"I'm just fucking with you *Innocence*. You're far too baby for that." She lets out a harsh sigh of annoyance. We're still on rocky terms but that's an easy fix. Fucking is not an issue, but she is still angry that I won't give up my secret and I still want to lock her in the damn basement for entering it when I specifically told her not to. *Brat.*

"Top shelf in the cupboard." I smirk menacingly, knowing full well that is too high for her.

"I literally cannot reach that." I can feel the eye roll.

Play - 'Bathroom - Montell Fish'

"Then what do you say?" I rise from my seat, glaring at her endangered body beneath my towel and I can taste her in my mouth just by looking at her, creeping slowly towards the bathroom door thinking of all the despicable ways I could ruin her next, baring my teeth at her like she's my next meal when I grin.

"Please..." She hums softly, waiting for me to retrieve the box from the cabinet, clutching the towel like it will save her from me but she knows I could rip it away before she even had a chance to blink. I go to hand her the box but before she has a chance to take it I drop it on the floor, gripping the back of her neck as I bend her over the sink, twitching at the angelic gasp that leaves her throat.

"Hayden..." She warns as I trace the tips of my fingers lightly up the back of her inner thigh, dragging the towel up with me and she's already a dizzy mess.

"Shhhhh..." The tips of my tongue dance against her throat, cuddling her carotid artery between the cut as I listen to her breathing escalate knowing she is incapable of saying no to me.

"But I'm on my-" I encase her mouth with my hand, cutting off her sentence because *I don't give a shit.*

"And? You think a little blood is going to stop me? It's just blood, *Puppet*." I'll be honest, I've not tasted the sweet stain of someone's insides for over a month. I've not killed, *for her*. I'm attempting to be a better person but I'm biting at the bit to tear a cunts life away.

"You really are a bundle of *Innocence*. I thought you liked to get dirty?" I whisper down her ear, tempting the devil on her shoulder and she's seconds away from giving in already, I can feel it in the weight of her sinking into my mouth.

"That's gross. It will go everywhere." She whispers lightly, trying to find her balance and any sort of truth in her blatant lie as I gently untie her towel, letting it fall to the floor as goosebumps smother her nude complexion. Her perfection against all my imperfections.

"That's the point." I nudge my way into that sensitive spot behind her ear, tickling it with my breath, gliding my fingers against her arms as I tower over her watching her melt for me in the cracked mirror.

"Does it make you squeamish?..." She quite happily watched Saw with me but she can't handle a little blood?

"No- it, just..." I glide between her thighs watching her twitch, but I know she doesn't want me to stop. We've been playing this game for far too long.

"Haven't you wondered what it feels like...fucking your most sensitive parts? Reaching that peak as you look down at the mess you've made?" She swallows against my hand as my thumb and middle finger rub at the blood pumping beneath my palm, squeezing it gently to cut off her oxygen supply, watching her life vanish from her eyes as a ghost peers back at me through the shattered reflection, possessing her vulnerable body as she comes back to me.

"I'm not a murderer... I have no interest in watching myself bleed to death."

"*But I am.*" And I will happily watch her bleed out for me whilst a heavy pulse still keeps her heart beating. I want her to see how pretty death can be when executed correctly. "Let me do it for you as you cum all over my fingers *Puppet.*"

She goes to speak but my hand has her tongue tied, rubbing against the red velvet between her warm thighs as she whimpers like a dream.

"Let me show you how I rearrange guts. It feels good, I promise." It feels so fucking good against my fingers. Plunging my middle and ring finger inside to take more of her, already making a mess as she moans out for me covering my rings in wine and its fucking *divine*.

I pull out, glaring at her through the mirror, swiping her blood length ways across my cheek, over my lips and against my scar, licking my bottom lip to taste her in my mouth.

Play - 'See You bleed - Ramsey'

"You're sick..." She watches me intensely, but she doesn't budge or pull away, captivated in my fucked up desire to taste every damn part of her.

"And you fuck this sickness like a drug *baby*. So who's worse?..." Her complexion goes almost the same colour as her insides painting my face. She loves that I'm messed up. It makes her feel less guilty for indulging in these desires I've planted in her head.

"Drugs are an antidote to pain..." She speaks truths and my eye twitches. We are both using each other to numb our past.

"Is that what I am *baby*... Your antidote?" My free hand grips her head tightly to face the ceiling watching her squeeze the china sink as I slide my fingers back inside, just teasing her entrance listening to her stuttered sigh behind my ear. She is my undoing. The blood on my hands. I've killed her once and I'll do it again until she realises that even in death. *Her body belongs to me.*

"Bleed for me."

My fingers curl deep inside, smothering my flesh in red satin, relishing in how wet my hand is between her succulent thighs, sucking out those bittersweet whimpers she hates.

"You're not fighting this very hard, *Love*." My teeth nip her tender throat as a whisper, tasting her bare skin as she sings my favourite song, creeping her legs open wider to take more of me. "Let me bleed you dry *baby*." I rock my fingers deeper, steady with my rhythm and she's already twitching her tight little cunt around me like a needy little whore, pushing into my hand as she rides that insatiable relief.

"Choke me..." She mummers quietly, and my lip curls as she uses her voice *for me.*

"My *Puppet* has a voice." My tatted claw crawls up her throat, applying pressure at the sides and her eyes disappear in our reflection, already crumbling like granite, melting against the basin of the sink as I grind my bulge up against her ass forcing a gasp from her throat.

"My belt." I snarl through a gravelly whisper and she wastes no time reaching for it, undoing its buckle letting it hang loose. Her hormones must be treating her well, *such a slut for me.*

I let her go, unthreading the belt from its loops before wrapping it around her throat, looping it through the metal ring, throbbing at her gasps as I pull it tight to secure her neck.

"Kneel." I bite, and she does as instructed, kneeling at my boots, wearing my belt as a pretty noose as she awaits her death dangling before me, undoing my jeans to let my strap loose. I lubricate it with *her blood* smothering my hand as I kneel between her legs salivating at the sight, my knees digging into the tiled floor as I push her upper body gently until she finds the ground, teasing her aching hole ready to take me like a *good girl.*

"Let me ruin your insides *baby...*" She's trembling with adrenaline as I slide in carefully, gripping her thigh to ease myself in, painting her ass in crimson as I claw at her porcelain skin and she's totally unphased.

"Bleed on my cock, *Innocence.*" My words escalated her jagged moans as she struggles to take my length, choking on my belt as it restricts her airways. I tug her to face the ceiling, making her pray to me as I loom over her, curving into the ridges of my body against her as I fill up her velvet cunt, bringing her to new heights as I breach her most sensitive parts. Overwhelming relief surges through her like anaesthetic as my cock now slides effortlessly through her arousal, burying my kill inside her pussy.

"*Fuck-*" I hiss in relief, watching her take my strap like it was built to fit inside her, she sounds so fucking pretty when she's dying *for me*, making me ravage her further, thrusting into her to seek out her cries as she clings onto her submission. She bows into my motion as she arches her back, her chest flush against the tiled floor and I must admit, it feels euphoric to tear down the archway to heaven. She won't be making it there unfortunately. She will fall with me where she belongs as I fill her with her greatest sin.

"H-ayde-n..." I've learnt her body and the way it responds to me, all her buttons to tip her over the edge. *My Little Puppet* likes to chase death when she cums on me, letting me pull the strings to keep her going as my grip tightens on the leather belt, slamming down around her throat to hike her back up on her hands as my tongue trails the length of her spine, tasting her sweet and salty pallet.

"*Filthy Princess,* make a *bloody* mess for me. Don't be shy." My hunger gnaws down her ear as she touches herself for me, whimpering at the sensation against her fingers, trying to stay balanced with her entire body weight shaking on one arm but my belt has her secured, fighting to keep her head up so she doesn't pass out as she grabs that impending orgasm, pushing into me with no repentance.

"Die for me." I will kill her body, mind and soul if it means I get to see her at my mercy like this. Her bloodied hand tears at the white tiles beneath her as the pressure gets too much, smearing it like my own personal horror movie. A husky moan slips out my mouth as she lets me suck up her essence, cumming all over my cock, trying to claw her way out from beneath me as her lifeless body slides against the cold floor trying to catch her breath that's quickly stolen from her as I hoist her up against my chest, choking on the humid air.

"See... Murder can be just as beautiful..." My distasteful words grate against her ear as she fights all the reasons she should hate me right now for violating her. I slowly pull out of her to reveal the destruction smothered between her thighs, patch work of a sinner's stain blanketing her flesh like wet roses.

"I hate you..." Those words are music to my ears.

"*Good.*" I pull her up by her abdomen, caressing her soft clammy skin, wiping the sweaty locks from her face as her back meets my front, chasing her breath as I run it off, kissing the shell of her ear.

"The harder you hate me the harder I'll fuck you."

CHAPTER 46

MY CONSTELLATION

Puppet

Play - 'Out of the picture pt.1 - Kilu'

She's been in and out all day lugging god knows what back and forth, I have no idea what she's doing. I felt I needed space after the last few days. She violated me in the best way and I'm still beating myself up over it yet again, giving into my weird compulsion to fall into her arms like a helpless princess. Even after everything, I find myself aching for all of her sick and twisted desires just to please her. It pleases me, but sex is not the answer. I know I shouldn't be but I'm hurting and I don't know why. I'm sure this is a silly little crush that will go away but my heart is aching. I just want her to see what I see in her and she refuses to. Refuses to let me see that vulnerable side of her but I see it anyway, it's just who I am. I can't ignore these feelings and no amount of writing or keeping out of her way is helping.

SHASSII

I'm stuck in the same house as her. I can't exactly avoid her forever and deep down I don't want to. I want a hug. I want her to hold me in her arms and tell me all the things I want to hear and I know it's unrealistic. She said it herself. She would never *Love* me back and I think I'm finally going through my first heartbreak. A heartbreak that was not even intentional or planned. But I guess that's what heartbreak is, no one prepares for that. She is trying to teach me that love is pain but she's wrong. It can be beautiful if you plant it in the right soil, this soil is just dry and has been left to wither away. I can't even get my words out, I've been trying to write for the last three hours and I want to throw the book, thinking of all the vile ways I want her to sin on my body just to feel close to her. She doesn't love, she shatters. She's shattered my perception on life. She's shattered the girl I once was and this new version of me now glues to excitement like I might die tomorrow.

A knock brings me out of my head, glaring at the door as she pushes it open and she's in fairly clean and presentable attire, *that's unlike her*? But I'm gawking like a schoolgirl. I will never not drool at her in a black shirt.

"What's the occasion?" There is sorrow in her attempted smile.

"I want to show you something. Get dressed." She leans her head on the frame of the door, running her fingers against the wood as she twitches the corner of her mouth before walking towards the living room and I swallow my feelings, trying to ignore this physical tension in my chest every time I look at her.

I slip into a turtleneck and my black frilly skirt, sliding on my knee highs as I tiptoe out the bedroom. The front door is wide open like it's calling to me and she's not in the house so I make my way outside the building, following Shep who rubs his wet snout against my bare leg as we wander out the front door where a metal guard dog signs hangs from a rusty nail. *'BEWARE'* in bold letters causes me to look at the fluff ball and grin comically. I could never see Shep being scary, he's only ever shown me devoted love. I exit the door as the outside chill hits my skin and it feels so foreign. It's dusk and the sun is cracking across the horizon, lighting up my face with a fading warmth as it sets behind the tree. I turn to see her waiting for me on the bonnet of the rust bucket sat in the front yard, a cigarette hanging out her mouth as she hops off it towards me and my body stiffens, swallowing my want to run into her arms. She smiles softly at me and my insides knot, walking around me as she closes in behind, making me hitch with curiosity, encasing my eyes with fabric restricting my view and tying a knot to keep it tight but I can feel this is not malicious or ill willed.

"Hayden, what the hell are you doing?" She places her hand on my lower back, pushing with delicate force to entice me to move with her.

"Just- trust me." That's the problem. All I've done is trust her and now I've become unstuck. My feet move, letting her guide me, hoping I don't trip over my feet.

"Is this where you kill me?"

A huff forces through her nose in amusement. *"I already did that."*

Her sly mouth really gets under my skin in the best way. We walk for what feels like maybe 20ft until she draws me to a halt and I can feel her against the back of my neck.

"Are your eyes closed?" I squeeze them shut along with my palms. I'm not scared, just beaming with anticipation as I nod, giving her the ok to remove my blindfold as she tugs the knot letting it loosen, pulling it away from my face. "*Open.*"

I squint with one eye first, but my jaw falls low as I finally focus on my surroundings. Her trailer sits amongst tall grass with a small gravel path leading up to the little steps, smothered in fairy lights looping the roof extending off into the bushes. A small bench sits in front of the window with snacks and beers. *She finally finished it.*

"Oh my god- Hayden this is beautiful." I admire the new coat of cream paint, glowing a warm pink against the sunset with stars scattering the wires and everything in me lights up, even underneath that hard shell I can see exactly what she's thinking about right now. "She would have loved it."

I glance over at her sitting on the table of the bench with one leg up on the seat and she stares intently at me, relighting her dead cigarette.

"Yeah...She would have." I stand awkwardly, waiting for her to say something but we mellow in the silence I think she needs right now. You could cut the tension with your teeth.

....

"Today is her birthday." My heart stops, swallowing my guilt for feeling so entitled to my feelings right now. She glares up at the empty sky and I wonder if she still talks to her when I'm not around. Hears her in the calmness of the gentle wind.

"Well, this is a pretty epic birthday present." All of this for someone who is no longer with us. Her bond is indescribable. *She is capable of love,* it's written in her actions and devotion to the woman who never stopped loving her. The only woman who never gave up on her, even till her very last breath. Me and my mom had a great relationship but I guess we never had that bond through pain to connect us. A bond I now understand. It's unlike anything I've ever felt, this overwhelming connection that pulls your souls closer together.

She continues her silence, popping the cap off a beer before handing it to me, saying thank you through a smile.

"Which one is my panel?" She points to the panel by the door and I smirk gently. Being part of this project makes my chest throb. It has nothing to do with me yet a piece of me still resides here in her hard work. "So. Are you going to give me a tour?"

She finishes the last draw, crushing the cigarette in the palm of her hands and I shouldn't have found that as attractive as I did. *She has absolutely no fear of pain and I find myself wanting to know why more and more each day.*

"Are you going to keep avoiding me?" *Fuck, she's noticed.* She stands to her feet, creeping towards me and I scrunch my shoulders into my neck. She just consumes my entire being when I'm in her vicinity.

"Hayden... I'm not. I just-" I glare at the floor where her boots fall into frame, too afraid to look back up at her but she tucks her index fingers underneath my chin, guiding me to face *My Nightmare.*

"You're hurt." She interrupts me. Her touch has the ability to make my eyes water as she caresses my jaw line delicately.

"Yeah... I guess so..." I feel so silly. She must think I'm absolutely ridiculous falling for her in these circumstances, but it's not exactly like she's pushed this possibility away. We had sex? She's been inside me? I thought that was *meant* to mean something. I push this to the back of my mind. Now is not the time to be arguing. Today is about her mom.

"Well, think of this as an apology." I look around at the effort and maybe this isn't just about her mom. She did this to try and remove the awkward tension in the house. To make up for hurting me.

"I'm starting to like apologies..."

Play - 'Star Shopping – Lil Peep'

The sun had finally set and we sat there for hours bringing up old stories, reminiscing on happy memories, the handful she had anyway. I had a few but we are more alike than we like to admit. I was only allowed one beer this time but I snuck a few sips from hers, playing fetch with Shep to keep him from snoring at our feet in boredom.

She stares at the trailer intensely, lost in thought and I study her thinking face admiring the emptiness she holds in her expression when she's lost in the clouds. She's a *dreamer,* but what she dare dream about may terrify me. Her features are softer when she's not here with me, when she allows herself to breathe and I gawk at her in the gentle glow that cascades the trees above us. In the stillness we don't get to experience as I study the features I'd never noticed before. Besides the gash in her cheek, there is a gentle nip in her lip, the word above her eyebrow etches into her skin and I can finally read, *Exile*. Wondering what it means and where it came from. All these questions I've still yet to ask.

She stands abruptly, walking towards the trailer and jumps on the arch of the wheel, lifting herself up onto the roof leaving my jaw on the floor. *She did that so effortlessly.*

"What are you doing up there?!" I face her, scowling up looking over to see Shep scowling right along with me, baffled that she thinks I have the strength to lift myself up there on my own. "Up there! I won't even be able to get on the wheel!"

She doesn't have to say a word, staring at me with her answer like I can read her thoughts. I get up slowly, shaking my head in disbelief as I make my way to the arch, managing to climb on until my foot slips. *I really shouldn't be in socks.* I fully prepare to land on my ass until her hand grips my wrist, hoisting my bodyweight up like it's nothing. Her strength makes me ache. *And I don't mean my heart.*

"Lie with me." She plants her ass down on the roof, laying back into her hands as she cups the back of her neck, peering up at me with nothing but admiration and the cool breeze taints my flush cheeks, joining as I lay beside her, fighting everything in me not to cuddle up to her as we lay there gazing at the midnight sky as if it's our last day on earth. Like we are the last one's left.

...

"I hated astrology." She confesses dryly and I burst into a snigger at the irony.

"Really? Because you have a funny way of showing it." Sarcasm splits the air, giggling under my breath.

"She was so obsessed with it, she'd talk my ear off for hours. And now I'd do anything to listen to those mind-numbing conversations again." My face contorts, finding peace in this happy memory but mourning for the little girl inside her so desperately trying to find peace after all these years.

"Well, I know nothing about astrology. Tell me something." I wiggle to get comfortable, willing to listen. Open to learn if it means I can listen to her.

"You see where those stars align? The three dots?" She points towards the dust scattering the void above us and I have absolutely no idea where she's pointing.

"Where? I can't see?" She shuffles closer and my entire body tightens, pressing her temple against mine to try and line up our sight until I finally see it.

"Oh! I see it, I see it!" There is something so crazy about looking up at an entire universe beyond us. Like we are all imprisoned to endless worlds and possibilities. A grain of sand in the Pacific Ocean.

"That's Orion's belt." Her useless but meaningful knowledge makes my heartbeat faster and I can feel her lips grazing my cheek innocently as she smiles.

"Do you think aliens exist?" I question her jokingly.

Play - 'Pretty When You Cry - Lana Del Rey'

"Oh absolutely. I've actually been abducted by one. They told me that I had no heart and sent me back down to earth." A disgusting laugh falls out of my mouth and I hiccup on air as she abruptly puts her lips to mine, dripping with tenderness, melting into her much needed touch. It's now insufferable to be away from her. These past few days have been nothing short of unbearable and all I've wanted is this.

She detaches, licking my taste from her lips and an uninvited throb cripples my flower.

I have no idea what she's doing but she's hurting my head with all these emotions we are both clearly feeling. I gaze at her like my own constellation, grazing my thumb against her faded tattoo curving her brow. She flinches slightly, scrunching her forehead as she glares at me like she wants to cut my thumb off.

"*Exile*. What does it mean?" Her throat bobs, like she's reluctant to tell me but I refuse to let go of her vulnerability I seem to be grasping at right now.

"It's what I am, *Princess*." There is pain etched into her tongue as she speaks down to me.

"I don't understand?" My tongue finds the roof of my mouth as her rough fingers drape behind the shell of my ear, still trying to accustom to this sweetness slipping through the cracks.

"I'm banished. From this life. From my home. From my heart. I've been exiled, or more I've exiled myself." My brows dip, trying to read her face, wondering why on earth she would say something so silly.

"Why?"

"Because I simply do not belong." I wait for her to laugh but she remains cold in the face. *She truly believes that.* And I gaze up at her trying to figure out where she is going to go from here if she doesn't even belong with me.

"So. Where will you go now? Or- we. If you'd have me." She peers down at me through her hooded brows.

"And how do you suppose I travel around with someone who's supposedly missing?" *There are ways around these things, right?*

"I'll wear a wig, change my name or something." I laugh off my delusion, but her facial expression quickly brings it to a halt.

"Are you serious?" *Is that so crazy?* To want to travel the world and explore? I thought that is what she wanted. Isn't that why she built this?

"Deadly."

She rubs the bridge of her nose with irritation, pondering on my proposition. "I don't think so, *Puppet*. That is no life for you."

My eye's peer to the back of my head as I roll them in irritation. *Who is she to dictate my life?*

"And what is exactly? This?" My tone is snappy, trying desperately to understand what more she wants from me if all of this means nothing.

"No. And I've already told you, when I've sorted shit out, I will get out of your hair for good. *You'll be free.* Living a normal life." My stomach sinks at the thought. Three months ago I couldn't wait to get out of here, *away from her,* back to normality, but now I can't think of anything worse. Why would I want to go back to a life with no freedom? *This is freedom.* I've done more in the last four months with her than I have my entire life. What happened to chasing me to the ends of the earth and haunting my dreams?

"I don't want a normal life anymore." Normality Frightens me. There is no adventure, no excitement. What is normal anyway? working a 9-5 job with responsibility pouring out your ass?

"*Alora*... You have a whole life to get back to. You're so smart and you have so much ahead of you, I will not keep you from that." She is complimenting me, four months ago she wanted me to suffer, to experience all my pain and endure her spiteful nature. But now? Now she's trying to push me to do something with my life. Something that doesn't involve her but I can only focus on the negatives right now. *I have no life to go back to.* Go back to court cases, people calling me names, conspiracies of the girl I once was and where I've been? Being plastered all over the news? I would prefer to stay in the clouds. Here. *With her.*

"Don't I get a say? You're starting to sound like my parents." I lift my upper body to meet her in a standoff and the tranquil night has turned into a storm between us.

"I'm just trying to do what is best for you. And it's certainly not me." Every time she doubts her worth it shatters me just a little more.

"Well, that is for me to decide. *Not you.*" I push her roughly and although I know I can't psychically move her, she moves anyway to give me space.

"*Alora*. I care about you. I do. But you need to leave it alone." Is this what dating a fuck boy high school varsity jock is like? Because if so I really didn't miss out on much, this is exhausting.

"You just, expect me to ignore the fact you made love to me? You took my virginity?" Everything writing her expression is screaming the words I dread to hear.

...

"I shouldn't have done it..." My mouth gapes, feeling physical pain invade my lungs as I suddenly struggle to catch my breath, feeling my heart bleed into my bloodstream.

"Wow... You really are like everyone else." She can't even look at me. My fury grows against her fire, smouldering me in agony worse than her wrath. "You told me when I was ready, Hayden. And I was ready. Ready to give myself to you. Was that all just part of your sick, twisted ego? Your quick fix?"

She is holding guilt on the tip of her tongue, eyes filled with absent words her mouth cannot find as she avoids my every emotion.

"You told me I wasn't an object." I slide out from underneath her, crawling to try and find my feet as she grabs my waist, pulling me back into her slightly.

"*You're not.*" My death stare meets her, ripping her arm off my body.

"*Then why do I feel like one?...*"

"*Alo-*"

SHASSII

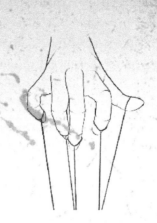

CHAPTER 47

FEED MY VIOLENCE

Puppeteer

Play - 'Numb - Linkin Park'

It's because she is not an object that I cannot bring myself to harm her further. She's been avoiding me and for good reason, I want her to resent me but there is a part of me yearning for this life she so desperately sees with me and I don't understand what she can see. Logistically, we would never work. The only option is to do time and I'm not prepared to commit to something like that again just yet. I've done what I needed to do, why the hell would I get myself thrown in there when I could stay here and live out my sad little life doing what I do best. She needs to let it the fuck go. She needs to let us go. *There is no us.* That sex meant more to me than I will ever admit to her because it keeps her tied to me. She needs to fear me, *hate me*. The way she used to, but I don't know why I am struggling to treat her the way my mind intends.

SHASSII

I grip my nails into the palms of my hand as she jumps down off the roof making her way inside, shaking in inner irritation. *I'm a fucking idiot. I don't know why the hell I fucking said that.*

I should probably run after her but that is not me. Like none of this is fucking me. I'm turning into a fucking pussy and I need a damn drink. Preferably not in her vicinity or I may do something I regret.

I jump off and head straight for the truck, following my intrusive thoughts until I reach the nearest bar, pulling up outside a rundown shack with a singular neon bottle hanging on for dear life to the brick wall. The stench of beer and boisterous men lingers in the air as I light a cigarette, drowning in my numbness as I stare at the door contemplating whether this is a good idea but quite frankly, I don't give a shit and I need to take my mind off her for five fucking minutes *before I lose it.*

I crush the cigarette in my palm and make my way inside with my hands in my pockets. It's not a bar I've personally visited, but there is a first time for everything and I'd rather not bump into company. As long as I can drown my sorrows I couldn't give a fuck what it looks like.

I reach the bar, slamming dollars down before taking a seat, hanging my head with the overwhelming thought of her like a lingering cold that won't leave me alone.

"JD. Neat." I demand as a dominant but feminine voice drips down my ear, looking back up to a woman with long ginger hair and a prideful smile, wiping out a glass before grabbing my poison.

"You've seen better days." She places the whole bottle in front of me with a shot glass to compliment it as she pours one out like she knows one drink is not all I'll be asking for.

"Not really." I drag it to my mouth, letting it heal my harm as it glides down my throat, burning me from the inside and god I forgot how good it feels.

"Dark and mysterious. Beats the regulars I get in here." I eye her curiously, in her tight black jeans and pretty throat exposed with a cute little owl necklace, glaring around the room at all the drunk fucks gawking at her over the bar.

"Someone like you shouldn't be working in here." She pours me another, smiling at me with serenity, leaning on the bar to get more comfortable.

"And has a way with words." She confesses, making me huff out loud as I neck another, tapping it on the wood as I roll my eyes in disagreement. My way with words is clearly riveting. It's why I'm bloody here.

"You can say that again..." She mimes an *'ohhhhhh'* as she reads me, filling the glass back up.

"That can only mean one thing. Whose heart did you break?" I look up at her, properly this time, analysing her eyes as she analyses mine like she can read my every thought and it's slightly terrifying.

"What makes you say that?" I scoff, taking another.

"Only people as handsome as you, who are drowning themselves in JD and wallowing in their own egotistical pity at midnight in the middle of the week are pining over a stupidly pretty girl they couldn't win over with their dick." Her words nearly make me crumble the shot glass in my fingers as she nails me with her scarily accurate accusation.

"*Ouch*. Remind me never to ask you a question again."

"What can I say? I've been here a long time. And you were a fool and didn't wrap your tool." *Clearly too long.* The girl needs a life or something. But her little dig does make me grin with amusement, *and I did technically win her over with my cock. That's the problem.*

"Hate to break it to you, but my cock is detachable." I look at her, expecting to see her laugh but she doesn't. Instead, she raises a brow with this seriousness that I'm not ready to listen to.

"I wasn't talking about what's between your legs. I was talking about the thing in your chest." Another slides down my throat, trying to ignore the way she just tried to point out I could possibly care when I literally kill for sport.

"It doesn't work." It hasn't worked for years. It's why it doesn't matter what I do. This will never work. *We* would never work. I was built to destroy, not mend.

"It does. You just gotta find the right part." People have so much hope. This unbearably annoying notion that love conquers all. That it's possible in everyone. But it's not, and I'm sick of fucking hearing it.

"What if it's broken." How the hell is someone meant to fix my engine when it's well and truly seized.

"Everything can be fixed. Whatever you did. It's fixable." I ponder on her optimism, wishing it was that simple. But then I relive everything I've done to her and suddenly it doesn't look so easy. I can't bring her parents back. I can't give her virginity back. I can't give the last god damn half a year back to her.

"What if you stole her parts to try and fix your own."

...

I grab the bottle, giving up with the glass as I swig it, glaring at her for an answer and she has one sitting on the end of her tongue.

"Then I'd suggest you stop being a selfish cunt and make up for being a jerk." Her fiery spirit makes me smile and even though I'm meant to be forgetting about her right now, I'm getting bitchy dating advice from a bartender, and all I can think about is her as I rub the scar on the inside of my hand.

"That mouth will get you in trouble, you know that-" I search respectfully for her name badge on her top.

...

"*Ellie.*" I mutter deeply as I peer back up at her glued eye contact, holding it for a little and I can see her turning slightly red, even in the warm lighting. Her eyes are entirely different from my *Little Puppets*. They are a void. A deep brown that harbours pain, so full of death. A look I know all too well. She's seen it all and she thrives in it. It's a look I'm familiar with. Someone I should be interested in but now my interests have changed.

Play - 'Coming Undone - korn'

"Is this lowlife disturbing you *baby*?" A husky groan emerges from behind me, leaning over the bar to try and intimidate me with the stench of liquor. I don't react, and she says nothing. "Hey, get your own, *jackass.*"

I side eye him through my bottle, nearly spitting it out in amusement. As beautiful as she is, she isn't my *Little Dreamer.* Nor will anyone else ever fucking be.

"Paranoid much? Worried a *lowlifes* gonna steal your girl?" He reacts exactly how I expected. *Threatened*.

"And an idiot." He snorts like a pig at his own humour and he's so punchable, my fist may just fly.

"You guys really like to throw accusations around huh?" It doesn't take him long before he's in my face, nearly spitting on me with his vile breath. Whatever she sees in him. It's clearly not his looks.

"Don't hit on my woman and we won't have a problem." My hands raise, admitting defeat so he's calms the fuck down.

"Look man. I'm just here to drink and she was aiding my request. *Cool it. That's her job.*" That clearly has no effect on his intoxicated craving for a fight, but I haven't had a good brawl in a while, and I'm urging to quiet my demons.

"Beat it." He's slightly shorter than me and he's far thinner than me so this confidence is truly admirable, he won't think so though when he wakes up with a broken nose tomorrow if he keeps getting in my fucking face.

"Paranoid *and* insecure. *That's cute.*" I spit, as he steps closer, practically inside me as he leans into my frame, challenging me with his feeble attempt at pushing my buttons and all I can do is kiss my teeth with excitement. *This is gonna be good.*

"You wanna watch your mo-"

His nose crunches as I crack it with my forehead, I ain't dealing with his obnoxious mouth tonight, finding his face in the bar as I grip the back of his neck slamming his sorry ass into the surface listening to the snap in the wood. Apparently neither is he as he wipes the blood streaming down his lip before aimlessly swinging for me, knocking me across the jaw catching my silverware, sending my head to nearly dislocate but I laugh under my breath, feeling the instant throb of torn skin where my piercing tried to dislodge itself. He's awoken a beast and my liquors starting to interrupt my bloodstream, moving solely on its hunger to feed my violence.

"You *FREAK*!" It only makes me cackle more, forcing my steel toe boot to his stomach, feeling him crush underneath me as he launches into the standing tables licking the gash where my tooth caught my lip, rolling in the sensation it gives me. The pulse is feeding me like I've snorted a line of coke as the metallic taste fills up my mouth.

Only I would get into a fucking bar fight with an incompetent drunk over a girl I wasn't even remotely interested in, all whilst trying to drown my feelings for the girl I am losing myself completely over. I'm drowning in this uninvited redemption she's trying to shove down my throat and my body won't allow it. I'm throwing it back up along with my *kindness*. This is who I fucking am and she needs to just get the fuck over it already. The quicker she does the better, because this nice act is only making me restless for blood.

"Hit me." I allow him to find his feet, giving him false security as he swings for me again, inflicting pain I oh so crave, grinning like the Devil as he hits me again, making me feel. Making me consume pain as he lets his pathetic tantrum out on my face before I grab him by the scruff of his neck and pummel his stomach with my knee, listening to him choke on his empty threats. Does he really think his little love taps are going to have any effect on me? *They are kisses.* "That's enough of that…"

Play – 'Can I – Genevieve Stokes'

I let him go, knocking him clean out with a final blow to the chin before grabbing the bottle of JD and dragging it off the counter. I coat my tongue in it as I tend to my mouth and lick it clean, feeling the torn hole under my already swelling lip throb, embracing its sting like I embrace her, drowning in the affliction as I picture her sweet little dimples and the beaming life still so hopeful in her eyes. The adrenaline is wearing off, leaving only my vulnerable body left to fend for itself as I sink into a pit of inflicted sorrow, intoxicated with only a longing for her in my arms and it's pissing me off how intensely I mourn for her when she is now not by my side. The past few days she's literally tried to avoid me and it's been agonising. This distance and silence is getting to my head. I said what I said so she'd hate me but it backfired heavily because now I'm the one getting hit the hardest. I bet she's over this shit by now, probably watching TV or asleep or something while I grovel like an idiot.

I glance over at Ellie gawking back at me, but not with fear. With spiritual excitement. I just beat her man to a pulp and she liked it. Sucks for him. But at least I could be entertainment, *as usual*.

My main worry now is that I've picked a fight and now I've drawn attention but the rest of the bar seem too gone to notice there was even a dispute.

"Have a good rest of your evening *Sweetheart*." I leave her with a gentle wink as I catch the blood dripping down my chin with my thumb and she fixates on me like I'm a foreign language, trying to understand me now. The truth is, no one ever truly did. Not even my mom. There is lots I never told her out of fear but most was so I could keep her from danger. Keep her from the truth which was inevitable. The gift he so graciously gave me across my cheek, I told her was from falling off my bike and although she never questioned further, the deceit in her eyes assured me that she always knew the truth. She wore it painfully behind the facade she performed. But she knew. She always knew.

For a little while I resented her for letting it happen when I found out she knew. Until one day I found burns etched into her shoulders and realised it was never just me being punished by the Devil and I began to endure it all so she didn't have to.

It was never enough. He was never satisfied. Hungry for my screams until I'd pass out and wake up in bed with an incurable migraine and marking so heavy I didn't understand how it never killed me at that age. *I was just a fucking kid.*

I hover over his pointless excuse for air as I spit on his mangled face, digging my heel into his ribs waiting to hear them crack beneath my boot but I refrain just this once, only pinning him down with the notion I might as that fearful glare I long for is staring back at me, feeling the pressure burning under my foot.

"Next time. Pick on someone your own size. *Jackass.*" I remove my foot, letting him breath again as he crawls away, clinging to the foot of a stool and I exit swiftly, bottle in hand, knowing this will be gone by the time I get back. I might just sleep in the truck, lock myself in so I don't do something dumb. *Like try and apologise.*

I plant my ass in the truck leaning back in the seat, letting my head hang as the blood pumps, burning my open wounds with a loving touch. I'm barely able to see as I turn the key, rolling out my dull ache in my jaw as it throbs, licking the sweet pennies from my teeth.

I picture my mom. And this is why I don't drink. Because in my most vulnerable moments, she's the only person to comfort me and she's not

SHASSII

fucking here. *Because of me*. So I cradle my pain, imagining her next to me as I hold out my bottle.

"*Happy birthday Mom...*"

CHAPTER 48

LUSTFUL QUARREL

Puppet

Play – 'Changes – XXXTENTACION'

I wake with sore eyes to the sound of shuffling and things breaking, peering at Sheps ears perked up knowing it wasn't just me that heard that. I drag myself out of bed, trying to recall what even happened before I passed out and I realise she never came back in the house. It's dark out and I haven't a clue what the time is but I know this racket is definitely not necessary at this time of night. I glare at Shep, scratching at the door to let him out. I reach for it, opening it as I poke my head round, adjusting to the darkness consuming the room with only the moonlight highlighting her silver jewellery, trying to read the clock in the dull lighting knowing it can only be one person or Shep would be ripping their throat out.

"Hayden?" I reach for the little lamp on the side table, glaring at her from across the room, her face completely mashed up, bloody and bruised as she attempts to look at me.

"M-om..." She mumbles under her shallow breath as she stumbles over her own feet and my stomach plummets, dropping the keys as she slams the door shut trying to hold her body weight completely unaware that Shep sits at her feet.

"Oh my god. Your face, what the hell happened?!" I run for her instinctively, reaching out for her face before she grabs my wrists, restraining me with little energy and she reeks of alcohol, barely keeping her head straight as it flops around like a dead body.

"Are you drunk?" I question. My affection is thrown as I'd expect, and logistically the only person who should be angry right now is me, but here I am aiding her drunk ass with concern.

"Ge-t off me..." She attempts to push me away lightly, backing into the door trying to keep herself up, smacking her head into the wood but I try to find her in her mass destruction, grabbing her chin, pulling her back down to earth to look at me.

"Hey! Hays. Look at me." She certainly didn't fight very hard. I know she's better than this. I know she can hit. This was intentional infliction and it only makes me more infuriated that she was so bloody stupid, wiping the bloodied mess from her cheek.

"Stop." She barely whispers through trembling lips, my hands find my sides as she throws them, hissing through the pain she's clearly suffering.

"Jesus... What the hell did they do to you?" More an accusation than a question as I tug her head around, analysing the damage but she resists me. Snatching her face from my light clasp.

"What i-s it to you.." I'm rejected once more, but her attempts are weaker as she actually begins to use me for support.

"Stop being silly. Let me look." The gash on her lip is still bleeding, crawling down her chin and I hate that I'm even blushing at the thought of kissing her right now. *Is that wrong of me?*

"I don't need your he-lp." She is still fighting me. Even now when she's vulnerable and fragile. She's still finding reasons to build a wall that's practically broken. We've been through this. And right now is the worst time to push me away.

"You're bleeding. Sit down." I gently reach for her forearms, trying to guide her to the sofa but I'm left with a hole as she rips her arms out of my hold.

"I s-aid I'm fine..." Sometimes I really wish I could beat some sense into her. Maybe this is a good thing. A lesson on stupidity.

"Where did you go? How the hell did you get home? Did you drive?" She's acting like a child as she sniggers, incoherent movement as she sways trying to find her feet but she's completely out of it and this is not something I wanted to be dealing with. *For Gods sake.*

"No, I flewwww." She's being absolutely ridiculous, finding amusement in her joke but I glare at her blankly, trying to figure out what the hell she finds so funny. This impulsive spurt of idiocy could have gone terribly wrong.

"Hayden. This isn't funny." I cross my arms, watching her make a complete fool of herself as she giggles at nothing, pinching her fingers together as she peers at me through one intact eye.

"Tis ju-st ah lilllllll-ll bi-t." I'm glad she's finding this amusing, collapsing into her own body as she belly laughs into me, pushing me down with her weight and I think she forgets she's three times the size of me, almost crushing me as she is completely oblivious to her own strength.

"Woah there. Easy does it big guy. I'm only small." Her laughs turn silent, trying to catch up with her own muddled up emotions as we usher towards the sofa, letting her fall almost on her face as she crawls into the cushions like an animal for closure, kicking her head back, hanging off the arm of the chair and I can tell she is not here right now.

"Don't move." She lets a huffed out laugh escape, trying to focus on the ceiling as her head spins, I can physically see her world turning as she struggles to look straight, rolling into the back of her head whilst I head to the sink, grabbing the nearest tea towel, drowning it under the cold water along with a glass.

"Yes, Mom..." She mumbles, groaning at her uncomfortable aches and pains, trying to adjust in the seat as she continues to whisper into the nothingness and my heart sinks. *"I'm s-orry mom..."* I stand by the sink wanting to wrap my arms around her in the tightest embrace, but I stand stationary with the cloth dripping on the tiled floor as I watch her head role.

"F-for-give me..." A tear follows until I blink, wiping my wet cheek before making my way back to her, watching her eyes now on me upside down as I approach her.

"Why were you so stupid?" I lift her head, surprised to see her let me, but by the whites in her eyes, she's fading fast, struggling to keep her eyes open.

"Becaausee-... I am..." I grip her chin gently, trying to tend to her wounds, dabbing the cuts delicately not to harm her but she's too off it to care, instead peering back at me like a lovesick puppy and I hate what she does to me. How no matter how hard I try to resent her; she looks at me and suddenly none of it matters.

"No. You're careless. There is a difference." I try to avoid eye contact but I can feel her burning a hole in the side of my head as I glare at the gash in her mouth, wiping it gently, trying to figure out why the hell she would get into a fight with someone on the most important day of the year.

Play - 'Drugs - EDEN'

"I'm sorry..." My heart sinks to the trenches of the ocean, where I'd been crying so many tears earlier today. I'd like to say I know she is but I'm finding it so hard to understand why she chooses to be so cold. So stagnant. Emotionally unavailable. When all I've done is show her I'm right here. *Why can't she see that?* It's like she is trying to be difficult to love so I'll give up. *But I'm not giving up.*

"For what?" She slumps back in the chair, admitting defeat as I eventually lock eyes with her, trying to draw her responsibility out but her eyes are the definition of a calm before the storm. So bright they could blind you, leaving you star struck by their beauty but filled with a heavy darkness untold just waiting to consume you with its wrath.

...

"I g-et it...I hate, me to-" My anger softens behind my eyes, letting my empathy slide through as I stare at her heavy lids, trying to hold back my impulsive need to shut her up with my mouth. *I do hate her.* But only because she makes it so easy to *love* her. When I really shouldn't. When I really don't want to. Right now I should be sitting in a police station, filling out forms and trying to escape this trauma. *Escape her.* I've had so many opportunities to walk out that door but I'm still here. Doesn't that tell her something? *Isn't that enough?*

"I didn-t use you..." She mumbles, only just making out the syllables as I wipe the blood from her nose, cleaning up her self-harm. I don't know why I'm trying to decipher what she's saying when she's intoxicated like it means anything right now.

"I'm- just af-raid..." She confesses. My jaw hangs low, eyeing her as she glances at my bottom lip like a chew toy stirring an unknowing guilt to let her have it.

"Afraid of what." I play on her vulnerability slightly, cooing the words out of her as the gap between us closes and I probably shouldn't. But she makes even the darkest of temptations seem feasible when adrenaline is your new power hungry, sucking in the familiar stench of metal under my nose as her open wounds still bleed.

"Who- I'll be if I- let you in..." She jolts through her pain as she tenses her jaw muscles like she's forcing herself to hold back just as much as I am. She'll be free if she lets me in, she just needs to realise that feelings are not terrifying. Caring for someone is not a death sentence and Love is *not* punishable.

"I can handle it." Truthfully. I'm terrified to learn more of her monsters lurking in the shadows, but she doesn't scare me anymore. My chest tightens as she leans in, gripping the back of my hair with sloppy temperance as her blooded lip grazes mine, smearing it against my fleshy skin and I can feel myself burning up, licking it off slowly so eager to taste it. *I don't know what that says about me.* But it only leaves me craving more and I slowly latch onto her wound, tugging it with my teeth before sucking it gently in my mouth. I let my tongue dance against the ball of metal as she hisses, tasting her sweet metallic wine on my tongue, throbbing as she groans into my mouth with nothing but pure satisfaction, feeding her sickness with more pain. I can't deny, the way she's reacting is making me feral to hurt her harder. Let her feel my storm as I claw at her face with my fingers, dragging her into a kiss so ferocious it's barely a kiss. It's emotions far greater than lust can comprehend. A vexation for understanding through the only way we know how. The only way she will understand.

Anger.

Her hands ride up my back, sitting up in the seat as she pulls me into her body making me straddle her waist, cupping her hips with my thighs and her bulge sends waves up my spine as I sit, pressing into me, drawing out an unexpected whimper. I know we shouldn't. I know this goes against everything I'm trying so desperately to hate her for. She said it herself; sex means nothing to her but the way she's clawing at me like I'm her oxygen is driving me beyond insanity. She's insatiable and I'm foolish enough to give in.

"*Alora...*" She groans down my neck filled with pent up resentment and I can tell she is trying to fight this just as much as I am but we are both thirsty to feel *numb*.

"*Don't...*" I whine breathlessly through her kisses; I don't want her to stop. I'll figure out my feelings tomorrow but for right now I need to lose myself in her touch. This drive to let go in her arms is taking up my moral compass and she doesn't fight it. *How do you fight someone you have found freedom inside?*

She kisses me harder, sloppier, panting like a dog as she sucks my skin into her mouth, gnawing at my neck as she sinks her teeth into my flesh and it's a pain I've fallen in love with. It's euphoric, drowning out my head as I flop into her dominant hand cupping my throat, feeding on my jugular like a starved night eater, tugging at my hips guiding them to grind against her cock only forcing my irrational greed.

"Fuck me..." I nearly choke on her words as she whispers into my mouth only intensifying my throb, burning bright red with anxiety. "Ride me *baby*. Show me how you hate me..."

She bucks her hips into me, pushing into my sweet spot to lift me up, giving us a gap as she takes her free hand, undoing her belt lazily and my heart beats faster. She's giving me some sort of control and I freeze, nervous to comply but she wastes no time pushing me down onto her cock, sliding in effortlessly as she catches my moan in her mouth. I sit down on her length until it fills me up, trying to catch my breath at the way she's stretching me out to fit all of her, but I relax, finding sick pleasure in the way I'm taking every inch and I soon loosen, giving me more movement to grind against her, blushing as she gazes up at me with pride.

"Fuck *baby-*" She whispers and my breaths crack, seeing her underneath me, unable to feel anything yet it's like she feels everything, reacting to the way I'm driving her dick inside me with broken moans and fingers digging so deeply into my hips they may bruise tomorrow. I throw my hands to grab the back of the sofa as she grips my ass, pushing me down until I hiss with spite. *I'm so full I can't see straight.*

"Take me- take me *Puppet*. Such a good girl." her praise only drives me harder, chasing it like it's keeping me breathing, doing as she says to hear it again, and again. She kisses me like it's a reward for doing so well but I'm breaking as her split tongue lines my collar bones, nipping up my neck with this passionate hunger, biting harder as I begin to slide up and down around her strap, quickening my pace to grab that high I desperately crave. Letting her find her home inside me, *where she belongs.*

"Hurt me *Innocence*..." Her words cut down my ears and I want her to hurt. I want her to feel my rage. How angry it makes me that she won't let me in. I dig my nails, applying more and more pressure into her shoulder blades but she doesn't even notice, too dosed up on her high, moaning deeply against my skin, so divine I want to let go already as it rings through my muffled ears. She only allows me to inflict pain, not tenderness. She only knows physical pain, so if that's what she wants, I'll give it to her.

I tug roughly on her bottom lip, biting her wound harder causing blood to pool into my mouth, riding her length deeper as she rumbles into my mouth, tasting herself on my tongue as it coats in copper. She's like a vampire, drawing it from my mouth as she licks every inch, only pushing my orgasm to surface, whining to let go on her cock as I use her to release my frustrations knowing she wants me to ask for permission but I use her vulnerability to show her how I feel inside, how she makes want to scream and cry. How her resistance makes me hate myself for craving attention so toxic, so damaging yet she is the thing keeping me alive. She is like water. Something so capable of killing you, drowning you until your heart stops beating, but you need it to survive. *I need her to survive.*

Play - 'Guest room - Echo'

"Don't you dare-" She snaps. I don't know how, but she can feel me close as I grip her skin until it's practically tearing. Giving in to my hate, ignoring her command, I cum all over her cock as I disobey her orders, making her feel my rage, denying her the way she denies me every damn day and it feels good. Her hazy gaze glares back at me, kissing her teeth in irritation, too tired to fight it as she watches me use her dick like a toy, resting her head on the back of the couch listening to me scream into the dead silence.

"Fuc-k You!..." I moan out, finishing off as I come down, pushing her in and out of me but the air is knocked from my lungs as she grabs my throat, squeezing tighter, tugging me to look into her state of fury and I try to swallow, suddenly glaring at someone else. Her entire demeanour shifts and her eyes become the storm, making my chest rattle like birds trying to get out of its wake, bulging in the sockets at her sudden strength. Like she's snapped back into reality, back to her incessant need to control everything around her.

"You shouldn't have done that..." My heart constricts, peering death in the face as she licks the side of my cheek, smearing her blooded lip against my salty flesh, still heaving from my first orgasm trying to catch a breath but she doesn't allow me. She squeezes tighter until I'm almost passing out before throwing me off her, gripping me by my scalp to throw me down, lying on the sofa underneath her as she crawl on top of me like a vice giving me no space to run as she forces herself inside me crying out at the sensitive ache as she rips me in half with her length. She claws my clothes off like an animal to access my body but I accustom to the throb quickly, quivering as she nails my sweet spot still sore, holding my leg up to push in deeper as I scream out in blissful pain but my palms retaliate, smashing against her solid frame in protest that is useless against the hold she has on me, physically and mentally.

"You want to hate me? Hate me *baby*. Scream it. Let me fucking hear it." She grips my chin, slapping me with enough force to hiss at the sting, pounding into my limp body mercilessly as she grabs my hand, forcing it on my clit. "Show me how I make you feel, *baby*. Fucking swear at me again."

Her alcohol has clearly worn off, feeling her cup my throat with malice as I begin to play with my swollen pussy, rubbing it to ease the burn, quickly coating her in my arousal as she pushes me to my second orgasm. I should know by now one round never quenches her thirst for my body and that thought alone is tipping me to suffocate her cock.

"Fuck you! Fu-ck, YOU!" My staggered words break up the thick tension of hatred lingering in the air as we glare through one another, lost in the depths of our own pain, our own feelings that make no sense. None of this makes sense, but when we are this close it feels so right. She's trying to make me resent her but she's doing the complete opposite. She's only showing me that I can't function without her.

Unwanted tears creep up my throat, so mangled with broken emotions I'm cracking. Gasping as she goes even deeper, leaning in between my legs to kiss me dreadfully slowly only drawing out my cries with an overwhelming amount of pressure between my legs and in my heart. My free hand reaches for her throat, barely covering it but I grip anyway as her tongue searches for mine.

"You are the reason I breathe." She whispers so full of frustration, spitting it through gritted teeth like she loathes it. Only confirming that I was right that day when she told me her plans had changed. That I am the reason she never went through with it. She is still here because of me. Yet she is still trying to deny her own heart of what it desperately craves. What it needs.

Love.

"Cum on my fucking cock." Her anger consumes her, only making us both squeeze tighter on each other's airways through a patchwork kiss as I finally let go of everything, screaming into her mouth, letting her consume my fury like an entity. Making her absorb it. Feed on it. Her love language is suffering. So, I'll make her suffer. I'll push her until she realises she needs me just as much as I need her.

SHASSII

CHAPTER 49

GUILTY CONSCIENCE

Puppeteer

I wake to the heavy weight of the sun blinding me through the kitchen window, trying to shift the stiffness in my face suddenly realising what the hell happened last night. I rub my eyes to adjust to the light as I drag my body weight to sit up, my face pulsing with a drilling ache, my lip throbbing feeling two times bigger. *The prick got a good hit. I'll give him that.*

I barely even remember getting home but I know someone is going to be mad at me. Rolling my eyes as I stare around the room, they land on the glass of water and painkillers on the coffee table with a little note stuck to the side.

I huff in amusement, squinting at the sting as I stretch out my wound from smiling before doing as I'm told and popping my pills. Not that it will make any difference. My face is busted, I'm going to need a lot more than a few painkillers, more like another bottle of J.D.

My feet find their strength, getting up to find the bathroom, rolling out my seized muscles as I make my way to the door. *I really was a punching bag last night.* I turn to see her already awake, standing in the doorway analysing her prep for her insulin, grabbing at her skin like there is something wrong with her and my jaw locks. I vaguely remember us fucking and an immediate wave of guilt washes over me. *God dammit Hayden. I told you to lock yourself in the fucking truck.*

Play - 'Let Me Down - Jorja Smith, Stormzy'

"May I?" I speak calmly in hopes not to startle her but she still lightly jumps up off the bed. I need to push her away so she can let go but I don't know what the hell I said yesterday. She glares at me still full of this clearly bottled-up frustration.

"You sober?" She bites, looking dead in the eyes. I should have said something yesterday but I couldn't. Not without hurting her further and I can't tell who's feelings I'm protecting anymore, *hers or mine.*

Eventually she holds out the pen for me to take, reluctant to let go for a mere moment. I sit beside her and adorn the beautiful work of bodily art against her skin and the bridge of her nose as her freckles highlight the golden accents in her eyes, staring intensely at the saturated necklace around her throat I vaguely remember gifting her last night. I graze my fingertips against the flesh on her higher abdomen, curling my lip at the fact she is finally, after almost five months, letting me do this for her.

"I'm fine, *Puppet*." She rolls her eyes and I can tell there are so many things she wants to say to me but she's holding back. "Does it hurt?"

I line the needle to push into her flesh and apply pressure, she doesn't even blink.

"No. I've become accustomed to the pain." Her words are so dry it makes me gulp slowly, lacking empathy for either of us where she refuses to look in my direction and I know she isn't just talking about her pen.

"What's wrong?" Suddenly, I hate the thought of us fighting. I remove the pen, placing it down beside her, wiping the pin prick delicately with my thumb.

"Nothing-" She evades the question and she forgets I've studied her since the day she stepped foot in my house. I know exactly what she is thinking, feeling, wanting. She isn't exactly the best at hiding her emotions.

"You don't think I know you by now?" The floor becomes her target, glaring at it like sun to a mirror, trying to burn a hole in it. "When you said you were broken the other day. It got me thinking-" I cock my brow, patiently waiting for her to speak.

"I was born into a broken body. Hayden. Nothing about me is fixable. So what's different? Why won't you let me in?" *What's different*? Everything is different. She didn't have a choice. I had a choice to be a better person and I chose pain and vengeance. I chose this life, I chose to be the worst version of myself to appease my name, I could have bettered my life once I stepped outside of that prison cell but I didn't, I went straight to the horse's mouth and I shot him right between the eyes, because it's who I fucking am and I like it that way.

"*Alora*. You're far from broken." My hand instinctively finds her thigh, squeezing it gently with reassurance.

"I was born into a dying body, Hayden." She pulls away from my touch and my heart drops to the floor.

"We all are *Puppet*." If she is trying to fight that we are equally as broken purely because she was given an illness that was out of her control, I don't know if I will be able to keep my mouth shut.

"But we are both still here. Because you are fighting for something." I'm fighting to stay alive even when I should have let death swallow me months ago and it's taken me a while to figure out why but now that I have, I need to rectify that.

"You tell me not to care for you. That you're bad for me. But we are both broken in different ways. I just have no wounds to wear my pain but it doesn't mean I'm not." she peers at my battered skin and my throat tightens with this wave of betrayal.

"Do you think I enjoy wearing these memories?" I'm trying my hardest not to blow the fuck up right now but she's poking the wrong bear.

"That's not what I meant…" Her anger slowly becomes sympathetic but she's already struck a nerve in me I can't shake.

"Then what are you getting at?"

"That they don't define who you are. They are a graveyard of loss. But every grave is dug because something that once bloomed has died." There was never a point in my life where I *bloomed*. I was dead the moment I got out of my mother's womb and I endured pain I have now consumed. It is now a part of me that she just needs to accept. She needs to stop trying to fix me.

"Me? I'm the dirt already embedded in the soil, giving people growth, happiness. While I get trampled on." Every moment she doubts herself is another shed of my dignity lost, nothing she just said is true. None of it.

That is what I am.

"I may not wear my pain. But I'm certainly not perfect."

She is perfect.

To me.

And that is why she cannot stoop to the kind of *monsters* like me.

"*Love* is not the solution." I see her eye line spill silver, she is so fixated on feeling nothing but empathy and love for people that do not deserve it. *I do not deserve it.*

"Then what is? If not *Love*? Because I hate this. Hayden, I'm ready to Love you broken. Let me touch you? Hold you?" Her cold little fingertips graze the craters along my shoulder blade through the gap in my tank top and a chill runs up the back of my spine, burning tension sitting in my mouth as she caresses the trauma in my face and my hands snatch at hers, ready to snap them in half.

"Enough!...." I jump up off the bed, my body crawling with memories every time I close my eyes. I walk towards the door but she follows me, gripping at my arm in anguish as she digs her nails into my skin.

"Why?! Why can't you even let us try?! I know you want to!" Her face is beaming with desperation, clinging onto the premonition of a person who is no longer with her and she needs to realise that that little girl inside me is never fucking coming home! *How does she expect us to work?!*

"Because you deserve better!" I spin to face her, clasping her wrists in the palm of my sweaty hands, squeezing at the pain in her eyes.

"I don't want better!? Don't you get it! Why do you punish yourself like this?!" She lets me channel my rage through her feeble bones, taking it like she always does. Taking everything I have to give. Taking my anger, my pain, my grief. Even now she is looking at me like there is no one else on earth.

"Because *Alora*! *Loving* me is a death sentence!"

Everything and everyone I've ever loved has been ripped from underneath me and I don't know if I'm doing this for me, or I'm doing this for her. I don't think I could go through that again. That insufferable loneliness that eats away at you as you search for them in everything you touch. In the stars. In sunsets. In faded memories with gaps missing. In the stillness of the ocean before a storm.

"Not understanding you is killing me! I need to understand! Please. Help me understand! I know there is so much more to you than this monster you try to let control you." The only way she will ever understand is if I show her the monster who created me and if she keeps pushing me that is exactly what I will do. "You need to stop blaming yourself for her!"

...

Her words cut through my heart like her bullet wound, ripping away at my kindness as the Devil speaks down my ear. Everything happened because of me and it will forever be my greatest burden to bear. I punish myself because that is my trophy for letting the only women who loved me, *down*.

"Don't!..." I push away, trying to give myself space before I do something stupid but she is reluctant, clawing at my sanity, trying to crawl inside of me.

"Let me in! What is it going to take for you to let me in?! Do I have to break that door down myself?!" I freeze, glaring at her in hysterics, watching her bleak fit of pain explode in front of my very eyes but my vision only tunnels red as she screams at my absence, thrashing at my forearm as white noise invades my ears. *She is not going to let this go until one of us is dead.* I clear my throat, seeing his face and his words breath down my neck.

"Once people realise how worthless you really are. They will see you the way I do.

An abomination. People do not play with broken toys, baby girl. They discard them."

"This is your funeral. Don't expect a burial." I grip her wrist, crushing her with my demons, heading straight for *the door.*

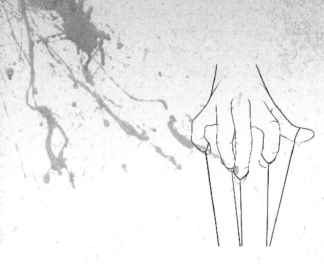

CHAPTER 50

CONSUMING HER MONSTERS

Puppeteer

I break the basement door open with the force of my boot, opening it up to the trauma laying heavy in the air as I push her in front of me, making our way down the creaky stairs until we are in front of the barricaded cell glaring at it with distant strength. I try to break my fear as I rip the panels off the door frame, clicking the key in the door with difficulty where it's seized up leaving it free to enter, smothered in cobwebs and dust a decade old.

My chest shakes my upper body with anxiety as she peers at me with unknowing resistance. I turn the knob and let the door swing open. A black void of desolate screams echo back to me as she walks through it, finding her way to my calls, carving crescents into my palms as she disappears into the room, holding my breath as I follow her in.

The atmosphere holds such a heavy weight on my shoulders I feel nauseous, fumbling for the light switch on the concrete wall, lighting up my past with nothing to hide behind. I haven't been in this room since he died.

I'd been avoiding it. I thought if I pretended it wasn't here that this ache would eventually dissipate but it never has. This room carries haunting memories hard wired like the night I lost her. A box filled with all my forbidden whispers. My cries seeped into the walls casing this asylum that is meant to be my home.

Play - 'The Line – Twenty One Pilots'

She freezes, soaking in my secret, glaring at the chair in the middle of the room. A wooden structure with no back, braced with heavy duty metal buckles on the arms and legs. Walls scattered with various tools. *My own personal torture chamber.*

"I don't understand? You do this? To people?" She studies my vice, tracing the grubby wood with her fingers making me squint like she's wedged a knife inside me.

"No." Of course that would be her first thought. I have kept it from her after all so she's bound to assume the worst of me. Exactly like she should.

...

"Oh my god..." The penny drops. Staring at me in disbelief. The face of a girl who is regretting digging up my grave. Exposing the rotting bones and spirits that keep me tied here, closing in on her ears, bringing her to tears. She's absent-minded as she glares at me with disturbance bleeding from her eyes.

"Hays..." I don't want to hear her pity. I don't want her sympathy. I don't want any of it. She pushed this. She wanted to see my demons in the flesh and now she can sink in her fucking guilt.

"You just couldn't leave it alone." Her face is painted with shame, swallowing all those unspoken words as she gawks at my demise. Right here. In this room. I am an apparition of myself. A ghost haunting my own grounds. Stuck in an eternity of suffering with my own devil and angel, and now she knows that too.

"I'm so sorry- Hays..." She moves towards me and I step back, she doesn't want to come near me right now.

"Bit late for that now, don't you think?" I can feel unwelcome tears trying to cut through my face, tightening my jaw in frustration.

"Show me." My brow burrows, glaring at her with utter shock, trying to make sense of her words. "Show me Hayden. I want to feel it. I want to harbour your pain." I stare blankly in disbelief.

"*Don't be fucking ridiculous.*"

"*I want to understand your suffering!*"

"You think experiencing just a glimpse of my suffering is going to fix things?! I'm not laying a hand on you, *Alora*." She ignores me, placing her ass in the seat and my temperature rises, feeling my blood boil beneath my skin as I stare at myself.

"*You're a clown baby girl. A circus act of disappointment.*"

"What more do you want from me?!" Being in here is ringing my ears with a need to destroy my own mind, blanking as she refuses to move.

"*Alora.* You need to get out, right now." My blood buzzes underneath my flesh, crawling out of my wounds as I look down at my palms, hallucinating my harm as the back of my hands burn.

"No." My back itches, trying to think of all the reasons I should let her breathe right now.

"*Fucking hold still. You burn so pretty for me.*"

"I'm not going anywhere. I want to feel what you feel. If that is the only way you'll let me in, I'll do it." She is out of her god damn fucking mind and I'm losing mine being down here. I'm suffocating.

"You just don't quit, do you," She's tampering with raw, destructive fire and I will burn her alive until she's merely a skeleton if she's not careful. "do you realise what you're asking of me?!" She hasn't got a clue, but she's too delusional to care right now, she is so high on this redemption, dormant inside me that she is so desperately clinging on to, it's pathetic. It's agonising how deeply she finds worth in me.

"I know that you need to face whatever it is that you're running from. He is no longer here to harm you." My knuckles whiten, channelling my frustration into my palms so I don't unload it into her pure, untouched face, sculpted to haunt my dreams, reminding me of the man I stole from her. I'm beginning to hate the fucking sight of her in all her naive, untainted glory.

"I would be very careful with what you say if I were you..." Her ability to push my buttons is impressive but it won't be when I cut off her fucking oxygen.

"Hurt me..." I'm trembling with this vile need to prove to her I am the monster she doesn't think I am, just to prove a point. I am tired of being something I am not, *for her*. She's clinging to this lust for affliction I've barely begun to play with but this is not *lust*. This is the work of a Devil. This is cruelty beyond my comprehension. Insidious nature even I can't understand. Harm to a child meant to be yours purely for fun, to fill your own twisted and sick desires. I'm a killer. But the real Devils who walk amongst us will always be the likes of men like him.

"*Alora...*" My fuse is about to run out, storming towards her, clutching at her throat so she looks at me, and she's ready to take everything, her eyes pooling with plead, knotting my throat with fury. Her fucking tears make me sick. She makes me sick. Begging for my suffering like it is going to somehow bring us closer together. She will run. Maybe this is what she needs, maybe this is the answer. Maybe inflicting my laceration will finally stop her digging for my coffin. It needs to stay fucking buried.

"*Let me be broken with you.*" I squeeze her throat tighter, surging my rage at her arrogant stupidity as she sobs helplessly, running on adrenaline, asking for death to come knocking and suddenly, *her life means nothing to me*. I snap the back of my hand across her cheek but she doesn't look at me with anger, just that face full of empathy for the broken woman standing in front of her.

I grip her wrists to lie against the arms of the chair, clamping them down to keep her restrained. Consuming this darkness seeping into my lungs. This room. This house. Everything that I am. Everything this room made me.

"*No one can hear you scream down here Hayley. No one. But I won't stop you. Maybe you'll scream so much you'll give out soon.*"

It's like a part of him is crawling out of my mouth, manipulating my body like a puppeteer, unable to see her in front of me as I head to the back wall and pick out from the various selection of whips. Only tunnelling a pitch-black void as I run it through my fingers, breathing in that old familiar sting, remembering the way it felt to scream into nothingness. Knowing that no one was coming to save me. The way no one is coming to save my *Little Dreamer*.

"This is *Love* Alora. Let me show you why I will never *Love* you." My heart thuds my eardrums, drowning out the sound of her cries of apprehension as I lift the back of her top up and over her head to cover her eyes. I never wanted this. I never wanted her to get this close, I never wanted to care for her, I never wanted to feel, to be a fucking hero, I never wanted her to see this part of my life but she will not, *STOP*. I just need her to stop, I need this all to stop. I need these feelings I cannot understand to go away. She will not give up on me, so I will give her a reason to. I will show her exactly who holds my life on strings. Still, even 6ft underground. She wants it to be her. She wants to think that she is curing the sickness inside of me but she's not and she never will.

"Show her baby girl. Show her what love is."

With one swift motion the whip snaps through the air, striking her flesh, slashing a light incision into her upper back on impact and nausea creeps up the back of my throat hearing her yelp, trying to hold in her cries just as I did.

"Punishment is only discipline. You will learn, this is for your own good. Daddy is just trying to help you."

Another follows. Not holding back. I feel her my demons through her wounds, piercing her skin with my *LOVE*. Hearing the understanding weep from her mouth as she cradles her heart, leaning into the seat, protecting it. *From ME*.

"Daddy loves you. I'm just trying to make you better? Can't you see?"

I strike once more, blowing her unconscious due to the pain. She falls limp into her lap, hanging there like a corpse as I catch my breath, snapping back into reality once her crying stops, leaving me in deserted silence.

"What have you done, Hayley."

My grip loosens, letting the whip fall to the floor heaving with culpability, glaring at her gashes realising what the hell I've done, stumbling for the vices around her wrists as I free her from their grasp. I cup her lifeless body in the palm of my hands as I push the fabric out of her eyes, moving the sweaty strands of hair from her face, checking for signs of survival as I lift her lids but she's out of it.

"You are broken. Not even Daddy can fix you."

"Oh my god... Alora... *Baby* I'm sorry. I'm so sorry." I'm trembling with hatred, drowning in guilt as I hold her deadweight in my hands, cupping her hair behind the shell of her ears as I fight back the overwhelming surge of nausea, pulling her close to my chest, gripping her so tightly she might suffocate.

"I got you *baby... I* got you." I lift her frail body from the seat, dragging her ghost into my arms as I walk her out of the room, cradling her like she's never coming back and in this exact moment I realise, *I need to let her go.*

Now.

Today.

She needs to get away from here. She needs to spread her wings for me. She needs to run and have the pleasure of living the life I never had. *I owe that to her.*

I climb up the stairs, met with Shep waiting at the top patiently behind the door, following me to the bedroom as I place her on the bed resting on her side, memorising the Orion's belt across her shoulder blade, tracing it with my fingers. My stars on the darkest of nights. *My light.* She has no idea what she's done to me. But I care enough about her to let her find her own light. A life she deserves. *A life without me in it.*

Nausea breaks me into a hot sweat as I stare at her harm, finally running for the bathroom, hurling up my emotions as I gag on my wrong doings, vomiting into the toilet trying to figure out where the hell it all went wrong, where I'm meant to fit into this life and the answer is, I don't. I don't fit anywhere, and I've come to terms with the fact that there is no place for me. Not even in hell. *And certainly not in her arms.* This crossed so many lines I never thought I'd cross. I hurt her, I became the Devil himself and I don't think I will ever forgive myself for that.

I've truly become what I feared the most.

SHASSII

CHAPTER 51

BETRAYAL

Puppet

I'm woke abruptly to the sound of glass smashing and china bracing the walls, jumping out of my skin as I stare towards the door finding Shep licking at my stagnant face. I squint at the forceful pull on my back realising I have been patched up but the harm still remains, stinging the incisions she left on my body and every part of me wants to scream and cry and hate her for this. But I can't. I pushed this. I asked for this. And now I understand her more than I thought I ever would. I'm bearing her suffering like *I wanted*. We are in this together now. I will do everything I can to help her realise that the little girl stuck inside of that room is worth more than the clown her father painted her to be. I feel violently ill as the ache stuns my entire back trying desperately to stand on my feet. I don't know how many I endured, I don't even remember passing out but I know she didn't mean it, she didn't mean any of it. I'm drawn to the anger swallowing the air from behind the bedroom door. *She needs me, now more than ever.* I dread to think how she is feeling right now and I need her to know I'm not angry. *I'm not going anywhere.*

I creep open the door slowly, peaking round the corner to an obliteration, broken glass, picture frames, the lamp and coffee table completely destroyed, plastered all over the floor as she throws yet another object at the wall, groaning out a deep roar. She's an animal stuck behind bars trying to fight her inner demons and everything in me seizes at the sight of her raw unfiltered rage. She's finally cracked. I've opened the red door and it's consuming her from the inside out.

"Hayden?..." As I speak softly, a picture frame is thrown millimetres from my head, fracturing against the door frame as I stun in place falling back inside the room away from the blast, crawling back out to see her standing there in complete absence, staring straight through me as unstoppable tears cut down her cheeks.

She's crying.

I've never seen her cry.

Play - 'Let Me Go - NF'

Tears crawl up my throat as I begin to feel this pain with her, suffocating on this agony we both now share. There is so much guilt on her face, like she doesn't even deserve to look at me and it's breaking me. This was all my fault. I pushed her to face her demons and she warned me there would be consequences but I didn't listen.

I was selfish.

I do the only thing I know how without thinking, chasing my feet, catching her in a hug as she buckles to the floor, smashing her knees into the wood as she collapses into my embrace.

"I'm so sorry! I'm sorry, I'm s-o sorr-y!..." Sobs tear through her staggered throat, bleeding into my hold as she claws at my shoulders, tensing as she handles the gashing on my back but right now this embrace is what we both needed, holding her so tightly as my fingers run up the back of her head. *She's letting me hold her.*

"Hey! Hey!.. It's OK, you're OK. I'm right here. I'm here." Her arms mould round my tiny frame and I've never felt more at home than I do right here in her arms, holding her head against my beating heart. Letting her know I'm right here. She makes it easier to breathe. Easier to face hardships when she's by my side. She's spent so long being strong. Pushing down all her hurt, never giving herself a chance to face those closed doors but she's not doing this alone. *She has me.*

She slowly pulls away, gazing into my eyes like I'm dying as her warm familiar touch cups my cheeks, tearing at the sight of me.

"I need you to do something for me…" Her voice cracks, trying to speak and I'm shaking at her hesitation. *I'll do anything to make this better.*

"Ok - ok." She tucks my hair out of my face, stroking the tenderness in my flush cheeks and her tears are tearing me apart. I didn't know seeing her cry would break me so much.

"Listen to me, very carefully." Everything inside me is screaming, gripping the straps of her top, trying to understand through the sorrow in her eyes, like she's about to say something I'll hate.

"You're scaring me!" Her hands clasp at my skull with firm pressure, channelling this hostility through her voice as she bleeds words I never expected to come out of her mouth.

"I need you to walk out that door. *Do you hear me?*" I can tell she doesn't want this through the way she's squeezing me with desperation, rubbing at my skin like we will somehow morph together.

"What?-" My vision goes fuzzy, becoming a blur, trying to focus on her skin against mine.

"I need you to run. And I don't want you to look back. Ok?" No. I can't do that. I can't run away now. I can't run away from this. We've come so far and she expects me to walk away? I'm not scared of her and she wants me to be.

"I'm not going anywhere. I'm staying right here. With you!" My resilience to stay is fighting her resistance to let me go because I know neither of us want this, I know she doesn't think she's fixable. But she doesn't need to be fixed, she just needs someone to love her the way she is. To care for her the way she has cared for me. I'm not giving up on *us.*

"Alora. This is not. Debatable." Her fingers become more forceful, sinking into me with irritation. "You're going to walk out of that door and you're going to forget about me. I need you to do that. For me."

She is crazy. The last five months of my life has been right here. I have nowhere to go, no place to call home, this is my home now. I don't want to be anywhere else and the thought leaves stones in my throat.

"Hayden. Please don't do this to me-" I weep uncontrollably. Drowning in my own sea of tears as she joins me, wiping mine away, hating to see me cry.

"I want you to be happy. And I - I can't do that, for you." She has it all wrong! If she would just let me in she would see that being in her arms has never made me happier! I've experienced so many happy moments with her, happiness I sometimes doubted I'd have the privilege to feel but when I look at her now. I see my refuge, I see peace. I don't want to fight anymore!

"I am happy! I am happy, here, with you!" She grabs my wrists tightly, pulling me off her frame with durability and her voice shifts, no longer laced in pain but vexation.

"You need to leave." My heart falls from great heights, shattering as it hits the bottom. She's pushing me away because she thinks this will solve her problems, so she can keep her image, keep being the monster she so desperately wants to be, but letting me go will solve nothing. Pushing me away will only make this worse. She wants to wallow in self-hate, break herself down to feel numb. Feel nothing, because feeling nothing is easier than facing your mistakes.

"Hayden - please, please do-n't do this- don't, don't do this-" She shoves my hands away, slowly standing back on her feet as she wipes away her grief, looking at an imposter as she glares at me with nothingness and my soul seeps into the foundations of this building.

"I don't want you here." None of this was expected. I never planned to fall for someone like her, the way she never planned to find me that night. I lost my life, my family, my home. I'm not losing her too; she doesn't get to just run away from this.

"You don't mean that-"

"Get out." I cling to her face, forcing her to feel me on her skin. I don't care if it burns. *This burns.*

"Why, why are you doing this. After everything, you're just letting me go? *Letting us go?"*

"There is no US!" She bites, clamping her fists together and it feels like I'm in the palm of her hand, crushing me with her hurtful words.

"If you do this Hayden, that is it. I'm gone. For good. *DO YOU HEAR ME!* Don't come for me! Don't look for me!" I try to make her see sense, make her remember the words she spoke the day I tried to run away, but she's numb, glaring at a stranger with carelessness and my heart mourns for her to *come back to me*. I'm looking at her ghost. The ghost that's been here all along but I was too blind to see it. She wants me to hate her, so it will be easier to walk away. Because it's easier to walk away from someone when you loathe them and right now I do. I loathe everything that she is, everything that she's done to me, everything she's made me feel. All to push me away to. I wish I died that day so I didn't have to experience heartbreak and grief hand in hand as she tortures me with emotions I never fucking asked for!

"GET OUT!" She snaps. "GET THE FUCK OUT!" Raising her voice at me making me jolt as she points towards the door and my dam breaks, letting everything go, pouring on to the floor waiting for her to scoop me up but she doesn't. I look up to find an empty space as she disappears into the garage, slamming it behind her.

I've lost her.

SHASSII

CHAPTER 52

KARMA IN BLOOD

Puppet

Play - 'WILDFLOWER - Billie Eilish'

I left not long after our fight, packed a bag with my shit and walked out the door. I'm so angry, I can't regulate my emotions right now. I'm fighting everything in me not to turn around, storm back in there and crash my lips into hers. She's letting me go, I should be grateful but now I fear for a life without her in it by my side. I'm so tired of grieving for the absence of people I love. Does it ever get better? Is this what life is like? How many times will I have to deal with this? I've been walking for what I can assume is about an hour and I've not reached any sort of civilization.

It's hot out and it will be dark soon. I should have stayed there, this was a bad idea but I didn't know what else to do. I miss her stupid smile and her stupid fucking laugh and the way she looks at me like I'm an idiot when I do literally anything but I hate the way she makes me feel when she's like this, like no matter what I do it is never good enough for her. But now it's over. *We are over.* We were never anything to begin with, just two broken pieces from different puzzles trying to fit together. I just need to suck it up and move on, get to the next town and find my way back into the city. I just need a police station or a phone.

Will I tell them where I've been? What the hell do I say? I don't want her thrown behind bars but it's where she should be for the murder of my parents. What if I have to face her in court? Maybe she will kill me before that point. If I tell them her name she will hate me and suddenly part of me wants her too. Do I tell them I know who did this? Do I rat her out? Do I lie and pretend I know nothing? Say I never saw their face? That is a heavy lie to bear, what if they don't even believe me?

I pause for a moment, not realising how out of breath I am just from thinking to loud. I'm caked in sweat and my head is beginning to pound against my temple. How long will I be walking for? I have no food or water and nowhere to sleep. At least I have my medication but I need to find food before the morning. Why did I take no food with me? I'm an idiot. *Silly Puppet.* Her voice rings through my head, causing me to pause once more, heaving as I bend over feeling a hot flush surge through my body. I think *I'm going to throw up.* I'm terrified. Even in her presence I was never this terrified to face the world. A world I can now see clearly since she opened my eyes to the ugly that lies within it and I begin to think of all the awful things that could happen to me out here, getting even more frustrated that she would just let me walk out on my own. Was this another lesson? Was this punishment? Does she want me to die? What is wrong with her?

My body is huddled over, cradling my stomach trying to figure out if I am going to hurl when noise approaches me from the distance, glancing up to see a truck coming my way. My face lights up but my heart rattles in its cage. *Civilisation.* Although I've not interacted with anyone besides her for five months. I feel like an alien to society. A silly part of me thinks it may even be her but I'd be dumb to believe she'd come and find me now, she's probably already forgotten about me, getting back to her old habits to channel her rage I should be taking, not other people's lives.

The truck pulls up beside me with the window already down as they lean into the car to talk to me from the other side of the bench seat.

"Hey, you need a ride? What's a pretty little thing like you doing all the way out here?" It's a man with a friendly smile, charismatic and charming, but I'm also not stupid.

"I'm visiting family." *I lie.* Standing there like a fish out of water as he glares at me in confusion. *He knows I'm lying.*

"Ma'am, there are no houses for miles?" He knows the area. Maybe this is a good thing but I can't exactly ask him now that he thinks I'm from round here.

"Are you sure you're ok, you don't need me to take you anywhere?" I'd say yes. Because I desperately need a ride but I am also not about to jump in a random man's car with absolutely nothing to defend myself.

"I like to walk." He scans me up and down, like I look familiar, and I probably do. I've probably been all over the news for months.

"With a bag like that?" I clutch my arms, hugging myself trying to contain my crippling anxiety right now. For some reason, I don't want to be noticed.

"I don't want to sound weird or anything, but I couldn't bear leaving you out here on your own, it's getting late. Let me drive you to a motel at least." My mind is screaming yes. But my heart is screaming no. Something is telling me to stay here, and I can't tell if it's my gut or the fact I'm clinging onto the hopes she will come and find me. *Stop being so ridiculous Alora.*

"Really, I am fine. Thank you though." I nervously fiddle with my fingers, trying to avoid contact with him but I know my face screams discomfort right now and my back is stinging heavily under this heat.

"I've just come from the nearest town about ten miles from here, on my way to go retreating, I have some supplies if you're interested, food, water? It's hot out." Ten miles? I can make that before it gets too dark. That's roughly a two to three hour walk if I pace myself but as he's offering, it will be easier with something in my system.

"Wouldn't hurt, if you don't mind." We exchange a fake smile, knowing I will feel a whole lot better when he's gone.

"Course. They are in the trunk." He wastes no time jumping out, pulling his keys from the ignition as we both walk to the back of the truck. I don't need a lot, just something to last me till morning.

He opens the trunk and my expression contorts, glaring at an empty space with no supplies to be found.

...

Shit.

...

Play - *'Can You Hold Me - NF, Britt Nicole'*

His hold grips the back of my neck tightly, digging his nails into my skin with malice as I squirm underneath his grubby hold, beginning to scream out for someone to hear me, a*nyone. H*e fights to throw me in the back of the truck and I can feel my heart in the back of my throat trying to find all the strength in me to kick this sick freak off me but it's no use.

"No one can hear you princess. Keep screaming. I like it when they scream." His words are laced with venom, ready to poison me slowly and my stomach curdles at the vile thoughts plaguing my mind.

"LET ME GO!" He doesn't restrict my mouth, only hurting me further so I scream as he bends my arm back until it's on the verge of snapping.

"Don't you know not to take help from strangers?" I can only rip my throat out, hoping I'm heard but I begin to sob profusely knowing no one is coming for me. Ten miles cannot be heard from here. He smells of musk and whiskey, stinging at my nose. "You sound so pretty."

I hurl in my mouth, fighting not to choke on my fear as he grips my scalp tightly, spitting on my chest as he claws at my clothes, ripping them to expose my bare skin, feeling over my curves like I belong to him. I picture her face, squeezing my eyes shut trying to imagine it's her. Anything to take my mind off the way I'm about to be violated.

"PLEASE DON'T!" He pinches my tits sharply and I shriek at the pain, bent over the back of the trunk as my bare backside sits on show and he's hard against my ass.

"That's it, beg for me." He gets off using my body like his own personal fucking toy. But I'm not his fucking toy. *I'm hers.* I find more strength but it's only exhausting me further as he unzips his trousers sending my body into paralysis. I concentrate on her words. How she touched me, how she made me feel. All the ways she violated my body to quieten my mind and numb my impending pain.

"I'm going to fuck you till you pass out sweetheart, doesn't that sound fun?" She doesn't like to share. I wonder if she would even touch me if I was touched by another man. Beads of fatigue stream down my cheeks, finally giving up, I laying there trying to relax as I pray for death. Wishing I'd died on her cock when she asked me to. So we could be phantoms and haunt her sanctuary together. My soul is with her, it's no longer a part of me.

I dissociate, peering at the rust caking the back of his trunk, realising I don't think I will ever be myself again. I close my eyes to take my punishment when suddenly my muffled hearing comes back to me and barking breaks my silence followed by bones crunching against my ears, repeatedly, relieving weight off my behind giving me the ability to move. I turn around to see him getting what he deserves, weeping in relief as I crawl out from the trunk, stumbling on my feet trying to muster up the strength in my legs once more where he'd cut off their circulation.

My Nightmare is becoming my *knight in shining armour* as she pummels mercilessly into his thick skull until he's merely conscious, hanging lifeless as she holds his dead weight by the scruff of his tattered flannel shirt now caked in his innards as it spews from his nose and I've never been so relieved to see someone hurt. Suffering at the hands of *My Puppeteer.* She's not even wearing a mask.

"Heal." My heart is pounding against my rib cage as I grab for Shep, sneering with his hackles up as he heals at her command and I'm strangely feeling comfort in the state of the mans face, barely recognisable.

She takes a blade from her pocket and I study her making a painting out of his face, giving him a cheshire smile, feeling my stomach tense with nausea as the muscles in his face protrude through the gapes in his cheeks. Bones and blood mesh into one gruesome picture as his screams ring through my ears like a lullaby. For once I feel no remorse. No sadness. Nothing. Purely hunger for the justice she's feeding him, and it feels good.

Part of me wants to end him myself but I shove that thought to the back of my head and watch instead. I've never watched someone die but she's right. *It can be beautiful.* He gargles up his final words, choking on his blood as it clogs his throat creating a sea of red to blanket his face, laying there lifeless on the rocky gravel as it spews over her exposed forearm. She takes her fingers, wiping them in his blood before smearing them over her eyes and across her mouth, branding her kill and I swallow my distant arousal creeping in, now understanding all her symbolisms and only wanting her more.

She stands, gazing at me with that admiration I crave, her freakish nature plastered over her makeshift mask, pleading a sorry with her eyes as she holds her hands out for me to take, wasting no time as I fall into her tight embrace.

"Come here *baby*... I got you. I got you. You're ok, I'm right here. I'm so sorry." My entire body relaxes into her, morphing into her grip, exhaling a content sigh followed by silent weeping as my brain tries to process what the hell just happened. I nudge my tears into her tee as she runs her bloodied fingers through my sweaty scalp, gripping the remnants of my ripped top to cover my dignity.

Home.

She feels like Home.

"I never said anyone else could hurt you, you're my *Innocence* to harm." Her words are the glue to my shattered heart. I would happily endure all of her pain, all of her hurt, all of her wrath if it meant being here in her arms until my last dying breath.

"Never do that to me again!..." I screech as she squeezes me tighter, quivering with adrenaline like she is never going to let go and I sob harder. She is the only person I need. Without her I don't want to spend another day breathing. I don't want to be anywhere else but right here.

"*Never.*" She whispers quickly as I chase her mouth in the chaos, seeking her lips on mine with desperation, tasting her murder in my mouth and it's bittersweet, lustful with vengeance as her tongue dances with mine. I want her to show me just how sorry she is. "I also told you. I would stop at nothing to hurt anyone who tried to take you away from me."

She was following me. And she acknowledged my last words to her before she slammed the door in my face. Her kisses draw a whimper from my mouth, removing his stains with her hands caressing every inch of my body as she lifts me up, wrapping me into a bear hug and I can feel her tension subside as our hearts beat in sync.

She'll never say those words to me, but this. This is enough. She doesn't need to say those words for me to feel that love she's wrapping around my tongue; I just need to feel it as she speaks to me through her body.

CHAPTER 53

CONSUMING MY MONSTERS

Puppet

I must have blacked out because I don't remember getting home.
Home.
I say the word like I truly belong here, but this is *her* home and I want her to feel that too.

I space out, glaring at the blanket wrapped around me as I sit up on the bed listening to her shuffling around in the living room, most likely cleaning up her mess and I can't help but wonder why. Why did she let me go, or more importantly, why did she come and find me? I'm trying to be angry at her but I'm too focused on his hands against my skin as I tremble feeling the dried-up tears stiffening my cheeks.

"I'm going to fuck you till you pass out sweetheart, doesn't that sound fun?"

I shriek into my skin, feeling a new tear roll down my face, so caught up in the moment dissociating that I don't even see her standing in front of me.

"*Baby?*" She whispers calmly until I fall back into the present, jumping at the sight of her. I didn't know it was possible to capture anger and sadness in one expression but it's exactly what she's giving me. Once again punishing herself for my suffering, slowly edging towards me, crouching down to my level with her hands gently on my thighs. "You with me?"

She catches my tear like a feather against her thumb, consuming it with her tongue like holy water as she licks it but I push another one out. I nod timidly, glaring at the pain in her face and is it wrong for me to want her right now? I just want to forget. I just want her to consume me, fight away my nightmares. She saved my life, *again*. And she's making it every bit harder to fight her away when she's proved to me that my life belongs to her. That my sanity and everything I hold belong to her now.

She still has his blood smothering her face and she looks so disgustingly handsome I'm squeezing my thighs together feeling disgusting in my own body at the thought.

"What if someone finds him?" I whimper through broken sniffles. I'm more afraid to be found than anything. I don't want to face the world; I don't want to face a world without her ever again.

"I've dealt with it." She murmurs confidently and I have no doubt she did, probably another fire but it's easy to disguise these incidents in heat like this and I feel calmer knowing we are in the clear. I skip the details, I've seen enough for one day but I wasn't exactly frightened by his demise, it only pushed this sickening desire to let her animalistic nature destroy me. She pulls out my insulin, refusing to let me do it and my heart tightens, watching her tend to my skin so delicately. I will never get over how gentle she is with me but for right now, I don't want her to be.

"*Make me forget.*" I whisper. She tries to read through my words, rationalise my thinking but there is nothing rational about any of this. I'm a prisoner in love with a killer, I don't think this is exactly farfetched after the months I've had.

"*Innocence...*" She warns, and I know how weird that sounds, I don't even understand why I want her but *I need this*. I'm still buzzing on adrenaline and shock, maybe this is a coping mechanism for my trauma but right now all I can think about is how I want her to ravish me and strip me bare of the *innocence* I may have left, I want her to show me how filthy I am for *her,* how much I desire to sin for *her*, defy god and worship the devil for *her*, obey her every command for *her*, unwrap all my layers of insecurities and make me trust completely in *her*, say words only to fuel my submission for *her*, corrupt my imagination for *her*.

I want her to make me touch myself in ways that would make ancestors turn in their grave, I want her to feel how deep inside me she can get until I can't feel the air around me, I want to feel the blood rush to my head as she breaks the last of me, as she clutches to my throat like I'm someone she loathes, pushing me closer to hell with every tavy hrust. Where my legs are immobile and I'm quivering around her length, praying to hell that she pulls me under and shows me no mercy.

"Please." She is glaring at me like my words are the words of a mad man but the bob in her throat only indicates she wants to give me what I'm asking for as she caresses my thighs with her thumbs.

"What do you want?" She asks calmly and I nudge into her fingers as she begins to caress my cheekbone. I suck up my nerves, reaching for her face as she squints at my touch.

Play - 'Hypnosis – Sleep Token'

"I want you to make me *yours*." Her chest rises and falls, like she is trying to hold back her hunger, but I don't want her to hold back, pressing my lips against her letting more tears crack down my red cheeks. "I don't want you to hold back."

My body is frail and damaged, beaten and broken, exactly how it should be. I finally understand what it means to *feel alive*. That moment when pain conquers all. When you are no longer afraid of pain, you can take on the world. He didn't enter me. But it makes this need all the more prominent. I need her to show me that she is the only one who will EVER belong inside me. I want her to claim me and show me no mercy.

I can feel her depravity through the way she's gripping me like we are sinking and I'm not holding my breath anymore, I'm ready to drown in her seas.

"You're unbelievably foolish." Her words crack through our heated kiss and I clamp my eyes shut focusing only on her hands against my frail body.

"*Why?*"

"Because when I'm done with you, there will be nothing left to save." It's a good job I don't want saving. I let her embrace the fragmented pieces of me only she can put back together as she squeezes me in her arms, leaning me back on the bed to devour my mouth. "Do you trust me, Alora?"

She peers down at me, searching for my fear but I'm no longer scared, I want to dance with her darkness, and I don't hesitate.

"With every breath I take." My words light up her face exposing that soft gaze she blesses me with, letting me know I am completely and entirely safe in her arms, taking both my hands and raising them up to her chest as she undoes her belt slowly. Something my pussy now reacts to with a painful throb between my thighs as she braids the leather around my wrists, pulling me up to meet the metal bars, tightening it through the metal hoop to trap me there, glaring at me with ominous intentions.

"You best spare those breaths then." I inhale deeply, trying to calm my nerves, trying to push back the endless nights I spent chained to this bed. Feeling my temperature rising as I relive it. She drags my jeans off my bottom half exposing my bare thighs and I can see on her face that what she's looking at is bringing out the monster buried inside her that I've been desperately trying to keep at bay but just for today, I'll allow it.

She runs her tacky thumbs gently over what I can only assume are the marks he left on me and I make an unpleasant face, squeezing the creases under my eyes at the dull pain. I've not looked down, I don't want to. I don't want to picture the devastation he's left on my skin, I just want her to replace it. It was only for a brief moment but his touch was palpable and dehumanising and it felt like an eternity I was trapped beneath him.

He never made his way inside my body but it doesn't matter, he made his way inside my mind and I don't know which is worse.

"Pick a word. Any word. And if you say it, everything stops I promise." I glare up at her in confusion, frustrated that even now she is so fixated on my safety and my feelings when I just want to switch off, but I think for a prolonged moment as she brushes the loose strands of hair out of my face,

"*Sunflower.*" I mumble through a gentle giggle and through the chaos she grins back before lowering her lips against my hot skin.

"Remember, you're in control, *Puppet*. Just say the word and I'll stop. I promise." I focus on my toes, her voice ringing in my ear as she reassures me I'm *not* trapped. That I can let go beneath her. Something I desperately crave.

She exits the room for a moment, trundling back in with a duffle bag that clanks as it hits the wooden floor making my stomach drop, glaring at her with suspense, drawing out a sharp gasp when bloodied tools are pulled from the opening of the bag.

She dismembered him?!

"Monsters are real *Puppet*. But luckily you have one who'd kill for you." I gape, blinking in shock but part of me aches at the thought. All this because he put his hands on me. *Because he touched what belongs to her.*

She runs her fingers against the metal, collecting the blood on the tips, staring at me through the murder on her face and I shudder, concentrating solely on her as she approaches the bed, straddling my hips, pinning me with her weight.

"You are a *Clown, Alora.*" My breath hitches, spacing out as I peer into her void at the clown above me, feeling violated as her ring finger and thumb find my face, trailing his innards against my skin to mimic her like a reflection.

"Give me a smile." She coos, baring her teeth in the corner of her abused cheek and every moral thought I was clinging to makes my blood run molten hot with a sickly ill desire to play in her crazy, my dimples making an appearance underneath her as she paints my smile with her thumb.

"You are *Mine.*" Her confession makes her ill acts of service flood to the back of my mind, wearing his blood proudly as she thrusts between my thighs, drawing out an unspoken moan, the stench of iron churning my stomach.

"You're foolish to *Love* me." She thrusts harder against my pants and I can feel myself dripping to feel her inside my walls, to let her burrow her anguish and love inside me as she grinds forcefully against my clit. I break out in whimpers, pushing against her to cure this throbbing that's crushing me, succumbing to her sadistic nature to feel something. To erase my memories and replace it with her.

I'm safe. I'm in control. I'm hers.

A switch blade peers into view, flicking it to slide against the remnants of my battered top and my bra with it, sucking in every time she exposes my flesh like it's the first time. Heat plagues my flesh as I coy away, wanting desperately for her to smother me in her skin.

"I'm going to shatter every perfect inch of your body until you break for me to fix." She thinks I'm perfect even though I'm already broken and it's infuriating that she can't understand why I see what I see in her.

"Fix me *Hayden.*" Her blade grazes my throat and I feel my airways close with adrenaline, nearly choking on her as she kisses me, sucking the little oxygen I have left and I've already broken. This is just the beginning, and I will shatter *over and over again* if it means I get to feel her tear me apart. I'd let her end me in every sense of the word.

Her pressure builds as she leans her weight on me, escalating my need to suck back in air, panicking at the thought of not being able to move.

"I'm right here. Breathe. In and out for me." She's pushing me to control my body under pressure, to find my grip when I feel like I'm losing it, to find my strength when I'm weakest. This is not just about dominance or claiming her territory. This is a lesson in control. She's helping me to fight my own demons. To let them know they cannot suffocate me when I am the one holding the gun.

I do as she says, one breath after another until my heart slows to a rhythmic symphony against her tongue on mine, reminding me that she's right here.

"You will be the death of me, *Alora Blackthorne.*" My heart palpitates, knowing that I am her weakness but that gives me the opportunity to become her biggest strength if she allowed me to show her just how heavily I care for her.

"And I'll happily die right with you." She kisses me harder and I didn't know it was possible to feel a connection so deep through just our lips but it's transcending and I'm moulding to her like wax. Burnt by her fire melting at her touch as she hurts me slowly, completely lost in our kiss that I don't register the metal running the length of my frame, gliding between my slick thighs freezing me in place making her grin from ear to ear as she slices yet another pair of my pants leaving me bare and vulnerable. I blush with embarrassment as she places it beside her and begins to toy with my pussy, taking my nipple in her mouth with subtle force, sucking it until I buck, arching into her with a gentle sigh.

"Beg for my cock *baby*, beg me like you're going to fucking die without it." I will fucking die without it. *Without her.* Without hesitating my mouth moves.

"Please Hayden…" She grinds harder, unzipping her button and I buzz with an ache worse than death.

"Louder." She growls down my ear, teasing my entrance and I'm buckling with excitement.

"Fuck me Hayden!…" Her grip clamps around my airways as she slides in with no remorse and I feel her ripping against my walls, wrapping around her as she shatters them to pieces inside me, tightening around my throat the deeper she goes until I can't fucking breathe, until her constellation is the only thing I can see as my vision disappears. Is this what death feels like? Or have I just been reborn.

"Atta *Fucking* girl, I want to hear you." She thrusts to my pleads, filling me up until I relax around her, fucking me senseless and I can barely see her through my hazy vision. I grip the leather of the belt, feeling it tearing into my skin the tighter I hold it for stability along with the burn against my back as my wounds graze against the fabric beneath us, hissing through the pain I'm secretly losing it over. "Only I can make you feel like this, do you hear me?"

I try to respond through staggered moans, her possessive nature only pushing my orgasm to surface with every word she whispers to me. My Devil on my shoulder as she sinks her jaws into the pocket of my porcelain skin so deeply I cry out only driving her to fuck me harder. I'm at her mercy and it's the most freedom I've ever felt.

"You sound so fucking beautiful when I'm inside of you." Her praise almost tips me over the edge, whining louder to let go and she can read my body language like a book, watching me crash under the pressure, struggling to keep my eyes open. "Don't you dare fucking cum. Don't you dare. Look at me."

A yelp of distress bleeds from my mouth as I try my hardest to hold back my orgasm but all I want to do is defy her, break her demand just to see her break me again as I glare at her with heavy lids. My mouth hangs open trying to keep my eyes on her as I drag my bottom lip through my teeth, clamping down trying to restrain from release leaving teeth marks in my skin.

"Such a needy *Little girl.*" She undoes the belt around my wrists, freeing me of my restraints and my curiosity peaks, still finding it difficult to focus on her as she keeps her rhythm, unsure what to do with my hands, gasping as she takes the air from my lungs when she pulls me into her cock pushing out a scream as she sinks her fingers into my thighs holding them high up above me. "What are you *Alora*?"

I glare at her and I can tell this is a trick question, confirming my suspicions as she halts, sliding in and out of my pussy painfully slowly as she pulls her pockets from her jeans, smirking as my legs quiver against her torso.

"Your *bitch*." I can feel my cheeks burning at my vulgar words that seep from my tongue like acid.

"Show me." Instinctively I reach for her pockets, gripping them with the last of the strength I can conjure up, dripping in a cold sweat as she secures my throat and her look alone makes me want to cum, so full of lust and death. A combination I've grown fonder of, as I lay there ready for her to kill me *again*, taking her until I can only murmur profanities.

"*Now,* *Y*ou're going to be a *good girl,* and cum on my fucking cock." Without giving me a second to catch my breath she rips into me, hitting my sweet spot with her length as she leans into the back of my legs, almost forcing my thighs to my stomach, driving herself inside my wet hole, loose and sore until I scream to break. "There we go!..."

It takes no time for me to lose myself, gripping so tightly I swear I'm going to rip these pockets off as I ride her waves as much as she's riding mine, like she can feel me tighten around her, growling down my ear as my release only makes her choke me tighter. I don't think there is anything more attractive in this world than a woman who is simply so adorn by you that she can feel pleasure purely through your body and not her own.

We are one of the same now and I intend on giving her every piece of me.

CHAPTER 54

MY BEGINNING

Puppeteer

Play - 'I'll be good - James Young'

After years of searching for a reason, a purpose, constantly a means to an end, chasing my revenge to fuel my ugly appetite, I never stopped to admire the beauty life captures when you're not looking. How it grows and is constantly changing. You cannot grow if you're stuck in time dwelling on shit that cannot be changed. This? This can be changed. And suddenly I'm ready to sacrifice everything I have to be by her side until the day I leave this god forsaken world. I tried to do the right thing. I tried to be selfless and it almost got her fucking killed. I almost lost her and now I realize, that pain. It doesn't ever leave, no matter what road you try and take, no matter how deeply you try to avoid it, even letting them go leaves a gaping hole in your heart. I refuse to feel that kind of pain again. So I'll be selfish and I'll give her what she wants.

Me.

I'll give her Me.

"Run away with me." Her eyes bulge, peering up at me with puffy cheeks and bloodshot eyes as her pupils dilate.

"But you-"

"I know what I said. And I've changed my mind." I cup her hair behind her ear, admiring every inch of her in my shirt, hot and messy from taking every inch of me and if she wasn't so exhausted I'd happily go again just to hear her cry my name again. And again. Until she had no voice left. "I almost lost you today. And I haven't felt that frightened since the night my mom died." I can see tears creep into her waterline, like she's relieved to finally hear me confess my feelings and I hate it but that realisation she's holding on her face is a picture I'll never get tired of looking at.

"I realise now that I can't breathe without you. And I'm selfish. I want this. *I want us*, I want you, I was just afraid you would run when you learnt the depths of my past so I pushed you away before you could hurt me first and in doing so I hurt you further. I was wrong to ever let you go. I was wrong to push you away, I was wrong to hurt you like I did. *Alora*. And because of me, you were almost -" I choke back the words I was going to say, hurting my jaw at how tightly I'm clenching it, knowing that it all could have gone all so terribly fucking wrong if I hadn't of trusted my gut. It's like I could feel her crying out to me. I left not long after she did and I know that deep down I wouldn't have let her get far but just the thought that I could have stared at that door for hours before eventually letting my heart speak for me, knowing that if I left it ten minutes, thirty minutes, an hour. *Hours.* If I was a minute longer he would have ploughed himself inside of her and I would have been too late. What if it was hours later?

My attention is diverted as tears break down her temples, reaching for my cheek like she can see I'm lost in my own head and I brave it just this once and let her, grinding my teeth at the sensation.

"It's not your fault..." She whispers through the silence and her words alone make me want to cry. I want to cry. Fuck I want to cry. But I can't. She doesn't realise how all of this is my fucking fault. She can't see the damage I leave behind. She's so glued to this redemption inside of me that everything else is irrelevant. Her empathy will kill her. *I will kill her.*

"Even broken you continue to find something in me worth fighting for. Even after everything, you look at me like I'm somebody." Like right now. She's looking at me like I'm her entire fucking existence and it's a power I cannot compete against. Her *Love* is finally gripping me by the fucking throat and I'll happily choke just to feel it. "I will never let you out of my sight again, do you hear me?" I slide my forearm underneath her upper body to grip her scalp, drowning in her sighs as she sings for me. I barely have to touch her and she's a pile of mush.

I never thought it would come to this, she wasn't even supposed to exist but here she is in my bed ready to sacrifice everything her life has to offer her just to be with me and I'm still trying to get my head around it. But I'm sure we'll make it work. I'll make it fucking work. Because for the first time in a long time I see something worth fighting for and I'll happily destroy anything that tries to get in the way of that.

"Where would we go?"

"Anywhere you want." I'm fuelled with this sickness she's pumping inside me, chasing her mouth to taste her again. Her body is my elixir and I can't get enough. Gripping her head tighter with every stroke of my tongue. I feel my heart escalate as her hands find my torso, caressing me gently but it feels like razor blades against my skin. Biting down on her bottom lip I transfer my irritation as I brace her warm fingers, trying to focus on our kiss.

"I don't care as long as it's with you." My chest throbs and I don't think it's possible to devour her any more than I have but I want to. I want to be her fucking throne.

Play – 'Over me – Camylio'

I roll onto my side, dragging her with me until she's straddling my waist, squinting at my size as I stretch her out, knowing she is already too fucked out, gripping my abs to keep her up right.

"Oh- my god! Hayden! What are you-"

"Sit on my face." She glares at me, terrified to move and it's adorable, really. *But I'm not fucking joking.* "Sit on my fucking face."

I need her in my mouth, I need to show her how sorry I am with my tongue. I want her to suffocate me with her pleasure as she rides my jewels. I want her to know that I will happily fall underneath her mercy. I grip underneath her thighs, pulling myself down between her legs as I hoist her up the bed until she stumbles for the bedframe.

"*Hayden!*-" My hands run the length of her frame, memorising her curves as I grip the squishy flesh on her hips, sinking my fingers into the warm creases of her thighs as she hovers above my face, still dripping for me, I lap up her arousal with the tip of my tongue already drawing out a sigh as she clings to the metal work.

"Sit down and shut up." She gasps as I force her to meet my mouth, sliding my tongue through her folds with sheer depravity, cuddling her clit between the slit, already groaning at her honey in my mouth making her relax into me like a good girl. She is already quivering as I attack her sensitive parts, sucking her clit softly to force a whine out of her that makes me throb painfully.

"Ha-ys..." Her whimpers make me dizzy, tightening my hold as she begins to grind against my face, smirking as her needy cunt rides my tongue.

"I want you to show me just how needy you are for me *baby girl*." She grips the metal, quickening her pace as she gets lost in this euphoria between her legs, giving her body to me once more. Its fucking delicious, looking up at my shrine dancing against my face like a goddess, moving like water as she rolls her body to the rhythm of my strokes.

"Good girl *Puppet*. Tell me you're *Mine*." My thumbs run her centre line, cupping her tits in my hands, a perfect fit as they mould to my hold. I graze her nipples lightly almost immediately pushing her over the edge, watching her kick her head back, filling up the rooms with my new favourite sound.

"*Tell me.*" I plead, craving to hear those words pour from her lips as she whimpers.

"I'm all yours!-"

She's near on about to break already and this control I have over her body has me nearly cumming in my boxers. I curl into her cunt as I take my dominant hand and rub it against her dripping hole, teasing her entrance, pushing it in slightly to let more run down my digit before smirking against her pretty pussy. I run my fingers between the crease of her ass, wetting it as I massage her other hole feeling her jolt as she gasps in shock. I can feel her wanting to stop as she glares down at me with warning in her eyes but her hips keep moving as my thumb eases in and out of her pussy effortlessly, curling my middle and ring finger in circles against her tight little hole before pushing one in slightly.

"Hay-den-" She hates to admit it feels good but I can feel how much she secretly enjoys it through my tongue. She cannot hide her pleasure from me. It's all fucking mine. Like all of her will be mine, even her perky little ass. She tries to pull away, met with a smack against her tits causing her to sit back down on my mouth, pushing my fingers deep in both holes and she's quivering. *So, fucking perfect, so mine.*

"You're all mine. Remember?" I murmur against her clit, reminding her that she wanted me to claim her, make her mine and she is as she takes me so well, riding me harder letting me dig deeper. "Cum on my tongue *baby*. I'm thirsty."

My other thumb circles her breast, teasing her rose bud as she jolts into my chin, chasing that high on the tip of my tongue like cocaine. Addictive and dangerous, quivering for release as she trembles against my mouth, so flustered her hand finds my hair, gripping it so tightly my entire body tenses, refraining from ripping her off me and pounding her tight ass into the bed.

"That's it, let go *baby*, such a slut for my tongue." My broken words between her slit only push her to cum for me and perfect doesn't even begin to describe the view as she cups my face vigorously, crying out for me as her perky little tit brushes up against the palm of my hand, fisting the bed frame so tightly she might actually break it.

"Ye-s Yes! Yes! Fu-ck!" She slows her pace as her soul leaves her body. I clamp her in place so she can't move to intensify her orgasm as I ravish her clit with my piercings, fighting against her resistance as she tries to push off my face, whining like an injured puppy as half my tongue lashes against her clit and the other runs the soft velvet to her throbbing hole that's currently inhabited by my finger she won't let go of as I feel her contract.

"It's too much! Please! Hayden please!" She sounds so God damn pretty when she is begging. I grip her ass and pull myself back between her legs before flipping her over, making her taste herself on my tongue, grinding against her weeping pussy as she soaks the thigh of my jeans, hiccupping into my mouth as I push against her sensitive flower.

"*Shit-*" I slip out a moan, fighting everything in me not to plunge myself back inside her but she's heaving, trying to catch her breath and due for some heavy sugar overload. My little princess needs a breather and we both need a clean-up.

Play - 'In Your Arms - Sombr'

My fingers find her in the ridiculous amount of bubbles she's put in this bath, her stomach full of food she definitely shouldn't be eating but she does this adorable little happy dance that makes it hard to resist. I'm not exactly the romantic bath type but it's as romantic as it's gonna get. She is lying against my chest completely content, her wet strands of overgrown hair swimming over her curves and I realise just how much her hair has grown, it's almost twice the length now. *More to pull on.*

I fiddle with her fingers as my other hand traces her skin under the water and she grabs my wrist softly, staring at my hand, swallowing my pride I expect her to ask me about my burns.

"Do they hurt?" Her fingertips trace the patterns in my skin, following the thick art dancing against my battered shell.

"No. But for you, maybe." I think she would well and truly cry if she got a tattoo. She's far too baby for that.

"How did you stay so sane? In prison, I mean." Her question catches me off guard, playing with her wet strands against my fingers as I raise a brow, whispering into her hair.

"*You think I'm sane?*" I am far from sane, and I don't know whether I enjoy the fact that I'm not, or if I live for the way I'm slightly crazy. *A lot crazy.*

"I think you're damaged but fixable. I've never met anyone quite like you." I smile into her wet mane, finding an ugly beauty in the way she perceives the person that I am.

"Because there is no one like me *Baby,*" I growl into her neck before pausing and pulling back, mocking her slightly with my next words. "Plus the fact, you've barely met anyone else."

Logistically, there is so much I do not know about her besides what she's told me and the bits and pieces I put together when going through her things but it doesn't take a person with two brain cells to realise that she has never really had true friends, nor has she had a partner or intimacy.

"Hey!-" She whines, tapping me gently on the forearm making the water splash onto the tiled floor as she giggles into its echo and I wish I could tape it and listen to it over and over again. "What does that say?"

My lip tugs, finding the irony in her innocent question as she grabs for my hand trying to decipher what it says on the back of my fingers, patiently waiting for her to figure it out as she plays with them between her own, tracing the ink in my skin.

"Go on *Puppet*, you tell me. What does it say?" She looks harder, scrunching her face until the penny drops, dropping her mouth in confusion.

"*Say it.*"

She peers up at me, nervous to say the word, understandably so. But my baby girl needs to learn, it's just me now.

"*Daddy...*" She mumbles, chewing on her finger and I can see the uncertainty in her beady eyes.

"Good girl, now remember that when you call out my name." She pushes my hand away playfully, rolling her face away from me.

"I'm not calling you that." *Oh she will.*

"You won't have a choice. You've said it now. *Puppet*. I want it bleeding from your mouth." She rolls her eyes, crossing her arms like a stroppy toddler and I can't help but hold back a laugh as I suck my lips together.

"Why do you even have that anyway?" *Oh wouldn't she like to know.*

"So when my hand wraps around your pretty little throat you know who your *Daddy* is." I raise my hand, sliding it up her chest until it's clutching her airways and her chest rises and falls just that little bit quicker, falling mute under my hold. "*Daddy* will take care of you now *baby...*" I whisper sweetly and she's trying to fight how her heart is feeling but her mind is winning this one as she squeezes her thighs together between mine. Her subconscious is melting into me, finding comfort in my protection. Finding solace in my ability to keep her safe in my arms. I will be her rock. Her provider. I will show her what it means to be truly vulnerable. How freeing it can be when you no longer have to fend but live, because *nothing*. will harm her ever again.

"If you even think to try and escape me now, I will not hesitate to fuck you till you can't feel your legs, *Puppet*." Her cheeks glow just waiting for me to kiss them, pushing her body forward to wash her back and my heart drops as I glare at my harm slicing across her shoulder blades, healing but still raw as I kiss them softly.

"I forgive you..." She whispers, looking back at me with nothing but pure admiration.

"Well, you shouldn't." She shouldn't forgive me for any of this because behind it all, it's me. I'm the cause of all her pain as well as her happiness and it's the most dangerous potion for disaster. I'm toxic and she's drinking me up.

"I feel stronger than I've ever felt. But I wouldn't be without you. You've shown me that pain is strength. Not a weakness." For people who deserve it like me. *Not angels like her.*

"Realistically. Where do you see yourself in five years *Puppet*..." She smiles, turning in the tub to face me and I melt like the butter in her eyes staring back at me.

"Well. This house needs some upgrades, but it's nothing we can't do *together*? You walk amongst civilisation with no problems at all. I'm sure we can figure something out." Her optimism almost deters me from the bigger picture but she still has her head in the clouds.

"*Alora. Baby...* You can't live cooped up away with me forever." My thumb runs her bottom lip fighting my urges to say *fuck logistics*.

"I said, we'll figure something out. But you have to be careful what you do." She's not wrong. I can't be so careless with my *work* now that she is my priority.

"You're crazy..." I nuzzle her nose, resting my forehead against hers as my thumb grazes her jawline.

"*For you.*" It's impossible to say no to her when she looks at me with so much hope. Hope I am terrified I will never be able to give her but I can do my bloody best to try. Try to be better for her. Try and give her what I can until I can figure out a way of getting us out of here. But I don't exactly have expertise in moving a girl I've kidnapped across the world.

CHAPTER 55

HOPES AND DREAMS

Puppeteer

Play 'Bad Luck – Noah Kahan'

After cooking my life away for the last two hours I place the plate in front of her and smile ear to ear as her face lights up like the stars. I can't lie, it's been a while since I've done roast chicken and vegetables. She's not even tried it yet but she's drooling over the plate like a dog.

"Holy HELL. This looks amazing!" She wastes no time digging in like she can't shovel it quick enough. I guess food is my love language or as good as it's gonna get anyway but I'll make her any meal she wants if this is her reaction. She's dripping gravy everywhere like a heathen.

"Oh my god- mouthgasm." I lean back in the chair and observe her child like nature, watching her enjoy these moments. How happy she is at the smallest things in life, imagining her face if I took her anywhere but here.

She's never experienced anything beyond her father's confinement and I intend to change that.

"If you had five things you wanted to do, what would they be?" She swallows her mouthful of potato, staring at me in a daze and by her expression it's not something even she has thought about in great detail.

"*Er-*"

"Anything." My thumb wipes the droplet of gravy from her chin, licking it off slowly just to watch her blush.

She plays with her food, tossing it around the plate as she's deep in thought. "Well- I've always wanted to dance in the rain?" *She's so simple it pains me.*

"And?" She scrunches her forehead at my careless response, rolling her eyes as she thinks a little harder.

"I'd love to go to the beach?" *She's never been to the beach?!* Jesus Christ, they really did keep her under lock and key. "Or drive a car?"

I smile, beaming with nostalgia and these won't be too difficult to knock off her list. Maybe not professionally but she can't exactly bust up an already butchered truck.

"Think bigger." A disgusting adorable kitten snarls at me across the table trying to think of something bigger but she can't.

"I- I don't know..." I exhale slowly, saddened to see how deeply her gift has been hidden from the world. Her gift to bring happiness and something special to any room, town or country she steps in. A girl capable of amazing things if she wasn't so sheltered.

...

"Publish a book." She glares into the abyss, doubt smothering her expression and that is something I unfortunately cannot help her with. Nor can she achieve it if she wants to stay by my side. It's a sliver of regret I can read through anyone. A sudden realisation that her dreams may never be, because she'd rather choose me and I sink in more guilt. She should have her name plastered all over billboards and book covers. Not missing posters and the news.

She gawks at me with absolutely no thought behind her eyes, smiling through a sympathetic grin and it physically hurts when my lips aren't on hers, fixated on the thought of how soft her mouth is against mine.

"Are you ever going to show me your writing? Or am I going to have to read it when you're asleep." I shouldn't but her pout is so kissable I might just have to.

"If you even try, I'll run away." *Ouch*. She's definitely writing about how good I make her feel when I'm between her legs.

"How do you expect to publish a book if you won't even let me read your writing?" I challenge her, mocking her with my eyes but she's persistent.

"It's not happening." She stabs her potato with malice before taking a ferocious bite. I can never take her seriously, wanting to squeeze her little cheeks.

"*Hayden's tongue felt so soft against my-*" I tease but am swiftly met with remnants of a mangled potato as she throws it at me.

"OH MY GOD NO!" By the redness on her face I am only led to believe I wasn't exactly wrong.

"That was a perfectly good potato you just wasted." Her dimples suck my annoyance up like a sponge as she giggles like a mischievous toddler. "I'll make you wear it in a minute." Cooking for her and she's wasting my blood, sweat and tears. *How disrespectful.*

"How do you know I won't?" She leans back in the chair, staring straight through me as she calms her words.

"*Won't what?*"

"Run away. Aren't you afraid I might?" I'm terrified. There is a possibility that tomorrow she may wake up and realise how crazy this is. She might miss normality. I know she said that isn't what she wants but I don't think even she truly knows what she wants right now. I wouldn't and I certainly never did at her age. If it was up to me, I'd make sure she never shed another tear again but I can never promise that won't happen considering the situation. She deserves to see everything life can offer.

"My luck has run out *Puppet*. If you do then that only solidifies how delusional I am about you." Hearing those words leave my mouth is still so unfamiliar to me. This affection. This longing for her to be mine. A strange chapter to this new life we have and I've never felt this *happy*. It's like I've been reborn. This new beginning with her is teaching me that there is hope and a recipe for redemption if you find the right ingredients. When I look at her I can suddenly see a future that doesn't involve me in a grave. She's teaching me that this sickness can be curable if treated correctly. This talk of *Love*. It can be gentle and kind. The way my mom would hold my hand on a stormy night. Or give me the last slice of pizza. The small things that begin to shape why they have an embedded place in your heart that now cannot be erased.

"Then I guess we are both delusional..." She whispers to me.

Play 'Time - NF'

I've managed to get through to some contacts who know their way in and out of the country. It isn't exactly legal but what do I ever do that's legal.

Being in jail had its perks and it's not just me trying to get the hell out of here now. I can't exactly grab her passport and wander through the airport so an off-radar aircraft is the next best option. I know this sounds ridiculous. *It is ridiculous* but she seems to be drawing more of that out of me lately. The lengths I will go to see her smile worries me. Because I may not be there to see those dimples one day. I want her to experience life the way I never could. *I owe that to her.*

I glare at the computer screen, realising I've abandoned all these cases I was meant to clear and my skin is itching at the thought but I suck it up, trying to remember why.

Because I'm trying to be a *better person* and if my body could reject it, it would. Because I'm feeling nauseous just thinking about it and it almost does come up when her scream rattles my ears from the bedroom and I'm suddenly ten again. Feeling my heart in my throat as I nearly take doors out on my way to her.

Her night terrors are back. Only this time I can't stand to hear her cry and my blood boils below the surface at the thought of his body against hers. She is usually in a state of paralysis I have to desperately shake her out of and it makes me feel so helpless. Every wrong doing she's encountered is by my hand and sometimes I don't even feel like I deserve to touch her. I know I got there in time but what if I didn't? What if I was too late? What if I had been stubborn and ignored my gut. She'd probably be dead at the bottom of a ditch somewhere and I'd be none the wiser and that thought alone makes me want to die.

"Hey! *Baby*! Hey, it's me! I'm here, I'm here *baby* I'm here!" I withstand her violence as she thrashes against my hold, screeching down my ear in pure fear she has no conscious mind of as of right now. She's still in a dream and sometimes I feel like she'll never wake up.

"*HAYDEN*!" She yells my name, even subconsciously her dormant mind searches for me, trying to hold back tears as she weeps in her sleep that makes me grit my teeth.

"Come on *baby*. Come on. Wake up, I'm right here, you're OK!" She finally surfaces, choking as she sucks in air, grabbing for me, trembling like a frightened lamb as I scoop her up into my hold and fight away all her new nightmares.

"I got you...I got you. Shhhhh..." Even dismembered and burnt to ash his face still haunts me. I dread to imagine how this is affecting her. Death was too kind. I thought slicing him up would have relieved some of my fury but still now I hate that even in death he's still ruining her. Dulling her spark that I refuse to let her let go of.

"In and out with me *baby*." I take a deep breath, encouraging her to follow suit and she does with great difficulty, trying to take back control of her body and mind like I've been trying to teach her.

"There we go..." I will sit here all night with her if I have to. I've become my worst nightmare as of lately. I'm coddling her but it's my own way of coping. I just like to know that she's safe and the only way I can guarantee that is if she's here.

In my arms.

"No one's gonna hurt you. No one." Her stray strands of chocolate stick to her damp cheeks as she searches for my gaze and she eventually gets a hold of her breathing.

""Look at me, look at me *Baby*. I'm. Right. Here." I remind her, brushing her face clean of her trauma as I plant gentle kisses against her hot skin tasting her salt on my lips.

SHASSII

I've never wanted to protect something so deeply in my life. Like she is the reason I'm alive. My reason to keep going. To scare away all the darkness that wants to harm her.

CHAPTER 56

DESSERT

Puppet

Play – 'Look After You – The Fray'

"Hayden this is crazy!" I grip the wheel of her battered old truck in absolute hysterics, belly laughing as she tries to show me the ropes but I'm definitely not getting the hang of this.

"You've got this! Just listen!" I know she has a death wish but this is ridiculous! I know I said I wanted to drive a car but this isn't exactly what I pictured. This is a shit box. "Is my shitty old truck not good enough for you?" It's like she read my mind and her mischievous grin only makes me laugh harder, trying to concentrate on her instructions but it's hard to when she's looming over me, being all intelligent and hot.

"No! No it's lovely!"

"Concentrate *Puppet*. Foot all the way down on the clutch, then into first gear." I'm panicking with too much adrenaline, giggling like an idiot.

"I can't! I can't- I can't do it!"

"Yes you can!" She sniggers at my predicament and I'm about ready to jump out of this truck but she has me as I claw playfully at her to let me out, restraining me with her palm to my chest. "*Alora Blackthorne*. I didn't train a quitter. You put your bloody foot down right now."

I pout, trying to seduce her into letting me out but she's not falling for it. Giving up I slowly look down at my feet.

"Wait, which one is the clutch again?" She glares at me with heavy judgement, rubbing the bridge of her nose as she leans against the frame of the open door and my chest tightens, staring entirely too long at her muscles. "I think I can tick this off my bucket list."

She scowls at me, gripping the back of the seat as I laugh into her chest but she can't contain her smile that makes my heart ache. It's my favourite feature on her desolate face. It brings out her smile lines that give me butterflies. How can someone so deadly possess a smile so beautiful. The contrast leaves me breathless as I gaze up at her through my lashes.

"You've not even got it started yet!" Maybe driving is not for me. Not that I could drive anyway but I'm clearly a pussy and we are both clearly not cut out for teacher and student.

"Maybe youuuuuu should stick to the driving." I hiccup nervously, grinning at her as she shakes her head in disappointment, peering over towards the passenger seat when my entire bloodstream turns the cold tap, glaring at an apparition of myself as that day decides to make an uninvited visit, wrapping around my neck like a snake until I'm starved of oxygen.

"What's a pretty little thing like you doing all the way out here?"

His words cut through me replacing them with tears as I stare into a black hole, unaware of my surroundings, now completely and entirely alone like the ground has swallowed me whole, unable to speak or move. I feel his pressure on me, weighing me down until I'm gagging for air. Sitting in the driver's seat of her truck has completely evacuated from my mind as I now feel him inside me. Sitting right here with me.

"*Alora?*"

A hand grips my shoulder and immediately I shriek, yelping for help as his face stares back at me and all I can do is scream, scream until he gets off me as I thrash against his hold that left bruises against my skin for days.

"Hey! *Baby* it's me! It's me! I'm right here *baby*, look! Look at me!" My vision becomes clearer and her face reappears, gawking back at me with nothing but pure fright as she grips my arms with so much strength they may break, cupping my chin with haste as she finds me in this sea I'm lost in, calling for me to swim back to shore.

"You see me? I'm right here *Baby girl*. No one's going to hurt you, ok? You feel that?" She places my hand against her heart, clawing at my cheek with the other as she kisses my forehead with gentle violence, pulling me into her chest, securing me to regulate my breathing. "Like we practised, ok? In and out with me. Breathe for me. Calmly. Slow it right down."

My sudden wave of security unfolds into floods of tears as she holds me there, squeezing me with just enough force for me to let it all out into her white tee. Soaking it with embarrassment.

"Don't ever leave me again." I cannot contain my fear or my pain and my words come out a blubbery mess. He's buried his nails deeply inside my marrow and I need to learn to overcome this new monster taking up residence in my head. My Nightmare has become my hero and I'm entirely ok with that.

She wipes my tears, cradling my puffy cheeks and I kiss her slowly. To remind myself I'm right here with her. Grounding me to find safety.

"I'm not going anywhere." Words cannot explain the comfort I find in her tongue. My own personal sanctuary I would never leave if she gave me the chance. An intimate connection that's touched every inch of my body and worshipped every part of me I loathed.

She pulls away, pulling my lip down with her thumb and I can see how much patience she possesses. How desperately she wants to ruin me but she won't until I tell her to and it only makes me want it more. I want her to possess me until she fights all my scary monsters away.

"But…" She lets out a prolonged '*U*' before she pops the '*T*' like whatever she is about to say is going to disappoint me.

"I do need to go and drop something off." I let out a deep sigh, smiling at her terrible timing.

"I won't be long, I promise. Are you going to be ok? You have Shep to keep you company." She pecks my forehead, playing with my chocolate hair between her fingers and everything inside me wants to ask to go with her but we aren't even close to being at that stage yet. I just hope one day we are.

"I'm ok. Go and do your thing." My muscles relax as she smiles at me and suddenly I realise my breathing has calmed, along with the world around me.

She pulls me from the seat until I find my feet on the ground, leaning over my tiny body as she pushes my loose waves over my shoulder, running her tongue along the length of my neck.

"And when I come back... If you'll let me. I'm having dessert." My pussy throbs at her call, knowing exactly what she means and I picture riding her face until I couldn't breathe. How ethereal it felt between my legs. I drag my lip through my teeth as I pull her in by her white tee, wearing mischief on my face.

"Yes *Daddy*..." her devilish upturn makes my disgusting words just that little bit more tolerable when she looks at me like that.

Play – 'Those Eyes – New West'

I mean. I know this isn't quite the dessert she meant but I had to keep myself occupied so I decided to raid her cupboards and she had just enough ingredients to make cookies but I wasn't expecting her to be so fast.

The key goes in the door and she wanders in, being rugby tackled by Shep at her feet as she glares at the monstrosity I've spread over her kitchen counter. Butter, sugar, flour, pots and pans. Meanwhile I'm prancing around in her flannel shirt I've been living in.

"What on earth are you doing? I've not even been gone a few hours."

"Well, I was getting extremely bored. But seems as you're here now. You can help me." I pull a sarcastic grin and she shakes her head as she peels off her leather jacket, heading straight for me and I still don't understand how she wears that thing in this weather

"Baking really isn't my thing."

"Oh come on! It'll be fun! Even if they do taste terrible. And besides, you said you wanted dessert." Her hands wrap my waist, spinning me to face her, lifting me off the floor as she puts me on the island, running her palms over my hips as she nips at my collar bone, melting her waist between my thighs like we are one.

"My dessert is meant to be spread over the island with her legs open." *If she thinks we are getting out of baking cookies she's highly mistaken.*

"We are making cookies! Thennnn you can have your dessert." I shove her away from me, placing a finger over her mouth as I jump back off the counter in protest, giving her incentive with persuasion but she follows me like a sheep, making my hairs stand on end as she rides the back of my shirt to reveal my ass, gently tapping it to make me squeak.

"Yes Boss." Her mockery is maddening but I can't seem to get enough, nuzzling into her chest with a laugh that makes her laugh and it's my favourite sound on this planet. It's crazy to think I have someone as hauntingly terrifying and disturbing as her, wrapped around my little finger and I intend to keep it that way because when she is carefree like this, it is one of the most attractive things in the world and I'm fighting the temptation to forget about the cookies and let her dine away when she touches me with such delicate force.

I've managed to tap into the soft dough beneath her hard shell and as if I wasn't already stupidly in love with her, she seems to forever prove me wrong by doing the next disgustingly adorable thing that just breaks away all my defences.

The way she refuses to let me brush my hair and does my insulin three times a day. How she looks after my needs when my sugars are low and lies with me when I'm having an episode. These last few weeks have been nothing short of everything I've been searching for. But I'll be honest. I don't know what we are. If we are even anything at all. I could say we are merely co existing but that would be a lie. Yet I don't know how relationships work so I guess the knowledge that I am hers is more than enough for my paranoia niggling in my ear telling me I mean nothing to her.

"So. What are we doing?" she asks playfully, peering over my shoulder at my weapons of choice and I see her eyeing up that flour.

"Youuuu. Are going to be my mixer because I have no muscles." She looks almost offended as she looks down at me with one eyebrow knitted to her forehead.

"You mean I don't get to eat the chocolate chips so you have none left to put in the mix?" She goes to reach the bar of chocolate I found stashed away before swatting her hand away.

"Get!" ~smack~ "Off them!" *She is a big kid I swear to God.* "Did you drop off whatever you needed to drop off?" I ask hoping she will tell me what was so important she had to leave me to my own devices where I'm now baking cookies out of boredom, measuring out the mix as I add it to a big bowl.

"I did." She leans against the counter next to me and the combination of petrol and leather makes my head fuzzy. It is this normal to be almost intoxicated by the scent of somebody's aura alone?

"What did you drop off?"

"That's for me to know..." She leans in, lingering behind my earlobe before gently kissing my sensitive skin and I'm tingling like a spark of electricity.

"And for you, to *dot dot, dot...*" If she carries on, I'm never going to get these damn cookies done.

"You're a pain in my ass." I pass her the bowl of measured ingredients, placing a whisk in her hand as she smirks like a sinner.

"I can be a pain in your ass if you want." She raises her tatted brown, grazing her bottom lip as she sets her eyes on my behind and I realise what vile innuendo she's referring to as she starts whisking with little effort.

"Absolutely NOT.." My face crumples at the thought, remembering how it felt whilst she was devouring my soul the other day and I can feel my cheeks heating. *How can anyone actually enjoy that?* Wouldn't it hurt like hell?

"I'll claim it. One way or another." I'd say *in your dreams* but so far I've given her everything she's threatened and I've given it willingly. So I huff in annoyance, watching her work her arm as she stares at me like a naughty school boy, drooling over her artwork that I daydream of at least ten times a day, wishing she'd wrap it around my throat again.

She finishes mixing and I portion the dough into a tray. I'm surprised her oven even still works but it hasn't exploded yet so we're all good.

Play - 'Daddy - Ramsey'

"How long have we got?" I turn to find her cleaning out the bowl with her tongue split against the rim and my throat locks, gawking at her as she peers at me over the bowl.

"I- about twenty minutes. Why?" I fight the little whore inside of me she's created, gagging to feel it between my thighs as I stagger my words, tipping my chin with authority but inside I'm dying slowly, fixated on the movement of her tongue as she purposely tries to get under my skin. *It's working.*

"It's a good job I can make you cum in ten then." She places the bowl down, dragging me from the oven with no remorse, turning my back to her as she smacks my ass enough to make it echo a sting, gripping my throat tightly but it now makes me pool with arousal. I'm entirely unafraid of her as she peppers hot breaths against my neck. "I said I wanted dessert."

She grabs my cheek, pulling me to face her and my body responds, turning until my hands are against her chest but she doesn't push them away. She lifts me to place my sore cheek against the cold tiles as she undoes the buttons of her shirt I'm wearing, slowly revealing my hard nipples beneath and I'll never get tired of the way she looks at me with such soft admiration yet her body holds so much hunger she has the ability to break my tiny body in half. It's alluding. She is a force to be reckoned with but I will happily be her reckoning. I love it when she breaks me.

"Start counting." She petals kisses against my flustered skin, burning up at her touch as she plays with my breasts, opening my legs like an automated response as she pushes my torso down against the island, running her tongue along my centre line until she's hovering over my entrance, breathing against it to set me off. "What do you say?"

I know exactly what she wants me to say but I hesitate, pushing my pelvis into her face trying to feel her against me.

"Please—" Her hands smother my body and I'm already whining like a needy little bitch. It's embarrassing how deeply I need to feel her tongue inside me but she resists me, taunting my ache.

"Please what?" Out of desperation the words leave my mouth without consent but right now it's the least of my worries. I need her to get rid of this crippling pain she's unfairly given me.

"Please *Daddy*..." I don't even have to look at her to feel the smile she presses against my pussy as she tugs my knickers to the side, tasting me on her tongue.

"That's right *Baby*. *Daddy* will get rid of that ache for you." The air is taken from my lungs as she wastes no time pressing her mouth to my hole with force, devouring me like she promised. My head falls back, hanging off the side of the counter like a corpse, dead weight with empty thoughts unable to keep my mouth shut and I'm glad there are no other houses around because if this was a village, every man and his wife would hear how I cry out for her. *I also don't hate how that word sounds on her tongue.*

I've fallen in love with the nothingness I feel as she pulls me over the edge with her. That blissful minute of freedom I cling to as I let go of everything. It feels like you're falling with nothing to keep you from hitting the ground. It's adrenaline without consequences. *It's freedom without rules.* It's the best minute of my life.

Her tongue swims in my honey before pushing her fingers in, making me grip the edges of the counter as I gasp with pure euphoria, arching my back into her digits.

"Such a greedy *Whore* for *Daddy*..." Her insertion has me already quivering to cum all over her ungodly perfect face and she knows it as she keeps a steady rhythm, pushing in and out of me with ease as I soak her hand in my juices. "Clocks ticking."

I grind against her tongue, twitching as my clit runs underneath her piercings to hit that sensitive spot.

"Please can I cum?!..." She says nothing, still following my motion and I grind my teeth trying to hold back this orgasm I'm slowly losing myself in. "Please *Daddy*!" It slips but I could get used to how she responds when she audibly groans into my slit, gripping my thighs tighter, indenting my flesh.

"Cum for *Daddy baby girl*." I don't know what kind of chokehold this woman has me in but I don't even have time to brace myself for the velocity in which I shatter, coating her entire face in me as I grip her hair tightly, locking her against me so she can't cut my fun short but it only makes her moan louder and that noise alone is something of a dream I'd happily never wake up from. She's at my mercy, feeding me pleasure through the very thing that grounds me, dirties me, commands me. Her voice is my anchor and her tongue is the chain, binding us to one another. Without it I am lost.

"Six minutes and thirty-two seconds." I throw my head back up, nearly falling over at the whiplash trying to focus on her between my legs. *Was she counting that entire time?!*

She slaps my pussy gently, stunning me in place as she stands back up, rolling out her neck as she wipes my cum off her chin slowly with her forearm and my ovaries buckle, admiring her as she towers over my naked body and I sound crazy but it's my comfort place when she looks at me like I've been carved out from heaven and placed in front of her.

"Don't burn the cookies." She drags my body into her crotch, slamming me against her as she pulls me up to her level, squinting my eyes tightly as I adjust to the light letting the blood rush back into my body. She runs the tip of her tongue against my bottom lip like a freak before sucking it into her mouth only resurfacing my demons she's just put to bed as I taste myself on her tongue. "I'm going for a shower."

She tips my chin with her finger to look up at her and my mind wanders, frustrated that she did that on purpose so I couldn't join her. Only able to imagine her naked frame under the water as I sit here and stare aimlessly into this oven so they don't burn.

"Fuck you..." She kisses me softly, grinning against my mouth and slowly pulls away making me chase her, almost falling off the edge.

"I'll fuck you later *Baby* don't you worry." She catches my fall with her hand around my neck, peering down at me as she smiles disgustingly slowly and whispers into my mouth.

"Such a *good girl* for *Daddy*..."

She's lucky I have to watch these cookies.

Dear current reader!
I just want to say, if you have made it this far, *thank you* for pushing through the nail biting tension and I hope you have enjoyed this rollercoaster of a ride. I hope you have laughed and cried and nearly ripped your hair out screaming at the pages as well as smiled so big your jaw hurts.

For the foreseeable best experience, I suggest that If you **do not** have a few hours to spare to carry on then you **wait** to do so. I feel to get the full extent of this ending you need to push through until you can't turn anymore so I'm advising you that if you can't do that, to wait and I promise you it will be worth it.

If you do have the time to carry on, grab some pain killers, some water, an entire box of tissues, chow down on some chocolate and grab something to cuddle.

You're going to need it.

P.S PLEASE DO NOT SPOIL ANYTHING BEYOND THIS POINT.
THIS IS A BITTERSWEET ENDING.
AND IF YOU ARE NOT ALREADY DOING SO, I WOULD HIGHLY SUGGEST LISTENING TO THE CHOSEN SONGS FROM THIS POINT ONWARDS FOR THE BEST CINEMATIC EXPERIENCE.

Happy reading!

CHAPTER 57

THEN NEVER I'LL WAIT

Puppeteer

Play - 'End of beginning – Djo'

After months of looking I finally found a decent back tire and it was actually a bitch to find but the old girl is finally up and running, ready to go for a spin. I touch up the last of the imperfections, polishing the gloss like its glass, tidying up the garage a little that is smothered in tools and parts before calling for her as I stick my head out the garage door.

"Hey *Puppet*." She pops her head round the corner, running a towel through her freshly washed hair as she clings to the towel wrapped around her body.

"Yeah?"

"You want to go for a ride?" She glares at me in confusion. I've not told her the bike was ready purely to surprise her. Since she told me she's not gone to the beach before, it's been sitting at the back of my mind, nudging me to get the old girl back on the road. I think we are past the point of escaping.

it's as close as I've got round here.

"You mean like-"

"Yes *baby*. I mean, do you want to sit on the back of my bike?" Her little face explodes with excitement as she legs it to the bedroom, nearly falling over on her way there.

"Oh my god YES! Just give me five!" I can't see her but the sound of out of breath pants and tripping feet is very much beaming from the bedroom door as Shep sits by my feet, glaring in her direction as his head tilts like we are thinking the same thing. *What the hell is she doing?*

"Hurry up! Or I will leave without you!"

She wastes no time throwing on some clothes, it takes her no more than three minutes until she's leaning her head into the garage door wearing a cute little summer top and some loose jeans with her hair still wet in her face. I concentrate on her freckles dotting her flushed skin and her plump, pink little lips still swollen from the hot shower. *so fucking kissable* I'm seconds away from pulling her back in that house and making her sweat again.

"Oh my god oh my god on my god." I don't think excitement really encapsulates the way she's bouncing off the floor as I close the garage door behind her, giving Shep a nuzzled kiss with my hand before he goes to find his bed and take a nap. He's a lazy bastard for a Shepherd. I'd take him with us but I can't quite fit her and him on the back of my bike.

"Listen to me very carefully." I hold the helmet out for her to take but I keep a hold of it until I finish talking, gripping it tighter as she tries to take it from my hand. *"Are you listening?"*

"Yes! I'm listening."

"You need to keep this helmet on until I tell you otherwise, ok? And you need to wrap your arms tightly around my waist. Put your feet on these metal bars and kiss your ass goodbye." Her face is dripping with fear as I let go of the helmet. Now not so hesitant to take it.

"Don't I need a suit or something?" She questions, trying to hold back a laugh as I look down at her beady little eyes.

"Don't you trust me, *Puppet*?" Normal people would. But I'm not going to ride like an idiot and these roads are dead, although, just to put her mind at ease, I'll give her my jacket. I grab it from the workbench, holding it open for her to put her arms through, smirking at the way it drowns her entire body and I know that's heavy but she's putting on a brave face as she looks at me with empty thoughts.

"Oh. And you might need an extra pair of pants." I whisper, teasing her with something she will completely take out of context. But I know she doesn't exactly have a bikini lying around so extra pants will have to do. She frowns, storming back into the house to grab some, coming back out stuffing it in the pockets.

"So where are we going?" I light a cigarette, letting it hang in my mouth before taking the helmet and pushing it over her head, strapping it tightly underneath her chin before planting my ass in the seat, holding out a hand to hoist her up and over, catching her as she nearly falls over to the other side.

"You'll see. And don't you dare start saying are we there yet. I will leave you on the side of the road." Her muffled laugh echoes from the helmet, wrapping her arms around my waist, gripping my tee for extra support as I start the girl up with some heavy feet until she fires, making her squeak like a little mouse, squeezing me tighter. "Are you ready?" I feel her nod her head against my back as she hugs me from behind like her life depends on it.

"*Yes Boss.*" I snap the throttle back to jog the bike at her sarcastic little nickname, making her scream into an adorable giggle as she falls harder into my back before jolting the bike with a quick flick of my wrist, riding slowly out the property as I hold her hand like a belt across my stomach.

We are on the road for around an hour and she gets a little more comfortable by the end, taking in the sights and I can't see her face but I know she hasn't stopped smiling which only makes me smile harder as I grip her ankle for comfort.

It's been a while since I visited but it was heavily overdue and it's beautiful at sunset. We pull in down a long dirt track, surrounded by cranes and shipment containers until we reach a dead end underneath a giant bridge with large concrete pillars where I stop to get off, helping her off behind me, watching her struggle to take the helmet off.

"*Come here, you idiot.*"

"This is it isn't it. This is where you actually kill me." She murmurs as I slip the helmet off her head.

"Yeah, I'm going to chain you down and throw you in the river." Even after everything she still bulges at my statement like I still might change my mind but I kiss her to ease her worried little head. She doesn't realise I'd be chained too because fuck being here without her.

"Where are we?"

Play - 'I Found - Amber Run'

"*Follow me.*" I take her hand with one of mine and slide the other one in my pocket, leading her under the bridge that holds a few containers until you walk out onto an open dock that has a perfect view of Chicago over the lake, mirroring it against the water to make the perfect illusion of a world underneath us.

"Wow-" She gazes as the sun hits her face and I don't think she's ever looked more beautiful. I've never seen her eyes in the sun like this. They are like balls of molten magma. Her own reflection of the sun that heats you up when you look into them.

I walk to the edge of the dock, hanging my feet over the edge as she follows, mimicking me and we wallow in the sound of the water crashing against the concrete wall before I confess why I really brought her here. I guess it's less romantic when you put it into words. It's actually kind of depressing but she wanted to know me.

...

"Her ashes were spread here." I glare out over lake Michigan. And something's different. Like she's here with me or something. I can feel her in the air, like she's watching over me and I hate that she's not here right now to meet her. I look over to see her looking right back at me and suddenly I'm not afraid to feel vulnerable with her. I've never taken anyone here, nor have I ever shared that with anyone. "She'd have loved you."

I can feel tears creeping in but I try to swallow them back down, finding it harder as she looks at me like she's never been happier and right now. *Neither have I, as morbid as that is.*

"I'd have loved her too." Her words crack my shell, fumbling for her hand, keeping my focus on the water ahead of me because what I'm about to say will only make it harder if she's looking at me and I take a deep breath.

...

"She used to tell me this story. About happiness. About how at one point in her life, she couldn't find it. And she was told one day by some jackass that it didn't exist. That it was a myth. That happiness never amounted to anything. Although she kept fighting. Looking for it. She knew that this couldn't be it. There must be more out there for her. So, she looked him dead in the eyes and said. *'Then never, I'll wait.'* And she did. She waited. And waited. And then I came along. She used to tell me this because I was her *happiness*. And she told me when I couldn't find it, to hold on, because one day you'll find it in the most peculiar way." I squeeze her fingers between mine, struggling to catch my breath but her little fingers reach for my face, forcing me to face her, wiping my cheeks and I'd swat her hand away if she didn't look so sweet. "And she was absolutely right." My words bring her to tears and I guess that is as close as I'm going to get to saying the words I know she wants to hear. Maybe one day I'll say it. But just not today.

"You, *Alora D'Arcy Blackthorne*. Are my god damn fucking happiness." Her eyes scan mine full of questions. Like how I knew her middle name but I answer before she has a chance to ask. "I did some digging. Turns out there is some information if I have your name."

She chippers up, giggling into my shoulder as I wipe her eyes.

"It's beautiful here." It's not amazing but it's enough. And besides home, I'm close to her here. I guess this is sort of a goodbye. But a goodbye I know she'd want. Finally wanting to do something with my life hasn't exactly been easy and she knew that more than anyone.

I stand to my feet, pulling her up with me and I can't even believe I'm about to do this. *Again.*

"Dance with me." I tug her into my chest, locking my fingers with her left hand, wrapping her waist with mine as I rest my head on her and it's not the tango. But it's as much as I'll allow, so we slow dance and consume each other like the world is going to end tomorrow, a moment I wish I could relive on a loop. One of those memories that keep you clinging to hope. Her fingers dance between mine, playing with them as she runs along the creases in my palms like she's trying to read my future.

"What do you see?" I hum quietly into her neck.

"Us. In Spain. Drinking pina coladas and eating coconuts. As we slow dance in the sea." I smile against her temple, finding much amusement in how scarily specific that is and how I could quite easily see us there right now.

"Close your eyes..." I place my palm over her face, trying to make her imagine it and she can't for one second take it seriously, sniggering into my chest as I lick my teeth at this *blasphemy*.

"Fine. I'll just get a better set." She dips a brow, peering up at me as I pull away, making my way back to the bike.

"Hey! Wait for me!"

CHAPTER 58

FREEDOM

Puppet

Play - 'Paradise - Coldplay'

We pull up into an empty car park, surrounded by nothing but trees and bike racks that look out onto the most beautiful view of the beach as the sun is slowly setting between the sea and the sky. A view I've never had the pleasure of experiencing until this very moment and it's everything I hoped it would be.

I hop off, struggling to keep my balance as I throw my leg over, now a little more confident in myself but she still has to catch my fall.

"I thought you said you'd let me fall next time." Her brow peaks before momentarily moving her arm to let me fall, catching me again after I scream into the salty air.

"I'd rather your pretty little face stayed intact." Her compliment disguised with an insult makes me flush. Some things never change but I'd never change her witty nature. It's what got me in this mess in the first place.

"Last one there is a rotten egg." I waste no time sprinting towards the water as fast as my little legs will allow me to and nearly trip as I flip my shoes and socks off, feeling the sand between my toes, the remnants of its warmth against my skin as the cool evening breeze takes its place. It's so peaceful I could cry. This tranquillity amongst chaos is never something I will get bored of. I had so much in Indiana but there was something about the stillness and silence of a sleeping city that felt electronic inside of me. Its rarity was indescribable. Like an off switch for mother nature when she tires of us. A concrete jungle full of sleeping lions. Silence in a city is one of the rarest and most peculiar things but it's beautiful because it's still beaming with life.

I exhale a few exerted breaths. Realising how unfit I am as she rips me from the shore, dragging me towards the gentle waves.

"Hays! Oh my god! Hayden NO! No! NO PUT ME-" She dunks me in, fully clothed. I cringe at the sensation of wet, cold clothes against my skin. There is literally nothing worse, drenched from head to toe as I glare at her with annoyance but it doesn't stay long as she admires her drowned little rat. I want to slap her for being so hard to be angry at.

"I guess you're going to have to take those off." My head shakes at her pure audacity, trying to hide the smirk creeping up my cheek as she moves towards me against the water, grabbing my top that is now literally see through, stopping her as she goes to lift it up and over my head.

"Only if you do." She squints at me, taking on board my proposition before slowly pulling her tank top off from the back and I'll never get over how beautifully she's crafted. There are still so many stories embedded in her skin and I will learn every single one of them when she finally lets me. I stare with fascination, finally able to see her in a little more light than her house provides us in its gloomy essence, admiring her battles. Seeing her right now, like this, knowing she's come so far. How, as much as she hates to admit it, *I've found Hayley.*

Too fixated on gawking at her like a mean girl on a college campus, she closes the little space left between us, touching with feather weight against my skin as she undresses me slowly, biting my bottom lip as I look around for sign of life in case we are being watched but she quickly takes my chin, snapping me back.

"Look at me." My eyes lock with hers through my lashes and suddenly the world around me stops, so drawn to the currents pushing us against one another that its all I can feel as she undresses me with her heated gaze before slowly riding up my top, never breaking that hold on my throat with just her unspoken language that I finally understand and it's quite incredible. Telling me that my soul and my body is all she is craving right now as she bounces between my beady eyes.

"Is this set better?" Her remark makes me chuckle, running my fingers through her hands, smiling as she lets me.

"Ok, let's see." I squeeze my eyes shut, putting myself in our silly little getaway to Spain, feeling the water wrap around my waist, the dimming heat from the sun against my face, her fingers in mine. "Oooo! Yep. Yep! I'm definitely feeling it now." Sarcasm oozes from my lips, taunting her only to get splashed in the face with water. "I-!" *Lovely.*

"It's cold!"

"Best warm up then." She hits me with another, and another. Until we are playing water wars like little kids and I know this was for me. But she clearly needed this too.

Her mom was right about one thing. You really do find happiness in the more peculiar places. And I wish she was here to witness her little girl. Admiring her carefree spirit where suddenly nothing else matters but this very moment. She's not being weighed down by her past. By her demons, She's simply. *Free.*

We are just simply existing in our own little world amongst the clouds.

I catch my breath before attempting to run towards the sand, failing as I squeak at her grip on my lower body, crashing me down into the water.

"Where do you think you're going?!" She pulls me underneath her body, letting the waves swallow me as she cradles me. Now accustomed to the temperature of the water as I sit in her arms contently, with her body against mine and I wish I could stop time. Just to live in this moment a little longer. My entire life has led up to this very moment. All I've ever wanted was freedom and I finally feel it. Right here. *With her.*

I can't get enough of her kisses, letting them consume every part of me as she rests her lips against mine, softly playing with my mouth, chasing away my worries as I giggle into the white noise of pleasant waves, echoing against the sand as she spins me like one of those rom com movies and I can't help but laugh harder until it's broken with her lips against mine.

"How crazy are you feeling?"

I stop mid kiss, questioning her with my eyes. "Whyyy?" I hate that look on her face. Like she's about to do something stupid.

"Stay here." She makes her way towards the carpark and I admire the incredibly handsome view as I step deeper into the water, letting the sea take me, floating in its embrace.

I always pictured the sea as the current I needed. Something to sweep me away. I imagined it felt like home. Somewhere to get lost in, holding you above water like a bed of flowers and it's everything I imagined. It's strong, it's powerful, it's full of thousands of secrets only the brave will explore, it submerges your thoughts and lets you think clearly, it can be delicate or vigorous. It's peaceful. *This is peaceful.* This is what freedom feels like.

I float there for a while, closing my eyes listening to the muffled world beneath me until it's interrupted with the sound of her engine, rumbling louder as it approaches me. I pull my head from the water, watching her looking at me from the edge of the shore line and I feel like I'm drooling as I gaze at her, sat on the bike with a cigarette hanging from her mouth. Her wet hair forms gentle curls that fall loosely in front of her face as I try to suck in a grin at how adorable her hair looks when it's natural, understanding now why she gels it back. She's glowing in the depleting sunset as it reflects off the bike creating something of a dream.

I stand to wander towards her, trying to figure out what weird and crazy idea she has up her sleeve as I take the cigarette from her mouth, deciding to try again as we are in a rebellious fuck it moment and this time I inhale it a little better, too high on dopamine to care that its pretty gross. She smiles slowly, her teeth peeping through the crack of her side smirk and my butterflies rattle. That look that makes me fold, like she's infatuated with me, no matter what I do. I could be in a bin bag and she'd probably look at me like I am the next top model.

"Get on." She ushers her head to the back of the bike and I glare at her with light confusion. *We have no safety precautions?* "Trust me."

God dammit. I lunge to the back of the bike as she holds out her hand to help me, strapping myself to her like a backpack as she twists the throttle, riding the stretch of the beach and my grip slowly loosens the further we go, observing the sun going down as I rest my wet mop against her back feeling completely and entirely at peace as the wind takes my hair. I feel her move underneath me, both her hands grabbing for mine as she reaches them out to the side of me, only holding on to her hands and my heart beats out my chest realising she isn't holding the handlebars but she told me to trust her, and nothing bad has happened yet. If we die I am haunting her even in hell. I reach out my hands and she gently lets go, leaving me there to find my balance as I feel the fresh sea air against my damp skin, feeling like a bird and *The Notebook* springs to mind, making me smile. I want to quote the movie but I know she would not get the reference, giggling to myself trying to imagine putting her through that movie with me.

"WOOOOOW!" This probably isn't legal or safe but we are living in the moment and I'm starting to enjoy living life on the edge. This crazy life I've managed to end up in. I'm collateral damage but somehow I feel like it was fate that she found me. Freeing me from myself in ways I don't think anyone ever could. I've found peace in circumstances that were meant to kill me, in pain and sorrow, in ruin and destruction I've found a new lease of happiness where I am no longer afraid of living. I'm suddenly afraid of dying and I hope that I find death before she does because I fear an empty hollow world without her in it. Now I finally understand what it means to find an entire universe in one person.

SHASSII

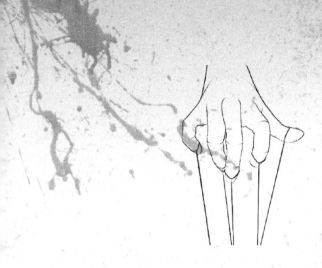

CHAPTER 59

SELFLESS

Puppeteer

Play - 'Beautiful Addiction - NF'

The sun suddenly looks redundant compared to her as I look out across the setting sea, leaving us in shallow rays as the clouds grab the last of the light, absorbing it until morning. Watching her dance away all her worries and in this moment, love and guilt dance hand in hand around my head. Staring at something greater than this. Something with potential to change the world. I can't explain it but its sat in my gut and it's now I realise that I no longer want to be selfish anymore. I want her to live a life better than this one. A life where she doesn't have to hide in the shadows and can spread her little wings. Where she chases her dreams and doesn't have to live in fear. She doesn't belong here with me anymore. She belongs out there, making the best of how special she is. I'm tying her down and it's not right. It's not fair. None of this was ever fair. She's still caged and it's not enough. I cannot give her the life she wants. I know that now. I clung to this hope that maybe we would work but seeing her like this.

Alive.

I've never seen her so fucking alive and I can't take it. This guilt chewing me up from the inside knowing that one day she will resent me for keeping her from a life far greater than this one.

I wipe the stray tear leaking down my cheek, admiring what may be the last and only, truly happy moment I've ever got the pleasure of experiencing. Something I'll cherish to my grave and tell people all about on the other side. The way her hair dances in the wind, her silhouette against the dim glow. Is this what heaven feels like? Maybe death won't be so bad after all, she's made living seem easy. Breathing is easier. Life is easier and this is what I want but I'm too broken to have it, I don't deserve it. I need to do my time and pray she'll be waiting for me on the other side. If she hasn't settled down with someone else by then. I'll wait the next twenty years if I have to. I exhale a deep, defeated sigh, staring at the next twenty years of my life, swallowing my pride, knowing it isn't going to be pretty. But for her I'll do anything. I'll do this. *For her.* She will live her life with or without me. I'll make sure of it.

My heart beats to the sounds of the waves and my knuckles whiten at the thought of living the next chapter of my life without her in it, trying to tell myself I'm being fucking ridiculous but I've never been more morally sane. She brings out the good in me I loathe but it's not so bad when *she's* my outcome. I'll suffer punishment worse than death if it means I get to *Love* her. I pause for a moment, realising, that is the first time I've admitted the word to myself and it terrifies me. How could she say it so carelessly? How does she even know the meaning of the word? But then again, how do I? I don't. But I know that I want to be by her side for the rest of my miserable life and I can't do that until I'm free from my sins, my burdens. My wrong doings. Something I cannot escape or run away from, it's never going to go away, I need to face this head on and take responsibility for my mistakes, I need to do good by her. She is my beginning for a better life. I need to cut this rope and set her free so I can heal, work on bettering myself for her. This change is needed for us both.

She smiles at me, laughing with nothing but raw joy and I know this won't be easy for her but she's a tough cookie, she's dealt with far worse than this. She's stronger than she thinks and I hope she'll keep the happy memories of me with her. These last few months have shown me that redemption is possible and I'll try to be the person she wants me to be. Even if it kills me, at least I know I tried to do something good, for once in my life.

I stand to my feet as she runs for me, her arms embrace me, hugging my neck as I lift her to wrap around my waist, she looks down at me and I'm finding it hard to keep my emotions in for once. *What the hell is this?*

"You ok?" She whispers to me, kissing my cheek gently and it takes everything in me not to break. I'll be ok when she's running into my arms a decade from now, telling me everything she's achieved while I've been gone.

"Have I ever told you how beautiful you are?" My words immediately bring her to tears, giggling into my shoulder to hide her bashful cheeks that warm up my soul. I won't ruin this moment. I'll leave it till tomorrow. Right now I just want her to taste this freedom, so it's easier. So she doesn't hate me completely. I swallow my unspoken words, listening to my favourite song as she sings to me wearing a smile so big it could scare my demons away.

"You're so silly."

"Promise me something." Her laugh fades into a soft smile, frowning her brows at me with curiosity. "Promise me, no matter what happens, you'll live the most epic twenty first birthday." Her curiosity turns to concern as she strokes my cheek, still making me twitch.

"Why are you saying it like that?" I wish I could tell her why. But it's better if I didn't.

"Just promise me?"

She looks for the doubt in my eyes and she agrees, pecking me on the lips softly and she knows not to ask more questions. "I promise..."

Her playful spirit is the only thing keeping my heart beating and that is why I know that this is the right thing to do. She's revived me. *My mission part.* She's given me a second chance to do better. The night I found her I never imagined she would be saving my life and all I've done in return is tear hers down.

"Don't get all sentimental on me now. I'll think I'm not enough." She giggles nervously, hanging off my neck and her words draw my mouth to crash against hers. She's more than enough. In this lifetime and the next. I hope I find her so I can tell her over and over again. So I can find myself inside her like a magnet to my soul. The karma I needed to see sense. I rub the softness in her tender cheeks still wet with salty water, brushing her oily strands from her face.

"*Alora*. You drive me to do unspeakable things." *Like hand myself in when I swore an oath to myself I'd never go back.*

Everything in the last eight months, I've done for her. My entire existence has been purely for her, so what's another ten years? I didn't understand at first, why I had this urge to keep my feet on the ground, why I couldn't let go. *Let her go.* But now I get it. I'm so stupidly *in Love* with her, I'll go to the ends of the earth just to give her everything I never had. Even if I don't know how, I'll learn. If I don't fit, I'll adapt. I'll mould myself into the person she needs me to be if it means I get to see the world and grow old with her. I thought I was incapable of Loving anyone. That it was a sickness, and it is, I'm lovesick for someone and I've found it's the most bittersweet remedy to cure this numbness. This *end* I worshipped, praying for it to cure my loneliness. It did. She is *my beginning* as well as *my end.*

A cool breeze grazes her skin as the sun finally falls behind the edge of the world leaving us in a shadow cast by my inner emotions only amplifying my hold on her. *My little light.* She's consumed it as I look into *my Sunflower*, soaking in her balls of paradise as I melt into her soft pools of honey. Holding the last of my hope in my hands never wanting to let it go as she quivers against me before I put her down, sitting down with her to capture the last few moments of this sunset.

She rests her head against my shoulder, looking just as at peace with the world as I am right now before she lets out a soft sigh.

"What now?" She asks softly, sounding just as frightened as I do on the inside as she runs her fingers against the art wrapped around my hand. I take a moment to try and find an answer to that. Because the answer I have, she isn't going to like. Biting my tongue as I lean against her, resting my head against her soft hair pressing into my cheek, taking in her sweet scent intertwined with the aura of salt and freedom.

"Let's go home *baby*." She nods her head underneath mine, sprawling out her arms for me to pick her back up, spreading them out as I walk her to the bike like a little bird, planting her ass down to straddle it as I wrap her up in my jacket, immediately warming her back up as I plant a kiss on her sticky little forehead.

We ride for a while when I notice I'm low on fuel, reaching the nearest 24 hour gas station still open on the way back. Its dead with only one person inside behind the tills jamming to their headphones. I cut the ignition, looking around for any other signs of life and we are completely alone besides the CCTV camera overlooking the petrol tanks from behind us and I bite my tongue with anxiety, finding it hard to get my words out.

"You can take your helmet off now."

"But won't someone see me?"

"This neighbourhood is dead. Besides, we are hours away from Indiana, the news is not as updated here." *I lie.* Squeezing my eyes shut trying to push back down my urge to stop her but she takes it off slowly, nervous to show her face where we could be seen, fluffing her damp hair to air it out and I breath out slowly, dismounting the bike, filling up the tank as I admire her looking incredibly beautiful on the back of my motor. "Wait here. I just gotta go pay."

I make my way inside, grabbing a Hershey's bar sat waiting for me to pick it up like it knew I was coming and I grin to myself, knowing this will light up her little face before making my way towards the till, watching him jamming out to whatever tunes he's listening to, almost completely unaware I'm standing here until I put it on the counter.

"Pump five mate." He peers up at me, swiftly removing his headphones to scan the bar. I look around to catch her face on the wall beside him staring straight back at me. *Her hair was so much shorter back then.*

```
Missing persons
Alora Blackthorne
Age 18
Last seen October 30th 2009
```

I glare at it intensely, completely lost in thought as he looks back on himself trying to see what I'm glaring at.

" *Sad isn't it. I hope she's ok. Anyway, is that everything?*" He pulls me back, waving in front of me. "Sir?... Is that everything?"

Trying not to look suspicious of kidnap when she's sitting outside the window is slightly difficult. My throat tightens, squeezing the words out as I look at her waiting patiently for me.

"Shit- yeah. Sorry." I turn to find him looking right at her and although I can tell he isn't exactly sure, he's still suspicious. She clearly looks familiar, trying to put the pieces together as he looks back at me, knowing my face is dripping with guilt, holding contact like he's trying to take a picture of my face in his mind and I drag my nerves back down my throat, slicing it open on the way down as he peers at the phone and back at me.

"That'll be $23.45" He keeps his composure, hearing the change in his tone as he passes the chocolate bar back to me, an over exaggerative smile gracing his tired face before taking my money. I'm trying to hold my culpability together, but this is wrong. *Everything about this is wrong.*

I sigh from exhaustion staring at her poster, coming to terms with the fact that what I'm about to do might be the end of everything but I do it anyway, nodding in a language I know he understands as I confirm with my eyes that he's doing the right thing, peering at the phone in front of him.

"Cheers. Keep the change. Have a good night."

...

I'm found only if I want to be found.

CHAPTER 60

MY FOREVER

Puppet

Play - 'Fields Of Elation - Sleep Token'

I scoff down my chocolate, ending off the perfect little adventure with my favourite treat as we pull up to the house. She's been fairly quiet the entire way back and I don't know whether to be frightened by that. Maybe she's just tired. Today has been a lot for people who never venture out of the house but it felt so incredible to feel the water wash away all my thoughts for a while, although I'm now in desperate need of a shower. I feel the sand in my hair as I run my fingers through it, *it's grosssss*.

She cuts the engine, sitting there in silence for a while outside the bungalow and I analyse her, trying to figure out what on earth she is doing, it's like she's waiting for something. Water begins to patter against my skin, looking up to feel a light shower against my cold cheeks, almost numb as it tingles my skin. *How did she know it was going to rain?* It literally never rains, what the hell are the chances.

She pulls me off the bike, lifting me like a feather and her strength is just ridiculously hot, planting me down on the ground as she wastes no time digging for my tongue, latching to me like I'm going to slip out of her grasp at any moment. *What has gotten into her?*

I melt like honey into her mouth, shuddering under the icy temperatures mixed with the chills she gives me without even trying, feeling the rain hit my skin harder as she grins against me, knowing that inside I'm cringing at the sensation but I wanted to dance in the rain. I'm smiling back when I remember our little slow dance earlier that took me completely by surprise.

Our lips finally detach and I look up at the sky as the heavens open, completely drenching us both from head to toe but we just stand there like idiots until she attacks under my arms causing me to yelp out into a helpless giggle as she tickles me to the ground trying to get away from her hold but I'm laughing so hard I can't breathe.

"HAYDEN! STOP! ST- STOP! I CAN'T BREATHEEE!"

She grabs my hand, pulling me into her torso feeling her attack my skin with her needy hands, grabbing my outer thighs as she lifts me to rest around her body like a koala. Walking us inside, she's unable to keep her lips off mine as she heads straight for the shower, paying no mind to Shep who's curled up in bed, glaring at us and if I didn't know any better it's almost like he's raising a brow as she rips her leather jacket off me with an animalistic nature I've never seen from her. Territorial and hungry for me in ways I never thought possible.

"You're fucking *Mine*. Do you hear me?" The water opens up as she flicks the handle, gasping as the freezing water frames to the curves of my body followed by her hands, completely careless to the fact she's fully clothed right now getting us both drenched under the shower but I'm too caught up in the taste of her to care, losing my head as her fragrant cologne stings my nose.

"Tell me *Alora*. Fucking tell me you're *Mine*. I need to hear you say it." I rush the words from my mouth, cracking to contain my oxygen as she pulls me under the water, nearly choking on it as my underwear disappears.

"I'm yours, all yours *Baby*." She lets me touch her body, hissing as I touch her like it physical burns but she's enduring it, panting heavier down my neck as I run my nails over her abs. I'm finally able to memorise every perfect imperfection in her skin as I pull her tank top up and over her head, hitching my breath as she presses me against the tiled wall, gasping at the ice burning my back, admiring her soppy wet hair falling in front of her demonic features that even the Devil himself would fear. She's so horrifically beautiful it haunts me, the bags under her eyes holding all her sleepless nights like trophies. My wounded monster is finally letting down her guard and I suddenly can't keep my hands off her, trying to claw my way inside her hollow body made just for me.

"Don't ever fucking forget it." She forces entry, pushing her fingers inside my aching hole, needy for her to fill me. How could I ever forget when she's my entire fucking existence, moaning at how easily she's sliding in and out, coating her fingers as I drip desperately. "You'll live for me. Do you understand me?"

Her words catch me off guard slightly, not responding as quickly as she'd like only to have my mouth filled with water as she dunks my head under the heavy flow of water.

"I said, do you understand me, *Puppet*?" She shakes me vigorously as I catch my breath once more, glaring at this emotion buried somewhere in her deep sea and I don't understand what is up with her but I reply abruptly as she orders me, trying to understand why she'd think I wouldn't want to when all I want to do is be here in her arms.

"Yes!..." She digs deeper for my submission, rewarding me as she pushes me closer, curling her digits inside me and I can't keep quiet, trying to clasp to her as she finger fucks me to draw out my whines, clawing into her flesh as I scream for her. It will only ever be her. I don't want anyone else. *Ever.* Just thinking about it makes me sick. My body, mind and soul belongs to her. *She is my forever.* Maybe this trip out has her thinking I'm going to walk away now that she's let me experience life outside these walls.

"I'm not going anywhere." I try to speak but it comes out as a whisper against her lips as I whimper through her kiss.

"*Promise me.*"

"*Why so many promises?*" She ignores my question, running her fingers through the knotty locks of my hair, tightening her grip to tug at my scalp with force to listen to her words, controlling what I see as she squeezes against the back of my neck, cutting through me with a look I've never seen on her face.

Fear.

She's scared?

"Promise me you will stay right here." She man handles me, rattling me with writing between the lines I don't understand. She's trying to say something, I can feel it. But what? She looks like I'm dying in front of her very eyes as she tries to pump life back inside me.

"Of course I will. With you."

She begins to speak to me with sentiment and it makes me uneasy seeing her so vulnerable. Being so raw, using words I've never heard come out of her mouth. "You need to know, that whatever happens, you made me a better woman."

She slowly feels my insides, dipping inside me, agonisingly slowly like she's savouring how I feel around her fingers as she rests her temple against mine, panting against the sensitive flesh behind my ear.

"What's wrong Hayden?" I hum, my tone laced with concern but she won't look at me, pressing her ear against my mouth to listen to my cries as she heaves against me, puffing out her chest to lay against mine, so close I can feel her heart vibrating through my rib cage.

"*Nothing*. I just wanted you to know." I'd believe her if she wasn't tugging me so tightly she was ripping my skin, clamping down on my neck like if she so much as lets go slightly I will fall out of her arms. I kiss softly against her cheek, warm and rough as I rub against her scars, breathing in her scent as I focus solely on the sound of her quivering groans, letting out a tiny yelp as she pulls out of me slowly, gripping underneath my legs to carry me like a bride to the bed. It's like our little rendezvous finally let her relax, allowing her to be soppy without fear of judgement as I kiss the creases in her cheeks where her smile lines sit before she lays me down against the sheets, worshipping me from the ankles up.

Play - 'Vertigo (Accoustic) – Jutes'

"A life without you in it terrifies me, *Alora*." She murmurs against my skin and those words terrify me. I can't picture a world where she's no longer by my side.

"Well I'm right here. I'm not going anywhere. *I promise.*"

She reaches my chest, smearing her bottom lip against my sweaty skin like kissing is not enough, like she needs to physically eat my essence and I ache at her yearning for me, letting my submission submerge me under that blissful blanket of freedom she feeds me. She's suffocating me with her entire being like we are now one and it's reminding me of the first time she took my body and soul. The only difference is this time, I know what to expect and I've never wanted anything more. I push my legs apart inviting her to find her salvation in me, clawing at the contorted bones that make up her face as I kiss her deeply, letting her work her way around my mouth. This connection we share is indescribable as much as it is soul crushing. She's now part of me and I don't think I've ever felt more complete which pinches at my chest as I realise she could be ripped away from me at any moment if we are not careful. This forbidden life we are living is dangerous but danger is my new Love language.

"Be my grave *baby girl*." My eyes flicker with lust and concern as she gives me no time to reply, undoing her jeans and pushing herself inside me, biting my bottom lip until I squeak like pain transfer, letting her in easier until she's coated. Hearing how wet I am she loses herself inside me and it's a sight I will never tire of, only whining for her voice like a needy puppy. I want to hear how I make her feel. I want her to show me what I do to her. How I make her question everything about herself through the velocity of her thrusts, pining for me like she cannot survive without me. I need to know I'm not crazy. That she is just as delusional as I as we run from our responsibilities like teenagers. Living in secret to rebel against this society set to destroy us.

"Let me bury myself 6ft inside your sweet *cunt*."

I jolt as the back of my head pushes into the pillow, feeling her indignation as she ploughs into me full of prominent frustration and I don't know what this feeling is. But it's not an average orgasm as I pool between my legs, crushing my thighs against her hips in embarrassment as I twitch against her. *Did I just squirt?* She forces my legs back open, pushing just her pelvis into my dripping pussy, gripping to my knees as she watches her length slide in and out of my hole painfully slowly, licking the curve underneath her lip like a freak as the Devil resurfaces through her grin, one I now strangely miss when it's not present on her kissable face.

"Dirty *Puppet*. Making such a mess for me." Her thumb finds my bud in my arousal, playing with me like velvet against her fingertips and I shudder, feeling that sensation creep back in with intent on ruining me. "Do it again."

She strums at my sensitive spot as she dips her strap inside, feeling myself shaking on the end of her cock.

"Look at that..." She hisses through her teeth, analysing my juices over her length, groaning in pure pleasure, admiring how she is my insatiable ruin as she pushes back inside me feeling each inch slide against my walls nudging a jolted gasp from my throat as she suddenly refuses to let me breathe. Her hand clamps down around my throat until I'm near on seeing the midnight constellations, focusing on only the brightest stars in front of me as she searches the adventure in my gleaming eyes, glossy with light tears but I'm grinning like a psychopath. *She really is rubbing off on me.*

"When you're not around me. This? This is all I feel." She squeezes tighter, looking at me like she's waiting for me to fight back but I lay there and take it until the corners of my eyes pinch black, embracing her emotions like they are my own, relishing in the guilty pleasure that cuts through me every time she confesses to me that I am her lifeline. Eight months ago she wanted to be the one to take my life but now she fears it so deeply I fear she wouldn't survive without me and it's sickly comforting. We are, in sickness and in health, hungry for vows to tie us to one another, in this life and the next but we don't need rings for that. Only our tongues.

She lets go letting me suck in air, still deep inside me. My hips buck as she gently builds pressure, her warm fingertips playing with my slit, gliding effortlessly against my cum as she coats her finger, tasting it between the slit in her tongue sending chills up my spine.

"What do I taste like?" I mumble with hesitance as she eyes me curiously, knowing I've tasted myself, but I want to know what I taste like *to her.*

"*Salvation.*" She says that word so seductively I may just cum, fixated on the way she cleans up my mess and it cramps up my entire torso as I tense to stop myself from letting go all over her cock but it's no use as another wave hits me, this time more violent, more desperate, making me rock into her to finish the job and she does as instructed, giving me that sweet release as she pushes me over the edge.

"Cum for me, *Alora,* be a *good girl baby* and show me how good *Daddy* takes care of you..." There is something in the way she says my name with such desperation that allows me to let go, trying to ignore why she said my name like she's never going to say it again, but I cool down, panting out my exhaustion. I convulse underneath her as she paints kisses all over my muggy skin, wiping my messy barnet from my face, unsticking it from my cheeks as she grins in amusement at my fatigue. "You're so cute."

She does nothing but peer down her nose at me, tilting her head as she watches me try to cover up my non-existent dignity, embarrassed to know I just made one hell of an unintentional mess and she loves that she has broken yet, another *first*. She's wearing a shit eating grin that makes my pussy clench, curious to know what she's thinking behind those sinister blades, stabbing me with force keeping me frozen as she leans in slowly, lining my top and bottom lip with her split tongue. It sucks a blissful moan from the depths of my fading orgasm, already pulsating to feel her again but I can feel my sugar levels depleting right now. I'm absolutely exhausted and I'm going to hurt tomorrow, trying to crawl back to the land of the living as the gentle caress of her lips send me immediately sleepy, shushing down my ear which has become a ritual to help me sleep. To scare my demons away.

"Hayden..." I barely get my words before her finger finds my lips as she lays down beside me, even though she has no idea what I want to say.

"Tell me tomorrow..."

Play - 'Carry You - Ruelle, Fleurie'

My subconscious wakes before my eyes, feeling my face rising and falling for a moment before I realise.
I'm lying on her chest -
I slowly crack open my eyes, trying not to move suddenly in case she pushes me away, discreetly adjusting my cheek as I nuzzle into her warmth, melting into her embrace as I become hyper aware of her muscular arm wrapped around my tiny waist and I don't know why but I want to cry. This overwhelming sense of pride and accomplishment makes me fight back a smile. I can hear her heart beating against my ear, slow and rhythmic like

mine, admiring my new favourite melody underneath her rib cage, beating just for me as I take in the scent of her, the REAL her, underneath the petrol and leather. Her bare essence fills me up like a drug, feeling my eyes well with a feeling so intense I don't know what to do with it. I've never felt so safe. *So at peace.* This is all I've wanted for months and she's finally comfortable enough to let us cuddle like, dare I say, a *couple*. As much as I wished for this the first time we slept together, I was not at all surprised to wake up to an empty bed. In fact I'd predicted that would have been the case. This is not her thing, *or it wasn't.* I don't know what has changed but she's finally letting her barrier down and content doesn't even begin to describe how I feel right now. She's still laying her hand underneath mine to keep me from touching her bare skin against her chest but this is more than enough for me. Wiggling to get more comfortable inside her, I barely even cover a quarter of her, even when laying on her frame like this.

She lets out a heavy sigh as she runs her delicate fingers through my still matted hair from earlier like she's about to say something and she does. Although not at all what I was expecting.

"He was a monster..." She knows I'm awake and she speaks as if she's been dwelling on it for hours. I don't know what the time is but it must be late, or early? As the birds are singing outside and the room is spilling with gold.

"Is that why you are sad? You're thinking about him?" I ask softly, squeezing her fingers in mine like a newborn baby to their mother.

"No. Just defeated." She sounds defeated. Is this why she's being this way? She's given up trying to punish herself, finally learning that love is far greater than suffering?

"Talk to me." I rub the pads of her fingers, letting us live deeply in probably the most intimate moment we've ever shared, feeling my throat knot, knowing how far she has come, how she's grown into the kind parts of her I saw from the beginning, admiring what a sight it is when she's accepting something that was ripped from her at such a young age. Physical, tender contact. *Love.* Her softness is so delicate it's slightly terrifying when I know of the blood she's spilt but her sins are now mine.

"I've spent my entire life trying to fill a void and in doing so I've become what I feared. It never made me feel better. It only left me more alone, I isolated myself by being destructive, believing I was doing the world a favour when really I was only destroying myself. Depriving myself of happiness and a chance at a new beginning. I ruined it and now it's too late." It's like the cloud over her head has finally disappeared and she's seeing clearly for the first time. Feeling her distress through her fingers as she presses them a little harder into my scalp, massaging it through my messy hair.

I lift my head to look up at her already looking down at me and her eyes make me fall off the edge, sinking deeper into her ocean where her current washes me away. *My Home.* Finally uncovering more of her.

"This is your new beginning. Us. I will help you to find whatever it is you need to find. You just have to let me all the way in." I gesture to her heart as I lift her hand with mine, placing it on her chest, smiling at the way she's looking at me like I'm her whole existence and I suppose now I am.

"It's not that simpl-" Before she has a chance to finish I pull myself out from under the blanket, dragging it with me as I hold it in front of my chest, sitting on my knees to face her as my thumb runs the length of her jawline.

"Sure it is. Being here with you is like breathing and I know you feel that too." She nuzzles into the palm of my hand and I could swear my heart stops for a moment, taking in this rare sight. *She's accepting my tenderness?* Intentionally seeking it out as she shuts her eyes, like she's focusing solely on my touch.

"Of course I do…" she confesses and a stray tear leaks down my hot cheeks, wiping it away quickly before her eyes meet mine again.

"What are you so afraid of?" I want her to tell me her deepest, darkest secrets, her biggest fears, her silly habits she has told no one. I want her to tell me everything.

"God, you make this seem so easy…" she blows out a worn-out breath, finally flopping into my hand as I cradle her defined cheekbone.

"It is easy. You just have to trust me." I crawl closer to her on my knees, leaning in so she can't look anywhere but me, my eyes sitting on her tongue for an answer. "Will you trust me?"

At first she doesn't reply. Resilient to my question as she lines the edges of her teeth with her tongue.

"This is *Love*, Hayden. Let me show you why I will always *Love* you."

She doesn't respond but I can read the answer in her face. It's become something I'm quite good at as she hates talking about her *emotions*. Maybe

I should buy her a journal and make her write down all her thoughts. It might quieten her mind.

I climb on top of her frame, for once not paying mind to how wide she stretches me out as I look down at her sitting against the metal bar, building up my courage as I place one hand followed by the other against her inky muscles, letting my fingers move against her ridges and I can feel her tensing underneath me like I'm about to stab her with a needle, rolling out the discomfort in her face as she squints.

"It's just me and you." I whisper to her ghost, coaxing her back out and she eventually breaths slower once more, putting her trust in me, passing her ghost to me as I crawl closer, now inches from her neck, wanting to lick and kiss all her beautiful artwork.

I kiss softly against the column and she sucks in a sharp breath, slowly letting it back out as my lips trail her shoulder and just under her chin. She lets me and I see no signs of distress so I keep going, relishing in the taste of her skin as her stomach muscles tense against my lips, blessing her battle scars with a pretty kiss and I didn't realise just how many she had coating her body, hidden beneath all her tattoos. It makes me want to weep. To cuddle her tightly and never let her go. *Ever*. I peer at the contrast between our bodies. Mine still so pure and full of life, so tender and untouched, against hers that has survived war and stood strong against its past. We are so entirely different but I long for her in ways I never thought possible. We may be opposites but there is something inside me that understands her in ways even I can't explain. A longing for acceptance. Our pasts are so different yet I'm drawn to this pain we both share. It's a magnet. It might simply be that I have no one else, but I know that it's more than that. And it has been for a long time, I was just too stubborn to see it. I trace the craters in her body delicately, feeling tears push against my lash line.

He really was a monster. But she was not. Only his prodigy. She is a victim to our bullshit system. Just thinking about it sets me in a flush of irritation as I absorb more of her and by the time I'm done, her head is back against the wall, almost like she is slightly enjoying it. And it's about time. *Who doesn't love kisses?* But I don't push it, stopping to respect the little I did get. I will eventually kiss every square inch of her. But not yet. Not today. We have a lifetime for this.

She pulls her head back up at me, giving me a look as if to say *why did you stop* but she pauses, wiping the stray tear I didn't catch before it escaped.

"No tears. We won't have that. You hear me?" I don't even know why I'm crying. *Relief? Peace?* Seeing her so natural with me. This normality in our own little world built on damage and pain. The life beyond these walls would call me crazy for the way I feel for her and I guess I am. But I'm not afraid to admit it anymore. Behind this journey she accidentally threw me into, it's been the most interesting part of my life. I don't know what that truly says about me and my sheltered life but I start living now. I never want to go back to being a bird in a cage. Here I have freedom as well as control and it's comforting.

There is not a day I don't think about what she did and I've mourned my parents in my own way. Sleepless nights and nightmares. Vomiting and neglecting my health. But they are all things she was there by my side for, holding my hair and holding my hand for and it's twisted. It's messed up. *I know that.* But my empathy runs so deeply that I see through my own pain to reach hers and I understand. Like I can finally tell she is understanding that everything she made herself was wrong and distasteful but it was to survive.

She was just trying to survive.

"When this stops beating. So will mine." I lean into her personal space, laying on her stomach waiting for her to nudge me off but she doesn't. Only speaks with concern.

"You promised me you'd live to see your 21st." Her words are heavy with worry and I don't understand why.

"You talk like we won't make it that far. We will. And you can make me a terrible birthday cake and tell me how beautiful I look in another yellow dress." I joke playfully, trailing my fingers against her chest, dancing with the patterns against her skin but I look up at her stern expression.

"Promise me baby." She says harshly but her eyes are soft and I knit my brows.

"Why is this so important to you?" She grabs my hand, locking her fingers with mine and they are muggy with sweat.

"Because I want you to experience normality. Go out, get drunk or something." I realise she never got to experience hers and my gaze softens watching her younger self talk to me.

"Because you couldn't?" I coo softly, watching her throat bob as I take her thoughts and put them into words.

"I went to prison at nineteen, but I was stripped of normality long before I was thrown behind bars. You have the chance to live like any other and I want that for you." Her attitude towards my life has completely shifted and I won't lie, it's slightly strange. She suddenly wants me to experience everything she couldn't and I know her guilt plays a huge part in that.

"Well on my 21st birthday you can tell yourself you did it, as we dance in a random club somewhere. Ok?" I grace her with a smile, waiting for her to smile back and she does, hesitantly for a brief moment before it disappears.

"Ok."

"*Ok.*" I whisper.

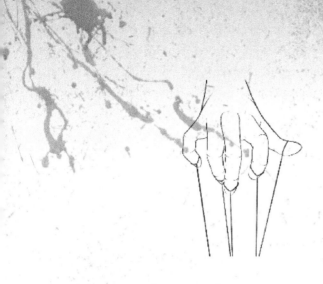

CHAPTER 61

REPEATING HISTORY

Puppeteer

Play - 'Sleepyhead (Acoustic) - Jutes'

I've not been to sleep. Glaring up at the ceiling as I caress every perfect inch of her in my arms and I've never felt so at peace. Taking in this blissful moment knowing it may soon be over. How do I tell her I want to walk away after last night?... Every word she spoke was so full of hope I think it really will break her. *I'm all she has left.*

   I contemplate my decision and even if I wanted to retract it, it's too late. I've put myself out there and now it's up to my fate. It's down to luck if that boy didn't pick up that phone and that is if the CCTV didn't catch me regardless. I knew what I was doing. It was the right thing to do. For once I'm doing the right thing, so why do I feel like I just made the worst mistake of my life? Why do I feel like this betrayal will shatter her until she cannot find any pieces of her inside me. The way I know she will loathe me because I've *broken* her heart yet again. All I can do is wait and as much as I'm telling myself luck is on my side. It never has been so why would it start now. Realistically we were never going to make it and my heart pinches with that horrific ache I've tried my hardest to run from. That pit of nothingness I'm feeling as I sink under water, gripping her tighter in my arms like she's going to keep me afloat, realising what I've already lost.

The truth is, I never had her in the first place. Our love was a waiting game. A chess board. A means to an end and I glance at everything that she is, everything she will be while I'm behind bars. Knowing she will do something good in the world, maybe she needs to loathe me so she can move on from this. *From me.*

I run my fingers over her constellation, memorising the little bumps underneath my fingertips, wishing I could forever etch her sense, her smile and her laugh into my skin. I made sure that last night I gave her as much of her as I could give. I held my tongue and promised her forever without words. Now she needs to trust me. Wait for me. I hope she forgives me for this.

I plan on taking myself to the station today but I feel that journey won't be necessary as my heart stops beating at the unfamiliar noise making itself known from behind the outside wall. So unfamiliar that it's too familiar. No one ever sets foot within a mile radius of this property and suddenly I can't breathe. I tune into faint doors slamming and gravel shifting underneath heavy boots, holding my lungs as emotions betray me, cutting down the scars in my cheek.

...

My time is up.

I don't move. I don't flinch. I lay here, admitting defeat as I look down at her so at peace with the world that's yet again, about to be ripped out from underneath her, I realise this was everything but the wrong decision. I deserve this. Maybe not even for the lives I've taken. But for her. I deserve to serve my time *for her.* For not just destroying her life once, *but twice.*

I close my eyes, awaiting the inevitable as whispers and shuffling approach the building, grating at my ears and I stroke her loose strands of oily hair, inhaling her sweet scent under my nose as she subconsciously squeezes me tighter and this time I don't fight it. In fact, I hate myself for not letting her in sooner. So I could remember her touch for the many years to come.

In another life maybe, things would have been so much simpler, but I was an idiot for ever bringing her into any of this. I should have let her go that night. I should have walked away. *I should have done better.* My jaw clenches, containing this internal rage building inside my chest cavity at all the fucking things I should have done but I didn't. But you never realise what you have until you lose it. And I've lost it.

I've lost it all.

Shep sits up, quietly growling at the commotion outside he can hear just as much as I can.

...

Three hard knocks rattle the front door, echoing through the house like the doubts in my mind

She jumps up abruptly, clinging to me like she's just woken from a bad dream, glaring at me trying to figure out if that knock was in her head, or very much real. But I don't flinch. I just stare at her trying to push down my urge to let the floodgates open as she looks at me for an answer. Shep begins to bark towards the bedroom door, raising his hackles with his brave face on.

Play - 'To Build A Home - Cinematic Orchestra'

"CHICAGO P.D OPEN UP."

Her eyes immediately bulge and within seconds she's tearing, like she's hoping she's going to wake up and this is all just a terrible dream, flinching as they bang again, harder, causing her to tug on the duvet. "Hayden, what is going on?"

They don't infiltrate. And they won't for a few minutes. The last few minutes I have to try and say goodbye, but I don't know how. I never have. How do you say goodbye to your entire life? How do you walk away from the thing that keeps you breathing? Not once, but twice?

"Hayden, you need to run. Now!" She forces a whisper as she clings onto my face. And so what if I did run? We wouldn't both get out, there is nothing we can do. I'd rather go with them than run for the rest of my life without her in it. At least this way I may see her again, behind a glass window.

"No..." I say gently, twitching my lip and my words slice through her, cutting me in the process. She is absolutely terrified and all I can do is say sorry for not doing this sooner. When she hated me, things were simpler. When I was not in *Love* with her. When she could have walked away and forgotten all about me.

"What do you mean?! Hayden they will take you away!" She looks almost angry as she tugs on my arm, trying to move me but I've already decided I'm not going anywhere, breaking my own heart as she tries desperately to save me from myself, *not realising that is exactly what I am doing.*

"Let me do this, *for you.*" Her forehead scrunches, trying to make sense of what seems ridiculous, clawing at my skin to get off the bed.

"Hayden no! No! Don't say that!" I hate seeing her cry. It crushes any ounce of kindness I have left. It's the reason we are in this mess. Seeing her cry as I left her to die. It made me realise how frightened she truly was and I saw every bit of myself in her.

"Let me do this. I need to do this. Listen to me." She refuses, shaking her head as her face becomes wet, clinging to my forearm with desperation. I grab her head as nicely as I can, trying to shake some sense into her. "Listen!...to me."

She stops thrashing, concentrating on me like she's dying.

"Let me. I'll serve my time and we will finally be free. Truly free, to live without fear, without hiding. I'll be able to give you the life you deserve. All I ask is that you wait for me... *Can you do that?*" Her soft admirable gaze shifts and my heart jams, dreading that her hatred has stemmed too quickly.

"You said to me, that you are only found if you want to be found." Her realisation seeps into her bloodshot eyes as she analyses the way I react to her words, swallowing slowly with guilt. "Was that what yesterday was? Is that what we were doing? Trying to out yourself?" In the beginning no. But I guess I did exactly that... There was always a possibility we were going to get caught. For a while now I'd thought she'd be better back to normality. I don't want to be selfish anymore. I want to do right by her and I just hope one day she'll see that.

"No..." I squeeze her harder but her expression doesn't let up, glaring at me with glossy eyes and a heavy anger burning within her.

"*Liar.* You're lying to me!" Her nails dig into my skin but I endure it. Letting her hate me. Letting her feel this, as much as I hate it, it would be easier this way.

"*Alora*, please understand, I'm doing this for you." I don't know what else to say and there is nothing really I can say to change the way she is feeling in this moment, only reassure her.

"You knew. You knew this whole time didn't you? That's why you made me take my helmet off, isn't it? *Why you were acting so strange? Why you made love to me? Made me promise? Let me in?*" I answer with a look that I know she understands, rubbing at her wet cheeks with defeat plastered all over my face. A sorry without words as I gently shake my head but she's slipping.

They bang again. More violently, carrying a heavy notion of destruction that sticks to us once they get through that door. She flinches out of her skin, clinging to me tighter trying to understand her own emotions.

"Hayden please, please don't do this- you said you'd never leave me again!..."

"*I did say that, didn't I.* And it's because I said that, I'm doing this." I'm just hoping one day she will understand it, when her head is clearer.

"WE ARE GOING TO GIVE YOU SIXTY SECONDS TO COME OUT WITH YOUR HANDS IN THE AIR OR WE ARE COMING IN!" they yell through the door, making her squeeze me desperately, knowing the entire property is most likely surrounded with weapons and armed men. She needs to cooperate with me or this may end in a blood bath.

"I'm so scared, Hayden I'm so scared!..." I pull her into a hug, clutching to her with everything I have left in me, realising she really will be starting all over again. *Maybe this was more trauma than it was worth. She doesn't deserve any of this...*

"*I'm so sorry...*" I whisper down her ear, before pulling her into a kiss I wish would last forever. A kiss I stain her lips with. A kiss I want a permanent reminder of while I wait for her on the other side. While I spend the next chapter of my life in a box until I can see her beautiful little face again. See her dimples again. Hear her angelic laugh again. Until I can have her in my arms again.

She pulls away slowly like she's angry to engage in our last moments and it pains me seeing her resent me.

"*Baby* look at me." She glares down at the floor like she's embarrassed to weep for a love that was impossible.

"Look. At. Me." I snatch her chin as I run my fingers through her knotted locks and I've never seen her look so fucking broken. "You're going to be, ok? *I promise.*" My words seem to snake up her spine as she tries to pull away from me trying to hug her own forearms.

"Don't! Don't make promises you can't keep!" I hate this, I hate this so much. I just want to take her pain away, I want to absorb her suffering until its part of my fucking DNA. I want to hold her so tightly and tell her why she's the best goddamn thing that has ever happened to me with words but we've ran out of time.

"This isn't about me. It's about you. You're so fucking strong. God I wish I had the strength you possessed." She grips at my wrists as I hold her cheeks firmly in my hands, wiping her stray rivers.

"I'm only strong because I have you! How do I stay strong if you're not here!" The cracking in her tears is only making this harder and this knot in my throat is threatening to suffocate me.

"It has nothing to do with me. This is all you. I am the root of everything that has caused you pain! All the strength you hold. It's all because you are a survivor!…" I'm looking for even a sliver of hope in her eyes but there is nothing. She's giving me absolutely nothing but betrayal.

"But I don't want to be!" Her words shatter the remnants of my fractured heart and I squeeze tighter, like that will mend her back together as I rest my head roughly against hers.

"Then you survive, *For me.*" She needs to hold on. It's not over, I'm not worth her life and one day she'll realise it but she needs to hold on. I know how empty loss can be. I know how much damage it can inflict on an already broken heart, but I refuse to let her walk that path again.

"I can't lose you again. I won't!" I'm seething through tears I despise trying to push past my lashline and it stings but she needs to see this. I need to be raw with her so she can understand how truly undeniable my words are. What she means to me. That everything I'm doing right now. *I'm doing for her.*

"They may never let me out... But If they do. I hope you'll be waiting for me." My dam breaks, as our soaked cheeks merge our tears, taking in her stupidly beautiful eyes, even puffy with silly tears meant for me.

"Then never, I'll wait..." She recites my mother's words and I realise, this is for her, but this is also for my mother and the justice she deserves. I need to pay for her death as well as my *Little Innocence* and all the pain that came with it.

"You are, without a doubt, the best thing that has ever graced my entire existence. I got to be loved by you, shown I'm more than just a monster, shown that love can be beautiful and it's so fucking beautiful. You brought *Hayley* back. And I will happily do whatever it takes to give you a better life, do you hear me?"

Silence fills the thick tension weighing us both down as her eyes brighten with that hope I've been searching for, never letting it dull before the front door bursts open, making us both flinch as we cling to one another harder, terrified to let go. *Has it really already been a minute?*

Several heavy boots infiltrate *my home,* Sheps protest becomes louder at the disruption from behind the bedroom door. I command him to come and sit next to us on the bed as I grab his collar and memories flood my mind. Memories I'd kept bottled up for years. The day they took me I fought like hell, I got a few hefty bruises and the shit kicked out of me. Another thing unethical about people wearing badges. But back then, I didn't feel I deserved it. I wanted justice, I didn't feel like I'd done wrong, I wanted my mom. I wanted to grieve in peace. Instead I was dragged to a station and thrown behind bars for the next six years.

Now? Now is different. Now I deserve it and I won't fight. I won't falter. *I'll simply Obey.*

"Sunflower!..." She whispers through broken cries and I feel all my promises fall out my mouth. Because I can't do anything. I can't stop this. I can't change the outcome. It's useless now.

"I'm afraid I can't stop this time *baby*... Neither of us are in control now." I whisper into her temple as my tears taint her loose hair framing her face, my hand gripped tightly around the back of her head like I'm never going to let her go.

They approach the bedroom door, busting it open and my heart leaps out my throat, grabbing at her tighter, barely able to hear myself think over Shep's barking but I run my fingers through his thick coat, saying my goodbye without words. *I'm already pushing it.*

"I'm going to need you to step away from the girl Miss. Moore!" he orders, as two or three more men enter the room, surrounding us on the edge of the bed.

"You need to let go *baby*... Let go. You need to hold Shep. Please." I squeeze her wrists, tugging them as I attempt to pull her off me but she resists, trying to cling to my neck. "*Baby* please, let go. He needs you, ok?"

She finally releases, reluctant but forces her hands away slowly as she grabs for his collar but I know she won't be able to hold him for long. She's glaring at me, as does Shep and I can't bare to look at either of them, hating that I may never see either of them again, wanting to kiss her again but we both know we can't and my chest tightens, hearing her say the words I dread to hear one last time.

"*I Love You. Hayden.*" She whispers quietly, quivering with fear and now I'm the one struggling to let go, as I back up off the bed towards the door, obeying their command. I let them lead me towards the living room with a gun firmly placed against the back of my head and my arms gripping the back of my neck. I still can't find the words to say it back. Because if I do. It will only be harder for her. So I don't say anything as I raise my hands, *going willingly*. At least this way I can vow to say it to her the day I get out. *What's a promise if you can't keep it?*

"*Hayden!*" The bedroom door locks with Shep inside, whining through the uncomfortable silence lingering inside my prison cell and her feet thud the floor as I hear her run from the bedroom and I squint with fear. *She needs to stay there. They are armed. This will have all been for nothing if they open fire!*

"Please! Listen to me!" She yells at the swat team, grabbing for me as she walks in front of me. Preventing me from leaving and even the night I infiltrated her home, the night I held her life in my hands, the day she almost got taken from me, I have never seen this level of fear on her face. I've never seen anything like it, *from anyone.*

"*Alora*. Let. Go. You need to let me go." I grab her with malice, trying to force her away but she fights, refusing to move and my heart rate thunders in my chest.

"You need to listen to me! She doesn't deserve this! You need to hear her out! Please!" She pleads, attempting to push me back but I know what officers are like and she's playing with her life. *She should know this.* Trying to contain my frustration at her stupidity. "I need her! Please don't take her away from me!" I scrunch my face in pain as my cheeks become swamped in tears, *fearing for her safety.*

"*Alora, baby.* Let me go. Just trust me." She makes her stand as the palms of her hands grip my waist. *She's willing to risk everything.* Shep's barks get frantic from the distance as he tries his hardest to claw his way through the door.

"You need to move Ma'am or we will not hesitate to shoot." My blood runs cold, watching her defend me until the very end, like her life is disposable to save my pathetic life and suddenly I don't see her.

I see my *mother*. I see her *father*. I see my past. My biggest mistake. I see all the things I didn't do. All the things that could have been avoided if I'd of just intervened. I could have saved her life that day but I didn't. I stood idly by as I watched them take the one good thing I had away from me like it was nothing. *Like she was nothing.* And I refuse to make that mistake again. After everything, I watch her put her life on the line to keep me and deep down, I envy the fight in her. Fight I wish I had. *The same fight my mom had.* The fight to defend the one you *Love* until the very end. *I should have died that day* but I'm still here.

She ignores them, still pleading my case but we are running out of time and I can see the annoyance on his face as he aims his weapon at her chest. History has a funny way of repeating itself. But it also gives you another chance to do the right thing. To redeem yourself.

To do better.

Well, this is me doing better,

...

SHASSII

This is for you, Mom.

I grab her arm, yanking her beside me as I use my body as a human shield, knowing she would never have moved, so I made that move for her, and I never really knew true pain until this very moment, as I mouth how sorry I am.

Love really does conquer all. And it also kills you. But some people are worth dying for.

I understand it now, as I look at her with nothing but peace.

This is my peace.

...

"I Love You. *Alora*."

~BANG~

White nose clasps at my ears as metal penetrates my back, squeezing her tightly with shock before I begin to lose grip. My hearing muffles, listening to only the beating of my shallow heart against the shriek that escapes her mouth, fading fast as I fall into her weak arms that struggle to hold me, both of us collapsing to the floor. Her echoed screams haunt me as her delicate fingers cradle my wounded skin and I hope she haunts me in my after life, so at least I get to see her once more. I let my tears run into the void with a sense of calming relief, drowning out my name on her tongue, hearing my mom in the whispers as my hearing dissipates, calling to me as the stench of gun powder invading my fading senses. *Blood. Theres so much blood.*

"HAYDEN!!!"

I take in my *angel* one last time feeling her squeeze my hand.

My *light.*

My *home.*

"Please, please don't leave me! Stay with me! Hayden!"

She's speaking to me but I can't hear anything. I can't make out her words. I can't feel anything.

"Get her out of here."

"WHY ISN'T SHE MOVING!"

Numb. I'm so numb.

"Help her! Please! Someone help her!"

I never wanted this, this is not how we were supposed to end. But karma finally caught up to me, I know I deserve it. I deserve this.

I can't see her anymore. I can't see anything.

"You're ok, you're ok! stay with me Hayden!"

Peace... That's all I feel as delicate fingers graze the abuse etched into my face.

"DON'T FUCKING TOUCH HER! GET OFF ME!"

In this moment, death is my *salvation.*

She was always going to be my *end.*

My *purpose.*

My *Freedom.*

And my death was merely, *Collateral Damage.*

SHASSII

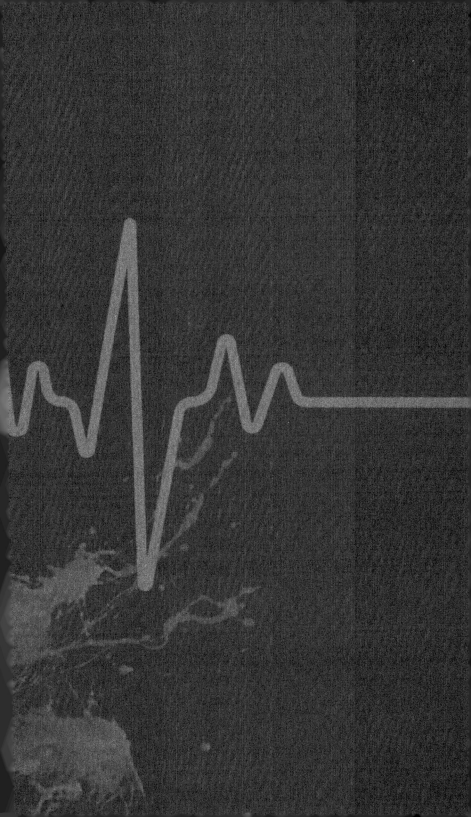

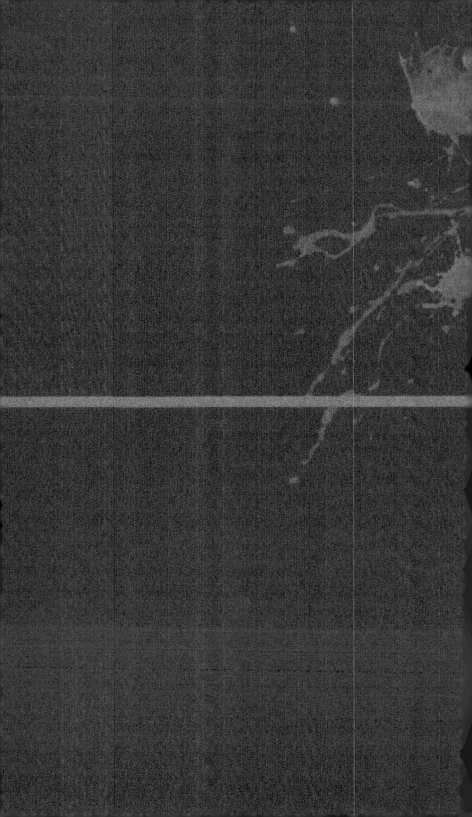

46 hours later...

CHAPTER 62

BLUE

Puppet

Play 'hurts Like Hell - Fleurie'

"Miss Blackthorne. Were you aware that Miss Moore was planning to transport you to a different state?" I stare blankly into the nothingness as their questions drill into the side of my head like a mind-numbing headache, hugging the itchy blanket wrapped around my trembling frame, still shivering and I can't see properly, with tears still breaking down my face no matter how hard I try to fight them back in. We've been at this for hours but I'm not cooperating. They think switching officers will make me give them a different answer. Anger and sadness are breaking my empty shell, glaring at the thick glass window disguised as a mirror casing the dull room, grey concrete walls closing me in as I refuse to look at the officer, feeling eyes on me like an animal in a cage. I dread to think how Shep feels right now. I screamed for him as I watched them take him away and shove him in the back of a van. All I've been told is that he is ok and he's been put in a kennel not far from here, I will get him back, even if it kills me. I made it very fucking clear that if they touch a hair on his head that I would find a way to sue them all in my stage of infuriated anger. It's highly unlikely in my state but they seemed to comply and tried to comfort me on the matter. I sob harder, knowing he's scared and alone, trapped in a room, on his own just like me right now and all I want to do is hold him and tell him everything is going to be ok.

"No." I murmur. *Lying.* I don't know why I'm lying. She's no longer alive to protect but I lie anyway, thinking about her dead corpse in my arms. How I watched her life fade away as her blood coated my hands trying to stop the bleeding and I can't get the image out of my head, feeling the front of my skull pulsate as I tense my jaw trying to contain more sobs as I remember her using the last of her energy to squeeze my hand until she stopped moving. *She told me forever.* She promised me we'd have more time. I grip the blanket harder, huddling my knees into my chest on the uncomfortable chair.

"Did Miss Moore harm you in any way?" He pushes, tapping the paper against the desk as he hangs over my anticipated words.

"No." I whisper, recalling the bickers eight months ago and even then, she wouldn't lay a hand on me. Even when I put my hands on her with anguish.

"Have I hurt you?"
"No..."
"Then I'd say you're pretty safe, wouldn't you?"

Her voice haunts me as I cling to her melody in my head, her deep, throaty engine, replaying it like a broken exhaust as I squeeze my eyes shut. I'm so tired, alone, scared. *I'm terrified.* Being in this room is making me so claustrophobic and I want to hurl being this close to a man right now, flinching at the thought of their hands on me as they dragged me off her lifeless body, unresponsive and pale. How they dragged her away like she was a bit of dirt.

I'm mourning for someone who was dead the moment this started and her face is a permanent picture in my head, looking right back at me. Smiling, but all I feel is an unbearable ache that's crippling me from sitting up straight.

She wouldn't even tell me she loved me until her last dying breath. A wave of insufferable anger washes over me, hating that those were her last words to me, gripping the seat either side of my feet as I dig my nails into the flimsy plastic.

"Did Miss Moore touch you inappropriately?" I swallow the truth down my throat as I spit out another lie, trying not to think about the way her hands felt against my skin, crushing my soul every passing second I think about the fact I'll never be able to feel it again. I won't be able to hold her again, or kiss every inch of her skin like I promised, as I graze my lips, realising her soft, sweaty skin is probably erased from my mouth by now and it's destroying me.

"No." He lets out an irritated huff, placing the papers down on the desk as he interlocks his fingers, feeling his fragile, sympathetic gaze on me as he leans into the table.

"You can be honest."

I know I can. But I won't. Channelling my inner rage, trying to find the strength in hating her as I dig for more lies, trying to cover up what really happened and I'm vibrating with an ache worse than my own end as I snap back, and I can't tell who I'm trying to lie to. Me or him.

"She never touched me." I hiss, nearly choking on my dishonesty as I finally look at him looking back at me like I am a compulsive liar. Water and painkillers sit perfectly in front of me and I'm refusing to take them. I almost didn't take my insulin but I was ordered by a nurse who was fairly kind to me, helping me as I couldn't even hold it steady but my food has already come up and I've not slept for almost 48 hours, terrified to let myself drift off into more nightmares. Terrified to see her dead eyes glaring back at me. Every time I close my eyes it's all I see.

"Did you share any sort of relationship with Miss Moore?" He asks confidently and I'm milliseconds from puking as the last few months of our lives replays on a agonising loop in my head like a happy movie which I thought would make me feel better but it only makes this worse and I can taste bile in my throat. I want to hate her. I want to scream, belt, throw this god damn fucking table across this room! *It should have been me!*

"No..." I contain my internal burning as he glares at me with visible annoyance, grinding his teeth in his pristine uniform and I used to feel so safe in the eyes of the law but I've never felt more unsafe. More repulsed by them, trying to get my head around the fact they were going to open fire on an innocent girl. How they opened fire when they know it's against the law unless it's self-defence. *Self-defence.* I squint at the words, realising the route of all of this. *This system. These people.* They are all frauds.

"Are you aware she killed your parents?" he bites, clearly trying to hit a nerve and it does. It's been almost a year and I'd nearly forgotten but their faces suddenly appear, screaming at me. Telling me how I betrayed them and guilt smothers my body.

"Yes." I did. And I don't know what will happen if I confess I was ever romantically involved with her. I myself may end up behind bars for willingly letting this go unnoticed. She gave me more than one opportunity to run away but I stayed.

"How does that make you feel?"

I don't know. I don't know how it makes me feel. I'm in no fit state to be answering questions right now, all I can think about is her and it makes me want to die, I'm frightened to live. The cameras, the press, the questions, the knife rammed into my chest, it's all too fucking much. I told her my heart would stop beating when hers did but I'm still breathing and I don't deserve to be.

I don't answer, glaring back at the invisible faces behind the glass that I know are watching me. Watching every move I make.

"Miss Blackthorne. It states here that you intervened during the time of breach. Can you tell me why?" If I told them why, I'd be in so much trouble. But If I lie they will be able to tell.

You are a terrible liar.

"I'm not sure." I chew the cuff of *her* hoodie, having ripped apart my lips and wipe my face dry of my grieving.

"Did you have feelings for Miss Moore?" My airways jam. Finally hit with reality, my feelings begin to suffocate me. I was in *Love* with the woman who ruined my entire life, not once but twice and my jaw locks as stray tears push over my lashes. Was it even *Love*? Infatuation? A bond by trauma? Did I just think I was because I had no one else?

"No..." He pulls a device from his pocket, placing it on the table. A recorder of sorts. But not the one we are already using to document this conversation. He presses play and her last moments begin playing out the crackly speaker, finding it hard to see as I hear the fear rip through my throat and her voice tears through my core like alcohol.

"Please! Listen to me!"
"Alora. Let. Go. You need to let me go."
"You need to listen to me! She doesn't deserve this! You need to hear her out! Please!"
"I need her! Please don't take her away from me!"
"Alora, baby. Let me go. Just trust me."

He glares at me, cocking his head slightly as his eyes narrow and my heart stops.

"That doesn't sound like you never had romantic feelings for her, Miss Blackthorne." His condescending slyness slips from his tongue and my eyes are burning trying to contain my fury. They are trying to corner me and *I can't fucking breathe.* "You told us to hear her out. Well I'm listening."

No one knows her story or the suffering she endured. Only me. I'm the only one who can fight for her. The only one who can let her voice be heard, her betrayal be known. But at what cost? I cannot beat the system. I have no power here, everything I say can be twisted, I realise that now and I will not be painted as a villain.

A loud buzzing fills the room as the door clicks open, and my tongue almost chokes me as I suck it down my throat, glaring at a man with a badge, the same man who ripped me from her, the same man who threw me in the back of the cop car place my journal on the table in front of me and the corners of my eyes fuzz.

Fuck.

"Does this belong to you?" He asks a question I already know he knows the answer to but I deny it anyway, staring down at it wishing I'd burn it like I should have.

"No."

"Miss. Blackthorne, do you realise with this you may end up behind bars?" He illiterates and my heart rattles thinking about all the awful things Hayden went through, gulping down my fear. I wouldn't last five seconds.

"You documented everything dating back from Christmas of 2009 and information even before that date. We need you to be honest with us or the court will see to it that you aided in criminal activity."

I scowl at him, trying to understand how the hell me being a hostage equates to me aiding in murders that had absolutely nothing to do with me. I was almost raped, possibly killed. *She saved my life?* But I guess that doesn't mean anything to them. *God forbid that ruin their reputation.* All they care about is her downfall. Being the *heroes*, ending the cycle of a deranged serial killer. Even if it means making me look bad. All the blood on her hands behind closed doors was not my doing, nor is it my fault but that is exactly how they will see it.

"Alora. This does not look good for you, am I making myself clear?" *Perfectly fucking clear.*

"I never aided in any murders. I was a victim." He scoffs at me, completely disregarding my trauma and it only makes me sob harder.

"Is that what you think? Miss Blackthorne. This woman murdered your parents? How do you think that will look for you? The night they died you just so happened to go missing. Found eight months later untouched with a clear indication you shared a romantic interest in your kidnapper? You infiltrated her arrest." His words are like poison, I'm finally out of my little clouds and I was a victim. But now? Now I'm lovesick for a convicted criminal who can't even keep me safe anymore. *Because she's dead.*

He opens a file filled with images and stacks of paper, morbid graphic pictures of mutated faces and gutted bodies, widening my eyes when it dawns on me.

These are all her victims.

Men, sliced up like vegetables, smiles of blood gracing their faces, just like hers. Just like the smile she carved into that asshole's face, dotted all over a fifty-mile radius. But for some reason, I'm not horrified anymore. This is no longer the Hayden I know. The Hayden I coaxed out. The Hayden that was ready to do better.

Now I know the real dangers out there, the man she dismembered for putting his hands on me, people who deserved it. People like her father. Pigs. *Fucking animals.* I glare at them, sifting through the pictures, clearly a tactic to try and weaken me.

And I realise my parents are not in this pile, *only making it more suspicious.* When I found them they only had one singular bullet wound through their skulls and nausea creeps up my throat. *She was clever.* This way they stayed off her scent, due to her relations with my father, they would have worked it out. She was a calculated woman. *She was only found when she wanted to be found.* She was found because of me. *For me.* This was for me and for some reason I hate every inch of her right now, because freeing me has only sentenced me to a life in a different box when I'd rather be in a box six feet underground with her.

She told me she'd taken fourteen lives, not including that prick's life or the remnants of another on her sleeves the day she brought me back my favourite chocolate. All her murders were to keep them off her scent after I came into the picture. She didn't leave them as a trophy or a message. She was in hiding, like she was frightened they would find us and my heart throbs heavier. *So how did they know these murders were her?*

"How do you know these were her doing?" I ask curiously. Trying to keep my composure.

"The mutations were a metaphor. The things you wrote in your journal only confirmed our suspicions. Her little acts. Her second identity you mentioned. It doesn't take a genius to put two and two together." I try to hold back a sarcastic laugh laced with amusement.

"Then you would also know that all those cases were all men in *your* records whose cases had been forgotten. Have you ever considered the possibility that they were deserved. Cases you left cold. Did you ever stop to think about why she finished what you couldn't?" I snap, squeezing my jagged nails into my palms, shocked at my own voice. He peers back at me, his eyes telling me everything I need to know. *He knows I'm right.* And he's struggling to find the words.

"She still murdered in cold blood." His tone now full of uncertainty as he backs away from me, leaning back in his chair trying to defend his own stupid laws.

"What, like your officers did?" Does he really think I don't know that in the last forty-eight hours, they haven't put all the pieces together. I now have no one to speak for me, the same way Hayden had no one speak for her. I'm silenceable If I say too much, so I refrain from talking further.

"Did your father deserve it? Your mother?" He stoops lower, trying to slither his cold scales underneath my skin but I'm already in a room full of snakes.

"I refuse to answer any more questions until I have a lawyer present." A fire burns inside me. A hunger for justice. Not just for me but for her. I will get her story out there. I will not be fucking silenced. *This system will fall. I will make sure of it.*

Play - 'Soul tied - Ashley Singh'

The first person I asked for once released on bail was Kacey. She is the only person that came to mind. The only person I really have left and her and her parents took the day to drive up and collect me. I would say she was thrilled to see me in one piece but by the sounds of it, it's like no one even cared I was gone. I could hear the ignorance in her voice and it hurt. I dread to think what she's put on social media in the last eight months. She's an attention whore and as much as I hate to see it, she's all I have left.

My time away made me realise she really isn't a friend at all, but her family welcomed me with open arms and lent me the spare room until my court case, they also promised me they would find Shep and bring him home safely which eased my panic slightly. He is all I want right now. The only part of her I have left.

I spent the majority of the car journey back to Indiana in silence staring out the window wanting the ground to swallow me whole as this concrete jungle merged into acres of nothingness, realising how petrified of the outside world I truly am. I feel like an alien on earth, in someone else's skin. I died in that house alongside her and I don't think I'll ever get me back.

She tried to talk to me but I couldn't find the words. I don't know what people know as of yet but these eyes on me is making my skin crawl. Desperate to get into the house and lock myself away.

We arrive at the house and I trundle inside feeling like a stranger. So out of place as they escort me to my room and I forget how made of money her family is.

"Here we are darling. The bed is freshly made and there are towels in the ensuite waiting for you. Please, if you need anything else, anything at all, don't be afraid to ask, ok?" Her mum says softly as she cradles my hands like my own mother and my swollen eyes pulse with the urge to push out tears I must have run out of by now. "Everyone is so happy to see you safe and sound."

I want to believe that but in the grand scheme of things, no one really even knew me. Not the real me anyway, and I'm sure they all jumped on the sympathy bandwagon once they caught wind of my disappearance. If there is one thing I've learnt. It's to see through the bullshit.

She rubs my cheek before leaving me standing in the doorway with nothing but the same clothes I've been wearing since her death, wrapped in her hoodie that I inhale, stinging at my eyes and a small bag of belongings they took from her house, my phone. my teddy and a few other bits.

I refused to change, even when they lent me new clothes at the station and I stare into the standing mirror propped up in the corner of the room, glaring at my own ghost as her hoodie is stained with saturated blood. *Her blood.* I can still smell the sea in my hair as I glare at the greasy mop on my head, tied in a loose bun wearing the heaviest bags, sighing as I glare at the bathroom door knowing I need to shower. But I don't want to. I don't want to erase her touch. Her smell, her last moments in my arms. The last remnants of her on my skin will be gone, something I'll never be able to get back and my knees buckle to the floor, cracking them with hard impact as I sob silently, clutching at the hoodie tightly in my fingers as I cradle my own body, praying for my death to come quickly. But I can't. Not yet. Not until I say my peace. I may be angry at her for leaving me on my own, but her story isn't over. *She is not a monster.* And I refuse to let the press paint her as one, so I will speak out in front of everyone if I have to. *I will be her voice.*

It's taken me three hours to finally run the shower. I stare at the bathroom door trying to move from the bed and the one thing I want right now is Shep. My pillow is drenched in my tears as I finally get up and make it inside, leaving her clothes on the floor beneath me and I weep as I walk underneath the flow of water, hoping I turn around and see her looking at me. Wanting her to hug me in a tight embrace and tell me everything's going to be ok but instead the bathroom is empty and I can no longer feel her by my side. I can't feel anything but the sweet calling of death whispering down my ear.

I'm completely alone and this pathetic muscle in my chest tenses, almost crippling me as I cup my knees, gliding down the wall onto the floor of the shower. I ignore how the tiles are burning my back, rocking to the shallow beating of my own heart as the water washes away *my soul*, watching it fall down the drain wishing it would take me with it as I glare at it for at least ten minutes, completely lost in my own head.

I thought I knew grief. I thought I knew pain. *But this?* This suffering is torture I wouldn't wish on anyone. Losing a part of yourself, a connection so deep that you feel completely empty inside. I feel so empty it physically hurts to breathe in oxygen. I rub my discoloured flesh, wiping the bags under my eyes from lack of sleep and my absence of rest and food is kicking my side effects up a notch. I feel so drowsy I might pass out so I crawl out the shower, wrapping myself in a towel and make my way to the bed, dragging her hoodie along with me as I huddle it into a ball underneath my head, using it as a pillow, trying to picture the rest of my life now. And all I see is darkness. Nothingness.

A dead end.

This is going to be a long night...

SHASSII

CHAPTER 63

JUSTICE

Puppet

Play - 'TV - Billie Eilish'

"Hey, Rara. Are you ready?" Kacey's voice seeps through the wood of the bedroom door and she sounds genuinely caring for once in her life. I've barely spoken a word to her since I got here. I scrolled through everything I missed while I was gone and it was as to be expected. Her sympathy card for me missing made me feel a little sick but I have no place to fight with her right now. I just want to get this damn court hearing over with.

I tug down my pencil skirt, feeling completely out of place and irritated already as I brush my hair out my face feeling way too claustrophobic in my clothes, applying a small amount of makeup to try and brighten up my dull face but I don't see much difference, clipping up my hair that is now almost down to my ass. I didn't realise how much it had grown until I was looking at pictures from last year. *When I thought I was happy.*

"Yeah." I've eaten the minimal and probably slept a total of six hours in the last five days. But I'm thankful for being taken in by her family. They have tried to make me feel as at home as they can and offered to let me stay until I figure out what the hell I'm going to do with my life. If it was up to me, I wouldn't spend much longer here, but I made a promise... I promised her I'd at least live to see my 21st birthday. Not that it means anything now as she couldn't keep hers, but I'll give it a go... Now understanding why she was so pushy with it, I let my anger out on the inside of my mouth, biting it until it bleeds. I don't think I'll ever forgive her for keeping that from me. She should have told me, we could have worked something out. Instead, she made love to me knowing it may be her last, giving me false hope that we were forever, *selfish bitch.*

I've spent the last week dwelling on every word she said to me but even in death it's impossible to truly hate her. Not when I crave her so deeply it physically hurts me and her last words continue to have me crying myself to sleep. She told me she would never say those words. Even when I said them to her, I was never expecting her to say them back. I told her I'd wait for it. But a part of me wishes she hadn't said it at all. It only confirmed everything I knew in those final moments. She was finally ready to feel. To be good. To start over. To do better. *For me.*

"We are ready when you are Rara, we will be waiting in the car."

I've not really come out of this room besides speaking to a local lawyer that has been visiting every day since my interrogation and I've probably worried them but I wanted to grieve in my own way. It has not been easy to talk about and she has not exactly been the best at making me feel better about my situation. She's advised me to plead guilty but I think that is absolutely ridiculous. The idea of death has been heavily high but I've refrained, staring at the razors in the bathroom just begging for me to use them, and I have, much to my detest... I never thought I'd find comfort in bleeding but it's the only way I seem to be able to control my pain and it takes my mind off everything for a while. I imagine drifting into a deep sleep where I can finally rest and not have to worry about tomorrow or this hearing or the press and the cameras in my face, my name all over the news.

I could run away from this ache, be by her side, be with my parents but I'm stronger than that. She told me how strong I was not even two days into my captivity. I've dealt with death. I've dealt with literal kidnapping, even my own death in a way. Something I wouldn't wish on anyone, *so why is this so fucking hard.*

I slip on some comfy shoes and make my way to the car, trying not to rub my makeup off as tears well against my eyeline, Kacey holding a coffee for me to take as I climb into the back.

"White chocolate mocha, extra hot with an extra pump and extra whipped cream!" The smell hits me like poison, immediately feeling nauseous and I'm suddenly back in her kitchen watching her drink it from her hideously ugly coffee cup and I freeze, glaring at it like it's dead.

"Get it away from me. *Please.*" She looks confused, knowing I loved coffee and I'm kind of surprised she remembered my order. She used to get me one before college everyday but now, the thought of it makes me want to bawl my eyes out. She jumps out the car, leaving it on the side of the pathway and jumps back in, staring at me like she wants to ask me a million questions but she holds them back, and I'm glad, because I'm nowhere close to talking about any of this yet. I don't think I'll ever be. It's still too fresh and everything is sore.

"Have you taken your insulin sweetheart?" her mom asks delicately, turning in the passenger seat. I nod in agreement but how am I meant to carry on living a normal life when everything reminds me of *her*. The leather seats sting at my nose and my senses are overwhelmed with the remnants of her in everything I see, touch and smell. Grinding my teeth together I try to concentrate on anything but being cooped up in this car for the next three hours.

"I have my headphones, would you like them?" Kacey asks gently, passing me them and I take them without hesitation. At least I can drown out my mind with music, hooking them over my ears as she glares at me, bewildered. I don't know what she was expecting when we were reunited but I'm not the sweet, bubbly little girl she once knew…Well, at least not now and I think it's frightened her. Although I'm surprised she doesn't prefer me like this. She is naive to think I'd be the same. Now I look at her and all I see is an insecure girl who uses me to make herself feel like she's a better person to fill her barbie doll ego. My mom and dad were so right but I can't believe it took me all I went through to finally see it.

"Would you like us to come in with you?" her mom asks timidly. I want to say no, but I think I need all the support I can get right now and as much as I feel completely uncomfortable, they are the closest I have to family left, so I nod gently.

"Also, good news! We found Shep and we will be picking him up from the kennel this evening!" she says joyfully and my heart beats heavily. They have no idea how much it means to me that they are not only taking me in but Shep too and I smile full of gleaming gratitude before focusing my attention out the window, playing *Beyonce - Halo* in my headphones, turning up the volume to drown everything out but this was a bad idea, as tears already fill my waterline, trying to suppress all my happy memories, the way she held me in her embrace, kept me warm on a cold night, washed my back in the shower, brushed my hair before bed, her gentle touch against my skin when she helped me sleep. Her essence, her everything. And now all I have left is the ghost of her.

Play – 'Fable – Gigi Perez'

We eventually arrive with half an hour to spare, walking inside to find a seat and my nerves are spiking. I've not been around this many people in almost a year and I was never good in crowds, which makes this even worse when I can feel everyone's eyes on me like a fish in a tank. Her mom holds my shoulder gently, caressing the fabric of my top to let me know she's here and it's comforting. It makes me sad to know how horribly Kacey speaks about her mother sometimes. She's been nothing but an angel.

"Miss. Blackthorne. Please. Follow me." An empathetic smile graces me as my lawyer escorts me to my seat in front of the judges stand, still empty and I sit, trying to chew on my anxiety but my lips are bruised and raw. I don't know how long this will take, but the officer who interrogated me is on the left side of the room, glaring at me with darkness behind his eyes that sends chills down my spine. I don't even know exactly what I'm going to say but the cycle of child abuse ends today. I will serve her justice. With or without her here. This is the right thing to do. For her and millions of other kids suffering. If I end up behind bars, so be it. But logistically they have nothing on me. I should be ok. *Right?*

Ten minutes go by and the court room fills up with strange faces. People who have simply come to watch and it bothers me, as they all gawk at the back of my head, shuffling to their seats. I suppose they are expecting to hear me break and admit to something I never did. I can tell by the funny faces I'm getting, no one in this room is feeling empathy or remorse for my disappearance and pressure builds in my chest, gripping on my heart, trying to control my nerves that have my leg shaking.

Breathe baby. In and out with me. Like we practised.

Her voice echoes through me like voices in an abandoned manor as I squeeze my eyes shut, imagining her pressed against me to slow my heart rate and it's working as I concentrate on the movement in my feet. *I'm in control.* Fighting to hold back more grievances.

The judge finally enters and the room falls silent as everyone raises to their feet, so silent you could hear a pin drop, making me hold my breath.

"Please be seated." He orders, and he doesn't waste any time.

"Alora D'arcy Blackthorne, age nineteen, birthday the fourteenth of February, year nineteen ninety. Do you solemnly swear that you will tell the truth, the whole truth, and nothing but the truth?" I glare at him, nodding as I pick at my fingers.

"Yes, your honour."

"Am I correct in saying, you have been missing since the thirtieth of October two thousand and nine?" *Has it really been that long?* It seems like only yesterday I went missing, even though when I was stuck in that house the first few months felt like years and then it went by too quickly. What is forever when you lose your forever in someone.

"Yes, your honour."

"And you have been held against your will since this time by someone you had no affiliation with until your abduction?"

"Yes, your honour."

"According to many officers as witnesses, you were seen infiltrating on the day of her arrest. Is that correct?" I breathe in sharply, trying not to shift my focus to the hundreds of eyes on me but I have to be honest. That is why I am here.

"Yes, your honour."

"And can you tell me why you tried to get in front of a gun to protect your kidnapper?" His words take me back there for a moment as the bullet ricochets in my ears, ringing with white noise as I stare into the void. *"Miss Blackthorne?"*

"Because she did not deserve to die." I blurt. And I don't have to see my lawyer to feel the disappointment in her face as she rubs the bridge of her nose.

"By this statement, I'm going to assume you were romantically involved with Miss Moore. Is that correct?" I can feel the judgement seeping from the audience, already disgusted by the question as I hold my head up and take a deeper breath.

"Yes, your honour." An array of gasps and low whispers stretch across the courtroom and I clamp my eyes shut trying to block them out. Trying to remember I'm not here for me. I'm here for her. *This is all for her.*

"I have your journal here that has been analysed in great detail. Am I correct in thinking you were sexually and intimately involved with Miss Moore?" My shame expands and I suddenly feel so small, afraid to look at anyone but the judge who doesn't seem to be too patronising, easy on his words with me.

"Yes, your honour." Not only was I sexually intimate with my kidnapper. It was a woman, and I can feel the judgement pounding the back of my head.

"And do you understand why you are in court today?" He asks gently, holding my journal in his hand.

"Yes, your honour."

"Can you tell me why?" I can't exactly be angry at a judge if they don't have the correct information. It's the CPD I have issues with. They are the ones breaking rules and not sticking to their words.

"Because you think I was somehow aiding her criminal activity."

"And were you?" He says it without judgement, letting a tiny sincere smile slip from the corner of his lip, like he already knows I was never a sinister part in any of this.

"No, your honour."

I startle at the abrupt reply from beside me at the man I have no recollection of. He's in a dark suit and slicked back hair. Not as pristine as Hays though, and I turn my nose up at him as he forces his voice to us.

"Objection! Miss Blackthorne went missing the week her parents were reported missing, only to be found without a scratch, sharing intimate moments with the criminal your honour. That leaves suspicion!" I kiss my canine underneath my lip in irritation. I know this is his job but the way they think I look like I'd even be capable of having a hand in my parents deaths sets my blood on fire.

"I had no hand in my parents' death, your honour. I found them dead before being attacked in my own home the night before Halloween." I bite, trying to contain my obvious frustration. I don't want to show too much, or it could show signs of guilt.

"And you are not aware why they would have spared you?" He collars and at the time I did not. But now I do.

"I am aware, your honour. Everything is in that book. Maybe things that were perhaps missed." I say coyly. They are asking me questions that are all clearly in my journal if they look hard enough.

"You said that Miss Moore did not harm you, is that correct?" I don't think I ever mentioned the basement in my journal. But even so, that was personally inflicted.

"Yes, your honour."

"So how did she get you out of the house? Are you saying you went willingly?" It would be easier for them if I agreed but I didn't and I will not give them what they want to hear.

"No, your honour. I was drugged from what I can remem-" I jump as the man beside me almost shouts over me, grinding against my thoughts with his raspy tone.

"Objection!" The judge does not look amused, silencing him with just his index finger as he lifts it in his direction, still heavily set on me and part of me feels grateful to have someone that will actually listen to me.

"Please. Continue." He coaxes me, asking me another question respectfully. "Is there a reason Miss Moore did not harm you?"

Because as much as she hated to admit it. She had a bigger heart than she liked to let on and somehow, I ended up loving that about her. Tapping into that hard exterior was an achievement for me.

"Because she is not a *monster,* your honour." I say softly and disagreement echoes through the crowd like my words are blasphemous.

"Were you aware of the number of victims she killed?" *Fourteen.* But that was when she told me. From what I can remember, I don't know how many were after that.

"Yes but I only knew the number, not whom or how your honour." I talk calmly, trying to get my words out.

"Did that not frighten you?"

It should have. At first it did, slightly. But for some reason when she told me, it didn't exactly shock me. Maybe I've watched too many documentaries. Should I have been frightened? Shown weakness? Given her a reason to retaliate? Would she have, if I had? I don't believe she would have. I rammed a knife into her hand and she ended up wrapping my harm where I clipped my own flesh. *What about that should terrify me?*

"If I am to be truthful, your honour. I am more terrified of the monsters that walk among us in plain sight than I was of her. I trusted she would not harm me, even with blood on her hands. She never gave me reason to fear her, she only ever tried to make the situation more comfortable for me, your honour." I explain, swallowing my absurd words slipping from my mouth knowing how absolutely ridiculous I sound right now. I know I do, and maybe I am just as to blame. Maybe I'm crazy, but her devotion to take a life in order to protect mine didn't scare me at all. I'd never felt safer in her arms.

"From her long list of victims, I find that hard to believe. I'm curious to know why you do not think she was a threat." I feel my eyes welling, sucking them back in with a sharp hitch in my breathing. *This is it.*

"Do you know why she killed my father?" I ask with a little more confidence filling my tone. Knowing that most people in this room did not do their research before prying on an innocent girl.

"Records state they had relations, ye-" I respond abruptly, cutting him off without meaning to, but he doesn't seem annoyed, only raising his brows in surprise, almost prideful.

"Because he killed her mother." Neither are alive, so speaking these words is a little easier on my heart knowing I won't have to face any of them tomorrow. Maybe I shouldn't visit the afterlife just yet. I don't particularly want to be hounded in hell. *Even though I know she'll be there waiting for me.*

"Objection! Detective Blackthorne's demotion from CPD was due to self-defence. The woman he murdered was justified." *Justified? The woman?* I try to hold back a scoff at the disrespect alone dripping from his mouth as he raises his voice sharply, slamming his papers against the desk and the judge does not seem to want to entertain his temper.

"And I bet that is what Miss Moore's killer also claimed, don't tell me." I face my left to look at him scowling at me so I scowl harder, standing off to him. I won't back down. I finally have a voice. I finally have control and I quite. Like. It.

"Would you like to elaborate?" the judge asks curiously, as if he himself is interested in this new take on their web of lies.

"Mrs Moore's murder was intentional. By my father." I explain, feeling slightly guilty that I'm dragging my father through the dirt but it's about time people knew the man he was. The man he kept hidden, even from me. A man I am still furious at for keeping me locked away for his own selfish reasons. A man I no longer recognise.

"Are you telling me that your father killed Mrs Moore with ill intentions?" He questions, furrowing his brows as he leans further over his table. We all know she was accused of being mentally unstable on the day of her death.

"*Yes.* Your honour. And he breached case laws by investigating undercover, involving himself romantically with her mother in hopes to uncover her husband's death." If Hayden was alive right now to hear me she would probably break her jaw with anger. But she's not. It's me and I'm done doing what everyone else says anymore.

"*And why do you say that?*"

"Because my father believed Lillie Moore was the cause behind Richard Moore's disappearance." He gazes at me, bewildered as we hold a strangely understanding stare before being interrupted.

"Objection! Mrs Moore went for Detective Blackthorne!" *He's really starting to get on my nerves* but my nerves are sucked out of me as the Judge raises his voice abruptly.

"*Silence!*" He ushers me to carry on, nodding his head for me to speak, and I can feel my tears crawling up my throat just thinking about my next words.

"Mrs Moore would not move, even after my father threatened to take her life, she pleaded for him to listen and he did not. He ignored her and he fired. Straight into her heart." I clutch my arms, looking at my lawyer for support, meeting her comforting gaze as she rubs my arm delicately.

"Is this what Miss Moore informed you?"

"*Yes, your honour,*"

"She saw everything. She died in her arms. And my father lied to get out of jail time, where he ran with me. To Indiana." Only now is everything making so much sense. The day she told me it was still so chaotic, I was so angry that it was all a blur, I never sat and processed it properly but thinking about it now, he did run. He seemed frightened for a while. Nervous, constantly checking over his shoulder. Paranoid, until he met my stepmom.

"Were you at all aware of your Fathers involvement in this?" Part of me wishes I had known but it would never have changed anything. And he would probably have lied to me too, so I guess not knowing at all was better than living through his deception and suffering for it.

"No your honour. Not until I was informed by Miss Moore." Her name is bitter in my mouth, hard to say, hard to swallow, tasting like liquor you want to sink in but it burns the back of your throat as you indulge in it. All I want to do is wrap my arms around her but I glance down at my hands and for a moment my skin is tainted strawberry red, her redemption smothering me, bleeding out on the matted carpet, imbedded with her soul as I shake my head to release me of my hallucination.

"And because of this you believe it was justified? Even though it was your father and your mother?"

Is it wrong of me for saying yes? My mother not so much. But if I was never in the picture, I guess her death makes sense. She was also *collateral damage* my father caused. It was inevitable.

She was fuelled with vengeance; she lived off it. It's what kept her heart beating when she wanted to give up. The love she had for her mother ran so deeply she would kill for her and she did. The way she did it for me. The way I feel she would do for anyone she loved. But where do we draw the line when we are robbed of everything we have? *When is it truly acceptable to take a life?*

"I believe it was justified. But it was not ok. She was failed by the system, your honour. But she did everything she could in the time that we had to try and make things right." I squeeze my nails into my flesh, trying to keep myself grounded but all I can picture is her skin against my fingers as I listen to my favourite song, singing from her chest. She was finally letting me in. *We were finally getting somewhere.*

"Please elaborate."

I look up at him, feeling sweat smothering my lower back and I don't know why I am so nervous to tell her story when her trauma isn't exactly new, it was just overlooked and forgotten, so I suck in a deeply shaken inhale and stand straight.

"Hayden was abused by her father for years, beaten and tortured, *silenced*. Not only her but her mother also. And so, she took his life to protect their own and was thrown behind bars for six years, charged with involuntary murder because she had no voice in the courtroom to defend her side. Because *my father* killed her only family. In a room full of people who preach the safety of women and children. People who were meant to be there for her and her mother and listen to her words when she explained why she took a life. Yet my father walked free because he claimed self defence, wearing a badge? What part of that is justified? Because he was a cop he got privileges? No one ever took Hayden's allegations against her father seriously after his death." I can feel anger spilling from the tip of my tongue, my words heated and swollen with bottled up hatred as I suck my tongue to the roof of my mouth.

"You have to understand it was her words against your fathers." He exclaims, and I shake my head in disappointment, hoping he would realise what stupidity just came out of his mouth.

"What does that tell you, your honour? Power has priority. My father lied through his teeth whilst Hayden rotted in a cell for six years. Tell me, would you settle for that? Will you silence me now because I have no one to speak for me? If my father told the truth would the consequences be reversed? Would my father pay for the death of Mrs Moore? Would he be plastered all over the news and called a monster? Or would that ruin their reputation?" I ask, waiting for a response I know will never satisfy me as I hold my chin up high, proud that I've left him, dare I say speechless and there is not a peep from my audience.

...

"We understand this all must be difficult for you-" he speaks slyly, trying to change the subject but it's too late for that now, I've found my feet. My Voice. *I can smell justice.*

"Please do not belittle me. She took the lives of monsters as horrid and as ruthless as her father. Cases turned cold by CPD, cases that could be protecting children like her. She was doing what you could not do. Is that a villain? Or a hero, your honour?" I glare at him before turning to face the room of strangers, totally taken by my words. Their jaws are hanging low, gawking at me in disbelief and I feel prideful. "Our system claims to be heroes, to keep us safe, to save lives but they didn't save hers or her mothers. Yet they were both punished. She stood in front of me to try and save me from making the same mistake her mother did. She blamed herself every day for not intervening and stopping it where she could. She was never going to hurt me. She was trying to save my life before the CPD opened fire on me. The people of this city, sworn to protect us. *Is that a monster? Or a saviour, your honour?"*

"Objection your honour! She aided in the death of a man that was stated in her journal!" he spits, and I can almost see his hackles up as he stares me down, feeling almost pitiful that he is this naive to his cause.

"A man that was going to rape me your honour. *Again*, she was saving my life. I never aided in her behaviour, she had let me walk free that day but if she hadn't stepped in, I would most likely not be here today. And it would not have been by her hand. Where do we draw the line? Where is death acceptable? Because from where I'm standing, murder is only acceptable in the eyes of the law. So they can reap the reward of being a hero when really, some are monsters walking amongst us and don't deserve their badge." I exhale my trapped anxiety, feeling a little lighter now that I've got that off my chest, and faces are beginning to change. *Understanding. Sympathy.* Whatever I'm doing seems to be working.

"Do you believe her sins were redeemable?"

Eight months ago, I would have said no. Out of hurt and spite. But I had the same urges to kill when she took my life from right under my feet. I wanted to make her pay, make her bleed. Hell, I thought about all the gruesome ways I could take her life. And then I realised, it's natural to feel like the only solution to your pain is to eradicate it. But who's to say it works? Will it make you feel better? Will it bring them back? *No*. But for that single moment, even only for a little, vengeance can take a form so hungry for blood you'll do anything to get rid of that hole in your chest. Even if it means taking someone else's life.

"I do your honour."

"Objection! How do we know any of this is the truth?"

I roll my eyes heavily, like a loose cannon before the judge leaves me speechless.

"Because she has no reason to lie, and everything she speaks she's documented inside this journal."

My lip parts, letting out a gentle breath as a tiny smile tugs at my lip, feeling my dimples form in my cheeks. *"Correct your honour."*

"Do you believe she had changed?"

The lump in the back of my throat grows, struggling to form words as I recall the last night we spent together. Knowing that the woman I was looking at was not Hayden anymore. It was *Hayley*. She was in there somewhere; I just had to find her and bring her back to me. She got so close, so fucking close until this fucking storm pulled her under.

"I do. She was just broken and needed to see that life was not as mean as it had treated her. All she knew was pain and suffering, your honour."

"Very well."

"Objection. Murder is murder. She murdered in cold blood, no matter the reason, she still took multiple lives! Miss Blackthorne clearly needs to be aided by a professional psychiatrist. She is only nineteen and has gone through something no young adult should endure. Who's to say she was not brainwashed? Drugged? She is clearly unwell. She was fornicating with a killer, your honour!"

He clasps at already cut strings and the voices behind me get louder. Whispers stretching across the length of the room but somehow, I just know they are no longer for me.

"But it was ok for my father to kill an innocent woman on the wim that she was guilty? Was it ok for an officer to open fire on Miss Moore for trying to protect me? Those were acceptable? Will he get punished for that? Will he spend the next six years behind bars?" I spit, slamming my arms down harshly on my desk, half expecting the judge to correct me but instead he says nothing, holding his chin as he peers at this arrogant ass hat prosecutor like he's the one who's lost it.

"She should be charged, your honour, we will be setting a terrible example."

"*I object.*   *I object.*   *I object.*   *I object.*
   I object.   *I object*
         I object.
I object.   *I object.*   *I object.*
         I object.   *I object.*
I object.   *I object.*   *I object.*   *I object.*"

The entire room sings words that leave my jaw grounded, all standing like a wave crashing into my heavy heart, bringing pools to my eyes as I rest my gaze on Kacey, who stands with her parents, smiling gently at me like they have never been prouder.

"We object."

"At this point, I would ordinarily give a detailed review and an assessment of all the evidence that has been given to me today. However, given the nature of this circumstance. I am going to keep this very brief. Miss Blackthorne, has been trialled today for indulging in the likes of criminal activity with a woman who is now not here to plead her case, shot on sight by a member of the CPD during infiltration where Miss Hayley Moore did in fact go willingly. It is alleged that on the evening of October thirtieth, Miss Blackthorne was abducted and held against her will. Since such events Miss Blackthorne has documented everything, she has done from that time to current date and all would have been raw, honest and are all justified. I have no doubt that Miss Blackthorne was in fact held against her will and is indeed a victim to an unfortunate circumstance, but she has not only told the truth, she has come forward and shared her story as well as Miss Moore's. She has in no way denied her feelings or relations with her kidnapper during her time held captive and has given a solid argument as to why. There is an unfortunate number of cases in which individuals have been wrongfully convicted on the basis of eyewitness testimony, which Miss Blackthorne has elaborated with us all today. I also find Miss Blackthorne to be a credible victim in such an unexpected situation. I accept her testimony that she did indeed share an intimate relationship with Miss Moore during her disappearance. But we have enough evidence to back up why Miss Blackthorne was not in any way in danger by her kidnapper. I appreciate that Miss Blackthorne must have had a horrible experience, and her trauma shall not go unnoticed, as will not many other cases, *starting today.*" My eyes bulge out my sockets, watching as he speaks to the audience with an emotion I can't put my finger on. Frustration? Familiarity? *Starting today?* Was that him making a stand with me?

"Miss Blackthorne has made it very clear to me that there are far bigger issues at hand besides the killing and passing of Miss Moore and with that. Our criminal justice system requires that before someone can be found guilty of a criminal offence, their guilt must be established beyond reasonable doubt. In the circumstances of this case, based on the evidence I have seen and heard by Miss Blackthorne today. I conclude that the crown has not established this case beyond reasonable doubt. Miss Blackthorne, I will ask you to stand now."

I rise to my feet, as my knees buckle with anticipation, looking back at Kacey who has a smile growing across her face from ear to ear and I realise that this is really happening.

"I can confirm, I find you *not guilty* of your allegations during the time of your disappearance. You are free to leave. This case is closed." A loud bang graces the room, filling my ears with an uproar of applause that push water out my eyes. *I really did it.* I fought my case and in doing so I hope that maybe now something will change. That the justice system will listen. That domestics and child abuse will be taken seriously. That it will no longer get swept under the rug. That kids like her may see happier days and will not be brought up to know only pain and suffering. That they will have a voice.

Like I was hers.

And I know she would probably want to strangle me just as much as want to kiss me right now, a bittersweet smile forming on my face at the thought as I look around the room all cheering for me, so loud I can barely hear myself think. I search for Kacey who is already running at me to catch me in a warm hug and I want to pull away but my arms fall around her, weeping into her little salmon pink dress.

Things are going to change.

Starting now.

COLLATERAL DAMAGE

SHASSII

2 years later...

Epilogue

Play - 'BLUE - Billie Eilish'

"Thanks for the rideeeeee!" Kacey hangs off my arm like a dead body as she waves to the handsome chauffeur. She is adamant he is a taxi driver but she is too drunk to comprehend that we did not, in fact, get into the back of a taxi to get home.

She didn't drink as much as usual, but her tolerance is clearly gone because she can barely walk on a few vodkas that I also had and I caught myself wanting a bottle of corona which made me smile for a moment before I had to hold back the waterworks. It was a good birthday and I made sure I did what *she* wanted. I went out like normal girls do for their 21st with a few other girls I've made friends with.

Friends. It's still such a foreign concept to me but it has been nice to have girly company. Girlhood is definitely something now that I can actually experience it. Besides being hit on by every Tom Dick and Harry. I'm not interested. My phones always blowing up with messages but I leave them on read.

"Come on, you cripple, let's get you inside."

She groans with disapproval as I drag her through her overly large door, greeted by her mom who patiently waited for us to get home safely before she went to bed. In many ways I see so much of my mom in her that my loss was never completely lost. She lives on through her and it's been nice to have a mother figure in my life again. Her father is just as kind and has done nothing but make life as easy as possible. They offered for me to stay with them permanently after my trial and I accepted. I was not sure at first and spent many weeks telling myself it was the wrong decision, that I knew where I wanted to be, but logistically it was not feasible, so I stayed and I am happy I did. It's been easier to get through the past two years *but not easy enough.*

"I see you ladies had a good evening! Happy birthday Alo. I didn't catch you in time to say it before I left for work this morning!" Her mom gawks at us as I yank Kacey's dead weight into the front door, smiling with amusement as she helps her off me.

"Thats ok! I had a good time, *besides babysitting.*"

I was angry at her for a while after settling in. I couldn't let go of her behaviour and I was in no mood for her company but since the trial, she became less, *bitchy*? More laid back. She stopped going out as much and being reckless, spending more time with me doing things I wanted to do like helping me with my writing journey. She even apologised for the way she treated me and it took a while but I slowly let her back in. It was hypocritical for me to preach about second chances that day and not give her a chance to show me she saw me as more than just an ego boost but it's been two years and we've never been closer. She even dyed her hair brown! I barely recognise her but I adore this new, compassionate version of her. She no longer judges or pushes me or belittles me. She's become a sister I never had and truthfully, if it was not for her and the Calloway's, I don't think I would have made it.

"I'll take her off your hand's sweetie. I'm sure you're exhausted!" Her mom takes her from my hip, placing her grumbly butt on the couch as I move to ascend the stairs. "Oh! Alora, this came in the post for you. I'm not exactly sure who it's from, I wasn't aware anyone knew of your new address."

She grabs a brown envelope from the side table sat beside the door, almost running for it so I don't run upstairs before she can give it to me and holds it out for me to take.

"That's strange?" I murmur. I have had no contact with my family? And my address has stayed extremely confidential for security reasons since my books been published. Sharing my story with the world is good and all but it doesn't keep the weirdos away.

"Goodnight darling."

I glare at the delicate paper, feeling worn down and grainy against my fingertips as I run them over my name, handwritten but almost faded with my address stickered against the envelope.

"Goodnight Mrs. Calloway." I say, still staring down at the anonymous parcel.

"Please. Call me *Selene*. We are family now, ok?" *Family*. Yeah, I guess we are. They treat me as if I was their own daughter and it's been so healing. For part of me anyway.

"Goodnight Selene!" I say chirpily, as I bound up the stairs nearly drifting as she shouts up to me.

"Don't forget your meds! And there are some snacks on your bed in case you get peckish! Drunk munchies are the best."

I wouldn't exactly say I was drunk, not even tipsy. I learnt my lesson and just thinking about it consumes me. I couldn't let anything distract me tonight so drinking was not exactly on my agenda, and I guess you could say I am still slightly level-headed. Alcohol and medication aren't exactly the best combination.

We exchange a polite smile before I make my way to my bedroom, placing the envelope upright on my bedside table in front of a fresh vase of sunflowers, smiling as I run the soft petals through my fingertips.

"Hey *baby...*" I sigh softly, turning to look at my best friend. "Hey boy."

Shep is laying on the bed being the goodest boy not eating my snacks but everything in his face is pleading I let him have a nibble as I sit beside him, running my fingers through the scruff of his neck as he attempts to lick my face and I suddenly feel so guilty but he'll be ok. He has the Calloway's.

"I miss her too..." I whisper against his fluffy ear and it's like he can feel my pain as he attempts to lick away my tears. I glare at the letter but whoever it is, they can wait. If I can even be bothered to open it. I can't be arsed to hear from some relative that is clearly only interested in my wellbeing now that I have made a name for myself. And an interesting one at that. But I've achieved a hell of a lot in the last two years. I made it my goal to achieve as much as I possibly could before my 21st and my name has been nothing short of quiet, almost everywhere. I've had almost everything, but the best one has to be *The ghost girl*. I ache to be a ghost. *I ache to be with her.* I've written almost every single day since, beside the last week because apparently birthdays are a huge deal in this family. But it helps me to let out my feelings. Maybe someone can turn this into a book too when they find it.

I waste no time jumping into comfy clothes, removing the snacks she left me from the bed onto the floor as I grab my journal and a pen.

Play – 'Still Mine – Ashley Singh'

Day 589   *02 14-2012*

I made it. I got to 21. And I can assure you, you didn't miss much turning 21. I definitely couldn't picture you clubbing but I imagined it anyway to make me giggle.

Shep is still ok and safe by my side. For months he was practically lifeless, crying for you every night by the bedroom door until he realised you were never coming back and those months were restless. We both cried so hard that I don't understand how I still have tears left but two years in and it doesn't hurt any less. He got me through it and I think I pumped some life back into him but he's not the same and I don't think he ever will be. The way I never will be.

I carried your end of the deal, but I never carried mine. So today I am going to do just that. I am going to be with you soon. I told you that when your heart stopped beating so would mine, and I've tried so hard to live a hollow shell of a life without you and it doesn't matter what I fill it with, a part of me is still empty. A part of me I will never get back. A part of me that belongs in that grave with you.

I passed my driving test last week. I know you'd be so proud of me but even the simplest things like driving become a pill I cannot swallow when I remember you are not in the passenger seat next to me. You're not in my bed. You're not in the shower with me, you're not inside me. You're not even three hours away. You're just. **Gone**. An absence so consuming that even in a room full of people. I see no one.

I thought this pain would eventually subside. That it would become easier. That waking up every day would feel lighter the more the sun rose a new day but it's only seemed to have gotten harder. Knowing that I will never be able to live a fulfilled life. I've tried. I've done it all and It's still not enough to fill this hole you left me. I published our story. It's called **Collateral Damage**. I thought it was only fitting considering how many times you liked to throw it in my face until you suddenly became the very thing that was meant for me. We were both Collateral Damage in a broken system I have tried to mend, for you.

60% of its earnings goes to foster homes or charity for children's programs and the crime rates for child abuse has skyrocketed. I guess my voice was finally heard and I thought this is what I'd want. This accomplishment should make me feel better but I'm finding it harder to breathe. This pressure is suffocating me. And peace is calling to me from the shore. Freedom is no longer fun when you're not here to experience it with me. My laughter, my smile, my happiness all resides inside of you.

Your mom forgot to mention a vital part in her story. How do you find happiness when you'd already found it in somebody and now it's gone. I try to move on, to let myself feel something other than grievance but anytime I catch myself smiling, I picture you smiling back at me and suddenly there's a noose around my throat, calling for me to take that leap. You're right there but I can't touch you. I can't hear you. I can only cling to this apparition of you that greets me in my dreams if I'm lucky and I now seek comfort through sleeping my consciousness away hoping that one day I won't wake up.

I'm not afraid of dying anymore. I'm afraid of living an unfulfilled life without you in it, where I still see you in the walls, in the current of shallow waters, in the ripples against the basin of the shower. In my bed on a stormy night. I can smell you everywhere. Every time I fill up petrol or get in the car. And every time, another fraction of me dies.

I want to be with you. I want to hold you; I want to hear you tell me you **Love** me again. I didn't understand it at first. Why you were so selfish. Why you left me on my own but then I finally came to the realisation, that the only time we would truly ever be at peace together, is 6ft under. We were doomed from the start and the older I get the more I realise that. I'm not over you and I never will be. I don't want to settle down and move on. I don't want to date. I just want to be with you.

This guilt I carry, this blame I hold everyday knowing that if I'd of just listened to you, if I had just let you go, you might still be alive. Behind a glass box maybe but you'd be here so I could see you. Instead, my own stupidity got you killed, and I will never forgive myself for that. I don't deserve to be here, and I hope that once I get to the other side, you'll forgive me?

So just know that when I do this. I lived as fully as I could. And I went willingly. That this was my decision and this time, **you can't save my life**.

I have nothing left.

I Love You Hayley. X x x

I exhale a worn sigh, glaring at the blob of transparent liquid where my tears are bleeding onto the page, like I'm trying to reach her through my words and I close it. I glare at the bathroom door for a moment before looking back at Shep. I kiss him deeply on his nose, smothering him in all the love as I cuddle him, feeling his warm embrace so I can share it with her once I get there.

"I'm sorry boy…" I walk to the bedroom door and let him out so he can run for the garden like our usual routine and smile gently at him before heading for the bathroom and making my way inside to grab my medication and a glass of water. I peer into the glass as I hold it in the shaky mould of my hand to fill it before placing it on the side of the sink, glaring at all this medication I'm on as I spill it across the basin. *I never liked medication.* The pills create a seabed of stones against the white china, feeling a strangely comforting relief wash over me. Living every day in a world you no longer feel welcome in is the hardest burden to bear but it will all stop soon. I'll be able to drift off and feel her warm embrace as she cradles me in her arms and tells me how silly I am for giving up so soon. But I think I'm ok with that.

I glare at the capsules, reminding me that they are to aid me. And aid me they will as they lead me to their biggest accomplishment. They are about to save my life as I roll one against my fingertips ready to rest the first on my tongue when a gentle noise makes itself known by my left. I turn my head slowly to find the envelope by the bathroom door near Sheps paw, clawing at it like he too wants answers, whining in distress that causes my brows to knit as he manages to pick it up in his mouth and drops it at my feet. I peer at it for a good minute. Trying to understand who the hell I would get a letter from but at least it distracts me for a minute, dragging my feet to pick it up as I go to sit back on the bed, glaring at my name before opening it gently, watching it tear at the smallest of movement, frail and stale as I slide it out from its blanket and my eyes lock, almost immediately pooling with uncontrollable tears.

Play – 'Would've been you - Sombr'

My Little Dreamer,

If you are reading this, it means I was unfortunately not here to say this to you in person. And for that I am so sorry. But I needed you to know all the things I never had the nerve to tell you in person if I haven't said them already and I know wherever I am right now I am kicking myself for not saying them to you sooner.

I hope you had an epic 21st birthday Puppet but God I hope you were sensible with your alcohol. Wouldn't want you falling asleep in someone else's arms now. That place is only reserved for me and I wish I was there with you, to tell you how beautiful you look tonight and kiss you at midnight but I'm not, so I can only write it on paper.

You look beautiful Alora.

I can't predict the future, but If I'm gonna take a wild guess, I probably didn't make it to that cell did I?

I hope you are taking good care of my boy. I knew as soon as he met you that I'd lost him to you but I was ok with that. He loves you so much, maybe more than me and that's saying something. He's a good boy and I hope he's keeping out of trouble.

I really was ready to risk it all for you. I knew it had to be done, the only way we could have worked was if I tried to right my wrongs, even if death was inevitable, and I'm assuming it didn't quite go to plan but that is ok. Because that means you have all the more reason to get your ass to Spain. With or without me. Got it?

Call me old fashioned but I put everything I own in your name. I don't exactly have anyone else to leave anything to, so this is your birthday present from me. I instructed for you to receive this letter on your birthday and my spare key is in the little pouch to my pile of junk. If I don't end up giving you this letter, knowing you it would be painted and smothered in plants by now and I'm totally ok with that. Just don't put them in my garage.

But if not, I understand if you don't want any of it. Sell it, burn it. It's totally up to you.

I just want you to know, I don't regret a damn fucking second with you. Even when you were trying to rip my head off, when you pushed me to find my worth again. At the beginning I resented it. I didn't understand why you were fighting so hard for something broken. Until you showed me what being loved by someone truly felt like. Never giving up on me. Never letting me sink when I felt like I was drowning. But most importantly, I got to be loved by you. So I guess my luck wasn't so bad after all. I found my light I'd happily let take my life. You took my life by storm baby. I'd happily let you end me. But most importantly, I'd live for you. I want to spend the rest of my broken little life with you by my side and it means I'll probably have to spend the next ten years of my life in a box but it doesn't seem so daunting when you have something to fight for. Like I want you to fight for me now. You better have published that book! I'm still mad you never let me read anything you wrote, so I may have been sneaky and took a look while you were sleeping.

And I. Love. You. Too. Alora. I Love You so fucking much my heart physically swells at the thought of you. I wish I let you in sooner. I wish I let you Love me like you wanted to. I wish I wasn't so frightened to love you in fear I'd fail you or hurt you further. I was a sinking ship.

The truth is, I knew I loved you the day you wore that silly little dress. I just didn't understand it. I didn't know I was capable of adoring someone so deeply I'd fish for the light lost inside my darkness in hopes you'd chase it like a moth. The same light I saw in you. That glimmer of momentary happiness I'd been searching for my whole life. I wasn't sure if you'd chase it but you did more than chase it. You gave me yours and since you walked into my life, I saw colours clearer.

What I'm trying to say is. You are so fucking special, and I hope you never waste that. You light up a room just by standing in it. So I want you to stand in as many damn rooms as you can.

I hope this clarified just how crazy I am about you. And how I'm beginning to see why people search for Love.

It's not a disease. It's a cure. It's not painful, it's healing. It's not punishable. It's a reward.

So don't you dare let mine go to waste. You will fucking live for me. You will do everything you set out to do and I will be right here with you. You hear me?

Or I may just have to haunt you in your nightmares, although I'm sure you'd like that.

This is not goodbye, Little Dreamer. We will see each other again, I promise. Maybe it's a good job I'm dead. I may of just popped it from second hand embarrassment. You know this is not my thing and I hope you're crying happy tears at how silly I sound as I bleed on paper for you. If you even remember me. Maybe you have moved on and now I'm just a stranger.

But you, Alora D'arcy Blackthorne.

You were my beginning. And you will be my end. I'd fucking die for you. And If you're reading this, it probably isn't far from the truth. I can't wait to tell you the very reason my **'never'** came true and I hope I get to by the time you read this, and I know you said you'd wait for me, but **'never'** is a very long time to wait for a love that may falter when it was doomed from the start. So I need you to do something for me. Ok?

I need you to let me go. I need you to know it's ok to move on. I want you to bloom, my **Little Sunflower.**

And I know that right now, whatever happened, you're blaming yourself for it. I know you're saying sorry but don't. I don't want you to blame yourself for something that was inevitable. I deserved this. I owed this to you. My life was an apology to you and I should have gone a long time ago. It would have saved you so much pain so please, do not feel guilty for my surrender. I'm at peace now. I finally did the right thing. **For You.**

Don't ever stop searching for that happiness Innocence. It's out there. It may just look different.

I'm right here. You just have to listen to the whistling in the trees and the way the leaves dance in the wind, the ripples in the sea and the voices in your beating heart.

Until we meet again baby. In another life. I'll be waiting. But right now, it's not your time. Ok? Don't wait for me, live for me. Live like every day may be your last so you have thousands of stories to tell when I get to kiss you again.

Then never, I'll wait.

Hayley.

I can barely see the paper in front of me through my sea of tears, as the pouch with the key falls into my lap, reading it over and over and over again until I memorise every word, wishing she was here to say this all to me in person and I could kiss her until our lips were sore and my eyes dried up. I stare at it for what feels like hours, imagining her sitting in front of me and I think this closure is what I needed. It's like she's suddenly still here beside me, undeniably present through her words even though she is no longer physically with me and I clutch at the paper trying to fuse myself into the parts of her she finally let me see. Being vulnerable and kind. I was never sure how she really felt and I know I said it never bothered me but this, this is what I needed to hear all along. I just wish it was not through paper. But her words of encouragement are working as I beam a smile I cannot control and I wet my pyjama top with my rivers suddenly feeling an emotion so overwhelming it stuns me and my cheeks begin to hurt from grinning so wide. A genuine smile. Not a fake image people want to see to make themselves feel better. I've spent my entire life smiling my way through this numbness that seems to take a hold of me. I've not smiled in so long this is giving me jaw ache.

Hope.

For the first time in two years, I can feel it, brewing inside me like boiling oil. I know what I want to do. I know what I need. My life is not over yet.

Play - 'Wait - M83'

"Wow. This really does look like a junkyard." Kacey blurts out as we drop our belongings on the gravel outside the car door, glaring like she's slightly terrified.

"Hey!" I scowl at her, nudging her in the shoulder playfully as I shake my head, clutching the letter in my hand as I look at her grave.

Since reading her letter, it took some convincing but Kacey and her parents allowed me to go through the paperwork and get her home in my name, so it's now officially mine and I can't remember the last time I smiled this big as I stare at it in its miserable state, overgrown and even more tatted with broken walls and dirty exterior. It needs heavy TLC but that is ok.

Being here feels like my missing piece has finally slotted into place. The place I should loathe has unknowingly been my cure. I didn't come back, purely because I was not allowed, not because I didn't want to. But it's been two years and the house was left to me so I'll be damned if they try to keep me away from it any longer. I belong here. *With her.* With our memories and our trauma embedded in the paint and soil.

"Are you sure you want to do this?" She questions me softly, rubbing my arm as she smiles delicately.

"I've never been more sure about anything." I can feel her, she's right here with me and it's making my eyes water as the familiar air wafts under my nose and through my chocolate hair that I've refused to cut, no matter how much Kacey pleads to chop it off. My hair is the only remnant of our growth I have left. I play with it excessively, almost ripping it out as if it's a coping mechanism but I guess that's better than drinking or drugs.

"My skin is crawlingggg." Kacey has matured rapidly in the last couple of years, but you will never take the privilege out of her. This place must be making her feel like a peasant and I can't help but snigger as she rubs her skin trying to shake her chills.

"You scared of ghosts Cici?"

"Rara!"

"I'm kidding! There are no bodies buried on the property. *I promise.*" She rolls her eyes, clutching to her bags as she picks up my belongings off the stone. The same stone she pinned me down on with a gun in my mouth and I flush strawberry red at the thought.

"Well that's comforting." She didn't have to come, I told her I'd go on my own but she insisted she come with me and it was weirdly comforting, knowing she is willing to step into my trauma with me full force without judgement. "SO! You gonna give me a tour or what?"

Something inside me ignites, realising I'm about to walk back in and I thought I'd be terrified but I feel strangely content as I look back at Shep who's practically jumping out the window trying to reach the house. He knows where we are and as I open the car door he bolts for the porch like his life depends on it. I grab my bags and we make our way towards the door where he's impatiently waiting, whining as he claws underneath it. I open it with the key she provided me and the door creaks open revealing the heart of the house as well as the grave, trying to suppress those memories only to realise that suddenly I cannot feel that weighted pressure or see her blood on my hands anymore. *We are moving forward Alo...This is good. This is a good thing. Just breathe.*

Call me crazy but I can still smell her like she's standing right next to me. I'm about to throw the whole painting idea out the window just to hoard the smell as long as I can, hoping it seeps into the walls a while longer, shutting the door quickly to trap it in and Kacey looks at me in shock, trying to slip a silly smile when Shep immediately lays in a specific spot that takes my breath away.

The spot she lay as she died in my arms.

"Where am I sleeping?" She pulls me out of my thoughts as I pick up my jaw and if I am honest, I was so fixated on getting here that sleeping arrangements weren't exactly on my list of priorities, nor did I think she would even want to stay, it's why she followed me in her own car.

"Cici, you don't have to stay, I'll be fine I promise." I grab her hands, looking up at her to try and make her see that I am totally fine. I haven't felt this good in a long time.

"You meannnnn, leave my best friend here in an abandoned bungalow that was previously owned by a literal serial killer that, did I forget to mention, was my best friend's girlfriend and could kidnap you while you're sleeping in ghost form? No thank you. I'm staying."

I let a little snort slip, followed by her cute little laughs as we imagine being kidnapped by a ghost of all things and laughing feels so good. I forgot how much it warms your soul, feeling more comfortable laughing now that I'm where I belong, and she can see me laughing only for her.

"Fineeeeee." I drag out a sigh, smiling with her and I'm so grateful I have had her through this. She's made it bearable.

"Is this really where you stayed for eight months?" Her eyes wander but for once I don't see judgement. I just see empathy and sorrow which I'll admit is slightly strange coming from someone so hot headed and cold to anyone that is now not me. Especially a serial killer she has had to warm to over the years. It's the only way I could remotely cope but I've still never told her too much. All she knows is what she's read and she has never been a reader, she said it was for nerds. She'd rather hear it from me or she's read bits and pieces on the internet.

I nod sincerely as she gawks over at the kitchen.

"Is that the infamous kitchen islandddd?" I suck in my lips, trying to contain my embarrassment feeling my cheeks burn and she glares at me to spill as I just barely nod a *yes*. "Rara!!! Was it good?..."

My lip falls beneath my top teeth, grazing it at the thought and I suddenly don't feel nausea creeping up my throat when I think about her worshipping my body, smiling a little harder at the relief as I look over to the kitchen. The sun leaks through the forest of grass outside the back window barely letting it in and suddenly we are baking cookies and she's licking the mix out the bowl.

"More than good." I say coyly, trying to mumble, realising that we have never had this sort of conversation before even though I'd sit there for hours listening to her talk about her sex life. Now that I can finally reciprocate it feels so strange. Girlhood really is peculiar.

"You know, now thinking about it, getting down and dirty with a serial killer doesn't sound so bad." Her fingers find her chin, pulling the smuggest face and I want to say that's gross, but I hold my tongue, realising why she's even considering it. If there is one thing Kacey likes about Hayden. It's that she loosened me up and made me live a little.

"What! All rugged and dangerous! It's kinda hot. Better than the idiots I sleep with. Sounds like you had a better sex life than me while you were awayyyy." *I guess I did?* "I like this new you."

She looks at me, this time a little more seriously but it takes me a little to clock on as I reply.

"You meannnnn, the sad and depressed version?"

"No. I mean the fearless version. You are changing lives Alora. You're inspirational. Never forget that. I can't even begin to imagine what you went through but you survived and you're here, sharing your story and helping others view the system differently." My eyes perk up, quickly losing the humour as I catch her in what I can only describe as a vulnerable moment from her. *This is rare.* But she soon catches onto her own behaviour, squeezing me tightly as she pulls me in with excitement and she whispers.

"Did she really have a split tongue?!...." I bead my eyes at her, scrunching my brows in confusion but not at the question. At the way she's talking.

"Why are you whispering?" I ask with soft amusement.

"Because. She might hear us. She's in the wallllllls."

Suddenly, being haunted by a ghost doesn't sound so bad. And it warms my heart how she's being about all of this. How normal she's being when I know this is by far the strangest friendship she's ever had. Wallowing with a depressed best friend who's mourning over a serial killer in a creepy bungalow in the middle of butt fuck nowhere who is my ex-girlfriend probably wasn't quite what she was signing up for the day she hugged me outside the police station. But a lot has changed since then. We've grown, individually and as friends, and I wouldn't be here without her pushing me to keep going.

"You're ridiculous."

"I wanna know everything. Spill the tea!" I guess it's about time we did what girls do. Exhaling my dignity.

"Grab a beer and I'll tell you everything." I exclaim and her face lights with beaming excitement as she jumps for the crates in the back of my car, leaving me alone to take in the place I will now spend the rest of my life, until I decide to finally be with her. But today is not that day. *I heard you baby.*

I glide my fingers against the thick dust laying on every surface and I can feel her behind me, breathing down my neck.

"Why on earth did you bring Corona? It's vile!" I roll my eyes as I look over at her in the doorway, knowing why I brought the beer she probably hates the most, chuckling as I lean over the island.

"Call it, n*ostalgia."* She doesn't question me, only staring blankly at me, blinking slowly a few times.

"I'm not even going to ask." Oh she will. And I think I'm finally ready to tell her all about it, as I make my way over and brush the sofa down to sit, patting for her to sit next to me watching her face scrunch as the discomfort weighs heavy, smiling through it.

"Here's toooooo. Alora and her crazy sex life with a murderer." We exchange a heated but absent glare at one another before bursting into laughter. "And Hayden. I know you can hear me. Thank you for not killing my best friend. I'll look after her. I promise." I don't even register the tears beginning to stream from my eyes as she wraps her arm around me, squeezing me for a big embrace.

"To new beginnings!" I guess this is. A new chapter of my life without her in it. But now? Somehow, breathing is a little easier. And I can see tomorrow. I can finally see a new dawn. Whether she is not physically next to me. I know she will be watching over me. And that? That is enough for me. I promise I will look after your soul until my last dying breath. We are one. And our story has only just begun.

"I'm home *Baby.*"

COLLATERAL DAMAGE

SHASSII

12 years later...

Play - 'Outro - M83'

I gaze down at the marble stones lining a patch of dirt where I just recently planted some baby sunflowers, trying to hold in my sobs but it's too much.

"Hey. Come here you." Kacey wraps me in her arms tightly as I weep into her pink cardigan trying to collect myself. Trying to find the words but I have none for the pain I feel and it's like I'm living it all over again. "He was the best boy and he loved you. He had the best life because of you and now he's up there with her. Now she isn't alone, she has her boy." I know she's just trying to make me feel better but I weep harder because she's right.

Shep passed away of old age on my birthday. I found him curled up in his favourite spot. *Her spot,* in the middle of the living room floor. The shriek that left my throat was nothing short of devastating and I felt like I was reliving my past all over again as I held his cold, lifeless body in my arms. He was physically well but either old age or heart break finally made him let go and for a long while I sat with him and contemplated pulling the plug too but Kacey's right. He's with her now and I have to find some comfort in that. I couldn't be selfish forever, I just wish I could join them.

We decided to make him a burial in the garden next to her. I buried her ashes. I was contemplating letting her go across Lake Michigan with her mother but I suppose now I'm the one being selfish. I just couldn't bring myself to do it. She belongs here, *with me.* With *us.* A family that loves her and somehow, I know that is what her mom would have wanted too.

I couldn't bare the thought of having her grave in some random burial site knowing it would most likely get vandalised. So now she's here, both visible from the kitchen window in the garden that is now tidy and full of life so I can stare at it as I sit on the kitchen counter, at five in the morning, eating pancakes and drinking coffee from her hideous mug I found when unpacking.

Life hasn't been easy but Shep and the Calloway's have kept me afloat and the last twelve years have been somewhat back to normal. I haven't needed therapy for the last three years and the nightmares and sleepless nights have finally stopped. I'm still on medication but I have a full-time job and I'm still writing books. I guess this is me finally saying goodbye to the only living piece of her I had left. I didn't think grief could get any worse, but I was wrong. It hurts more when you know that you should be happy they are ok but you're left feeling broken and left behind.

I am keeping my promise. As much as I so desperately want to drift off and reunite with both of them, I promised I'd live for her so that is what I'm going to do. I knew this day was coming and I thought I was prepared for it but I was nothing but. If I can get through this? I can get through anything. I owe that to myself and I want to make her proud. So, I'll live. I'll live it to the fullest and know they are both looking down on me. *My guardian Angels.*

"Hey Rara. You wanna go get some ice cream?" She asks lightly into my ear, still clutching onto me like her life depends on it. I envy the life she has but I'm so happy to be a part of it. She's getting married in a month and the chaos will definitely keep me distracted. She's almost been a bridezilla and I've had to keep her grounded so she doesn't rip peoples heads off. Her man is an angel and I have no doubt in my mind he loves her the way Hays loved me which makes me smile that she can experience that sort of love. I thought I'd be jealous, envious. *But I'm just happy.*

They've occupied a seat on the day for her next to me and that gesture alone made me bawl into both of their arms before dropping the B word on me. She's pregnant and the scream that came out of my mouth probably deafened them. I wondered for a moment if Hays would ever have kids, what she would have been like around them considering she made it her life's mission to protect them. Part of me thinks she'd want nothing more, but she'd be terrified that she wouldn't be a good parent and that is the furthest thing from the truth.

"We thought of some names." she whispers as I cuddle into her chest, both gazing at the sun hitting where they lay in front of us and I realise what she's referring to.

"Please don't be anything stupid. I might have to bop you around the head." I blubber through a snotty nose. "Do you know the gender yet?" I ask, giggling softly.

"Nope, so we've accommodated for both." She says with confidence.

"Oh?" I can feel her smile against my hair and she squeezes me tighter.

SHASSII

"How does, Hayden and Hayley sound?"

HAYDEN-HAYLEY MOORE
In loving memory of a survivor, an incredible daughter and the love of my life.
1980 - 2010

SHEP
In loving memory of a best friend, the goodest boy, and my guardian angel.
2005 – 2024

HARLEY
In loving memory of a best friend, the goodest boy, and my guardian angel.
2009 - 2024

To the readers and to the people who knew of Shep before release. I know I said I wouldn't kill him off but during the writing of this book I got a call to let me know that my boy Harley unfortunately passed away on the 14th of February 2024 which just so happened to be Alora's birthday and I never got a chance to say goodbye. So this is me.
Saying goodbye.

Harley and my past as well as my partners have had a heavy impact on this book. Harley was named after a Harley Davidson that, as you know, is Hayden's bike and that is just the tip of the iceberg.

I won't go into detail about our past but I hope that this book heals a part of you
the way it healed us.

ACKNOWLEDGMENT

Where to even begin! We want to start off by saying the biggest **thank you** for reading this book. None of this would have been possible without your support towards my little dream and I can't believe I've written my first ever book. But most importantly, a book that others also enjoy! It's still such an incredible feeling and I hope you loved this book just as much as I enjoyed writing it. If I told myself a couple of years ago that I'd written a book, past me would have laughed at the thought. If anyone takes anything away from this. *Writers I'm looking at you!*
WRITE THAT BOOK!
I want to first off say thank you to the rock that got me here. **The love of my life.** I want you to know how much I appreciate everything you have done for me this past year to give me the time to work on this book. For doing the background of the cover, to editing the early drafts, for helping me with all the business aspects and keeping me stress free through this entire process, for letting me stay up till 5am working on god knows what, to spending our days off to write and edit, to brainstorm ideas and doing everything around the house so I can concentrate on this, your efforts never go unnoticed and I am so lucky to have the most incredible partner. I also want to say thank you for letting me share your past and creativity through Hayden. I hope I did her justice, and I hope people forgive me for the ending! (Ops) **I Love You** so much and I cannot wait to create more incredible stories with you.
To my main **Alpha** reader *Selene.*
Thank you for putting up with my endless late night spams, my constant questions, simping over the babies every day with me and going through the wars with me, experiencing pain with me and loving them just as deeply as we do. Your love for Hayden and Alora will be something we will forever cherish. I don't think anyone will ever love them as deeply as you and I am so happy I could create an experience you will never forget! You really have

become one of my bestest friends and I am blessed that I could share this journey with you! I still can't believe you did everything you did for me!

To my **Beta** readers,

Celeste, Cris, Dilan, Chlo, Lizz, Ame, Jake, Bri, Jess & Aly.

I cannot express how grateful I am that you took the time to beta read for us! I knew it would be an incredible experience and an experience it was! I hope you forgive me and don't have too much of a book hangover. But also, I hope you do because you can all suffer with me now. I would say I'm sorry but that would be a lie. I'm not.

To ***Jake*** *(From work)*, thank you for listening to me blabber about this book at work for the last year. I know I've gnawed your ear off but I appreciate you listening and showing so much interest in my little dream. Not only did you listen but you took the time to read the entire thing and you enjoyed it which is a bonus!

To ***Jake*** (*From insta*), thank you for sharing your raw unfiltered personal experiences with me throughout this book, you really did get me back, playing that UNO reverse card on my heart but I am so grateful I could touch you in ways this book intended, we cried together and I learnt so much more about you as a person.

To ***Bri & Alex,*** my living breathing ***Haylo***. Thank you from the bottom of my heart for reading this, I am so happy it touched you in the ways I intended, thank you for all the kind words and effort you bled into your review, LITERALLY! I can't believe you got it tattooed. I will never get over your rating or the fact it was your favourite book of the year, the way this story has changed your life has also contributed to changing mine and I'm forever grateful.

To ***Chloebear***, my twinny, my beautiful friend, what a journey it has been getting to know your beautiful soul and all the kindness you hold. I know I've said it a million times before but thank you always for showing me how touching this story is through your incredible narration. It was the most surreal experience and I will never forget it. You touched me in ways I never knew possible and I am forever grateful for everything you have done for me.

To ***Wik***, thank you for coming with me on this journey, from the old gaming days to now, you have been nothing but supportive and shown me nothing but kindness and admiration. Thank you for your beautiful illustrations that helped everyone to fall in love with Hayden & Alora.

To *Ame,* you promised me and till this day you continue to never break that promise that this journey would forever be my greatest turning point in life, I am so grateful to of met you, you calm me on bad days, you help me when I'm overwhelmed and you have been right by my side through all of this.

To my biggest inspiration *Aly,* not only have you been with me every step of the way, you were one of the first people to welcome me into this community and you're not only my biggest inspiration but I have the honour to call you one of my closest writer friends I've got the privilege to know. You show me every day that the hard graft and our dreams are achievable. I've never seen anything quite like it, your drive to be a writer surpasses anything I've ever witnessed, and you keep us writers hanging on so thank you for being that pillar for me and thank you for reading this book baby.

To my spooky, mysterious vampy lady, *Ophelia*, I honestly could not have gotten through half of this without you guiding me and being the voice I needed through this process. You've not only taken your own personal time to help me chase my dream but you've been the most amazing friend and support to me, regardless of my idiocy sometimes that you put up with. (You love your British weirdo really) I hope you know, words will never begin to explain how grateful I am to have met you and how much of an amazing person you are! You continue to amaze me with everything that you achieve, everything you strive for you nail and it makes me so unbelievably proud of you.

To *Fai,* what an absolute light you have been since meeting you. I cannot begin to tell you how deeply your love for Haylo means to me. I will never get over the ring you engraved for them, and the countless hours of voice notes you left me, how you picked apart my brain and voiced exactly how I felt whilst writing this book. I'm so glad my words shifted your aspect on life and made you realise you are not a bird in a cage. You are human and you deserve to fly. Chase that freedom, for us.

To all my ***bookish baddies & ARC readers***! You know who you are, I would write to you all but it would take up an entire page. I just want to let you know that every like, comment, share, DM, review, sign up and buzz of excitement you have shown towards this project has been a blessing and we are so happy we got to share this story. You ladies make me feel so seen, so heard, so understood. This community has given me a space to express myself in ways I never could and to have a group of people to share that with feels so amazing!

You guys really are incredible!

To my Editor **Boo**, thank you for taking the time to use your insanely nerdy brain and edit this book for us. I wouldn't have trusted anyone else if I'm honest. This is your element and I hope it was all we hyped it up to be for you and I hope you know this will not be the last time. You are now our designated book Editor as well as the coolest step mum on earth.

I Love You!

COLLATERAL DAMAGE

ABOUT THE AUTHOR:

Am I doing this on my own?

NO. I may be the writer for the stories we create, network and control the social media side of things but everything I write has a soul, and that is the love me and my partner share, along with every dark part of our lives we've unfortunately had to experience prior to finding one another. Every story and character is a part of us that we create together to give you love so deep it seems real. Because it is real. Its every shared an unspoken emotion we express that I've had the pleasure of putting into words for not only the readers but for us. Every broken and shattered MFMC I write was moulded and created from her. When you fall in love when them, you're also connecting with a piece of us, and as a writer that is very much important to me.

We have been on this book journey since we met back in 2020, but only decided on really pursuing this back in 2023. We live in England and are both extremely artistic which we found creates art like this. If we aren't working or building on this publication we are gaming or out on long night drives with the music blaring, attending car shows or eating yummy food. I actually used to hate English in school so becoming an indie author is as much of a surprise to me than it is to anyone I know personally but I feel I've finally found my purpose and I've never been so motivated and driven to achieve something. To the 17 year old me who was so close to giving up on the world and letting go. I am so proud of you for staying. Look what you achieved, and look how many lives you are already changing.

SHASSII

Love creates art, pain creates strength and acceptance creates healing. Just two broken souls trying to give you all three! Me and my partner have always both been artistic in our own nature and we have found a way to blend those pieces of us together and create something magical.

From all the children ever harmed by the hands of evil all in the name of **'Family'**.

Sincerely,

F *the Justice system.*

CONNECT WITH US!

Feel free to slide into our direct messages anytime you like! I am always up for a chat and I'll talk your ear off for hours if you let me. I adore receiving messages regardless of the context, it could be about CD, it could be a simple hello, it could be to bond over another book or simple to get to know one another! Please don't be afraid to shoot me a message and I will always reply!
You can find us as **@shassiiwrites** on all platforms!

Until next time Little Dreamers!

@SHASSIIWRITES

Printed in Great Britain
by Amazon